DAMMIT, SARA

The fingers on her shoulder bit into her flesh. Suddenly, he was looming over her, his eyes usually as dark as coals, now were burning fiercely. Sara was aware of a weakness in her limbs and a fluttery feeling in the pit of her belly that was unlike anything she had ever felt before.

"Perhaps—" she began, but he cut her off.

"Perhaps, nothing! Meaning you no disrespect, Sara, but if I don't kiss you once more before I leave, it will weigh on my mind for as long as I live. Which might not . . ."

But he didn't finish the statement. Instead, he lowered her to the bed and leaned over her, his chest crushing her bosom, his hard body pinning her beneath him. Sara's eyes grew wider. Her breathing ceased altogether as she waited for what was to come. She couldn't have moved if the bed had suddenly caught fire.

Which, she thought, it might well do.

# HALFWAY HOME

by

## Bronwyn Williams

A TOPAZ BOOK

TOPAZ
Published by the Penguin Group
Penguin Books USA Inc., 375 Hudson Street,
New York, New York 10014, U.S.A.
Penguin Books Ltd, 27 Wrights Lane,
London W8 5TZ, England
Penguin Books Australia Ltd, Ringwood,
Victoria, Australia
Penguin Books Canada Ltd, 10 Alcorn Avenue,
Toronto, Ontario, Canada M4V 3B2
Penguin Books (N.Z.) Ltd, 182–190 Wairau Road,
Auckland 10, New Zealand

Penguin Books Ltd, Registered Offices:
Harmondsworth, Middlesex, England

First published by Topaz, an imprint of Dutton Signet,
a division of Penguin Books USA Inc.

First Printing, August, 1996
10  9  8  7  6  5  4  3  2  1

 REGISTERED TRADEMARK—MARCA REGISTRADA

Printed in the United States of America

To the Indian Ridge gang:
Lee, Greyson, Kyle, Andrea, Zac,
Felicia, and Matthew

# Chapter One

Sara Young folded her shawl and tucked it away on the shelf over her washstand. Carefully, she removed her Sunday-go-to-meeting hat, which differed little from her Monday-go-to-market hat except for the feather.

The snow had started on the way home from church, and before she'd gone the first mile, her stockings had been soaked, thanks to the cracks in her good patent-leather boots. They had belonged to her mother, and Sara wore them only on Sundays, but they were nearly ten years old, after all. Nothing lasted forever.

It wasn't supposed to snow in March, not here in southeastern Virginia. Sara had a bad feeling about seeing snow this late in the season. It had snowed the year her mother had died. Sara had been eleven years old at the time.

It had snowed the following March, too, when her father had brought home a new bride and a half-grown son. Noreen and Titus had joined forces to make her life miserable from the moment they'd set foot over the doorsill, not that her father had ever known.

Not that she would have wanted him to know, poor man.

It had been snowing that morning in March two years later when James Young had set out to go to a cockfight at the Lake Drummond Hotel, drunk too much and on the way home wandered off into the swamp, where he'd frozen to death.

Since then, it hadn't snowed once during March, but goodness knows, things had been about as bad as they could be. Between them, Noreen and Titus had managed to run the farm right smack dab into the ground. They were both spendthrifts. Titus gambled. Neither one of them knew doodley-squat about farming. They had sold off most of the land, the best of the furniture, and all the lovely paintings. Her father's field hands had gone along with the land, and now the only servants left were two free blacks, Maulsie and Big Simon, who had come south with Sara's mother and stayed on after her death to look after Sara.

Before heading down to help Maulsie serve dinner, Sara carefully removed her good gown, hung it on the peg, and then changed into her other one. After pulling on a dry pair of stockings, she reluctantly slid her feet into the ugly boots Titus had outgrown years ago. She would sooner have gone barefoot, even on cold floors, because her feet hurt something fierce, but Noreen would pitch a conniption fit, and Sara had had about all of her stepmother's tantrums she could take in one day.

Dinner was neither better nor worse than usual, the food being excellent, the company deplorable. Sara carried platters and bowls in to the dining room table, trying not to look at the bare places on the walls where her mother's portrait and a lovely landscape had once hung. That done, she rang the bell, removed her apron, and waited silently for Noreen to take her place at the head of the table before sliding unobtrusively into her own chair.

Titus was once more favoring them with his absence. He'd lit out courting again nearly two weeks ago, after wheedling another bit of pawnable jewelry from his mother. As much as Sara despised the man—for man he was—no longer the hateful boy who had tormented her for so long—at least his presence would have deflected some of Noreen's spiteful attention.

"I don't see why you have to be so stubborn about going to church every time the doors are thrown open," the older woman complained, helping herself to a big, fat sweet potato. The menu might be skimpy, but Maulsie did roast the best sweet potatoes in Norfolk County, cooking them real slow to bring out all the sugar.

"I've always gone to church," Sara said quietly. "It's the only way I get to see my friends." What few she had left.

"Well, it was downright embarrassing, watching you come traipsing up the hill all dusty and red in the face, like some cheap little peddler."

With Titus off courting in their only transport, Noreen enjoyed being driven to church by a widower who lived a few miles down the road. Even if she'd been invited to ride with them, Sara would have declined. Her fondest hope was that Noreen would remarry and move away, taking her lickspittle son with her.

Refusing to be drawn into another argument, she forked off what little meat she could find on the chicken back on her plate. What should she say? That if those two hadn't sold her father's perfectly good trap to buy that fancy new runabout, which Titus was using in his courting, why then, she wouldn't be forced to walk everywhere she went?

Noreen had never cottoned to criticism. Especially not from Sara. And most particularly not when it concerned her son.

More than once Sara had wondered where her father had found the woman and what had prompted him to marry her. For all she was still pretty, there was a coarseness about her that never failed to grate on Sara's nerves, and as for Titus . . .

Well. The less said, the better.

By midafternoon, the snow had dwindled to a random flake or two. By supper time, a few scraps of sunshine where actually beginning to break through the clouds. The afternoon had passed uneventfully, with Noreen snoring in the front parlor, having had one too many glasses of Big Simon's blackberry wine.

And then, like a noxious weed cropping up in the middle of the early peas, Titus came home. "Come give big brother a kiss," he taunted, catching Sara from behind.

She twisted out of his arms and glared at him. "Big *step*brother needs a bath. He smells like chicken droppings."

Titus laughed, but the laughter didn't carry to his eyes. "Ah, but I won this time. Now, don't you wish you'd given me that kiss?"

Sara didn't. She'd sooner kiss the rooster on which he had placed his money. She managed to stay out of his way by helping out in the kitchen with supper preparations, which was expected of her anyway. She slipped off her apron and slid quietly into her chair just as Titus was telling his mother about his latest efforts to find himself a rich wife.

"The James girl's got a tongue like a knife blade. Don't matter how much money her old man has, I'd sooner marry a fish crow."

From which evidence Sara surmised that the girl had the good sense to refuse his proposal. It was all she could do not to smile.

It was undeniably true that her stepbrother was just about the handsomest man in the entire county, what with his shiny yellow curls, his pale blue eyes and his small, perfect features. Sara happened to know that he rolled his hair every night in rags to produce those fashionable curls. She had once made the mistake of remarking on his efforts, and had quickly come to regret it. Since then she had learned to duck and dodge. Titus was stronger, but she was quicker. And Sara was nothing if not sensible.

But no amount of sensibility could rein in her stepfamily's insatiable appetite for fancy clothes and expensive geegaws, or Titus's ruinous habit of gambling on every card, horse, dog, or chicken in the commonwealth of Virginia. Between them they had managed in five years to go through every cent her father had left. The house and the small portion of land that remained were deeply mortgaged. They had only the small vegetable plot Sara maintained with Big Simon's help, but that would soon have to be sold along with everything else unless a miracle happened. Where once dozens of hands had worked her father's fields and her mother's staff had looked after the house, only Maulsie and Big Simon remained, and those two couldn't go on forever. There were days when it was all Big Simon could do to get around, his joints were that swollen, and Maulsie's hearing was failing her. They were too old to find work if they were turned off. Their only security lay in the fact that Noreen couldn't afford anyone else to take their place. There was simply no more money. She had sold everything of any value except for the few pieces of jewelry she doled out to placate her son. The sad truth was that unless Titus could find a rich wife, they would all end up in the poorhouse.

As for Maulsie and Big Simon, being free, they would likely starve. Norfolk had a large community of free blacks, but most folks, black and white alike, resented freed slaves.

It never occurred to Sara that she might find herself a husband and move into a home of her own, taking her two old friends with her. She wasn't a beauty. On the puny side, she had plain brown hair and plain brown eyes, and her skin was unfashionably tanned from working outdoors all year-round. She had no pretty clothes, having either worn out or outgrown most of her gowns long ago. The last time she'd been to a social had been four years ago, when she was only fifteen.

Since then, she'd been ashamed to go, aware that everyone knew of her situation and felt sorry for her. After a while, as her friends married and moved away or started families of their own, the invitations had stopped coming. The only man who still remained friendly was Archibald Ricketts, who came by every month or so peddling his wares from the back of his drummer's wagon. Although more than twice her age, Archibald, at least, enjoyed her company.

Rather more than enjoyed it, if his shyly flirtatious looks were any indication. Lately he had taken to writing her to let her know when he would be coming through so that she would be sure to be there.

Of course, Noreen read any letter that came addressed to Sara if Maulsie didn't get to it first. Not that she received all that many, for mail was dear, but she treasured the rare letters from her best friend Carrie, who had married and had moved to Illinois. And, of course, the notes from Archibald.

Impatiently she waited for Noreen and Titus to finish eating so that she could clear away the supper dishes. Noreen was enjoying a third glass of blackberry wine while Titus devoured the last of the chicken, spearing it off the platter with the wicked knife he used to pare his fingernails, and then fastidiously licking the blade when he was done.

"Careful," she said sweetly. "They say splitting a crow's tongue will make him talk, but I've never heard what it does to buzzards."

Glaring at her, he flashed the blade threateningly. He might look like a china doll, but she knew to her sorrow that he was a good deal more dangerous. No wonder every single woman in Norfolk County had turned him down. They must know him for the scoundrel he was, which was why he'd had to go so far afield to do his courting. All the way down into North Carolina, according to Big Simon.

Just as if he'd been following her train of thought, Titus said, "Mama, I'll be riding down to Pasquotank

County again come morning. I'll need the runabout for a few more days."

"A few more days! You've already had it for nearly two weeks! I'll not be stranded out here in the middle of nowhere another day! No sirree bob. This time, you'll just have to make other arrangements."

Titus leaned back in his chair, a smug smile on his grease-polished lips. "You know that big white house set back in the trees, with the two-story front porch on the road from New Lebanon to Elizabeth City? I was down in that neck of woods at a house party back last fall, and I met the woman that owns it. She's some older than me and nothing much to look at, but I've been sparking her up for a while." He punctuated the statement with a loud belch, and Sara wondered how on earth such an angelic-looking creature could be so utterly vile.

"How many acres? How many rooms in the house?" Noreen's small eyes narrowed speculatively.

"I've not seen the inside yet, but I reckon it's big enough to make this dump look like a two-hole privy."

Sara bridled at that, but bit back the retort that nearly jumped off the tip of her tongue. If only he *would* marry and move down to Carolina, and take his precious mother with him! She would go down on her knees and give thanks every night of her life if only she could be rid of the pair.

"Her folks is all dead except for a brother, and he's gone all the time. A sailor, I think she said. She's not got a lick of style, but she's grateful for the least little attention. If I was to ask her to walk to the moon, she'd bust her bustle trying."

"You going to marry her? How much you think she's worth?"

"Well, Mama, I can't hardly ask her that yet, but I reckon she'd jump at the chance to marry me. Like I said, she's not much to look at," Titus said with a smirk that made Sara want to shove his face into a gravy bowl and hold it there.

March went out like a lamb. April entered with seven days of rain, which made it impossible for Sara to get her rows hoed up for planting beans and sweet potatoes. Noreen whined and drank and argued over the use of the runabout whenever Titus came home.

April passed into May. Noreen complained constantly of a windy bowel and refused to eat any more sweet potatoes, beans or cabbage, which didn't leave much to choose from unless they slaughtered their only remaining pig or killed another of the laying hens.

In a rare streak of good luck, Big Simon acquired a neighbor's discarded two-wheel cart and managed to repair the broken wheel, which gave them another vehicle, even though all they had to pull it was old Blossom, the plow mule.

Titus was still courting, mostly down in Pasquotank County so far as Sara could tell. Lately he hadn't seemed quite so cocksure. From something she'd overheard, she rather thought he was running with a fast crowd and had piled up more gambling debts.

Lordy! If that wasn't just what they needed.

Archibald came by one morning in early June just as Sara was hanging out the wash, her hands reddened by the harsh lye soap. They both knew that she lacked the money to purchase any of his wares, yet he never failed to stop. They visited, and he lingered long enough to enjoy a tumbler full of water and a few of Maulsie's cold biscuits while he cast sheep's eyes at Sara. Life on the road, he told her, not for the first time, surely did get powerful wearisome for a man traveling alone.

"Couldn't your wife ride with you?" she asked, and he blushed so hard she was afraid he was going to lapse into an apopleptic fit.

From which she gathered that, just as she'd suspected, the poor man was single. And too bashful, even at his age, ever to do anything about it.

Sara felt sorry for him, for he was one of the gentlest, most thoughtful men she had ever known, despite the fact that he was rather homely and frequently smelled of rum, even in the middle of the day. He talked often of the neat little cottage he owned near Portsmouth, and about the flowers his mother used to grow in the garden there. Oh, yes, indeed, he did enjoy gardening, he said, although Sara didn't know when he found time.

But he was kind and hardworking. And generous. As often as not, he left her with some small gift—a length of ribbon or a jar of cream for her hands—saying it was only a sample he had left over. Which, unless Sara was both quick and clever, Noreen usually managed to claim.

Watching him drive off in his gaudy peddler's wagon, she sighed, almost wishing she could go with him. It would be heaven simply to climb aboard and not look back.

Instead she turned to go back inside with her empty clothes basket, consoling herself that at least she still

"You wants me to open it fo' you?"

As bad as things were, Sara knew they could get worse. She also knew that she would be the one to bear the burden, if there was a burden to be borne.

"Best get on with it, chile. Bad news jes' festers less'n it's let out into the open."

But it wasn't bad news. What it was, was . . .

Well, she wasn't entirely sure what it was, because of all the flowery roundaboutness. "Get to the point, get to the point," she muttered, having always been a believer in plain talk. "I think it's about my grandfather," she said finally, having read through the entire epistle twice. "Maulsie, would you hang my Sunday gown out to air? I'm going to have to go into town and find out what this is all about."

# Chapter Two

Big Simon had driven her into town in the mule cart the very day after the letter had come. At Blossom's sleepy pace, it had taken nearly all morning. When they'd finally rumbled up before the fine brick bank building on Granby Street, Sara commenced to set herself to rights. Her coal-skuttle bonnet—the one with the feather—had slipped sideways so many times as they'd jounced along the muddy road, she had finally removed it. What could the sun do to her face that it hadn't already done?

"We's here, Miss Sara. You wait right here while I go knock on the do'. Ain't no use in you standin' outside in the hot no longer'n you has to."

So Sara waited in the "hot" on the splintery wooden bench seat in the delapidated mule cart. Several minutes later, she was shown into the building, with Simon assuring her he would be right there waiting when she came out again. " 'Ceptin' if you don't mind, Miss Sara, I'll jes' walk ol' Blossom 'round the square a time or two to keep the flies from settlin'."

Sara would rather have climbed back up in the cart and headed home, but that wouldn't prevent bad news from catching up with her. If bad news it was, and

"Just how well off is this girl you told me about last time you were home? Is her money free and clear?"

"Which one, Louisa? She ain't no girl, I can tell you that much. Must be thirty if she's a day—plain as a mud fence." Titus hawked and spat in the chamber pot. "Might be worth it if the place was good as it looked from a distance, but it ain't. Besides, it all belongs to the brother. She just lives there, but she can't keep it up. Roof leaks and word is the fields don't yield more'n seed money anymore. Something about drainage. Anyhow, forget Louisa. I've already dumped her. Got my sights set on this widow over near—"

"Forget all that and listen here to me, you lazy good for naught. The brat's come into a fortune. I don't know how big it is—couldn't get a word out of that pinch-purse banker, but talk around here is that one of her Yankee kinfolk on her mama's side died and left her enough money to buy her way through the pearly gates."

"Sara?" Titus gawked. "Our Sara's got *money*?"

"Yes, our Sara's got money! Didn't you hear a word I said? Why do you think I sent for you? Now get out of that bed and either bathe or douse yourself with Bay Rum—you smell like you've been sleeping in a chicken pound!"

"Stopped off at a cockfight, that's all," he grumbled. "Would've won, too, but somebody was cheating."

Sara wondered on hearing the conversation repeated just how anyone could cheat at a cockfight. She decided she didn't even want to know.

"Damned woman's got a filthy beast of a dog, anyhow," Titus mumbled.

"Sara?" Noreen squawked.

"No, not Sara," Titus retorted. "Louisa. Big old bastard bit me last month, nearly tore my best coat right off my back. She had to lock him in the barn every time I come around, which is one more reason why I quit . . ." He yawned.

"Don't you *dare* go back to sleep, Titus Smithers!" his mother screeched. "Forget all your other women, you've got one right under your nose. I'm not about to let all that good money go to waste, so you can just get yourself cleaned up and set to courting before the brat walks off with one of those stupid clods that's been sniffing around her skirts ever since word leaked out. If she up and marries Joe Baker or that Culler boy, you and me'll be singing for our supper, I can tell you that. And right now, the way you smell, I wouldn't blame the twit if she won't even have you."

According to Maulsie, Titus had that "greasy" look about his eyes, which usually meant he was either planning mischief or had already accomplished it.

The next few weeks were like a bad dream as far as Sara was concerned. Titus was one step behind her everywhere she went, holding her chair, smirking at her, bringing her lemonade when she so much as remarked on the heat, and plastering her with compliments that would have made her laugh if she hadn't been so irritated.

She wasn't really worried, even though she knew very well what he was up to. No man, Sara assured herself, could force her to do anything against her will. She might not know all there was to know about everything in the world, but she did know Titus. And she knew the strength of her own backbone.

Noreen was constantly reminding her of what a fine-looking man Titus was, and how he could have had most any woman he wanted for the asking.

Well, then why hadn't he? Sara wanted to ask.

But she took it all with a grain of salt. Her stepmother seemed to forget that she had heard all about his women, not a one of whom would have him when push came to shove. Sara hadn't a doubt in the world that Titus would have married an elephant if it had a trunk full of gold.

But then Noreen started in on Sara's conscience, telling her that poor dear Titus needed someone who understood him, and that Sara's dear departed papa would rest so much easier for knowing his family would always be together.

As Sara told Maulsie later on that evening, "As if I gave two hoots of a night owl how Papa is resting. He buttered his bread; now let him lie in it."

Guiltily, she reminded herself that her papa couldn't help being weak anymore than Noreen could help being greedy and spiteful. Any more than she herself could help being quick-tempered, stubborn and intolerant of other people's weaknesses.

For Titus, she made no excuses. The man was vicious as a weasel and every bit as sly, and if there was one thing Sara couldn't abide—and actually, there were several—it was slyness. He knew precisely where she was most vulnerable and never failed to make the most of it.

Her biggest weakness was Simon and Maulsie. Titus was forever watching Simon struggle to do his work. The poor old man seemed to move slower each day, and to make matters worse, he always seemed to be working somewhere nearby whenever Titus was home. It was almost as if he was deliberately taunting the younger man.

Or watching over Sara.

Titus would shake his head and mutter something about old fools who ate their heads off but couldn't pull their weight any longer. And then he would say something to Maulsie in a voice that was little more than a whisper and swear at her when she didn't jump fast enough to fetch whatever it was he wanted fetched.

It was plain as day what he was up to. Both Maulsie and Simon were outgrowing their usefulness, but they were all the family Sara had left. If Titus ran them off, they would have nowhere to go. Worse still, a word in the proper ear and he could have them both taken up as runaway slaves, even though they weren't. Such things happened all too often.

Viciously, Sara chopped at a strangling growth of morning glory vines that had invaded her squash hills. Frowning, she thought about her troubles, mopped her sweating forehead, chopped some more, and thought some more. For all the good it did.

If only she could get away. If only she had somewhere else to go. *Anywhere!* She could afford to pay off the mortgage now, but there was no way she could force Noreen and Titus to move out.

It never even occurred to her that she might look for a small cottage of her very own, where she could take care of Simon and Maulsie while they took care of her. Unlike men, a woman couldn't simply go out and buy herself a house. Legal or not, no man would deal with her. There had to be a father, a brother, an uncle, or a husband to act as a go-between.

A husband.

Merciful saints alive, but it was tempting. There was Joe Baker. He had brought her flowers from his mama's garden. If only he weren't so slow-witted. The poor boy wouldn't hurt a fly, but she wasn't sure she could tolerate a lifetime of Joe's lengthy silences interspersed with his self-conscious giggles.

Theo Culler wasn't so awfully boring, but there was something a bit off-putting about the way his gaze always seemed to settle on her bosom and linger there until she felt like wrapping herself in a blanket.

Besides, he smelled like lard. Especially on a hot day. She was almost sure he used it to dress his boots, and probably his hair as well. He had certainly left a big enough grease stain on the antimacassar of the only good parlor chair they had left.

Leaning on her hoe, Sara stared out over the distant woods, hazed with the smoke that had hung over the entire area since lightning had set off another peat fire somewhere in the nearby Dismal Swamp. Like all the other peat fires as far back as she could remember, it would likely burn just beneath the surface for years. She was so used to the smell and the haze that she hardly even noticed it now.

No, not Joe Baker. And not Theo, either, nor any of the others who had snickered at her for years when she walked into church, puffing and red-faced from her three-mile walk. Not a one of them had been interested in courting her when she was poor; otherwise they could have collected her in their buggies and driven her to Sunday service instead of making fun of her for being all sweaty and dusty and out of breath when she finally arrived.

Being poor wasn't easy, but neither was being rich. Both took some getting used to. It occurred to Sara for the first time that she could afford to buy her own buggy, as well as a horse to draw it. A matched pair, in fact.

The trouble was, she would have to buy three. One for Noreen, and a new one for Titus. And two more horses, and there would be constant squabbles about who would get which one.

Mercy, she'd be better off marrying Archibald. At least she would have his big wagon to get around in and a house where she could take Maulsie and Big Simon.

Which might be worth considering, because unless she had misunderstood Mr. Wallace at the bank, it would take the largest portion of her inheritance just to pay the mortgage on her father's property. Where would that leave her when Titus and Noreen spent them into the poorhouse again?

Decisions, decisions . . .

It was pitch-dark outside when Sara suddenly became wide-awake. Lying in her narrow bed, her heart pounding like a woodpecker, she listened for whatever sound had aroused her.

If that blasted fox was trying to get at her hens again, she was going to nail his hide to the barn door!

And then she saw the glow on the sloping ceiling above the attic stairwell. "Maulsie?" she called softly. The old woman hadn't been up to Sara's bedroom since she had helped her move in.

The top of a lamp chimney came into view, followed

by Titus's pale curls. He was all ready for bed, but he hadn't yet rolled up his hair.

"Is someone sick?" It was the one thing she could think of that would have brought him up to the cramped attic room. "It is Noreen? Wait a minute and I'll be right down."

Gaining the floor level, Titus lurched toward the window and stuck his head outside, breathing deeply of the cool, smoke-scented night air. "Mama's fine. It's me that couldn't sleep."

"Well, for heaven's sake, being up here certainly won't help. What do you expect me to do, sing you a lullaby?" His nightshirt, she noticed, was of the finest quality handkerchief linen, certainly finer than any nightshirt she possessed. But then, Noreen had always said that her boy had delicate skin.

"I thought we might keep one another company for a spell."

"In the middle of the night?" Sara scoffed.

It occurred to her that he seemed to be having trouble with his breathing. She wondered if it was the smoke, the exertion of climbing the steep attic stairs or his claustrophobic tendencies. Titus couldn't abide close places, which was one of the reasons Sara had moved up to the tiny attic room.

She didn't want him here, for whatever reason. It was her private place. She had made it her own with freshly painted furniture, pictures she had made herself with pressed flowers and her mother's dresser set. She didn't want him here for any reason.

"Titus? Go back to bed," she said dampeningly.

Turning, he suddenly lunged toward her, causing the lamp to tilt dangerously. "Oh, for heaven's sake!" she cried, grabbing the cut class bowl just as the chimney crashed to the floor. Oil sloshed over her hand, and she quickly turned down the flame and set the thing on the tiny chest beside her cot. "What in heaven's name are you trying to do, burn down the house? Get out, you fool! Go on back where you came from before I call Big Simon to throw you out!"

Which was an empty threat, and they both knew it.

When a hand clamped onto her knee, she brushed it aside, but before she could scramble to the far side of her bed, he was at her again, both hands clawing at her night shift. All the while he was wrestling with her, he was grunting something about the different ways to skin a cat. "We'll see how damned proud you are when your belly starts poking out under your apron. Oww, you bitch! You bit me!"

"I'll do worse than that if you don't get—off—me!"

He hadn't brought his knife. If he had, she didn't know what she would have done. Cracked him over the head with the lamp, probably.

Twisting suddenly, Sara managed to get a foot against his chest. She shoved, and he fell to the floor, knocking the lamp over on his way down. Spilled oil flared up and quickly she flung a pillow down, smothering the flames. Scrambling to her feet on the bed, she bent over under the sloping ceiling and whispered fiercely, "If you ever, *ever*—lay another hand on me, I'll stuff you in a trunk and bury you under the biggest pile of manure I can find! Now get out of here before I tell your mama on you!"

Two weeks later, some twenty-odd miles to the south, a grim-faced man dressed all in black headed north along the corduroy road that led to the state line. Mounted on a rawboned gelding that stood a full seventeen hands high and answered to the name of Bones, Jericho Wilde stared unseeingly into the smoky distance. His eyes burned, but that was most likely due to the fact that he hadn't slept in so long, he'd lost track of time.

He'd gone by the graveyard again and come away feeling empty and guilty and angry. The earth was still raw. He'd thought about spreading a blanket over her grave, but it wouldn't have helped.

Her dog had been there, too. God, that had torn him apart. The mutt had howled every night since it had happened. Last night, Jericho had been tempted to use one of the dueling pistols he'd been cleaning to put the poor bastard out of his misery.

He had felt like howling, himself. Instead, he'd poured himself a single drink, put away the decanter, and got on with setting his affairs in order.

As the sky to the east began to pale, signs of traffic appeared. Two lumber barges made their way up the canal, warped by a team of oxen on the canal-side road. Alligator River lumber, Jericho noted absently, headed to Norfolk and points north most likely. He'd hauled enough lumber himself, mostly logwood from Honduras.

As daylight grew strong enough to cut through the peat smoke, the road traffic began to pick up. He passed a few horsemen, a few buggies—a freight wagon. A mile or so farther on he came upon two boys herding a gaggle of geese—God knows where or why. Bones stamped and snorted indignantly while the boys rounded up their scattered charges and cleared the road, and then he plodded on toward the border.

Jericho's belly rumbled, reminding him that he hadn't eaten since yesterday. Or maybe the day before. Guilt, laced with anger, was hard on the gut. If this was the way grief felt, he prayed he would never lose anyone else. Not that he had anyone left to lose.

Hunching his shoulders against the early-morning chill, he rode on to meet his fate. To meet the bastard who had courted his sister, got her with child, and then murdered her.

# Chapter Three

Sara waited as long as she dared for a reply before setting out. As she had explained in her letter—hastily scribbled the morning after Titus had come to her bedroom in the middle of the night, attempted to rape her, and ended up nearly burning down the house—if Archibald was still of a mind to take on a wife, why then she would come to him willingly and well dowered. In exchange for a home, she could offer companionship, a considerable inheritance as well as two dear and trustworthy servants who had been with her family since before she was born.

Not to mention the fact that, as he well knew, she was a hard worker, she could read and write, she was healthy as a horse, and she had always been known for her sensibility.

It hurt like everything to leave Maulsie behind, but it would only be for a little while. Big Simon would return after leaving her at the hotel where she had arranged to meet Mr. Ricketts. The Lake Drummond Hotel—also called the Halfway Hotel, as it was situated directly across the state line—was known as the Gretna Green of the South. It was popular with some Virginians because of North Carolina's lower marrying age.

It also served, unfortunately, as a rendezvous for duelers, gamblers, cockfighters, and travelers on both the Dismal Swamp Canal and the Canal Road, as well as a hiding place for criminals who might find it convenient to step from one state to the other at a moment's notice.

Regardless of its dubious reputation, it was not only the most convenient place Sara could think of at short notice, it also happened to be the most logical. There they should be able to get on with the business of marrying with scant delay, and once she became Mrs. Archibald Ricketts, she would be safe.

That is, if Archibald was still willing to marry her. To be perfectly truthful, he hadn't precisely mentioned marriage, but she was sure he'd been leading up to it. He had certainly hinted more than once about his lonely cottage.

Or was it his *lovely* cottage?

Well. She would find out soon enough. Meanwhile, there was the added benefit of being able to step into the next state should Titus come after her. Surely, there were laws in one state or another about dragging a woman off against her will.

"I wish it were all over and done with," she repeated for the third time since they had slipped away from the house at an early hour, before anyone else was awake.

"Yes'm."

Unlike Maulsie, Simon was not resigned to the arrangements, but none of the three had been able to come up with a better idea. Sara had wanted to take Maulsie with her, but someone had to stay behind, else Titus would have known she was up to something. She was almost certain Noreen had put him up to that wicked business the other night. And having failed the first time, they would only try again.

"You best git out'n dis house, chile," Maulsie had warned when Sara had told her what had happened the next morning. She'd had to explain her ruined pillow and the burn on her left hand. "I didn't raise you up for no yaller-haired devil to ruin."

She sighed now and fingered the bandage that held the lard and sugar poultice in place. It was only a small burn, nearly healed now, but Maulsie had insisted on dressing it one last time. There'd been tears in the old woman's eyes.

"Mr. Ricketts will likely be waiting for me at the hotel by the time we get there," she said now to Simon. Archibald probably knew not to send a reply in case it should fall into the wrong hands.

"Yes'm."

"He should have had my letter three days ago, which is surely time enough to arrange for the preacher and . . . well, whatever else is needed." A ring would be nice, but it was hardly necessary. It wasn't as though this were a love match. A *like* match, perhaps . . .

Which would suit her very well, Sara told herself. Of a practical nature, she'd never had a romantic bone in her body.

Big Simon cleared his throat, the sound reflecting an astonishing amount of skepticism, which she forced herself to disregard. It would all work out for the best. It simply had to.

"Now remember, you and Maulsie are to go with Mr. Ricketts when he comes for you in his wagon, whether or not I'm with him." She had already given both him and Maulsie traveling money. Neither of them had wanted to accept it. "Have your bundles all packed and ready to go at a moment's notice."

"Yes'm."

Sara sighed. With every mile they traveled, more doubts set in, but by the time they arrived, she had managed to convince herself that even an uncertain plan was better than no plan at all.

The hotel, an imposing structure some hundred and thirty feet long, rose up from the eastward shore of the canal bank, looking new and busy and prosperous with the bustle of activity all around. Sara sat up straight on the hard wooden seat, suddenly glad she had worn one of her two new gowns.

The best one she had saved to be married in.

Glancing uneasily over his shoulder, Simon helped Sara down from the cart. The area was notorious for the slave catchers who worked both sides of the state line. Nevertheless, he refused to leave until he saw his charge safely established, following her inside the lobby and standing, hat-in-hand, several respectable paces behind as she marched up to the desk.

Sara requested a room in the Carolina wing, signed the register with a flourish that was sheer bravado, and then listened with poorly concealed impatience as the clerk pointed out the many advantages of his fine new establishment. "Right over there's the dining room, ma'am, and a finer spread you'll not find between Charleston and Boston."

Sara took him at his word, having had little experience with any dining outside the occasional church social and her own table.

"That there's the barroom." He looked rather apologetic, as well he should, for a rougher-looking clientele than that hanging around the bat-wing doors would be hard to find. It occurred to her that the entire lobby seemed filled with men, with scarcely another female in sight, but before she could mention that fact the clerk said, "If you'll allow me, miss, I'll make you acquainted with a Mrs. Best, who stops off regular-like on her way to visit her children up Hampton way."

Relieved to learn that there was at least one other respectable woman in residence, Sara murmured an appropriate response.

"Now, as I was saying, we've got eight separate chambers, four in each wing, each with its own fireplace. Through that there door"—he pointed over his shoulder—"you'll find the necessary outhouses and our very own, never-failing juniper water spring, just a few convenient steps away from the back door."

Wondering if he rehearsed his speech every night before he went to bed, Sara nodded. "It all sounds lovely. Now, if I may be shown to my room, please? My man is waiting to bring my luggage inside."

A few minutes later, standing in the doorway of the busy hotel, Sara watched Big Simon rattle off down the corduroy road in the splintery, crudely patched cart. A feeling of despair swept over her, and she fought against the temptation to run out into the yard and call him back.

Well. She had burned her bridges, and that was that. Whatever lay ahead, it could hardly be worse than what she had left behind.

With that thought firmly in place, she turned back inside, steeling herself against the stares, some lascivious, some merely curious, of a number of men who seemed to have nothing better to do than lounge around the lobby making a spectacle of themselves.

Dinner that evening was more pleasant than Sara had anticipated. True, Archibald had not yet registered, nor had he reserved a room, but the woman whose table the clerk had arranged for her to join turned out to be a middle-aged widow from Elizabeth City who could talk cheerfully at great length about almost any topic, and did.

There were only two other women in sight, a pair of elderly sisters from New Lebanon who, according to Cordelia Best, were the biggest gossips in three counties. "Name of Jones. Brother's a traveling preacher. Spreads their gossip along with the Lord's gospel. By the time he comes by to collect them, they'll likely have more tales than one of them Grimm's storybooks, with just about as much truth to 'em."

Sara had dressed modestly in her new brown wool broadcloth, with a touch of ecru lace at the high neckline. It was nicer than anything she had had for years, but certainly nothing out of the ordinary. Which made her wonder why their table seemed to be attracting so much attention from the noisy male contingent.

It certainly couldn't be her looks, she thought, because those had never been above passable. Her father used to tell her that one day she would grow up to be a real beauty, with her chestnut brown hair and her big amber eyes, but it hadn't happened. Brown was brown, no matter what fancy name you called it, and drab was drab.

"Don't look now, but I do believe the Jones sisters are whispering about one of us," Mrs. Best murmured.

She patted her elaborate hat. "Probably wondering where I got my new bonnet. Unless it's you they're talking about—wondering who you are and what you're doing here."

The widow was obviously dying to ask both questions, but had better manners. Just barely. With a quirk of amusement, Sara wondered what the woman would think if she knew that her dinner companion had not only proposed to a man more than twice her age—a man she hardly knew—but she had come alone to the hotel to meet him without even waiting for his acceptance.

"I'm sure it's your hat," she murmured. "It's lovely, with the ruffles and ribbons and all."

"Balderdash. More likely it's your face," the widow declared generously.

"My face?"

"You're pretty enough, but they're probably wondering if you've got—" Here she leaned over and whispered loudly. *"Foreign blood.* If I was you, I'd try a cucumber poultice. Some swears by buttermilk and honey, but I always say, don't put nothing on your face that draws flies, or you might end up in worse shape than you started out."

The woman was truly kind, and Sara tried not to laugh. "I suppose you mean my sunburn. I do a lot of gardening. It's what you might call my pastime." It was also what had kept them all from starvation. "A hat gets so bothersome with all this hair . . ."

They discussed hats and complexion aids and the best way to cure a sluggish liver, which Mrs. Best suffered from. After a rather watery rice flummery, which

Sara toyed with and the widow practically inhaled, Sara excused herself and returned to her room.

Methodically, she brushed her hair with the silver-backed brush that had belonged to her mother. That and the matching mirror, a blue-glass hairpin tray, a scent bottle, and the embroidered dresser scarf, which was the last thing her mother ever finished, had been neatly set out, along with the two silhouettes and the framed dried flowers she had brought with her in a wooden box. It was a small enough inheritance, but it had the effect of making the room somewhat more homelike. And for the moment, it was the only home she had.

Tomorrow, she whispered, standing in the window that opened out onto the verandah. Tomorrow Archibald would be here, Sara told herself, because she refused to consider the discouraging possibility that he wouldn't come at all—wouldn't have her.

He *would* come, and then they could get on with the wedding and she could send for Maulsie and Big Simon and they could all settle down to a brand-new life. Perhaps not an exciting life, but a safe one. Which was just as well, because Sara was beginning to suspect she was not cut out for adventure.

Noise from the taproom made it all but impossible to sleep. Worry didn't help much, either, for her mind was filled with doubts no matter how much she tried to convince herself that everything was going just as she had planned.

Utterly exhausted, she had almost succumbed when the sound of someone pounding on her door brought her bolt upright.

*He was here!* Swinging out of bed and fumbling to

light a lamp, she cried, "I'm coming, I'm coming, just be patient."

It would have been more seemly, she thought as she flung on her wrapper if he had taken a room and met her in the morning over breakfast, but perhaps they did need to talk. There were certain formalities, she supposed—it would be just as well to get them over with as quickly as possible.

Setting the lamp back on the washstand, she opened the door and then jumped back as a pair of drunken seamen practically tumbled inside her bedroom.

"I do beg your pardon, sirs, but you have the wrong room!"

Hanging onto the door frame, the tallest of the pair swayed toward her. She shoved him upright. They were both grinning, and the bolder of the two—the one with the earring—managed to get inside her room and fling an arm around her. He was stronger than he looked—and he looked strong as an ox. Fortunately, he was also quite drunk.

Sara was not without experience when it came to repelling unwanted attentions, having lived with Titus Smithers for nearly eight years. Barefooted, she could do little damage with her heels, but a fist thrust sharply upward under a bulbous nose and a finger poked into a bloodshot eye was enough to make any man hesitate.

A moment's hesitation was all she needed. Snatching her umbrella from the cane stand beside the door, she whacked the smaller man on the head, jabbed the big one in his soft belly, and shoved them both out into the hall before they could recover. The washstand would have done nicely as a barricade, but it was too heavy to move. Instead, she snatched one of the two straight chairs, jammed it under the doorknob and placed the washbowl and a tumbler on the seat. There, she thought smugly, standing back to admire her handiwork. Small she might be, but between Simon and Maulsie, she knew how to protect herself against bullies.

Tomorrow she would demand a key.

All night long the noise continued. Only through sheer exhaustion was Sara finally able to gain a few hours of sleep. She awoke early, filled with fresh doubts. What had seemed such a wonderful idea only a few days ago was beginning to lose its luster.

However, she reminded herself, hearing the constant sound of arrivals and departures from the courtyard just outside her window, Archibald was bound to come today. No doubt he had wanted to set his house to rights before he took her there. Bachelors, she suspected, were less than perfect housekeepers.

Or perhaps he had been on the road and had only just got her letter. . . .

The hours crawled by. Mrs. Best came by to inquire after her health, not having seen her in the dining room at breakfast.

"I wasn't hungry."

"Then, I'll just have a pot of chocolate and some macaroons sent up," the woman announced, clearly intending to join her.

"Thank you, but I've a slight headache," Sara murmured apologetically. And truly, she did. Waiting was sheer agony. It opened the door to too many doubts.

"It's that disgusting pack of rabble rousers, is what it is," the woman said knowingly. "A decent person can't rest easy without wondering when some drunken fool is going to come busting through her door. For six cents you can rent a key, but then, every key opens every lock in the hotel, so what's the use?"

"I've found a chair under the doorknob works quite well," Sara said, and was gratified when the other woman agreed with her.

"Smarter than you look, ain't you? All the same, if the packet don't come today, I'll stay here with you tonight. A single woman can't be too careful."

"That's awfully kind of you, ma'am, but—"

"I know, I know, your young man will likely come along any minute now and whisk you away, and the last thing you need is a meddling old busybody dogging your coattails."

Her *young man*? After a polite, if distracted response, Sara closed the door and leaned against it, wondering if everyone in the hotel knew why she was here and what had happened last night.

Archibald couldn't arrive soon enough to suit her, Sara thought fervently. A quiet cottage with flowers in the yard and a kind, elderly gentleman to keep her company sounded just fine to her; it surely did.

Jericho was in no mood for the convivial atmosphere he found when he finally arrived at the hotel. A fresh northeast wind had sprung up just after sunup, blowing the smoke inland for a change instead of allowing it to lay like a pall over the entire countryside. Horses milled around, the fresh ones stamping and tossing their heads, eager to be on their way, while the blown ones stood docilely, heads hanging while they waited to be unpoled and turned into the livery paddock. Around the courtyard, men in varying degrees of soberness prepared to set off by boat, carriage or horseback, while others greeted new arrivals.

As he led Bones over to the livery shed, Jericho dug out a coin. "Rub him down, water him and give him a decent feed," he told the boy who jumped forward to take the reins. "Mind his teeth, though. He's right partial to ears."

The boy stepped back, tugged his stocking cap down over his ears and led the big gelding away while Jericho leaned tiredly against the wall. For all he knew, Smithers could be waiting for him right now. He hoped he wasn't. He could use a good night's sleep before he faced the bastard over the barrel of a gun. He hadn't slept in so long, he had all but forgotten what it was like.

Not that there was any reason to believe that tonight would be any different. Still, he intended to try. He had a job to do. Killing Smithers wouldn't bring back his sister, but he was determined to send the bastard to hell, even if it meant escorting him there personally. As it very well might.

For a moment, the noise around him seemed to fall away. A hot sun beat down on his head, and he took off his leather-brimmed black wool hat with the tarnished brass braid and ran a hand through his hair. God, how he wished he were back aboard the *Wilde Wind*, pacing the bridge while the salt air blew clean and fresh in his face, with nothing more on his mind than outrunning the latest storm blowing up from the Caribbean.

But she was no longer his. It had fair broke his heart to put her on the market, for the sea had been his life for nearly two decades, the *Wind* his home for nearly as long. But when, eight months after the event, Louisa's letter had caught up with him informing him that their parents had been killed in a carriage accident on the old log road, he had lit out of Puerto Barrios without even waiting to arrange a return cargo.

It had been too long since he had been back home. He'd felt guilty over that. Louisa had said to come if he could, because she needed him. Their father had left things in an unbelievable mess.

It had been that, all right. He could scarcely believe it.

Located in northern Pasquotank County, the farm had been in Jericho's family ever since his great-grandfather had traded a horse, a hog, and a bushel of oysters to Okisko, king of the Weopomeioks, for the rich, fertile acres. Or so the story was told. The old man had then married a woman of the same tribe, which accounted for the Wildes' dark coloring.

As a boy, Jericho had clashed with his father often, their temperaments poles apart. His father had been bookish. Jericho had not. He'd been a disappointment to both his parents, for he'd had a great talent for getting into trouble. Louisa had been the good child, yet Jericho had never resented her for it. He'd only been sorry his parents couldn't like him for who he was, but then, that was the way of it, he supposed. Some folks were likable. Some weren't.

At any rate, he had lost little sleep over the matter. At the age of thirteen he had gone to sea with his great-uncle Ethelbert and quickly discovered a love for that life.

Since then he had visited infrequently, mostly to see his sister Louisa, who had grown from a shy girl into a sweet, if rather plain, young woman. She had been twenty-nine when she had . . .

God. Even now he had trouble believing she was gone.

During the weeks he remained at home that first time, he'd had his hands full settling his parents' estate. Wilde Oaks had still looked prosperous enough on the surface, but closer inspection had proved that the house was suffering from damp rot, termites, and a leaking roof. His father had spent all his time and energies studying some of the more obscure English poets, to the detriment of all else.

Most of the field hands had drifted off and were probably living as free men in the swamp now. Thanks to the scoundrel who had served as overseer before he'd lit out with the only decent horse left, the outbuildings were in sad need of repair and nearly all the drainage ditches were clogged to the point that the fields were rapidly returning to swampland.

What he'd needed was money. A lot of it. Unfortunately, every penny Jericho had and more had been tied up in his ship. Less than a year earlier he'd been forced to borrow heavily to pay for repairs after a storm had caught them in a port in Argentina.

Unable to borrow more to restore Wilde Oaks, he'd been desperate. The farm was all Louisa had. Her dowry, should she ever marry. Her home and her only source of income should she remain single.

The irony of it now was enough to make him weep.

While he had been struggling to make sense of the farm accounts, Louisa, quieter than usual, but as dear to him as his own heart, had spent hours out walking with her red Chester duck dog, Brig. The pair were inseparable, which made Jericho feel somewhat better for having left her alone, except for the housekeeper, for so long.

He had been distracted with trying to find some source of funds in the damnably mysterious account books when she had confided diffidently that she'd been keeping company for some time with a gentleman from Virginia, seeing him whenever he came down to visit Rafe Turbyfill on the adjoining farm.

Glad that she had found congenial company, though somewhat surprised that she hadn't seen fit to confide in him sooner, Jericho thought he'd better look the gentleman over.

"Shall I invite him to dinner?" he asked.

Shyly, she had stared at the tip of her boot. "I— we—that is . . ."

"Never mind," he'd dismissed. She'd been timid as a child. She was even worse now. The amazing thing was that she'd found herself a young man at all.

So he had set out to reacquaint himself with Rafael Turbyfill, whom he hadn't seen since they'd been boys on neighboring farms.

"Bless me, if you ain't a sight!" the man had exclaimed. "Look like a damned pirate. Sure that ain't what you been up to, Rico? Come in, come in—have a drink, meet my friends. We're having us a house party here. Cards, a little hunting, a little racing, a few women—you know how it is."

Jericho didn't. He'd been hard at work for the past twenty years. Rafe had grown into a flush-faced dandy. He was still a handsome man, all togged out in a red and gold brocade waistcoat with the fanciest cravat Jericho had ever seen, but his eyes looked old. He looked

tired. For a man who was hosting a party, he looked
. . . sad.

As a boy Rafe had been something of a bully, but
Jericho had more than held his own in their frequent
brangles.

God, it made him feel old even thinking about it.

Rafe had summoned the young Virginian, Titus
Smithers, and introduced the two men. Smithers had
seemed surprised. Possibly, even nervous, although Jericho had put it down to the boy's youth.

He had come away from that first meeting with an
uneasy feeling. Not that there had been anything
openly objectionable about the lad, although he was
obviously some years younger than Louisa. He was certainly handsome enough, and well dressed if one liked
pretty velvet suits and fancy neckwear.

Jericho had reservations, but he'd told himself the
choice was not his to make. Louisa was of age. If they
wanted each other—if young Smithers could make her
happy, why then, they would have his blessings.

All the same, he hoped the fellow had a decent bank
account and knew something about running a farm,
because otherwise, Jericho was going to have to put
the *Wind* up for sale.

Three days later, after making a few more inquiries,
he had been forced to face the truth. The man his
sister was riding out with was dirt poor and a known
philanderer, with a reputation for sponging off his
friends.

Which meant that not only was Jericho going to have
to sell his ship, he was going to have to break the news
to Louisa about her intended.

Eventually, he had told himself, he would get another ship. Or captain another man's ship if he had to.

His sister might not be so fortunate. A woman's choices were far more limited than those of a man.

It had been bad. She had refused to hear a word against the man, and when she burst into tears and locked herself in her room, Jericho had taken the coward's way out.

He had left. Telling Hester Renegar, the housekeeper who had been there forever, that he would be back as quickly as possible, he had taken the train to Baltimore, put his ship in the hands of a reputable broker and finally sold her for more than enough money to pay off his loan and restore Wilde Oaks. The process had taken longer than he'd expected, but finally he had headed south again, worried about Louisa, desolate over the loss of his ship, but ready to begin salvaging his family's heritage.

It was too late. It had been too late before he'd ever left Wilde Oaks in the first place, although neither he nor Louisa had realized that fact.

"Damn the bastard, and may his soul rot in hell," Jericho swore softly, his back braced against the whitewashed wall of the stable.

"You want I should take your bag in, cap'n?"

It was the livery lad, hoping for another coin. Jericho would just as soon have carried his own duffle, but he admired the avaricious gleam in the boy's eye. "Sure, son. Mind you don't drop it. Speak me a room while you're at it, name of Wilde."

"It'll have to be the common. All the rooms is took."

Jericho nodded, and the boy dashed off, tilting under the heavy duffle, which contained a matched pair of flawlessly balanced dueling pistols. As Wilde had issued the challenge, Smithers would get to choose the weapons, but what else would a man use to kill another man? No one used swords in this day and age.

Jericho would have preferred to use his bare hands.

Levering himself away from the wall of the livery stable, he ambled tiredly across the open courtyard. He was halfway to the main entrance when something prompted him to lift his gaze to the tall window on the Carolina side of the main entrance.

The face he encountered there flat-out stopped him in his tracks. Jericho stared. The woman stared right back. For one fleeting moment, something about her put him in mind of Louisa. He couldn't for the life of him figure out what it was. Something about her eyes . . .

Louisa, God rest her, had been on the plain side. This woman was a beauty, although not in the common mold. His sister had been pale, with dark hair and eyes. She'd been as gentle as a moth, timid and utterly trusting. Animals had loved her. Even now, that dog of hers was mourning himself to death.

What was it about this woman, then—she was hardly more than a girl, from the looks of her—that reminded him of Louisa? Was it the way she stood there, as if she were waiting for something and half afraid of whatever—or whoever—it was she was waiting for?

"Judas priest," he muttered, tearing his gaze away from the face in the window. That damned swamp fire smoke was rotting his brain!

Crossing the lobby toward the registration desk, Jericho nearly ran over a small, stout woman in the ugliest bonnet he had ever seen. She was talking up a storm to a pair of gray-haired sticks who were lapping up every word she said.

If there was one thing he didn't need right now, it was a run-in with a swarm of busy bees. He was here to kill a man, and the fewer who knew about it, the better he liked it. Louisa's misfortune had died with her. He was pretty sure no one knew, but duels always gave rise to speculation, and he wasn't about to take any chances.

He learned at the desk that Rafe wasn't yet registered. Nor was Smithers and whatever scum he had chosen to second him. Jericho went into the dining room in a somber mood, determined to enjoy his last meal, if such was to be his fate. Without meaning to, he glanced around, hoping for a glimpse of the mysterious young beauty, but she wasn't among the diners.

Which was just as well. The last thing he needed at this point was to be faced with another pair of big, reproachful eyes.

Politely, Sara listened as Mrs. Best rambled on about who was who in Pasquotank County, and exactly how they were related. Although the woman lived in Elizabeth City, she evidently had relatives scattered all the way up and down the eastern seaboard.

"I do like to travel," Cordelia Best confided over a dinner of baked shad and roasted potatoes. She had arranged to have their meal served in Sara's room. "Do you know, I'm almost certain I saw that young Wilde boy downstairs, the one that went to sea with his uncle ever so long ago?"

Sara had more on her mind than boys, wild or tame, but Cordelia needed little encouragement to continue her monologue. "I heard the poor Wilde girl passed away not long ago. They say she caught a fever and collapsed, and before old Doc Withers could even get to her, she was gone. My, it don't seem fair, does it? Her folks was killed little more than a year ago. Hit a boggy place in the log road, landed in the river, and the horse with 'em. That poor boy, I wonder if he brought the fever back with him from one of those heathen foreign places . . ."

It was the strangest thing, Sara thought as she toyed with her fork. Across the table, Cordelia's voice droned on and on about things and people in which Sara hadn't the least interest.

Instead, and against all reason, she was remembering the man who had stared at her from out in the courtyard.

And to her everlasting shame, she had stared right back. It was mostly because of the way he walked, although not entirely. Sara had never paid particular attention to the way a man walked, and certainly not to his . . . well, his *parts*.

But this man was different. The way he moved—the way his clothes fit him, as though they were a part of him. He had a way of walking that made her think he'd been riding for a long time. As if he weren't quite sure of the ground beneath his feet.

For the longest time after he had moved out of sight, she had thought about him. She'd even ventured a few swaggering steps in front of the looking glass to see if she could replicate his powerful, graceful stride, but either her limbs were too short or her shoulders too narrow, or she wasn't put together in the same way.

But it wasn't just the way he walked, nor the fact

that he was dressed entirely in black. There was something about his face. About his eyes. From where she'd been standing, she couldn't even determine the color, yet she was quite certain that if she saw those eyes again, even years from now, she would remember them. There was something incredibly sad about them.

Impulsively, Sara made up her mind to ask Archibald, as soon as he arrived, to look out for the man and see if there was anything they could do for him.

# Chapter Four

Sleep was impossible in the common room, even if Jericho had nothing more on his mind than whether to have herring or ham for breakfast. With only eight rooms in the hotel, most men bunked together, using bedrolls or blankets on the floor.

Among the shingle captains, swamp lumbermen and other rough customers, talk was crude, raucous, sometimes funny. Jericho was in no mood to be amused. Neither was he in any mood to put up with listening to speculations on the various attributes of the brown-haired beauty. Bets were placed on whether or not she was here to meet a lover, whether or not the lover would show up, whether he would marry her if he did show up, and whether or not she was ripe for a tumble in the meantime.

Momentarily distracted from his own dismal affairs, he flung down his saddle blanket in the farthest corner of the crowded room, stretched his six-foot, two-inch length on the thinly covered floor, crossed his arms over his chest and stared up at the smoke-darkened ceiling.

He tried not to listen. The woman, whoever she was, would be safe enough. She probably had a maid traveling with her. At any rate the doors had locks, didn't they? All she had to do was turn her key.

Yes, and every key would likely unlock every other door in the hotel, he thought ruefully. Skeleton keys were all but worthless.

Jericho told himself the woman was not his problem. He had never felt at ease around women—leastwise, not around respectable women. His entire adult life had been spent among men of the roughest sort.

Besides, he had too much on his mind to concern himself with some big-eyed waif with skin the color of sourwood honey and eyes as big as chestnuts. In a face that was too vulnerable by half.

Unbidden, his mind filled once more with the images that had haunted him for days. Louisa as a small child racing down the lane after a puppy, tripping over her shoelaces, tumbling headlong and then wailing for "Weeco" to come pick her up and chop off her hateful old shoestrings.

His had been the arms that had comforted her when the pup had died of the flux. She'd been seven at the time. Ten years later, when he had come home for a rare holiday visit, he had been the one to dry her tears when her best friend married the young man both girls had loved.

Oddly enough, they had remained close over the years, right up until he had taken command of his own ship, when his duties had multiplied a hundredfold. His father had never written to him. Not a single letter. His mother couldn't write, but Louisa had written to him often, her letters catching up to him in bunches. He had written back, but not, perhaps, as frequently as he should have. His only excuse was that he'd been busy, and the corn, tobacco and potato fields of Wilde Oaks had seemed a world away.

He had hated to leave her that last time, only partly because of what he would have to do. Perhaps even then, he'd had a premonition.

When he'd come back after selling his ship, with the funds in hand to hire carpenters, field hands and a new overseer to begin putting the farm back to rights, he had been greeted by a pale, desperately thin woman who was scarcely recognizable as the sister he had left behind little more than a month earlier.

Knowing something was badly amiss, he had suspected it had to do with that damned Virginian with whom she'd been keeping company. His first evening home he had persuaded Louisa to tell him what was wrong, expecting to hear the sad, if predictable tale of another broken romance.

Instead he'd been stunned to learn that she was with child. She had broken down and cried in his arms, explaining in gulps and gasps that she had only just found out, and had not yet had a chance to tell Smithers about the baby because he'd been called home by a sick mother and had been unable to return. He had forgotten to leave her his direction, and Rafe had not known how to reach him.

"But he's back now," she had said with a feverishly hopeful smile. "I saw his horse in the paddock with Rafe's big gray just before dark when I took Brig out for his evening walk. I'm sure he'll be seeking you out first thing tomorrow, because now that my year of mourning is up, there's no more reason to wait." Her eyes had pleaded with him for understanding. Or perhaps for reassurance.

Jericho's first impulse had been to hunt down the bastard and wring his neck for treating any woman, especially one so gentle and innocent, in such a shameful, disrespectful manner.

Evidently, Louisa had read his thoughts. "Don't be angry, Rico. I love him so much, and I—I'm sure he loves me, too, only his mother has been sick so much lately, and—and, well, it just happened, that's all. Besides, it's not as if I were in my first youth."

Grudgingly, Jericho had admitted that perhaps at Louisa's age, a certain amount of impatience was understandable, but damn it all, the rogue should have known better than to leave her with child. There were ways of protecting a woman. What if something had happened to him before he could marry her? She would have been ruined. Not only heartbroken, but flat-out *ruined*!

Jericho had wanted to collar the cad and haul the pair of them up before the nearest preacher before the sun set on another day.

Unfortunately, he had scheduled an interview with a possible overseer for the following morning. As the man was coming all the way from Perquimans County to meet him, he couldn't very well send him away and ask him to come back another time. Distracted, he had forced himself to go through with the interview, and after hiring the man, he'd had to take still more time to show him around the farm and try to answer his questions.

God alone knew if he'd made any sense, with his mind on far more vital matters.

"Where's Miss Louisa?" he'd demanded of the

housekeeper the moment he'd seen the man off the property.

Hester Renegar, a dour woman who had kept house for them for as long as Jericho could remember—who had been known irreverently as old Vinegar when they were children—had gone on breaking eggs into a big graniteware bowl. "Gone sparkin', I reckon. Buggy left out about an hour ago, with that mangy old hound of hers trotting alongside. Shut 'im up in the barn, but he dug out."

Brig wasn't mangy and he wasn't a hound, but defending the dog had been the last thing on Jericho's mind at the time. He had saddled up Bones and set off at a tooth-rattling gallop across the field toward the Turbyfill farm.

"Where's Smithers?" he'd demanded, bursting through the door.

Rafe Turbyfill was dozing over a brandy, a big, battered tomcat sprawled across his knees. "Titus? What's the young fool been up to now?"

"Never mind that, just tell me where to find him."

The older man tugged at the cat's ear, then dumped the animal when it clawed him. "Damned ingrate," he muttered. "Talking about me cat, Rico, not you. Last I saw of Smithers, he was headed down the lane. We were playing cards, and he spotted Louisa's buggy down by the pond and took off. Surprising, the way she took to him. She could do a lot better, even if she is getting a bit long in the tooth."

Rafael Turbyfill eyed the man who had bested him more often than not at racing, fighting, hunting, and gaming when they were boys. Weighing his words, he said, "If I was you, Rico, I wouldn't encourage nothing in that direction. Young Smithers is good enough for rough company, but he ain't good husband material, if you know what I mean. "

Jericho was afraid he did, although it was a little too late now. "Much obliged, Tubby," he said, absently dredging up a hated nickname. Taking the steps two at a time, he leapt on board the gelding and wheeled back down the long, pecan-lined road.

They weren't at the pond that had been a favorite fishing hole for all three as children. Feeling an odd sense of disquiet, Jericho headed home. Likely, he would find her in the kitchen, talking wedding plans with old Vinegar.

They'd damned well *better* be laying plans! Husband material or not, the bastard was going to marry her. What's more, if he so much as brought a frown to her face, he would answer to Jericho, because this time he wouldn't be halfway around the world; he would be right here to protect his sister's interests.

At least for a spell. Until he found himself another ship.

God, he was going to be an uncle, he thought, bemused as he rode home at a far slower pace than he'd set out.

The rest of the afternoon passed slowly. Hester Renegar served him a cold meal at his desk. Ignoring it, he asked again after Louisa.

"Still out. Lots to talk about, I reckon, poor young'un. Heard the dog a-barkin' up a storm not more'n an hour ago, sounded like he was down by the hedgerow."

"Likely run up a rabbit." He was glad she had taken the dog.

It was late in the afternoon when Jericho, caught up

in the farm account book, which was not so different from a logbook now that he'd had time to get a grip on it, heard Brig barking outside. Closing the book, he stood and rubbed the tense muscles at the back of his neck.

She was home. It was about time. Engaged or not, Smithers had no business keeping her out this late of an evening. They'd damned well better have scheduled a fast wedding, otherwise they were going to find themselves hustled off the nearest joiner so fast their shoe soles would smoke! No nephew of his was going to be born on the wrong side of the blanket and have to bear the shame of it for the rest of his life.

Erasing all signs of anger and worry from his face, Jericho headed outside to unhitch the buggy and rub down Louisa's mare. He'd expected to see Smithers with her, but there was no sign of the young jack-a-dandy.

"You're late," he said, careful to keep any hint of anger or disapproval from his voice. "Shouldn't you be resting more now that . . ." His voice had trailed off, and he'd stared at the creature who all but fell into his arms. "God almighty, Weezie, what happened?"

She'd been weeping hysterically, making barely a sound. Her hair was tumbled around her shoulders. She had always taken great pride in her hair, for it was long and lustrous, the color of a crow's wing. Now it was tangled and—Jesus, was that blood?

"Louisa! Hush now and tell me what happened! Did the buggy roll?" Of course the buggy hadn't rolled. She'd never have got it righted again without help.

She had clung to him, her fingers biting into his arms with surprising strength while the damned dog pranced around them, twisting and whining. Ignoring the mutt, Jericho had held her away to force her to look at him, to answer him, and then he wished to God he hadn't.

He had carried her into the house, trying not to stare at the bruises, the abrasions—at the place on her cheek where it looked as if she'd been caught by a vine.

Hester had taken over as soon as he'd laid her on her bed. "I was afraid of this," the stern-faced old woman had muttered. Jericho had wanted to know what she meant, but there'd been no time to ask.

Without bothering to saddle Bones, he had raced off bareback after old Doc Withers, who lived some four miles away. Barking out a few words of direction, he had sent the man back to Wilde Oaks and then set off for Rafe's farm to find Smithers. There had been not a single doubt in his mind as to who was responsible.

Before he had even reached the split-rail fence between the two properties, he'd seen a flashy red and black runabout wheel out of Rafe's driveway and head north at a rapid clip.

"Smithers! Damn your black soul, come back here!" he'd shouted, kicking up his winded mount.

The driver had glanced over his shoulder and had begun frantically whipping the blue roan, the flimsy vehicle bouncing on the rough road and nearly over-turning twice. With the slightest shift of his weight, Jericho had urged the gelding into a dirt-eating gallop. As if he'd known the desperate stakes—as if he hadn't already been lathered from racing to fetch the doctor—Bones had flattened out and given chase.

The race had ended almost as quickly as it had begun.

"Get down from there, you scurvy bastard." Jericho's voice had been soft, but the deadly threat was unmistakable. Panic had widened the other man's eyes. Under pale, arched brows, they were a perfect match for his blue velvet coat.

"Keep away from me, you madman!" Smithers had screamed. From atop the high seat of his fancy vehicle, he had snapped his whip at the devil dressed all in black—a devil with murder in his eyes.

With a lightning-like move, Jericho caught the weighted end of the braided leather whip and jerked hard, tumbling the younger man to the ground. Rolling off the back of his horse, he was on him instantly.

No fighter, Smithers had been paralyzed with fear. Dirt caught in a thread of spittle, marring his flawless features. Jericho had been within an inch of wrapping his hands around his lily-white throat when a voice behind him had coolly spoken. "You don't really want to do that, Rico. Kill him now and you'll only hang for your troubles, and then who'll look after Louisa?"

Bending over the cowering creature on the ground, Jericho had waited for the fire in his belly to cool. Rafe was right. This wasn't the way to do it, not if he intended to live long enough to look after his sister and her baby.

"You don't know what you're asking of me," he had growled.

"Probably not, but whatever you've got against the boy, this is no way to settle it." Rafe had still been mounted on his big gray. He had gazed down on the scene dispassionately, his face flushed from too many years of high living. "Back off, Rico."

"I want him dead."

The man on the ground had whimpered and tried to scramble away. Rising slowly, Jericho had placed a big, booted foot on his coattail.

It was Rafe who had issued the instructions. They would meet at the Halfway Hotel as soon as Smithers could find someone to act for him. Was that clear?

It was clear.

By the time the details had been settled, Smithers was puking his guts out in the middle of the road.

Jericho and Rafe had ridden back together. Neither man had spoken until they'd reached the place where the road turned off to enter Turbyfill's nine hundred acres.

"I'll act for you if you'll have me," the older man had said quietly. "I feel partly responsible. He was my guest."

Jericho had nodded. "Obliged," he'd said. "And Rafe—thanks for saving me from being buzzard bait. I'd have murdered the son of a bitch right there in the road."

"Louisa?"

He'd nodded. "He beat her."

Turbyfill's hooded eyes had darkened. "Jesus," he had muttered.

Jericho had remained silent. He'd seen no reason to mention the child. It would be common knowledge soon enough.

"Give Smithers a few days. Doubt if he'll find anyone real eager to second him."

"I'd rather go back and finish the job now," Jericho had said with a harsh laugh.

"Go home. If there's anything I can do, send word. Otherwise, I'll meet you at the hotel in about a week's time. And Rico—don't worry. I'll see the boy's there if I have to drag him there, myself."

Looking back, Jericho wished Rafe had never come along that day. Wished he had finished what he'd started—not that it would have changed anything. Louisa was gone, taking with her any need to save himself from the hangman's noose.

It had been too late by the time he'd got back home. He'd known it as soon as he'd seen old Doc Withers walking out to his buggy. The old man had looked a hundred years old. Jericho had felt his blood run cold, quite literally. He'd always thought that cold-running blood was merely a figure of speech. It wasn't.

He had flung himself to the ground and slapped the gelding on the rump. "What's wrong?" he'd demanded, catching up to the physician just as he was placing his black leather satchel in his old fashioned buggy.

"I'm sorry, son. I did all I could. I don't believe she wanted to live. Once the bleeding started, there was no way I could help her. I tried everything I knew to do, but sometimes, the Lord's will prevails."

Jericho had commenced to swearing. He had sworn to keep from crying, but he'd cried anyway.

"I take it you knew she was with child," the old man said quietly.

Lifting his wet face to a sky that had been streaked with the last remnants of a smoky sunset, Jericho said, "I knew."

And so he had buried her. Buried her on the low rise that passed for a hill in this flat country, under the big woods maple, beside their parents and the two babes that had died in infancy.

And now he was waiting to finish what had to be finished before he could go back to sea. God knows, he had no desire ever to see Wilde Oaks again. For all he cared, Hester and the new manager he had hired could split it between them.

Sometime after midnight, the noise abated. Jericho was on the verge of falling asleep when he heard two men speculating again about the woman in room three. It didn't take a whole lot of imagination to realize they were speaking of the brown-haired beauty he had glimpsed at the window on his arrival.

With a soft oath, he rolled over on the hard floor and stuffed his rolled-up coat under his head, but it was impossible to ignore what was being said.

"Way I heard it, she's alone over there in the Carolina wing. Don't even have a maid with 'er. Not but one kind o' woman stays in a hotel without a maid."

"Less'n she's waitin' for a husband."

"Either waitin' er runnin' away. Packet boats an' stages runs both ways."

"Aww, she ain't married. She ain't got that married look to 'er. I got me two dollars. Reck'n that's enough?" one young tough speculated.

Jericho had about all he could stomach. The lady, regardless of her situation, deserved to be treated with more respect. Sitting up, he eased one of his two pistols from his duffle and rested it across his lap.

"Gentlemen," he said with cutting calmness, "disturbing a lady's sleep is downright unmannerly. Not to mention unhealthy."

You could have heard a fly land. After a moment, one man cursed and spit. Another one gave a nervous laugh. Then they were at it again, boasting, threatening, calling for another bottle.

Resigned to a sleepless night, Jericho got to his feet and gathered up his blanket and duffle. He slept in his boots. It was either that or risk having them stolen.

"If you'll excuse me," he said politely. Stepping over two drunks who were passed out over a deck of grimy cards, he headed for the door.

"Hey, you ain't going after 'er, are ye? That ain't fair! I saw 'er first!" whined one young buck who was either bolder or drunker than his mates.

"Rest easy, gentlemen. The lady is entitled to her sleep."

As it happened, Jericho also slept well for the rest of the night. The hallway that ran along the bedrooms was considerably quieter, not to mention cleaner, than the common room.

But that hadn't been the sole reason he had done what he'd done. He had kept order among rougher crews than those in the common room, and without once resorting to the cat.

The woman was someone's sister. Or daughter.

Or wife.

Although, for no reason he could put his finger on, he rather thought she was unmarried. The drunk was right—she didn't have a married look about her.

But regardless of her status, he felt compelled to do what he could to protect her. For Louisa's sake, if not his own. And so he spent the remainder of the night stretched across her doorway, his head pillowed on his coat, arms crossed over his chest, a long-barreled pistol in his right hand.

# Chapter Five

On her way out to visit the necessary, Sara almost tripped over the man sprawled across her doorsill.

"Merciful saints alive," she exclaimed, "you're the man in black!"

He rose to his feet stiffly. And rose and rose and rose. He was taller than he had looked from a distance. "Beg pardon, ma'am. Didn't mean to block your passage."

"Did you drop something?" Sara stared up at a face that was all planes and angles, without a scrap of softness. Surely he hadn't been trying to peep through her keyhole. He hardly seemed the type.

"Truth to tell, I was sleeping. It's considerably quieter here than it is over in the common room."

In the shadowy hallway, the man loomed over her. His hair, his eyes and his clothing were as dark as sin, yet she felt not the least bit intimidated. "Yes, well . . . I suppose it is."

Oddly enough, she was inclined to believe him. He did have a blanket, after all, and a satchel. And his clothes, while plain and a bit worn, were of good quality. There was a gleam on his tall boots that bespoke the finest leather. Suspecting that he was unable to pay for a bed and too proud to say so, Sara went out of her way not to hurt his feelings. She did know the value of pride.

Hat in his hands, he seemed to make up his mind about something. "Ma'am, it occurred to me that a lady staying alone—that is, in a place like this, there's some that might misunderstand—"

Touched by the odd mixture of strength and diffidence, Sara said, "Thank you, sir. If you're offering to escort me through the lobby, I grant I would appreciate it. I don't relish having to pass by that rowdy taproom on my way outside to the, um—the spring."

Should she offer him money?

No, he would hate that. Besides, after giving Maulsie and Simon most of what she had on hand, she had scarcely enough to pay for her own board unless she wrote another bank draft. And if she did that, Titus might be able to trace her through the bank.

The truth was that if Archibald didn't come soon, she might be forced to sleep in the common room herself, wherever and whatever that was.

No one could have been more respectful than the tall, somber stranger. He was waiting beside the back door when she came out of the necessary, having done her business and set her skirts aright. They both pretended she had merely stepped outside to fetch a tumblerful of spring water. Sara remarked on the weather and the brilliance of the sun on the nearby canal, and he nodded thoughtfully.

"Yes, ma'am, it is indeed a fine day." He seemed to brace himself to say more. "Ma'am, it would please me greatly if you'd agree to take breakfast with me. My name is Jericho Wilde. I can ask the desk clerk to introduce us."

*Wilde. Wilde . . .*

Now why did that ring a bell? Sara pursed her lips thoughtfully while her companion waited for her answer. "Do you happen to know a Mrs. Best from Elizabeth City? I believe she left early this morning on the packet *Albemarle,* but she might have mentioned your name over dinner last night."

For a single moment, a look akin to panic crossed the man's lean, sun-browned face. "No, ma'am, I can't say as I do."

"Well. Never mind. I'm ashamed to say, I wasn't paying all that much attention, anyhow." Her eyes glinted with rueful amusement. "Breakfast, you say? To tell the truth, I don't really relish dining alone. I've learned that it's possible to have one's meals served in one's room, which is convenient if one happens to enjoy cold soup and congealed eggs."

"Then, shall we?"

And with the courtliest of all gestures he offered her the support of his arm, enabling her to enter the dining room feeling like a queen. Or at least a princess.

Or at the very least, someone who hadn't been abandoned on the far side of a whole string of burned bridges.

Breakfast was delightful. Sara learned, among other things, that his proper title was Captain. Captain Jericho Wilde.

"Although," he admitted, "I'm presently between ships."

Poor man. He was probably hoping to be taken on by one of the vessels that stopped regularly at the hotel.

She tried to think of some way she could help him, but nothing came to mind. They talked at length, although later, when she was standing at her window watching for Archibald, it occurred to Sara that for all he had gone on about foreign ports and the fascinating ways of different people around the world, she didn't know anything at all about the man himself.

Which made it all the more strange that she was so drawn to him. She did know that he was strong. Her father had been a weak man, her mother a semi-invalid for as long as Sara could remember. Titus and Noreen were even weaker. Sara got so very tired of having to be the strong one of the family. She would like, for just a little while, to be able to lean on someone stronger.

She knew, too, that he wasn't frightening. Perhaps it was because of the hint of despair that lurked in the depths of his dark eyes. She'd thought at first that she had imagined it, but it really was there. Sometimes only a shadow—sometimes more.

Whatever bothered him, it didn't keep him from treating her as if she were made of spun sugar and might shatter at the first harsh word. The novelty of that alone was enough to enchant her. If he only knew, she thought with amusement, that she could hitch up a mule and plow as straight a furrow as any man. She could bargain with the best for top price for her butterbeans and melons, and chase a weasel from her henhouse with no more than a willow switch.

Not that she'd been brought up to do all that. Once upon a time there had been servants to see to her every comfort, but times changed. It was just as well she'd had the chance to learn that she was perfectly capable of looking after herself.

\* \* \*

Jericho paced the yard fronting onto the canal road. Within the week, Rafe had said. It had already been five days. Or was it six? God, he had lost all sense of time.

From behind him came the steady din of water traffic; sail, steam, and oar. Absently, he watched two boys paddle by in a dugout, ducking into a feeder ditch as the *Lima* passed by with a blast from her steam whistle. Next came the *Only Son,* warped by two teams of oxen so slowly that her gentle wake barely disturbed the reeds along the shore.

He thought of his own ship and wondered if she was being refitted or if she was already under sail, under the command of another man.

And then he set his mind back on course and resumed his watch for Smithers. Sooner or later, the scurvy bastard would have to show up. Not even a sniveling coward could ignore a direct challenge, not with a witness standing by.

Setting aside his own anxiety, Jericho made it a point to be waiting in the hallway outside her door when Miss Young stepped out for the midday meal. She needed the protection. He needed the distraction.

Besides, he couldn't help but admire her gumption. She was at a disadvantage, being a young, respectable woman at a hotel that was none too respectable. At first, he'd figured she was too innocent to know the dangers. Now he was beginning to believe she knew, but was too plucky to be intimidated by them.

At any rate, she needed someone to stand between her and the scum from the common room. As long as he was at loose ends, he might as well take the position.

She stepped outside, turned and locked her door, then smiled ruefully at the shiny new skeleton key, indicating that she knew full well how ineffective such an instrument was likely to be.

"Better than no key at all," he said, tipping his cap.

"But not as good as a heavy piece of furniture," she countered, dropping the key into her reticule. She was wearing a pretty yellow dress that brought out glints of gold in her light brown hair. When he complimented her, she confided shyly that it was to be her wedding dress. "I would have liked something blue, but there was no time to have anything made up."

Her wedding?

Her wedding. He'd known she was waiting for someone. Everyone in the hotel knew that.

Jericho didn't want to talk about weddings or wedding gowns. Not that he begrudged Sara her happiness, but the thought of a wedding—any woman's wedding—brought back his sister's pitifully brief dreams.

Taking a deep breath, he closed a door in his mind. "If you've no other plans, may I escort you to the dining room?" He held out his arm, and she placed her small, shapely hand on his sleeve. Suddenly, he felt six inches taller.

Over bowls of thick cabbage soup, Sara explained that she had come to the hotel to meet her intended but was beginning to wonder if her letter setting the time and place could have gone astray.

Jericho choked on a bit of salt port. *She* had set the time and place? He wouldn't have thought her so forward, but then, his experience with women was admittedly limited.

"I simply can't go back home," she confessed once the soup plates were cleared away and they were served stewed chicken and dumplings with rutabagas.

"Burned bridges?" Jericho asked.

She nodded. "Something of the sort."

"Bridges can be mended."

"Some bridges are not worth mending."

From which he deduced that the lady had left behind an unhappy situation. It was none of his affair. Nor was the fact that she refused to allow him to pay for her meal and instead carefully counted out the correct amount and returned the rest to a rather flat purse.

The lady had her pride.

After leaving the crowded dining room, they strolled along the canal bank together. Jericho tried to think of a diplomatic way he could offer her money. God knows, he had no need of it, with Louisa gone and his own future uncertain. He had no intention of returning to Wilde Oaks. Not yet, at least. Not until the grass had had time to grow over Louisa's grave and he'd had time to heal.

Maybe not even then.

Gazing down at the small figure beside him, with her leaf brown hair and her warm brown eyes, Jericho told himself that until her Mr. Ricketts turned up, she was in need of a protector. That much, at least, he could do for her. Louisa had needed a protector, and he'd failed her, being too concerned over having to sell his ship to see what was going on right under his very nose.

This time, he would not fail.

As the *Albemarle* steamed away from the landing and new arrivals scattered, either to register at the hotel or catch the connecting stage, Sara heaved a wistful little sigh, then seemed to collect herself and smiled. "Well, that's that, I suppose. The packet has come and gone again, and no Archibald. Maybe tomorrow."

Jericho stopped himself just before he slipped an arm about her shoulders. "There's plenty of time," he said. "Next stage'll be along directly. Riders coming in all the time. Your young man will be along presently."

If he had a grain of sense, he would. The man must be a fool indeed to leave a woman like this alone in a hotel filled with transients and the roughest elements of society.

Over dinner that night, Sara kept up a sprightly conversation, her cheerfulness flagging only now and then. She was trying to cheer him up, Jericho realized in amazement. When had anyone ever done that? When had anyone even given a single damn as to how he felt?

Should he tell her he was a lost cause?

No. Let her ramble on. God knows he could do with the distraction, and until Smithers showed up, he had nothing better to do with his time.

"It's my stepmother, you see," she said, and he realized that he'd missed part of what she was saying. "I happened to come into some money awhile back. I'd thought to pay off the mortgage, only then there wouldn't be much left, and I do want to settle enough on Maulsie and Big Simon so they won't have to work until they drop in their tracks. Only my stepmother wants me to marry her son and keep it all in the family."

"You're not interested in the lad, I take it?"

Sara shuddered. "Mercy, no. I'd be penniless again in a week's time. He's a gambler of the worse sort, and besides, he drinks too much, and he has this way of—well, I suppose you could call it a mean streak."

Why she felt compelled to confide in this solemn stranger, Sara would never know. It wasn't her nature to burden others with her troubles—not that anyone had volunteered to shoulder the burden. It occurred to her that she and the captain were not unlike ships in the night, touching briefly, then each going its own way, never again to meet.

Which was sad, in a way, for she did like being with him. Liked looking at him, for while he was not strictly handsome—at least, not in the same way Titus was handsome—there was something reassuring about that square jaw and those steady dark eyes.

Even so, she must take care not to mention any more names. She was not all that far from home, and sooner or later most travelers in the Tidewater area had cause to pass this way, for it was the most direct route south—or north, as the case may be. Titus regularly came this way. Fortunately, he could seldom afford a hotel and usually managed to sponge off friends, or even friends of friends.

"But even if I liked him," she continued earnestly, "I would never want to be married for my money. The whole time Mr. Ricketts was paying me particular attention, I was poor as a church mouse. He liked me anyway."

Jericho murmured a response, his attention captured by the way her mouth moved when she talked. She had a remarkably expressive face. Not a face that could keep secrets easily. But she was keeping them. Or trying to. He didn't know what they were, nor did he want to know.

"—So I said to myself," she continued. Again he'd missed the first part of her statement. "I said, Sara Rebecca, that man is plumb hungry for companionship, but if you wait for him to pop the question, you'll be waiting until—" She clapped a hand over her mouth. "Oops! I never meant to tell you that. You won't tell anyone I did the asking, will you?"

Jericho's eyes sparkled with amusement. The little witch! She had proposed to her man as well as naming the place and day. He gave her full marks for gumption and only hoped her judgment was as sharp.

A short while later he saw her to her room, waited until he heard the key turn in the lock and the chair slide under the doorknob, and then went back out to the lobby, acutely aware of the curious gazes following his course. The same ones that followed them into and out of the dining room, and out along the canal bank.

It couldn't be helped. The lady needed protection, and until her young man arrived to keep her safe, why then, they would just have to contend with the whispers and speculative looks.

Striding purposefully toward the bat-wing doors, Jericho waved them open, crossed to the bar, ordered a whiskey, and then turned to face the crowd. He was wearing his usual garb, a plain black shirt and a black worsted suit. With his dark coloring, the effect was sobering. Having taken command of his first ship at the age of twenty-three, he had found it necessary to employ a few props to maintain order. Now, at the age of thirty-two, he no longer needed such things.

Command came as natural to him as breathing, but being a creature of habit, he still wore black.

Deliberately, Jericho allowed his gaze to move around the smoke-filled room, touching on first one rough customer, then another. He planted his hands on his hips and hooked his thumbs in the waist of his trousers, shoving his coat back just far enough to reveal his guns. In the days before he had set out from Wilde Oaks, he had practiced until he could hole a card at twenty paces and put out a candle at ten. He felt like a damn fool wearing the things—he had no need of guns to command authority—but in a place like this, a smart man didn't leave his valuables lying about for pilfering fingers to discover. Besides, a pair of fine weapons might discourage any would-be trouble-makers.

Early the following morning, Jericho was on his way to the dining room, Sara Young on his arm, when Rafe Turbyfill arrived. He paused in the doorway and Jericho looked past him, half expecting to see Smithers's girlish face. Not now, damn it, he thought, and turned to lead Sara into the dining room, hoping Turbyfill hadn't spotted him.

No such luck. The older man quickly crossed the crowded lobby and removed his beaver. "Morning, Rico. Care to present me to your friend?"

Alongside Rafe Turbyfill in his fancy claw hammer coat, his brocade waistcoat and his Polish cape, Jericho suddenly felt like a damned crow. Tight-lipped, he made the introductions. He told himself that the resentment he felt was only because he didn't want Sara to be touched by a single element of the nasty business that had brought him here.

Neither did he particularly care for the quick gleam of interest in Turbyfill's jaded eyes.

"You're on your way in to breakfast, I take it? Then I'm just in time, ain't I?" Turbyfill spoke as cheerfully as if he weren't there for the express purpose of watching a man die. Because they both knew Jericho had no intention of deloping. The law seldom punished scum like Smithers. That duty was left to the male members of the victim's family.

"Shall we?" Rafe Turbyfill extended an elbow to Sara. "That coffee smells downright paradisiacal."

*Paradisiacal?*

Jericho shot the man a scathing look. "If I was you, I'd be after securing a room," he said with false congeniality. "They seem to be at a premium around here."

"I thought I'd share your quarters."

"Then it'll be the common room. You might ask at the desk. Something could have opened up by now." So saying, Jericho turned to the now empty place where Sara had stood a moment ago.

"If you're looking for your ladybird, she's gone inside. Right now she's being seated a table with a pair of old haunts who must've ridden in on the last broomstick. Friends of yours?"

"Hell and damnation," Jericho said quietly. It was bad enough to have been forced to introduce her to Turbyfill. It was even worse to see her gathered to the scrawny bosoms of that pair of flap-jaws.

"Come outside for a spell," Rafe said, suddenly serious. The breakfast and the paradisiacal coffee were apparently forgotten. "We need to talk, and I'd just as lief not have an audience."

Neither of the men spoke until they had gained the relative privacy of a persimmon thicket on the far side of the road. Rafe pointed out a clearing some distance into the woods.

"That's the place, I believe. Road cuts off just below that big cypress there. It's wide enough for a cart to get through to haul the—uh . . ." He cleared his throat and turned his attention to the task of clipping the tip off a cigar.

"To haul the corpse off," Jericho finished for him. To think that inside the hotel, a few hundred feet away, Sara was having her breakfast, daintily sipping her tea and parrying prying questions from those two old biddies he'd seen in the lobby the day he'd arrived. And here he was, talking about hauling away the corpse of a man he was planning to kill in cold blood.

Not that it would be murder. Murder was killing without a cause. Or for gain. Or in anger.

Jericho was no longer burning with anger, but he was coldly set on justice. If he had to carry the stain on his soul for the rest of his days on earth, so be it. Smithers had taken Louisa's life. Justice required that he give up his own in return.

"The meeting's set for three days hence, but Rico—"

"Three days from now! You said a week, and it's already been more'n that!"

The woods around them, rich with muted autumn color, echoed with distant birdsong. The fragrant smell of Cuban tobacco drifted up to mingle with the gray Spanish moss and the ever present smell of burning peat. Rafe studied the ash forming on the tip of his stogie. "Fellow that usually stands up for him was hard to track down. Even harder to sober up. Rico, there's something I need to know."

"There's something I need to know first. Tell me this, Rafe—just how the hell did you and that lying, raping, murdering son of a bitch get to be such good friends? You and me, we've not run with the same crowd in many a year—not since I came home in '22 after Louisa fell into the pond and nearly drowned before you fished her out. But I don't ever remember you running with scum like Smithers. Judas priest, Tubby, if you hadn't brought him around—"

"I swear to you I never knew what the bastard was up to, Rico. With Weezie, I mean. I knew he'd met her—there was the usual round of house parties and socials last winter, on into the spring. Weezie never was a regular, but she and the Scott girl was friends. That's where they met the first time."

Jericho took off his hat, raked his fingers through his hair, and swore foully in three languages.

"First time I met him, I'd invited a few friends down for the dog races. He turned up with old man James's youngest boy. Seemed a decent enough sort. Dressed well. Didn't cheat at cards—leastwise, no more'n the rest of that bunch. No good with horses, but hell, that's no cause to kick a man out of the house. Later on he showed up a few times on his own, and with me rattling around in all those empty rooms, I couldn't see any good reason to turn him away." Rafe stubbed out his cigar on the sole of his boot. He seemed suddenly ill at ease. "Rico, how good are you with a knife?"

"A knife?" Jericho shrugged. "As good as the next man, I reckon. Why, you want a fresh cigar cut?"

"About this business with Smithers . . ."

"I know the rules. I've never fought a duel before, but I've fought my share of fights, and won most of 'em. This time, instead of fists, I'll be using a six-iron, but if you're worried about whether or not I can handle it—"

Rafe cut him off with an impatient gesture. "I know damned well you can shoot. That's not the trouble. Listen here to me, Rico, the man's fought five duels! You know how many he's lost?"

Jericho waited for the score. Smithers might be good, but Jericho knew he was better. He had to be.

"None. Not a frigging one! That whey-faced little pantywaist has killed five men in cold blood, and walked away without a curl out of place!"

Jericho drew a deep, steadying breath. "In case you've forgotten just what this is all about, that same whey-faced little pantywaist seduced my sister, got her with child, beat her to within an inch of her life, then let her bleed to death when she miscarried his whelp. I don't give one sweet damn in hell how many men he's killed. If I have to come back from the grave to put a bullet through his black heart, I'll do it."

Turning away, Rafe stared out over the gray-boled forest of cypress, gum, juniper, and persimmon. Smoke lay like sweet, spicy fog across the flat, swampy land, swirling in damp wisps around his knee-high boots.

Abruptly, he swung back. "Damn it all, Rico, the man fights with a knife! Have you ever killed a man with a knife?"

Jericho felt a bead of sweat start at the base of his

throat and work its way down his chest. He had never killed a man at all, but he'd seen many a man die. He could do it if he had to. *Because* he had to.

"Well? Answer me, damn it! Have you ever knifed a man to death?"

"The last time I used a knife in a fight, I near about sliced a man's liver out of his side trying to keep him from going for my throat with a broken bottle. But I didn't kill him. No, I've never done that."

"You know the rules," Rafe said with a tired finality.

"I know the rules. One to three seconds allowed each principal. Physician present. Sun and wind equally divided, choice of positions decided on the turn of a dollar. Ten paces, seconds to be armed, seconds to be permitted to examine clothing and weapon of each principal and to load each pistol with powder and a single ball in the presence of all parties."

"You got it right, all but one thing. The challenger chooses the time and place; the challenged chooses the weapons."

"Christ," Jericho said reverently.

"It ain't too soon to be praying, and that's the truth. The boy told me once he used to practice with his old man's knife by knocking sparrows off limbs, slicing their legs out from under 'em. What he didn't tell me, but I found out by digging around these past few days is that his old man was hanged for murder after he knifed a man to death for spitting on the toe of his boot. That was down in Tennessee. His widow changed her name, took the boy and moved to Virginia, and remarried."

Jericho swore again, the oath somewhere between a

prayer and a curse. For the first time it occurred to him that he just might not leave the swamp alive. He had toyed with the notion before, but it had never taken hold.

Now it did.

# Chapter Six

Thinking about what was to take place three days hence, Jericho couldn't sleep. Turbyfill had managed to find an acquaintance with a private room who was willing to share. They'd offered Jericho space on the floor, but he'd opted for the common room. He had thinking that needed to be done, and he couldn't do it among people he knew. Strangers were different. They were only noise, and noise could be shut out.

So he lay awake in his corner of the common room, trying to ignore the usual drunken revelry as he thought about his life: his home, his ship, and all he would be leaving behind if he failed to walk out of that clearing in the swamp three days from now.

It struck him as ironic that Rafe should be the one to stand up with him now. As a boy, Jericho had been jealous as hell, partly because Rafe was two years older and considerably more sophisticated. Or so it had seemed at the time.

But mostly because Rafe had got along well with his father. Jericho never had. He had envied his friend that relationship more than anything else.

Strange, the way things turned out. Old man Turbyfill had died of the French pox, although they had put it about that he'd died of a wasting fever. Jericho's father had died because he'd been trying to read poetry while he was tooling a pair down a dangerous stretch of road and had rolled his carriage. According to Hester Renegar, the book had still been in his hand when they'd found him.

Gradually, the din grew louder until it was impossible to ignore any longer. Jericho rolled over onto his side and covered his exposed ear with his cap. It didn't help.

"Oh, yeah?" challenged one lout, only slightly more sober than his mates, "I got me a eagle says I'c'n talk my way into 'er bed 'fore you can."

A bearded tough struggled to his feet and thrust out a pugnacious jaw. "You? You couldn't talk your way into a three-hole privy. My pack mule against your eagle I can bed 'er before—"

"Pipe down, damn it, else I'll geld th' both o' ye!"

The pair turned as one against the grizzled old shingle captain who was trying to sleep.

Glaring through the miasma of cigar and lamp smoke, Jericho propped himself up on one elbow and wondered if he could find a quiet place out in the livery stable. The air was bound to be fresher. He'd rather smell horseshit than two dozen swampers who hadn't bathed since President Jackson was inaugurated.

"Stow it, Keeler," growled one of the unwashed. "We all know you ain't got no more use for a woman since yer old lady caught ye in bed wi' that quim peddler an' cracked yer acorns wi' a frying pan."

Amid the general laughter, Jericho swore quietly and got to his feet. He stood about as much chance of grabbing forty winks in this place as rum did of freezing in hell. He was fairly sure these scoundrels were more talk than action. All the same, if they took a notion to do more than brag about their prowess, the lady in question might be in for an uncomfortable night, key or no key.

A few minutes later, using the broad veranda that ran along the front of the hotel for access, he let himself in through the window of her bedroom. The night air was damp and cool, rich with the ever present smell of peat smoke and swamp. He inhaled deeply, taking a moment to get his bearings.

Then, at the sight that met his eyes, he nearly crawled back out through the window again.

This was a mistake. The last thing he needed at this critical point in his life was a distraction. And the vision he saw in the feeble glow of a single candle was a distraction of a major order.

Sara had armed herself with an umbrella, positioned herself in a straight chair in front of the barricaded door, and fallen soundly asleep.

Even with his mind set on his own affairs, Jericho had noticed how delicately she was made the first time he'd ever laid eyes on her, standing by the window. She was small, tidily constructed, and so slight a loud whisper could knock her over. Since then, in spite of his own circumstances, he had begun to feel a strange upwelling of tenderness when he was with her. Tenderness well laced with desire. It was not a feeling he had ever experienced before, nor one he was comfortable with.

The first time he'd had a chance to look her over from stem to stern, she'd been all rigged out in full regalia—corset, bustle, high-tops, fancy headgear, and more rag than a five-masted schooner.

Tonight she was dressed only in two thin layers. A night shift and a worn wrapper that was both too small and thin enough to see through. Candlelight splintered off the hair that tumbled over her shoulders, thick as a waterfall. With her head tilted the way it was, she'd have a crick in her neck sure as the world come morning.

Gusting a sigh of resignation, Jericho moved silently across the room and disarmed her. Again he gave her full marks for spunk. With a good swing an umbrella the size of the one she carried, while it would hardly fell a man, would pretty well discourage him.

She was wearing shoes, not slippers. He eased them off her feet, feeling the cracks in the leather as he set them side by side under the chair. He didn't know much about the size of that inheritance she'd mentioned, but for an heiress, she wasn't any too well tricked out. Tenderly, he lifted her and crossed to the bed, his body quickening enthusiastically as he pressed the soft, warm bundle against him. Through it all, she never stirred.

She smelled of soap—the homemade lye kind, not the fancy French stuff. When her hair brushed against his face as he leaned over to fold back the covers, he caught a hint of something spicy and lemony that reminded him of the black-walnut husks Louisa used to delight in as a child, rubbing the scent on the skin of her wrist and demanding that he " 'Mell my wist."

Had Sara done that, too? Did all little girls?

Reluctantly, he laid her on the bed, stood and pulled

the covers up under her chin, trying hard to think of her not as a woman but as merely someone in need.

His body refused to be distracted. Mindlessly, it reacted to the womanly feel and the scent of her. Before he could block the thought, he found himself wondering how she would taste. Achingly aroused, it occurred to him that this might be the last night he would ever spend with a woman.

Judas priest, what a waste.

The thought was almost enough to cool his throbbing desire. Which was a good thing, he thought ruefully, because he would hate to believe he was no better than the scum against which he was trying to protect her.

He angled the chair she had vacated so that he could see both the window and the woman, and at the same time, keep an eye on the door. Then he settled down to stand watch until morning.

Gradually the din of late-night revelers faded into the background. From the banks of the nearby canal, a bullfrog croaked. And then another. Cheerful and commonplace, crickets chirped in the corner of the bedroom.

In the comparative quiet of the night, thoughts of what was to happen in a short time once again floated to the surface of Jericho's mind. It wasn't the first time he had faced death. Far from it. But other than the natural hazards of a seagoing life, the threat had usually been thrust at him suddenly, offering him no time to dwell on his own mortality.

Now there was time. Time to consider Wilde Oaks, the land that had been bought so cheaply and loved so dearly by generations of Wildes. Time to realize that he might never again know the joy of standing on his own deck with the scent of tar and salt in his nostrils, hearing the crack of canvas overhead and the rush of the sea beneath his hull, with a hold full of lumber bound for the West Indies. Or homeward bound again with a cargo of rum and molasses.

Might never again know the pleasure of undressing a woman, exploring her secrets, discovering what made her gasp and tremble with need, even though the gasping and trembling was seldom genuine. Might never again feel his own flesh hardening, rising to meet the sweet challenge. And then meeting it.

Was he truly never to know the joy of coming home to a wife of his own? He had never before even considered the possibility of marrying, yet now it suddenly seemed the most desirable goal a man could harbor. To watch his sons grow to manhood. To see a child of his flesh burst squalling and red-faced into the world.

Once in the North Atlantic, with forty-foot seas breaking over the decks, Jericho had helped birth a babe in the hold of his ship. A stowaway's child. The tiny girl child had entered the world kicking mad, both tiny fists waving and howling fit to wake the dead. He had thought it remarkable at the time.

Now he knew it was God's greatest miracle.

Drawing a deep breath, he stretched his long legs toward the door and rotated his head to ease the tension at the back of his neck. Fingering the cool hexagonal barrel of the pistol he had placed on his lap, he thought about the duel. He thought about fighting with knives and tried to recall all the tricks he had learned over the years aboard various ships and in waterfront dives around the world.

But no matter how hard he tried to concentrate on preparing himself for the upcoming event, his mind and his gaze kept straying back to the woman.

To Sara.

She slept deeply, almost as if she sensed she had nothing to fear. How long had it been since he had slept as well? A week? A month?

That and more.

What he wouldn't give to be able to slide into bed beside her for no other reason than to bask in her warmth, to let the scent of her lull him to sleep. It might be the last time in this life he would ever lie beside a woman.

Unbidden, the notion kindled and began to glow deep inside him. It wasn't as if he was asking anything more of her than the comfort of another warm body beside him while he slept. The bed was surely wide enough so that they would not even need to touch. God knows, he would never lay a finger on her while she slept—that would be dishonorable.

Besides, she would never miss the little he wanted from her—never even know. He would be gone long before she awoke.

In the darkest hour of the night, when reasonable men were asleep, and the minds of those who lay awake turned tentatively down twisted paths seldom visible in the light of day, Jericho made up his mind. Removing his boots, he placed them beside the bed. He unbuckled his gun belt and looped it over the bedpost. Sleeping in his clothes was no problem—he did it as often as not—but bedamned if he was going to sleep with a pair of smooth-bore, saw-handle pistols gouging him every time he turned over.

The sheets were coarse, but clean. They smelled of her scent, which he forced himself to ignore. Half expecting to lie awake, he drifted off within minutes, the sound of Sara's slow, even breaths offering the comforting knowledge that he was not alone in the night.

God knows, he had never felt more alone in his life than he had these past few days.

Sara came awake instantly at the sound of something being dragged across the floor. Her first thought was that she was back home and Titus was forcing open her door against the weight of the dresser she had used as a barricade, before she had moved to the attic.

Everything seemed to happen at once. The man in the bed beside her sat up.

*The man in the bed beside her?*

Merciful saints alive.

Standing in the doorway, bracketed by the bedposts, three drunks blinked owlishly. One of them started to come in and stumbled on the chair that had been toppled by the sweep of the door. Another one pointed at Jericho, who had somehow come to be sharing the bed with her, while the third one pointed at something dangling from the bedpost.

"Bejasus, boys, she's armed!" Two of the three drunks began fumbling frantically at their belts.

"But she's already got 'er a man! Tarnation, Murph, you said she wuz—"

At the same moment Sara felt the man beside her lunge for the foot of the bed, a shot rang out. Splinters and dust drifted down from the ceiling onto the counterpane. While Sara sat clasping her night shift to her throat, her eyes round as doorknobs, the whole world seemed to fracture and spin around like the kaleidoscope her father had given her for her thirteenth birthday—and that Titus had smashed with a hammer.

She saw a dark shadowy figure dive for the three drunks and shove them through the door. It was Jericho.

*Had he truly been in her bed, or had she only dreamed that?*

Someone lighted a lamp, and she flinched from the sudden glow. A crowd was already beginning to gather in the hallway. People she had never seen before in her life—and some she had—began pushing their way into her bedroom.

Sara, frightened, angry, confused, and embarrassed, reached for her wrapper, preparing to chase them all outside and lock the door after them. She slid her feet out onto the floor and promptly tripped over a pair of enormous boots that had somehow found their way into her bedroom.

"I never!" gasped one of the women she recognized.

"There, I told you so! And her looking so uppity butter wouldn't melt in her mouth."

The Jones sisters. Dear Lord, they were still here. They would talk, and their brother would spread the word up and down the canal, and sooner or later Titus would hear and come after her, and she would never manage to get away again. At least not until her money was all gone.

For the first time since her father had been brought home stiff as a mackerel on the bed of a farm wagon, Sara began to cry.

\* \* \*

Jericho managed to secure the three drunks with the help of a night clerk and a few colorful threats. Dead drunk, they would sleep it off and probably not even remember the event come morning.

But those two old flap-jaws were something else. He didn't know whether to go to their room and try to bribe them into silence or wring their scrawny necks.

Neck wringing might be more effective. Unfortunately, they hadn't been the only ones to see what happened. He could hardly silence the whole hotel.

With the best intentions in the world, he had compromised an innocent woman beyond salvation. If her Mr. Ricketts heard the tale, he would likely compound the sin by throwing her over.

Jericho stood in the doorway that led to the Carolina wing, his head bowed, his shoulders hunched. God help him, he had never meant her the least harm, yet harm her he had. And the trouble was, she was still vulnerable. After word of what had happened spread throughout the common room—as it was doing right now, and there was no way in hell he could stop it— they would come after her in droves. A woman alone and unprotected—a woman so damned beautiful, with her delicate features and her exotic coloring. There wasn't a man made who could look on her and not want her.

Jericho paced the hall. He considered waking Turbyfill and asking his advice, then dismissed it. Rafe might be two years older, but in a spot like this, Methuselah himself wouldn't be of any help.

He eyed the door of room number three. She was all alone in there. Probably flat-out terrified. The key was no good. They'd poked it out of the lock. Every schoolboy knew that trick. There wasn't a piece of furniture in the room heavy enough to withstand a serious assault, and besides, there was the window. He himself had merely raised the sash and stepped inside without a speck of trouble.

The way he saw it, there was only one course of action an honorable man could take. The damage to her reputation was already done. He would simply have to explain to her man when he came what had happened, and why. He would assure him that the lady was still as untouched as she had been when Jericho had first laid eyes on her, staring out her bedroom window as if she were watching for a ship she suspected had sailed without her.

It came to him then that back there in her bedroom, after the ruckus had started, she had backed up against him for one brief moment as if he were a wall, as if she knew he would protect her. It made him feel proud.

It also made him feel guilty.

On his southerly tack, Jericho passed her room again. A soft sound arrested him in his tracks. Kittens? A mouse?

Oh, hell, she was crying. If there was one thing he had never been able to deal with, it was a weeping female. But when he was the man responsible, there was nothing he could do save bear up under the burden.

"Sara?" He twisted the knob. The little fool had forgotten to lock her door after the place had cleared out. Not that it would have done much good. All the same . . .

Stepping inside, he closed the door behind him and charged her with not having the brains God gave a

turnip. "Are you hoping for another visitation? Is that
why you didn't bother to lock yourself in?" She wailed
again, and Jericho cursed himself for a clumsy fool.

"I c-couldn't find the k-k-key, and the chair is b-
b-broken. . . ."

He removed his hat and raked his fingers through
his hair, wishing he was somewhere else—*anywhere*
else. "It probably got kicked into a corner. Here now,
don't take on so, it's all over. You're safe."

She cried like a child. Noisily, gulping and wailing
and sniffling. It occurred to him that of all the women
who had cried in his arms, only two had shed honest
tears. The rest had wanted something from him.
Money. Jewelry. Once, a horse and buggy. And he, God
help him, had usually given it to them.

He gave this one his handkerchief.

And then, what could he do but give her the comfort
of his arms? "There now, girl, it's not so bad." Easing
his large frame onto the bed beside her, he drew her
against his chest and tucked her head under his chin.
"Your young man will understand when I explain that
I was only protecting his interests. He'll be thanking
me for it, and praising you for having the good sense
not to sleep unguarded."

"You d-don't understand," Sara whimpered.

What he didn't understand—what Sara didn't understand herself was that she didn't give a goose feather
what Archibald thought. She was only just now coming
to realize that she wanted more from marriage than
a comfortable life with a nice garden and an elderly
companion and a place for her two old friends.

The truth was, she wanted someone big and strong,
someone who smelled of soap and cigars and good

woolens rather than an old man who smelled of macassar oil, dipping tobacco and rum.

She heaved a deep, shuddering sigh, and the hand that had been patting her awkwardly on the arm closed over her shoulder, warm and comforting.

"Thank you," she said, her voice thin but quite steady. "I'm much better now."

All the same, she didn't move away, nor did he seem in any great hurry to let go of her. Gradually, she became aware of the reassuring beat of his heart. Ba-boom. Ba-boom. Ba-boom, ba-boom, boom, boom*boom*!

"Do you know your heart is beating fit to raise Jerusalem? Are you all right, sir?"

He allowed as how he was just fine, but to Sara, he didn't sound all that fine. The fact was, he sounded hoarse. As if he were coming down with a bad cold, and besides that, he was shifting on the bed like a feather stem was poking him in the backside.

"Well," she exclaimed decisively, "I'm just fine, myself—although I still feel a mite all-overish."

The hand on her shoulder curved upward. She felt the brush of fingers against her neck, and shivered.

"Are you cold? I could stoke up the fire . . ."

"No, I'm just fine," she said breathlessly. "What is it they say? Someone stepped on my shadow?"

Jericho retrieved his handkerchief, which was wet from her tears, and mopped his forehead. He had no business thinking what he was thinking. If he didn't get out of here right quick, he might end up doing more than just thinking it.

"Captain Wilde, do you think—"

"Jericho," he said. He was in bed with the woman, for God's sake! "Or Rico. Some call me Rico."

She twisted her face up to beam at him, lips moist and parted, her lashes still tangled with tears, and that was when he flat-out lost it. Lost his mind.

He didn't kiss her hard enough to scare her. At least he retained just enough common sense to go easy. All the same, he was shaking by the time he drew away. She tasted like tears and wild mint and honey. Her lips had trembled, but she hadn't drawn away. Eyes wide, she touched her lips with a finger and stared up at him, her eyes glistening like wet amber. Jericho broke off an oath by turning it into a cough.

"There now," she said in a thready little voice, "I thought you sounded hoarse. You're coming down with something."

"Sara, if you don't know what it is that ails me, I'm not the man to show you. Your Mr. Ricketts will take care of that." And he thought, damn the lucky fool.

Again she twisted around to stare up at him. Stubbornly, Jericho looked away, but he didn't remove his arm. Nor did he leave her bed.

"How would Archibald know what ails you? Oh— you mean, because he sells patent medicines?"

Under his breath Jericho muttered something about hatching out only yesterday, but Sara was too busy trying to regain her sensibility to pay much attention. "Well, he did prescribe a bismuth solution for my stepmother's bilious attacks that seemed to help. I could ask him—"

"Damn it, Sara—!"

The fingers on her shoulder bit into her flesh. Suddenly, he was looming over her, his eyes dark as coals and burning as fiercely. Sara was aware of a weakness in her limbs and a fluttery feeling in the pit of her belly that was unlike anything she had ever felt before.

"Perhaps—" she began when he cut her off.

"Perhaps nothing! Meaning you no disrespect, Sara, but if I don't kiss you once more before I leave, it will weigh on my mind for as long as I live. Which might not—"

But he didn't finish the statement. Instead, he lowered her to the bed and leaned over her, his chest crushing her bosom, one of his limbs moving heavily over her own. Sara's eyes grew wider. Her breathing ceased altogether as she waited for what was to come. She couldn't have moved if the bed had suddenly caught fire.

Which it well might do, she thought a little wildly. All at once, she felt terribly warm.

This time, there was nothing gentle about his kiss. His mouth came down hard, and she felt his teeth against her lips, and then his tongue, and then—oh, merciful saints—his tongue was inside her mouth, doing things that didn't make any sense at all, but it was wonderful. Quite magical, even though it made her want to squirm and press against something, only she didn't know what and she didn't know why.

And then he was touching her bosom, and she nearly cried out. How could he have possibly known she wanted him to touch her there when she hadn't even known it herself? But oh, it felt so good! So sweetly, achingly delicious, she didn't think she could stand it another moment!

She could feel the web of ropes through the feather ticking pressing against her back. Only then did she realize that his body was lying on top of hers, and that the weight of both their bodies had pressed the mattress flat.

Not only that, but he had bumps and ridges in places that she had never noticed before, even that first day when she had particularly noticed the generous swell of his *parts*, which had embarrassed her no end, because she *never* noticed things like that about a man.

Right now, one of those ridges was pressing against her in a way that made her want to press back. She wiggled her hips.

Jericho groaned.

Then his hips moved, and they both groaned.

Sara thought he might be hurting. Then again, perhaps he was feeling the same remarkable sensations she was feeling, feelings that took her breath away and made her want something . . . something that shimmered just out of reach.

"Judas priest."

The words, uttered harshly, sounded like tearing canvas in the sudden silence. The fire, banked for the night, glowed dimly. On the washstand, the candle guttered and went out. For long moments, the only sound to be heard was the faint creaking of overstressed rope under the mattress and the rasp of heavy breathing.

Abruptly, Jericho levered himself off her body, leaving a chill in his place. He stood beside the bed, not looking at her, shoving his shirttail back into his trousers.

Sara hadn't even known it was out. She couldn't see him very clearly, only his silhouette against the feeble glow from the fireplace. Not for the first time that evening, she felt confused, angry and embarrassed.

Felt, in fact, as if something infinitely precious had been snatched away at the last moment.

"Well," she said finally, the way she sometimes did when she needed to organize her thoughts. But before she could go on, he turned on her and told her to say no more.

"It's my place to apologize, Sara, and I do. Most sincerely. I took—wanted to take— That is, I had no business forcing my attentions on you when you're already spoken for, and I'm in no position to make you an honorable offer."

Sara started to tell him that it was all right, that he hadn't forced anything on her that she hadn't wanted, even if she wasn't quite certain what it was, but he hushed her again.

"I'll be right outside your door, madam. You have only to call out if anything disturbs you," he said, and before she could gather her wits, he was gone.

Jericho didn't even try to sleep. He had all but forgotten how. Instead, he sat down, braced his back against the cool paneled wall, crossed his booted ankles, and went to thinking over what he had just done.

Or rather, what he had come close to doing. It didn't help his conscience to know that he could probably have taken her and she wouldn't even have tried to stop him.

She was a complete innocent. A seaman didn't run into too many innocent women, not in the kind of places that usually sprung up along the waterfront of every port city in the world. Men who had been at sea for weeks, sometimes months, were a gold mine for the kind of women who made their living servicing their needs.

Fearing the French pox, Jericho had usually steered clear of the houses closest the docks, but even farther inland, he had never trafficked with an innocent.

In two days now, he was to meet a man and fight him to the death. He might, or might not walk out of the swamp alive. Which made it all the more puzzling—or maybe it didn't—that he should be so drawn to a woman like Sara.

Not a woman like Sara. To Sara, herself. To her warmth, her wit, her sweetness, and her pride. To the strength he sensed beneath that deceptively delicate framework.

Ricketts had better claim his woman fast, or he might just find himself in for a disappointment. Sight unseen, Jericho despised the man for leaving her here unprotected.

More like envied him, he admitted reluctantly. The truth was, he would like nothing better than to take care of her for the rest of his life, but she deserved a man with a lifespan longer than a couple of days.

And that was the one thing he couldn't promise her.

What he could offer her, however, was the protection of his name. Just in case Ricketts kicked up a fuss over the gossip that was bound to greet him on his arrival. He could promise her a home. Wilde Oakes needed a mistress if it couldn't have a master. Sara and Louisa would have liked one another, Jericho was sure of it.

He almost went back into her room and made his offer right then, to reassure her that she had nothing to worry about in case Ricketts sheared off.

But tomorrow would be soon enough. Tomorrow he would broach the subject, and if Ricketts backed off—if Sara was agreeable—he would fetch a joiner and see the deed done then and there. Before he went to face Smithers.

That decided, Jericho felt as if a half-ton anchor had dropped from his shoulders. For the first time in weeks, he looked forward to the dawn of a new day.

# Chapter Seven

The morning was half gone before Sara ventured from her room. She had waited until hunger drove her out, and then gone to the dining room, miserably conscious of the stares and whispers that followed her progress.

"Is there—is it too late—I mean, could I possibly get something to eat?" she inquired.

"Late for breakfast, early for dinner. Reck'n I can rustle up something," said the surly woman who waited on tables.

Sara hoped it would be whatever was left over from breakfast rather than what was already cooked for dinner. Breakfasts and suppers cost only thirty-seven and a half cents, while dinners cost fifty cents. If she had known she would be staying so long, she would have asked for weekly rates.

The grits were lumpy, the biscuits cold, the coffee too strong. However, she was in no position to complain. She spent the entire time seated alone at a table that was none too clean, staring out the window at the canal traffic and trying not to dwell on what had happened last night. And on what it all meant.

A stern-wheeler chugged past, with stacks billowing

and flags flying, packed with people headed south to Elizabeth City, or Fayetteville, or maybe even Charleston in South Carolina.

Sara told herself it was an exciting time to be alive and tried to be excited, but all she could think of was a grim, gun-wearing stranger who, against all reason, made her feel safe and cherished for the first time since her mother had died.

Made her feel, in some ways, anything but safe, but that was another matter. She didn't know how she was going to face him again. Perhaps he had already left. He had never said where he was bound, but then, she had never asked. Big Simon had warned her that one didn't ask questions of chance-met strangers in a place like the Halfway Hotel, that was as well-known for its criminal and duelistical arrangements as for its matrimonial ones.

Quite naturally, the very first person she ran into on leaving the dining room was Jericho Wilde.

He looked drawn. As if he hadn't slept at all. The shadows around his eyes reminded her of a raccoon.

"Good morning, is your cold—?"

"Sara, I have a proposition to put to you," he interrupted without even allowing her to inquire after his health.

She waited for him to go on. Two men passed by, both talking at once, neither of them listening. She placed them as drummers from the plaid suits they wore and the sample cases they carried.

"Not here," he said. Taking her arm, he led her outside.

The morning stage had not yet arrived, and the packet boat had already left. Except for two kitchen boys, dawdling on their way back from the chicken yard to chuck oyster shells into the canal, they were alone.

When that nice Mr. Turbyfill came outside and started toward them, Jericho waved him away. Which made Sara curious. "What did you want to talk to me about, mister—captain—that is, Jericho?"

For such an imposing man, he looked downright uncomfortable. He cleared his throat twice before he commenced to speak. "From what you've said, I take it you're not of a mind to go back home to your, uh—your stepmama, is that right?"

Sara nodded.

"And so far, your intended hasn't turned up."

Again she nodded. What could she say? He knew, to her everlasting shame, that she had been the one to do the proposing—not only that, she had set the time and place. "I'm sure he'll come soon. You see, he travels so much, and my letter probably arrived while he was away."

Rucking back his plain black wool coat, Jericho braced his hands on his narrow hips. He stared down at the dust that had drifted onto the toes of his tall black boots and then turned to face her, not quite meeting her eyes. "I would take it kindly, Miss Young, if you was to hear me out before you give me your answer."

*Miss Young? Only last night it had been Sara.*

Again he cleared his throat. "A few miles southwest of New Lebanon, there's a farm that's been in my family for a number of generations. It was prosperous once and could be again with the proper hand at the helm. I've set things in motion—that is, I recently hired on an overseer—a manager, you might say. There's him and the family he'll be bringing—a wife and a sister, if I recollect rightly—and the housekeeper, not to mention half a dozen or so new hands that have been hired on by now, I reckon. The thing is, I'll not be going back."

Jericho pondered over whether or not to tell her about the duel he was to fight and the very real possibility that he might not survive it.

He decided against mentioning it. Womanlike, she would probably try to talk him out of it, and there were some things a man had to do because they were the right thing to do.

"You'll be going back to sea?" she ventured, and he took her lead and allowed her to think what she would.

"Wilde Oaks needs a mistress. My sister—"

"I should think it needs a master, even more."

Ignoring that, he said, "My sister passed away recently. My folks died just over a year ago. There's no one left, so you see, you'd be doing me a real favor if you was to consider my proposition."

He shot her a quick glance, then stared down at his boots again, waiting.

Sara waited, too. And then she said, "Well. I reckon I might consider it, only you haven't yet said what it was."

If a man whose skin was tanned from years of exposure to the elements could be said to blush, Jericho did. "Marry me," he said.

Sara's jaw fell. That he should ask her that which all morning, ever since he had left her bed last night, she had been thinking about—

"It'd be to your advantage, Sara. You'd have a place to take those two old servants you set such store by."

"But what about—"

She meant to say, what about love, but it suddenly struck her that she had been planning all along to marry Archibald and she certainly didn't love him. Never had. Probably never would.

But this was different. She wanted far more from Jericho Wilde than she had ever wanted from Archibald, only she wasn't certain just what he was offering her.

"I'd not ask more of you than that, Sara. To look after my home. In return, I'm offering you a roof over your head and the protection of my name."

Well. That certainly spelled it out good and proper. Sara still wasn't sure what it was she had wanted, but whatever it was, it was certainly more than he was offering. Bristling with pride, she tipped back her head and looked him square in the eye. "No thank you, sir. It's very kind of you, I'm sure, but Mr. Ricketts has already offered me the same." Which was not precisely true, but she had to believe that he would.

"Sara, last night—"

"It was merely an unfortunate mistake." He *would* have to bring that up.

"The talk—your reputation, I mean . . ."

"My reputation will survive. I'm sure Mr. Ricketts will be reasonable once I explain what happened."

Jericho's dark eyes gleamed with something that looked almost like amusement. "All of it, Sara? How are you going to explain what happened between us in that bed?"

It was Sara's turn to flush, and flush she did. "I'll simply lay out the facts. I don't have to embroider them with all the details." She wasn't even sure she could, for she didn't understand much of what had happened, herself. "And while I thank you kindly for the honor you do me, sir, I believe I'll just wait for Archibald." Face burning, she lifted her skirts above the tops of her cracked patent leather high-tops and made her way back to the hotel. With every step, she could feel Jericho's eyes burning a spot right between her shoulder blades.

Let him look. The handsome devil might have been able to distract her momentarily, but she herself had chosen this path and she was obliged to follow it. It was the only sensible thing to do.

The trouble was, sensible no longer felt quite so . . . sensible.

Sara spent the remainder of the day in her room, ignoring knocks on her door, raps on her window and the raging headache she had developed, a result of the perpetual peat smoke, no doubt. It was getting so a body couldn't walk outdoors without coming in all covered with fly ash.

The Jones sisters came by twice, calling through the paneled door to inquire if she was all right. She assured them both times that she was just fine, thank you very much, only suffering from a slight headache.

"All that excitement last ni—" one of the sisters began, when her sister loudly shushed her and offered solicitously to bathe Sara's brow with lavender water.

Sara had to smile. She could imagine those two sharp noses twitching to sniff out every last detail of what had gone on before and after the grand spectacle.

And then Jericho came by to call through her door. When she ignored him, he went outside, rapped twice on her window and then raised the sash and poked his head inside.

"You set one foot inside this room, Jericho Wilde, and I'll crown you with the washbowl." The fact that she wanted nothing more than to fly into his arms and forget all about the Jones sisters and Titus and her obligation to Archibald made her angry, and she retaliated by glaring at him.

"I don't know why you're so upset," he said plaintively. "I never meant to insult you, you know. Sara, are you sure you're all right?"

"I'm fit as a fiddle. I wish you would just leave me alone and go about your own business—that is if you even have any business."

Jericho winced, but doggedly stuck to his guns. "I just thought you might want to know that the evening stage just got in, and unless your young man is about four foot tall and wearing drop-seat breeches, he's not among the passengers. There were two ladies, and I use the term loosely, one cleric who looks suspiciously like that pair of flap-jaws that's been haunting this place these past few days, and an old codger—" Jericho had spent the afternoon watching all the new arrivals, by land or water. He had it in mind to tackle the first young, good-looking fellow he saw and bribe him to move on.

Just then Sara threw a pillow at his head. With a look of mystification, Jericho ducked, closed her window, and went back to stand watch. The evening stage was due in most any time.

He watched the passengers alight. One old woman with a chicken in a basket. One half-grown girl, evidently the old woman's granddaughter. And one old man in a sweat-stained hat, a dusty coat and a pair of loose-fitting homespun breeches. No sign of a lusty young buck.

Jericho tried to be concerned for Sara's sake, but he couldn't repress a satisfied grin. The last stage left the yard, the last packet boat was long gone. Which meant he had tonight to plead his case.

The thought that Smithers, too, was due in before morning never even occurred to him, which was a sign of just how distracted a man could get when he was thrown off course by a pretty woman.

Sara saw her intended from the window of her room. Taking time only to smooth her hair, she hurried into the lobby and shoved her way past the hoard that was headed for the dining room. "Archibald, over here," she called out.

"Sara?" Clutching his hat in his hands, he glanced over his shoulder as if expecting someone else. "Sara. My dear, how pretty you look. Blessed land, that's the roughest ride I've had in many a day." By now they were standing in the middle of the lobby. "My old mare went lame on me, so I come in on the stage. Have you had supper yet?"

They dined together at a table for two. Sara was uncomfortably conscious of the stares and whispers directed their way. She tugged at the high collar of her brown wool and tried to ignore the gleam of oil that had oozed down into the creases of his neck from his sparse crop of graying hair.

Should she tell him about what had happened? Would he understand? If she didn't tell him, he was sure to hear it from someone else.

"I'd just as lief get on with it," Archibald said, smack-ing his lips over the stringy roast pork.

"Get on with it? Oh . . . you mean the wedding."

*Of course he means the wedding, you nitwit! What did you think he meant? Dessert?*

"I suppose tomorrow would be as good as any day," Sara ventured, although she felt strangely reluctant. If she had more time to think, though, she might lose her nerve altogether.

"I already bespoke us a joiner. He'll be here directly." The peddler sawed off another big bite of pork and shoved it in his mouth. His teeth were the color of rutabagas. Sara had never noticed it before.

"Do you have someone to stand up with you?" She was grasping for excuses to delay the ceremony, even though logic told her that the sooner they were wed and on their way to Portsmouth, the safer she would be.

And the sooner she could send for Maulsie and Big Simon.

*Be sensible, Sara! This is what you wanted, isn't it?*

And then, as if she weren't confused enough, Jericho chose that moment to show up. He bowed to her—actually bowed!—tipped his hat to Archibald, then swung a chair over from the next table and straddled it, without even a by-your-leave.

"I take it you're Sara's young man?" He dared the old coot to say he was anyone's young man. He'd been first disbelieving, and then mad as hell when he'd heard her call his name and watched her lead him into the dining room. *This* old relic was Archibald Ricketts? *This* was her young man?

She might not be willing to marry a chance-met

stranger who didn't know the first thing about sweet-talking a respectable lady, but he'd be damned if he was going to allow her to waste herself on a snuff-dipping, greasy-haired old sod who picked his teeth at the table—with a dirty fingernail!

Archibald looked as if he had swallowed his chunk of pork the wrong way. "Ricketts," he said when he was able to speak. "And who might you be, sir?"

Looking as if she wanted nothing so much as to kick him under the table, Sara did her best to smooth things over. "This is Captain Jericho Wilde. He, um—that is, Captain Wilde has been keeping me compa—that is, he's seen to my comfort while I've been waiting. For you, I mean. With the rougher element drinking and carousing till all hours, a lady can't be too careful."

"What Miss Young is trying to say, Ricketts, is that any lady left unattended in a place like this needs protection." The words were not precisely an accusation, but they weren't far off.

Archibald sawed off another chunk of meat. Sara glared across the table at Jericho. Jericho met her glare with a self-satisfied smirk.

Or at least she told herself it was a smirk. Truth be known, he was the handsomest man she had ever laid eyes on, and he probably couldn't have smirked if his life depended on it.

After wiping his mouth on his sleeve, Archibald recovered his manners enough to invite him to the wedding. "Won't be much of an affair, y'understand," he said diffidently. "Me'n Sara an' the joiner. Don't take no more'n that, not in these parts."

"Is this what you want, Sara?" Jericho's face gave away nothing.

Sara looked from one man to the other. She felt like weeping. What was Jericho offering her? Would it be enough? With Archibald, she knew what she was getting, knew she would never want more from him then he could give her.

Jericho took her silence for an affirmation. With a parody of a smile that never reached his eyes, he said jovially, "Then I don't see why we can't manage a small celebration. It's not every day a young lady gets herself married, is it, Sara? I wouldn't be much of a friend if I didn't arrange a suitable wedding celebration."

"Now that's right kindly of you," Archibald allowed. He belched discreetly behind a liver-spotted hand.

Sara wanted to tell Jericho what he could do with his celebration, but good manners prevailed. For all she had instinctively trusted him from the moment she'd first laid eyes on him, he had a wicked look about him right now that was making her distinctly uneasy.

Or maybe it was the pork.

It was widely known in that area of the Dismal Swamp that marriage was reckoned to be a lay contract in Carolina, and thus could be performed by a justice of the peace as well as a minister.

Sara, dressed in her yellow, with the brand-new pair of matching slippers she had been saving for special, wondered if the man who stood before them, swaying ever so slightly, his hands trembling as he read the few lines that made her Mrs. Archibald Ricketts, was a preacher or not. No one ever said for certain, and it didn't seem courteous to ask. He clutched a small black book in his hands, but it could just as well be one of Mr. Poe's detective stories.

"Now p'nouce man 'n' wife, 'cordin' t'th' mumble, mumble, mumble," the man gabbled, and then he lit out as if his coattails were on fire. Sara tried to convince herself it was merely because he had a busy schedule.

It was Jericho who first kissed the bride. Sara was so befuddled she wouldn't have noticed if the desk clerk had bussed her on the mouth, but Jericho she noticed. If he was trying to impress on her what she was giving up by marrying Archibald, he needn't have bothered. She knew. To her everlasting sorrow, she suspected she had just made the single most devastating mistake of her life.

He kissed her cheek. Then he stood back, still holding her by the shoulders, and looked searchingly into her eyes. "Be happy, Sara," he murmured, then leaned forward and kissed her again, this time on the mouth, so tenderly she felt like weeping.

Archibald had headed, directly after the deed was done, for the refreshment table Jericho had arranged to have set up in the lobby. There was already a crowd there, comprised mostly of the riffraff that frequented the taproom, with the two drummers and the two women who had come in on the evening stage.

And there in the middle of the table, amid the ham biscuits, the sweet potato biscuits, the salt herring, and the boiled potatoes, was a bouquet of goldenrod, swamp magnolia and marsh pinks.

Sara looked up at Jericho, her eyes brimming, and whispered her thanks, for she had no doubt he was the one responsible. He had been waiting just outside her door when she emerged a little while ago dressed in her wedding finery, such as it was. He had handed her a small bouquet of the same.

"Good luck, Sara," he'd said quietly, and she'd simply nodded. She would need it. "Are you sure this is what you want?"

Again she nodded. It had to be. She had thought out her plan very carefully, and this was the sensible thing to do. She knew Archibald. Had known him for years. She didn't know Jericho—not really. She didn't know how he could make her feel the way he made her feel, nor why, with a simple question, he could make her want to weep at her own wedding. It didn't make sense.

Maybe it was because her new yellow slippers were too tight.

Not for the first time, Sara wished her mother had lived long enough to advise her on the things every woman needed to know. About men. About love. About the mysterious marriage act.

The party lasted well into the night. Sara didn't. A fiddler had been engaged and played doggedly, but the noise level was such that Sara doubted if many people appreciated his efforts.

Sipping warm cider punch, Sara stood beside the elderly woman who had come in on the stage with her twelve-year-old grandson and watched the goings-on. Two shingle-getters fresh from the swamp, filth and all, danced a knee-lifting jig, sloshing ale from their tankards with every step.

Sara, desperately tired, searched the room for her husband. If he had any plans to leave on the morning stage, why then, he should consider getting a night's rest.

Ever since Jericho had kissed her, she had been thinking about her wedding night and what was soon to happen. Sara was innocent; she was not entirely ignorant. She had heard hushed whispers among her married friends so that she had some notion of what went on between a man and a woman after they were legally wed. Not the particulars, but enough to suspect that she wouldn't much care for the marriage act.

However, she was legally wed now, and facing an onerous duty, she would just as lief put it behind her and get on with the next step in her plan, which included settling into her new home and making arrangements to send for Maulsie and Big Simon.

That was what was important, she assured herself—not a few moments of discomfort and embarrassment, which was how her friend Carrie in Illinois had described her own wedding night.

At a table over near the edge of the room, Jericho pretended to concentrate on his cards. He was a fair hand at the game—nothing special. It took all his skill, not to mention a considerable sum of money, to allow Ricketts to win just enough to keep him playing.

And to keep him drinking. The old sot was already three sheets to the wind. Jericho dealt him the queen he needed and hoped to hell he was too drunk to even pick it up.

"Need m' spec-tickles," the old fool mumbled.

"No you don't, what you need is another drink." At Jericho's nod, a waiter refilled both glasses. The man must have a hollow leg. He had put away enough to fell an ox, yet he showed no signs of passing out.

It was Jericho's intention to drink the fool under the table for the simple reason that, legal or not, he couldn't bear the thought of those thick, none-too-clean hands on Sara's body.

"Jesus," he whispered.

"Wha's 'at? Bees? Where?" Archibald looked around wildly, then blinked and said, "M'woman. P'int her out to me, will you, boy? Can't see a blame thing through all this confounded smoke."

There was nothing he could do about it, Jericho told himself. Sooner or later—if not tonight, then tomorrow night—Ricketts was going to bed his wife.

Archibald struggled to his feet, raked a fistful of money off the table, crammed it in his pocket—spilling even more of it on the floor—then staggered away. Watching the old fool weave his way through the crowd in the general direction of the Carolina wing, Jericho reminded himself that no matter how he was feeling at the moment, he had more serious matters to consider than a newlywed couple celebrating their union.

When Smithers had not checked in by supper time, Rafe Turbyfill had set out to find him, missing the festivities. Likely they would all be riding in before midnight—Rafe, Smithers and whatever lowlife Smithers had coerced into seconding him. The meeting was set for break of day. In which case, Jericho told himself, he might not be around much longer to worry over who was bedding his Sara.

Not his Sara, damn it. Rickett's Sara!

With a heavy sigh signifying weariness and any number of mixed emotions, Jericho stood and stretched, his fingertips brushing the low ceiling. He might as well catch what little sleep he could. He had left word at the desk for Rafe to wake him an hour before dawn. Less than that and he might not be clearheaded.

More than that would allow him too much time to
think.

*Sara, damn your sweet soul, why didn't you have sense
enough to take what I offered you? It would have been
a damn sight better than what you're going through right
now . . .*

# Chapter Eight

There was no way on earth Sara could have gone to sleep, although she was drooping with fatigue. It had been a strenuous evening.

She had had a strenuous week!

Sitting up in bed, she thought about her new status as a married woman. She tried to picture the home Archibald had promised her, with the garden his mother had planted. They had that, at least, in common. Gardening. And he was kind. If nothing else, he was kind.

And there was always the possibility, according to her friend Carrie in Illinois, that after consummating their marriage, she would find herself with child. It had happened to Carrie, whose daughter had been born precisely eight months and two weeks after her wedding.

A baby. Sighing, Sara drew her knees up under her chin and tried to picture her baby. He would be dark, of course, with thick black hair and molasses-colored eyes that could be wistful or sad, or a glint with laughter in turn.

It occurred to her that she had no idea what color Archibald's hair had been before it had turned gray.

His eyes, however, were blue. Really a lovely shade of blue, if somewhat bloodshot.

She thought of names for a son. James, like her father. Or Joseph. Or Jeremiah. That had a substantial sound to it. Or . . .

As the sounds of partying continued, with the occasional louder burst as the levee spilled outside onto the veranda, she thought about Maulsie and Big Simon and wondered how they were faring in her absence. Sara had left a note saying she was off to visit with a friend in Hampton, and that she would return in a week or so. That, she had hoped, would be enough to keep her two old friends safe and secure until she could make arrangements to get them away.

Things would be unpleasant, to say the least. Titus would be spiteful to them, but Noreen would temper the worst of his cruelty, because both knew that with Sara gone, there was nothing to keep the two freed slaves from leaving. And if they left, Noreen would be unable to afford anyone to take their place.

Outside in the hallway, a loud, irreverent toast to the bride and groom was followed by the sound of breaking glass. Evidently, the party was a huge success. Perhaps she should have stayed on a while longer, but after Archibald had told her that to be perfectly legal a marriage had to be consummated, she had felt less and less like celebrating. In spite of all her common sense, she wasn't prepared for that. Not really. Companionship, yes. Shared interests, security—those were the things she had married for. But if consummating was what it took to make her marriage legal, then consummating was what she would do. After going this far, what choice did she have?

Unbidden came the thought that if it were Jericho waiting on the other side of that door, she wouldn't be quite so reluctant. And it could have been. He had asked her.

Was she a fool, or merely too stubborn to stray from a given path once she had set out upon it?

Both, she supposed. Mostly it was pride. She had discovered that she had too much pride to let herself be married out of pity and some misguided notion of duty. Especially to a man who affected her the way Jericho did.

Mercy, what if she came to love him? Her heart would be broken when he left her, which he had every intention of doing.

Better the safe, sensible path she had chosen. At least her heart wasn't involved.

The sounds of another fight breaking out on the grounds broke into her ruminations. Evidently her wedding celebration was still going strong. She shuddered, fingered the button on the high collar of her night shift and crossed her legs under the covers, trying not to think of the coming ordeal. According to her friend Carrie, it took less time than soft-boiling an egg and was just about as exciting.

Not that Sara was looking for excitement. All she wanted was to get the business over and done with. If she'd been looking for excitement, she would have—

Well. That was water under the bridge.

The rattle of the doorknob alerted her that the event she had been dreading was about to take place. Steeling herself to remain calm, she smoothed the covers over her lap and waited to take the final step toward legalizing her marriage.

*        *        *

Some twenty minutes later Sara lay on her back, staring up into the darkness while her bridegroom snored beside her. According to Carrie, the first time one performed the marriage act, it hurt like the dickens.

At least Archibald hadn't hurt her—except when his bony knee had accidentally landed on her hand and bent her fingers backward into the mattress.

Had they made a baby? It hardly seemed possible that a few embarrassing moments of grunting, puffing, swearing, and fumbling about under her night shift could produce a brand-new human being. But that was more or less the way it happened with animals. A rooster would grab a hen's comb in his beak, tread on her back for a few seconds until he fell off, and then, lo and behold—fertile eggs!

She couldn't sleep. No matter how hard she tried, each time she closed her eyes, thoughts came swarming in on her like a cloud of midges—thoughts she had tried so hard to keep at bay.

*How in heaven's name can I spend a lifetime with this poor old man when all I can think of is Jericho and what tonight would have been like in his arms?*


Sometime after midnight, long before the revelry had begun to die down, Jericho dragged a chair out onto the veranda, all the way to the far end on the Virginia side. There he spent the remainder of the evening brooding and drinking. He had looked for Turbyfill and Smithers's party to arrive before now. What kind of a fool would expect to ride all night, walk directly out onto the field without a moment's preparation, and come away the victor?

The kind of fool who had fought five duels and killed five men.

But then, was he any less a fool himself, Jericho wondered, to spend the night drinking and thinking about a woman—or rather, trying *not* to think about a woman—when he should have been resting? Or at least polishing his skills with a knife? He had spent countless hours practicing with a pistol, but when it came to dueling with a knife, he didn't even know the rules.

If there were any rules. In the only official knife fight he could recall seeing, the opponents had been instructed to brace right foot against right foot, place left arms at their backs, and then have at one another. Which they had done until one of the pair lay bleeding on the floor, too far gone to continue.

A shudder of disquiet, not to say distaste, rippled the skin on his back. The night air held more than a hint of the winter to come, along with the pervasive smell of smoke and swamp.

It occurred to Jericho that if he could recall any prayers, this might be a good time to haul them out and dust them off.

He tilted his chair back against the wall, propped his feet on the railing and closed his eyes, willing his mind to stillness. Damn it, he was tired of brooding over the past. Thinking about the present was no better, and as for the future, it was always a gamble, any way you looked at it.

Trouble was, he had a feeling the cards were running against him.

Daylight was just cutting through the early-morning

mixture of fog and smoke when Jericho awoke to the sound of clattering hooves and the squeak of an ungreased wheel. Yawning, he secured his hat on his head and prepared himself to meet his opponent, hoping Rafe would be riding in close behind Smithers's rackety runabout.

The minute he stood, a ton of ballast stones came down on his head, reminding him that he had overdone it last night. Temperate by nature, he had tried without much success to block out the next few hours. Or perhaps the last few years.

It had been a damn fool thing to do at any rate. His neck was stiff and his head felt like a watermelon that had fallen off a wagon onto the cobblestones.

Blinking to focus his red-rimmed eyes, he searched the yard for Smithers's rig. Except for a Dearborn, a dray and a gaudy peddler's wagon that had obviously just pulled in, as it was still hitched to a lathered pair of bays, the yard was empty. There was no sign of either Rafe's gray or Smithers's blue roan.

"Lemme at 'im, the horny ol' sot!" bellowed someone from inside the wagon. The wagon lurched, leather springs creaking, and out tumbled a red-faced, red-haired and extremely pregnant harridan who looked bent on mayhem. She was waving what appeared to be a letter in one hand.

"You there," she yelled.

"Who, me?" Jericho, still half asleep, blinked at her.

"No, you young fool, I was talkin' to President Jackson! Come hold these here horses fer me while I go wrassle my man out o' that crazy whore's bed!"

By then, the livery boy was staggering out of the tack room, rubbing his eyes. Jericho quickly delegated

responsibility for the winded bays and followed the
waddling woman up the steps, across the veranda,
barely managing to reach around her to open the heavy
front door.

Some poor devil was about to catch what for. If there
was one thing Jericho could use about now, besides a
hair of the dog, it was a distraction of any sort.

The woman came to a halt in the middle of the lobby
and planted her hands on her wide hips, her prominent
belly lifting her faded calico skirt well above her ankles.
She glared at the few late-night revelers sprawled
drunkenly around the room, the few more who staggered out of the taproom, and the pair of drummers
who appeared in the doorway of the common room.

"All right, where is he?" she challenged.

"Where's who, ma'am?" inquired the night clerk,
pulling on his coat with one hand and fumbling to
hook his spectacles over his ears with the other.

She had a voice like a steam whistle. Thus it was
no great surprise to Jericho when an assortment of
nightshirted guests came spilling out of both wings,
grumpily demanding to know where the fire was. Glaring at them all, the woman loudly expressed a warning
that could be heard three miles down the canal, the
gist of which was that if some miserable bastard didn't
trot his flea-bitten carcass out here this very minute,
she would burn the place down around his ears and
fry the lard off whatever floozy he'd been bedded
down with.

It occurred to Jericho that the Jones sisters had left
too soon. They could have dined out on this tale for
years to come.

Watching the performance from just inside the front

door, he found himself feeling vaguely sorry for the woman's philandering husband. It was easy to see why, with such a wife at home, the poor wretch might be tempted to stray.

Jericho's amusement, however, was short-lived when he spotted Archibald Ricketts elbowing his way through the crowded doorway, hastily ramming his shirttail into his trousers.

"Hush now, Ida Lou," the peddler grumbled. "Things ain't the way they look. I was just—"

"I know blamed well what you were *just,* you old fool! Ever' time you sober up enough to find the flap of yer britches, you go chasing after the first bitch in heat that twitches her tail in front of your nose!"

Roughly two dozen pairs of eyes swung back and forth between the two contenders. Bets were placed. "Half eagle says the old battle-ax has 'im hog-tied and outta here in two shakes of a coon's tail," offered a lumberman fresh in from the swamp.

"Got me a V-spot says he'll land 'er one on the chops," challenged someone else.

"You see who that ol' sot was a-bedding down with?" demanded one of the three men who had tried to break into Sara's room two nights earlier. "Whooee! Feller must be hung like Baily's boar hog!"

Tightening her lips, Sara forced herself to ignore the crude remarks as she hurried down the hall after her brand-new husband. The way he had jumped out of bed and rushed from the room, she was afraid something dreadful had happened. A fire or a robbery—or perhaps that awful cholera epidemic that had started way up in Canada and worked its way south had broken out among the guests.

She burst into the lobby just in time to see her husband being grabbed by the ear by a fire-breathing female who was ranting loudly about no-good husbands who leave their wives and nine children to go sniffing after every hellfired strumpet that comes long.

Wives? Children?

Merciful saints, where was she going with Archibald?

"Wait!" cried Sara as she shoved her way through the crowd. "Archibald, what—"

It was Jericho who caught her by the arm and pulled her against his side just as the pair disappeared through the front door. He was holding a rumpled note that looked depressingly familiar. "Shh," he said softly. "She's his wife."

"His *what*? Do you mean to tell me my Archibald is that woman's husband?"

"Not to mention being the father of her nine children."

"But—"

"Shh, we'll talk about it later. Right now, I expect you could do with a restorative."

But Sara didn't need a restorative. What she needed was the answer to a very simple question. "But—but if she's his wife, then what does that make me?"

Some twenty minutes later, Sara was huddled in the unbroken straight chair, staring blindly at the cold fireplace, when someone rapped on her door. "It's not locked," she said dully. What good would a lock do now? The damage was already done.

Early morning sunlight glinted on the dusty windowpane as Jericho let himself inside with a bottle and two glasses. "Drink this," he said after pouring her a tot of brandy and another for himself.

Numbly, she took the glass, downed the contents as if it were a dose of salts and gasped for breath. Then, wiping her stinging eyes with the tail of her wrapper, she resumed staring at the cold hearth as fire blossomed in her belly. What was she going to do now? Merciful saints alive, she was ruined. All her plans— her sensible plans to make a home for herself and Maulsie and Big Simon—what would become of them now?

For all she knew, she might even be carrying Archibald's child.

"Sara?"

Carefully, she placed her empty glass on the bedside table. "Jericho, I think I may be going to have a baby."

It was Jericho's turn to strangle on a swallow of the fiery spirits. He placed his glass beside hers. "You *what?*"

"I said—"

"I heard what you said!"

"Yes, well . . . it happened that way with my friend Carrie. Eight months and two weeks after her wedding night, she had a baby girl."

Jericho felt as if he'd been slammed in the gut with a belaying pin. "You slept with him?"

*Of course she slept with him, you dolt. What did you expect, that he'd married her to play dominoes?*

"You have to do the marriage act before the marriage is legal. Archibald explained it to me. He was a very kind man, in spite of . . ." She sighed lugubriously. "Well. Mostly, he was kind, anyway."

Kind. Was that truly what she thought? Jericho wondered whether any woman could be that innocent. "Did he—was it—that is, are you all right?" he asked tentatively.

Nodding, Sara said, "It didn't hurt nearly as much as I expected." She flexed her fingers and stared down at them.

Jericho stared at them, too. He didn't want to know what had happened between them, he really didn't. Lowering himself to the bed, he stared at the profile of the bride who wasn't a wife. In only a few days she had been at the hotel, her tanned skin had faded to the color of old ivory.

Or maybe it was the shock she must be feeling after finding herself wed to a bigamist.

"Sara, listen—you remember what we talked about before? About Wilde Oaks and the fact that if I—if something happens to me, it will all go to a scoundrel of a third cousin somewhere out west who might not even still be alive? He hates farming. He's a—a trapper."

"I don't remember about your cousin." She blinked owlishly and sighed again.

There wasn't any cousin. He'd only made that up so she wouldn't feel sorry for him being all alone. He wanted her to marry him, but damn it, he didn't want her feeling sorry for him. A man had his pride. But, God, it hurt like blazes to think of that scurvy bastard being the first to bed her. Hurt almost as much to think she might be carrying his seed.

"Sara, if you're already carrying a child, why then, that's all the more reason for you to marry me," he reasoned. He was pretty sure she wasn't, unless they'd had a rowdy old time of it, and he didn't think the old sot was up to more than a couple of pokes, if that.

Her eyes were taking on a glassy look. He knew he'd better talk fast, or else she'd be asleep. "Sara, about what I said—"

She yawned. "I still don't understand why you can't look after Wilde Oaks yourself. You said you were between ships, so why not go back home and do what needs doing?"

Jericho swore under his breath. He hadn't wanted to tell her the truth, but he didn't have time to waste on coaxing her to see reason. "There's something I didn't tell you," he said quietly. "The thing is, Sara, I'm engaged to fight a duel. That's why I came here in the first place." He heard her gasp, ignored it, and went on with what had to be said. "The man seduced my sister, got her with child, and when she went to speak to him, expecting marriage, he beat her so that she lost the babe and died."

Even as he watched, the last shred of color left her face. "Oh, no," she whispered. She turned to face him, and he could see the shock in the clear amber depths of her eyes.

"I'll likely come through it without a scratch, but in case I don't, it would please me to know you were safe, and that Wilde Oaks was in good hands. You might even find time to plant a pretty bush or something on the graveyard up the hill from the house."

She seemed to be struggling with something. He wished he had thought to bring a pot of coffee along with the brandy. Or not brought the brandy at all.

He poured her a tumblerful of water, and she gulped it down. "Of course I would. Plant a bush, I mean—

but Jericho, you don't have to marry me for that. I'll look after your home until you're ready to take it back, and then—"

"No. Sara, we do it my way or not at all. As my wife—or widow, if that's the way it turns out—what's mine now will be legally yours. You'll have a name and a home for your child, and money enough to take care of you and yours until the farm is productive again."

He could almost see the thoughts running through her mind as she twisted her hands in her lap. She had small square hands. Capable hands. Jericho tried not to think about the way those same hands had felt on his body. Here he was, trying his damnedest to get his affairs in order in case he died within the next few hours. She was half drunk and fighting it, and he was swelling up fit to burst his breeches.

Scowling, he cleared his throat. "Then if you're of a mind to help me out, I'd as soon get on with it. Smithers was due in—"

"Who?"

"The man I'm to meet on the field of honor."

She stared at him, mouth agape. "Did you say Smithers? Not *Titus Smithers?*"

She stood up, knocking over the chair in the process. Wild-eyed, she lurched for the door, then swung back. Jericho was at a complete loss. Rising slowly to his feet from the bed where he'd been sitting, he wondered if she had cracked under the strain of finding herself married, impregnated and deserted in less than a day's time, her reputation in shreds.

Or was it only the brandy? "Now, Sara—"

"Do you know who he *is?*"

"*Who?*"

"Titus! He's my stepbrother! The one who tried to rape me so that I'd be forced to marry him! The one I ran away from! The wastrel who's gambled and squandered every cent my father left when he died, and now that he knows about my inheritance, he wants to marry it!"

"Jesus," Jericho whispered reverently. Things like this didn't happen outside the storybooks.

On the other hand, was it so strange? To meet at a hotel that was known primarily for its matrimonial and dueling arrangements? Sara had come for the one; he had come for the other.

"Sara? I think you'd better marry me right fast, girl. Elsewise, your stepbrother might decide he'd rather take you and leave than stay here and pay his debt of honor."

# Chapter Nine

The bride wore brown. Her brown eyes held elements of both panic and determination. Her brown hair was twisted into a tight coil and anchored on top of her head with four tortoiseshell hairpins. On top of the coil was a hat after the style of French jockey's caps. It did not match her gown. Neither did it match her boots.

Neither did it match the pitiful bouquet of wilted flowers, too obscure even to have a name, that Jericho had snatched hastily from the ditch bank.

Nevertheless, neither hat nor gown nor these particular flowers had been a part of her first wedding. For some reason, that seemed important.

Standing rigidly side by side on the landing while the packet boat unloaded her passengers and took on those bound for points south, Sara stoically endured her second wedding in twenty-four hours, having still not quite recovered from her first. Under the green and yellow bonnet, her face was frozen into a mask. Slanting a look at the man standing beside her, a man dressed entirely in unrelieved black, she observed the same look on his stern face.

Had they both lost their wits?

Titus. Merciful saints alive, her own stepbrother had done that terrible thing to Jericho's sister, and was now about to die for it, and Sara couldn't even find it in her heart to feel sorry for the wretch. She had hated and feared him for too long.

And then she began wondering about the legality of her second marriage. Had she not repeated these very same lines only last evening? Shouldn't she unsay them before she said them again to someone else?

But then, Archibald and his other wife had probably said the same lines. Perhaps it was the intent that mattered, not the words.

"Hsst! Sara!" Jericho whispered. "Pay attention!"

Love, honor, and obey?

Sara wasn't sure she could promise to do all that . . .

"I said, do you, Sara Rebecca Young," repeated the impatient minister, if indeed he was such, "take this man—"

The rest of the phrase was lost in the blast of a steam whistle. Two men brushed past, nearly oversetting the small wedding party in their rush to leap aboard the boat.

"Well? Speak up, miss, do you or don't you?" Squire Abernathy, who had been hastily coerced to officiate for a price, glanced anxiously over his shoulder. He, too, was scheduled to depart on the packet *Albemarle*.

"Well, yes. Of course. I mean, I do."

"Do you, Jericho Jefferson Wilde, take this woman to be—"

"Yessir, that I do. I now pronounce us man and wife, thank 'ee, sir, here's your fee." He handed over a half eagle. "Sara, grab your satchel. Remember, now—Miss

Renegar will see that your people are sent for. Closest neighbor's Rafe Turbyfill—he'll call on you soon's he gets back home to see how you're going on. I'll be along by-and-by if I make it."

As if waking from a nightmare only to find that it was real, Sara grabbed his sleeve, wildly searching his face for some shred of reassurance. "Wait! Jericho, just wait a minute—how will I know?"

"Shh, hush now. I've already sent off a messenger to tell all them that needs to know that you're my wife. Rafe'll be close by, too. Remember to plant something pretty on the hill, will you? Oh, and there's Louisa's dog, name of Brig—if he's still around, you might want to give him a wide berth. He's not what you might call friendly, but I didn't have the heart to put him down."

A dog? What was he talking about? "Jericho, wait, don't leave yet!" Oh, for mercy's sake, if only her head wasn't pounding fit to wake Jerusalem.

Two dockhands began casting off as the *Albemarle* blew her final warning and made ready to depart. Jericho tossed Sara's luggage aboard, lifted her by the arms to swing her down, changed his mind in midstream, and brought her up hard against his body.

She thought she heard him swear, but then he was kissing her. The crowd aboard the packet began to cheer, and her heart started beating a tattoo to match her pounding head. Without even thinking, she wrapped her arms around his neck and hung on for dear life as the universe shrank to contain only the two of them—only those parts of her body that were in contact with the body of this stranger.

This stranger who was kissing her as if he would devour her very soul.

When Jericho finally lifted his mouth to stare down at her, Sara stared right back. He looked as if he'd been poleaxed. Sara, groping for security in a reeling world, grabbed hold of his gun belt. Her fingers curled under the worn leather, and she was instantly aware of two things at once. Hard, living flesh under a thin layer of cloth, and a heavy weight that could only be the two enormous pistols he wore at his side.

Gasping, she jerked back her hand as if she had grabbed hold of the wrong end of a red hot poker. She might have fallen had he not grabbed her by both elbows and swung her down onto the deck of the packet.

Before she could call him back, he stepped away from the edge of the wharf. He swallowed hard—Sara saw his Adam's apple move—and then he nodded to her as if they were no more than chance met acquaintances.

Which, in a way, she supposed they were, she thought dazedly.

There was no escaping the noisy bustle of getting underway. "Thank you, Sara," he said, and she read the words from his lips, straining to hear his voice one last time.

"Take care," she cried, pushing through to the stern rail for one last glimpse of the man who was her husband. "Jericho, please take care!"

The packet gathered speed, kicking up a wake in the coffee-colored water. "Oh, do take care," she whispered as the distance extended between them.

But the tall figure in black had already left the landing. Her newest husband had not even lingered long enough to wave her out of sight.

"You look like you been dug up and hung out to dry," Rafe observed dryly as he surveyed his friend's troubled countenance. He'd been waiting impatiently ever since he'd spotted Jericho's dark head above the throng down at the packet landing. For about half a minute he'd entertained the thought that his friend might be skipping out, but the thought had died almost as quickly as it was born. The two men had spent little time together over the past twenty years, but he'd lay odds that Wilde had not changed all that much. To Rafe's knowledge he had never ducked out on a fight in his life.

When the two men came together by the livery shed before the packet was even around the bend, Rafe wasted no time on pleasantries. "Got 'im! Finally located the scoundrel in a crib near Gosport, drunk as a lord. He sobered up quick enough when I dragged him outside, shoved his head in a horse trough and reminded him that he had an engagement at the Halfway Hotel."

Jericho, glancing around the yard at the handful of patrons going about their business, saw no sign of the young jack-a-dandy. "He's not here," Rafe said hastily. "Him and his man went ahead to the field to study the lay of the land. I told him I'd fetch you and we'd be along shortly. Late as it is, I figured you'd still want to get it over with instead of waiting another day."

It occurred to Jericho that with the morning barely underway, he had already accomplished quite a lot.

"I'm ready. But Rafe, first there's something you need to know." A solitary man both by nature and by calling, he had always found it hard to confide and damned near impossible to ask for help. But before he could broach the subject foremost in his mind, Turbyfill drew something from the pocket inside his Garrick.

"I don't know how good you are with a knife—ain't like you're an ordinary seaman anymore. Anyways, I bought this off a Spanish man I come across in a tavern while I was tracking Smithers." He unsheathed an efficient-looking weapon with a short cross guard and a clip point blade some ten inches long. "The heft of it feels about right. Man who sold it to me looks like he's been in a fight or two, and managed to survive. Maybe some of his luck'll rub off on you. For what it's worth, he says if you'll hold the knife in your right hand and your hat in your left, you can toss your hat in the other bloke's face if things get dicy. Might throw him off stride just long enough for you to get in under his guard."

"I don't need to use tricks, damn it. I'll win fair and square, or I'll not win at all."

"You think Smithers gives a hoot in hell for any stupid rules? You're fighting for Weezie, man. Don't forget that."

"My hat, huh? I'll try and remember, but Rafe—" Jericho cast a distracted look toward the canal, now empty save for the usual traffic of canal schooners, towboats, and barges. Clearing his throat, he tried again. "What I'm trying to tell you is that I went and married me a wife while I was waiting for Smithers to turn up. I just now set her aboard the southbound with letters of introduction to my housekeeper and old man

Kinfield in Elizabeth City. He was Papa's lawyer. He'll see she gets to the farm all right, but Rafe—I'd be much obliged if you'd look in on her when you get home. She's a sensible sort, but I left things in pretty much of a mess there, what with the new overseer and his family not even moved into their quarters yet."

Rafe stared, his somewhat jaded eyes bulging in their pouches as the knife fell unnoticed to the ground. "You *what*?" he drawled.

Jericho shrugged. "Yes, well—can't say much for my timing. Happened she was in a bind, and I didn't have anything else to do while I waited for you and Smithers to show up."

Turbyfill cursed a blue streak. He raked all ten fingers through his once tidy hair. And then he sighed in defeat. "I don't know why I even bother."

"Me, neither," said Jericho with a wintery smile. "Leastwise, if things don't turn out too good this morning, I can rest easy knowing the farm's in good hands."

"Good hands. Tarnation, Rico, if you ain't the most hellfired lamebrain I ever come across in all my days. Don't you know that once you let a female get her hands in your pocket, you could wind up piss pot poor? Who is she? How long have you known her? How'd she manage to get you by the short hairs so fast?"

"Damn it, Tubby, Sara's not like that! You met her. Name of Sara Young? As for winding up piss pot poor, I'm likely to wind up doornail dead anyhow, so what difference will it make in the end?"

"Jesus," Rafe muttered.

Jericho knew he might as well hoist sail and let it all flap in the wind. "That's not the half of it. Happens

Sara and Smithers are kin. Leastwise, not blood kin, but he's her stepbrother."

Rafe swore again. With a bleak and self-deprecating smile, Jericho went on to explain how Sara had run away from home at about the same time Wilde had come north to meet Smithers. "She's afeared of him. I'd take it right kindly if you'd look after her for me if I don't come through this morning. He'll go after her again, and this time he'll be getting more than just her inheritance, however much that is. We didn't talk about it."

Rafe's iron-gray hair, once neatly dressed and combed, stood on end. His fine linen collar was twisted awry, and he was pacing a tight circle on the dusty stable yard. "I don't believe any of this rigmarole, you know. Not a bloody damn word of it."

"Me, neither. Trouble is, it's all true."

Retrieving the knife from where it had fallen, Rafe wiped the blade off on the sleeve of his coat. "You ain't fit to be out alone without a leash. Here, take this blasted pigsticker. If I'm going to have to haul your carcass home and dump it out on your widow's doorstep, I'd just as lief get on with it. I figure if I get out of here within the next hour, I can drop off your remains, go home and get started on drinking myself blind before midnight. And yes, damn it, I'll look after your widow!"

Jericho didn't much like the look of the man Smithers had chosen to second him. But then, the bastard probably hadn't had much choice. The two were propped up against a big red bay tree that was riddled with mistletoe. Smithers, resplendent in a soiled and wrinkled blue velvet claw-hammer coat and buff-colored breeches, was picking his teeth with the blade of his knife. The other man was upending a jug, the gurgling sound of the white liquor audible all the way across the clearing.

Both men managed to get to their feet. Neither of them spoke. Jericho wasn't certain the second man could—he was barely able to stand. "You arrange for a burying man?" Smithers called out, the smirk on his pretty features looking somehow obscene in the harsh morning sunlight.

"Physician'll be along most any minute now," replied Turbyfill, his usual drawl clipped with distaste. "There's no wind to speak of, so we'll quarter the sun. Rico, you'll face yonder big cypress, sun on your left shoulder. Smithers, you take the sun on your right. Last chance to beg off, no honor lost." One of the duties of the second was to settle without bloodshed where there existed a possibility.

There existed none. Before either man could reach his appointed position, the physician arrived, his dusty black carryall rattling to a halt at the edge of the clearing. He stumbled from the buggy and Turbyfill swore roundly. "Is it too frigging much," he muttered, "to hope for just one sober man in this damned affair?"

Titus's second, a tavern tender by the unlikely name of Ladymore, staggered forward and began to speak. "Ten pastes—paches—shteps for'ard, fire in count o' three. Where's m' jug?"

"That isn't the way it goes, you old fool," Smithers said fiercely.

Rafe stepped forward and waved a hand for silence. "Center of the clearing, foot-to-foot, one hand only, at the count of three, commence to fight. Fight ends at first blood drawn."

Titus's face was as guileless as a hangman's smile. Running a thumb along the edge of his blade, he said, "As the challenged party, I choose the weapons. Man that chooses the weapons sets the rules, and s' far as I know, there ain't no set rules for knives. Reck'n we'll just have to make do with the reg'lar rules, which is, ten paces, weapons up, then turn, take aim, and cut loose."

"God in heaven," Rafe whispered. "He means to throw on you, Rico. Get ready to drop at the count of nine. No—better make that eight."

There was no pretense of examining the weapons. A knife was a knife. It could kill but once in a single throw. At a nod from Turbyfill, both men made their way to the center of the clearing. The sun had just topped the level of the surrounding trees. The smell of smoke hung heavy, but the air was clear enough.

Back-to-back they stood, each man intent only on killing his opponent. Jericho had fought before, more times than he could recall, but seldom with a knife and never with the intent to kill in cold blood.

The count began. In measured tones, both seconds called out the numbers, Ladymore's count slurred, Turbyfill's crisp and angry.

At the count of four, Jericho felt the muscles in his right arm begin to tense. At the call of six, he took a deep breath and flexed his throwing arm. At the call of eight he felt the hairs at the back of his neck stand up, and then Rafe shouted, and then someone else cried out—the physician, as it later turned out.

Before either cry had faded, he felt a bolt of lightning strike him in the back.

"No, damn you—*no!*" someone screamed.

Turning, Jericho staggered. On his knees, feeling strangely calm, he lifted his right arm, holding the knife by the tip of the blade, and let fly the instant before he collapsed. End over end the knife spun in the general direction, but wide of its intended target, falling a foot for every three it sped forward.

Titus stared in dumb paralysis as the tumbling blade came toward him. Not until it was almost too late did he jump to one side, which was probably why the thing caught him in the belly instead of missing him altogether.

Staring down in disbelief as blood gushed from the front of his well-cut buckskins, he commenced screaming obscenities. Twenty feet away, Jericho lay sprawled on his face in the rich, alluvial dirt. His last conscious thought was of Sara.


Jericho's first conscious thought was of Sara. It was followed by the surprising awareness that hell was somewhat cooler that he'd expected. "Water," he mumbled.

Someone lifted his head, and he cried out as pain shot through his upper body. He felt a tumbler pressed against his lower lip. Water dribbled down his chin and was tenderly wiped away.

He tried to say his thanks, but gave up and allowed blessed unconsciousness to claim him again.

Voices? Then he wasn't the only resident of hell. Although why he should have expected his own private quarters in the fiery region was beyond him. He'd never been particularly bad ... but then, he'd never been particularly good, either.

"Poor devil, he'll not last the night, I'm afraid."

*The devil was dying? Then who the hell was going to run his kingdom?*

"Don't relish having to tell his wife."

*Devil's wife? No, Sara. I never even got to try you, did I, sweetheart? Prob'ly a good thing—might've liked it a bit too much ...*

"Does he leave an heir?" Jericho didn't recognize that voice.

And then a voice he did recognize replied, "Not to my knowledge, only a wife, and her brand-new from what I understand."

*Jesus. Rickett's brat would inherit Wilde Oaks?* "Over m'dead body," groaned the pale figure on the bed. But then, Rickett's brat was Sara's, too. He couldn't be-grudge a child of Sara's anything.

Jericho felt as if he were hovering somewhere near the ceiling, gazing down on the three men in the room. His words were barely audible, but they had an electri-fying effect.

"Rico? Can you hear me? God, man, don't try to talk, just listen!"

" 'S all yours," the figure on the bed mumbled. "Sara, too. Good woman. Promise me, Tubby, take care of her'n Rickett's brat, y'hear?"

"Mind's wandering," said the elder of the two men.

"Laudanum?"

The physician, as nearly sober as he'd been in years, shook his head sadly. "Wore off by now. Takes 'em this way sometimes. Man just plum hates to die and leave loose ends. Sounds to me like you just inherited yourself a house and a woman. Not sure what a ricket sprat is, but it sounds to me like he wants you to have it."

Turbyfill shook his head impatiently. After watching over his friend for a day and a night, waiting for him to die, he looked as if he'd been on one of his own well-lubricated house parties, known far and wide for the high-stakes gambling, rough track racing, and the choicest light skirts in a three-state area.

"What about Smithers?" he inquired.

"Ladymore carted him off to his ma. Lad'll not last out the day. Belly wounds always putrify."

Considering Wilde might have the barest chance of surviving, as his heart was still beating and the blood was oozing rather than bubbling from the wound, the doctor had left the gut-stabbed man in the field while Jericho was driven to the hotel. Rafe had bribed two old women out of their room and had it set up as a sickroom.

"Hotel manager's found a woman to sit with Wilde."

"Hope she ain't plannin' to make a career of it," the physician retorted. "Boy's in a bad way, a real bad way. He could go most any minute."

Rafe concurred. They had not been close in years, but for old-times' sake, he was torn between staying to see Jericho off on his final journey and heading south to break the sad news to his widow.

Before he could make up his mind, the door burst open and a stout black woman carrying a red kerchief-wrapped bundle stepped inside. One hand on her hip, her feet planted firmly and widely apart, she looked from one man to the other and then directed her remarks to Turbyfill. "I be Princess Anne County. I's free as de rain, I's come t'rough de cholera, didn't take no part in de uprisin', I gets ten-cent a day for my nursin', and I don' take no orders from no buckras."

Goggle-eyed, Rafe looked to the physician, who nodded. "She'll do you fair and well. Miss County's about the best nurse around these parts, long's you don't ask what she's a-totin' in that sack o' hers."

# Chapter Ten

At her first glimpse of Wilde Oaks, Sara murmured, "Mercy, and I thought Papa's house was fine. This place is a regular wedding cake!"

It was late in the afternoon. A hazy pink sunset cast a flattering glow over a large white house surrounded by enormous water oaks. In the distance, beyond acres of lush farmland, a wall of somber pines was accented here and there by wine-colored gum trees. Most of the vast, rich fields were presently overgrown with weeds, as if they hadn't been planted in several years. A few tattered cornstalks stood brokenly in the field directly behind the house; the rest, unharvested, obviously trampled by marauding animals. How sad. But then, Jericho had said he had hired a new overseer. Perhaps things would soon improve.

Sara's gaze returned to the impressive house, and she quickly forgot the disturbing signs of neglect. At this point she would have welcomed the sight of a one-room cabin if it meant she could finally take off her bonnet, corset, and slippers and settle down for a spell.

She had been met the previous day at the packet landing in Elizabeth City by a clerk from a Mr. Kinfield's office, who said Captain Wilde had sent word ahead of her arrival. She didn't envy the messenger. The distance from the Halfway Hotel to the small riverside town was some twenty-odd miles over roads that made slower travel by way of the canal a blessing.

Brushing the wrinkles from her skirt, Sara had allowed as how she was glad to be met.

"I took the liberty of securing you a room at the Indian Queen Hotel, Miss—Mrs. Wilde," the unctuous attorney had informed her a few minutes later in his office one block off the riverfront. "I assure you it's the finest establishment in our fair city."

"Oh, but—"

"At Captain Wilde's suggestion, I made an appointment with his man of business for ten o'clock tomorrow morning. We're to meet right here in my office, and then when we're done with business, it was the captain's notion that you might want to do a bit of shopping while you're in town. There'll be a carriage ready to take you out to Wilde Oaks whenever you're ready to leave."

After a delicious evening meal at the hotel, which she barely touched, and a restless and largely sleepless night, Sara had been determined to set aside her worries and follow Jericho's instructions to the letter. It was the very least she could do.

But oh, how she had ached to know what had happened. At that very moment he might have been lying—

No. She refused to believe it. He had to survive. Even if she never saw him again—even if he boarded a ship and set sail for China and never came home again, God simply would not allow a man as decent and fine as Jericho Jefferson Wilde to be murdered by a mealy worm like Titus Smithers.

Arriving at the appointed time and place the following morning, Sara had been introduced by Mr. Kinfield, the attorney, to Mr. Willis, the banker. Between the two men she had learned the extent of her husband's wealth, most of it in land, but a considerable sum resulting from the recent sale of his ship. At her husband's direction, according to the banker, she was to have a quarterly allowance for her own personal use and another account from which to pay the servants and operate the household.

The management of the farm, according to the attorney, was to be left to a Mr. Hiram Moyer, who, along with his wife and a spinster sister, had recently taken up residence in the overseer's house.

When asked if she had any questions, Sara had thought it best to lay her own cards on the table. Briefly, she had explained her circumstances prior to her marriage to Jericho Wilde, leaving out the part Archibald had played and the troublesome business between her new husband and her stepbrother. Whatever the outcome, they would learn of it soon enough.

Poor Mr. Kinfield had swallowed so hard he'd nearly dislodged his necktie. "Do you mean to tell me, Miss— uh, Mrs. Wilde, that you have, er—that is, that you are—"

"An heiress," Sara had informed them grandly, looking from one nonplussed gentleman to the other. But then she had grinned, quite spoiling the effect. "Yes, indeed, sir, that I am, thanks to a grandfather I never even met. I'll not be dressing in diamonds and ermine, but at least I won't be having to peddle vegetables at the roadside."

Obviously, neither man had known what to make of that. She suspected they had thought her an adventuress, out to feather her own nest. Which she supposed in a way she was, only she never set out to marry a rich man for his money.

"I do have one very particular request, however. There are two servants at my father's home who need to be brought down to Wilde Oaks as quickly as possible. My, um—stepfamily may kick up a fuss, but Maulsie and Big Simon are free to go when and where they please."

Mr. Kinfield had promised to make arrangements that very morning, and then Mr. Willis had offered to drop her off at the shop of her choice on his way back to the bank. Not that there were many to choose from.

But Sara, after casting one longing look at a dressmaker's establishment on Main Street, had declined his offer. An hour later in front of the Indian Queen Hotel, she had followed her shabby luggage into the hired conveyance and set out on the last leg of her journey to her new home.

And now here she was. "Mercy, it's grand, isn't it?" she whispered, feeling just a tad intimidated by the two-story, square, hip-roofed, porticoed dwelling set at the end of a long, tree-lined driveway. The house, she was later to learn, had been built by a much earlier Wilde and elaborated on by succeeding generations.

Evidently, her arrival had been expected. As the carriage pulled up before the wide front steps, a young woman came outside and stood waiting.

The housekeeper? Sara wondered. The woman didn't

resemble any housekeeper Sara had ever seen. Although she supposed there was no rule that said housekeepers could not be tall and willowy, with shining blond hair and a face right off a cameo brooch.

At closer range, the house appeared somewhat rundown, the housekeeper even more beautiful. Sara, in her brown serge with her green and yellow coal-scuttle bonnet, felt rumpled and out of fashion, even though her outfit was scarcely a month old.

Feeling like a turnip in a rose garden, she wished now she had taken time to purchase a new trunk, a new pair of shoes, and to have a few more gowns made up before she had run away to marry Archibald.

"Mrs. Renegar?" she inquired timidly as the driver set off down the dusty driveway.

"I happen to be Miss Ivadelle Moyer, madam, and just who might you be?" It was plain as day the woman was on the verge of sending her around to the back door.

Well. Sara hadn't dealt with Noreen all these years without learning a thing or two about holding her own. "I," she announced in even loftier accents, "happen to be Mrs. Captain Jericho Wilde. Would you please be so good as to have someone collect my bags?"

Even while she was asking herself who in heaven's name Ivadelle Moyer was, Sara couldn't help but be pleased at the effect of her statement.

"But Mr.—that is, Captain Wilde—that is, madam, you must be mistaken. Captain Wilde is unmarried. Now, if you'll state your business?"

The door behind the self-proclaimed Miss Ivadelle Moyer opened silently. The woman who emerged was every inch the proper housekeeper, from her plain gray chemise under the enveloping white apron, to her stiff white house bonnet. "Miss—that is, ma'am, I just this morning got word you was coming. It'll take a few minutes to set your room to rights, but if you'd like a cup of something hot to drink, I'll see to it right away."

"Then *you* must be Miss Renegar," said Sara, relieved. She picked up the valise, only to have the older woman hurry down the steps and take it from her.

"Here, now, you're just a little thing, ain't you? What was that boy thinking about, sending you down here all by yourself?" The woman's face fell a mile. "Lordy, don't tell me—he's gone and got hisself hurt, ain't he?"

"Oh, no! He was just fine when I saw him last." Sara scampered up the front steps after the tall, beanstalk-thin housekeeper, wondering how she could reassure her when she was filled with dread herself.

They brushed past Miss Ivadelle Moyer, who looked considerably less lovely with her jaw hanging halfway down her gimp-edged collar. "The captain," she hissed, "was not married when he engaged my brother. If you're truly married to him, then where is he? Enjoying a honeymoon for one?"

Sara froze in her patent-leather boots. Assuming her haughtiest attitude, she turned and said sweetly, "If you will forgive me for not answering that question, Miss Mouser, I will forgive you for asking it."

"It's Moyer!"

"Oh, I *do* beg your pardon." Sara knew she was being childish, not to mention mean-spirited, but she was just too tired to deal with another Noreen at the moment. "If you must know, my husband is presently engaged in a—a business affair."

\*   \*   \*

The house was gloomy. Quite lovely, with all the dark paneling and dark wood floors, but gloomy. There was no other word for it. The first thing Sara did after being shown to her room was to unpack her mother's embroidered dresser scarf and spread it over the marble-topped dresser. Next she carefully positioned her brush and mirror, with the blue-glass pin tray and the matching scent bottle just so between them. And then she propped her framed pictures on a shelf, not quite daring to hang them on the walls.

Having settled in, she sought out the housekeeper, asked instructions to the family burying ground, and set out to pay her respects to Miss Louisa Wilde. If it weren't for that poor, unfortunate woman, she wouldn't even be here.

"And if it weren't for my wicked stepbrother," she whispered to the freshly turned earth beside a cluster of markers on a low rise near a grove of pine and hardwoods, "*you* wouldn't be lying *there*. Oh, my dear, I'm so very sorry. If I can make it up to you somehow, rest assured I will."

Rest assured. How perfectly awful. To be young and dead and forced to rest forevermore.

It wasn't a very worthy thought, but true, nevertheless. Dead was all very well when one was tired of living, but when one was young, with everything to look forward to, it was a wretched shame, that was what it was.

And then, in that quietest hour of the day, just as the first stars begin to creep out, Sara heard a sound that sent prickles up her spine. Cautiously, she cut her eyes toward the dense stand of oaks nearby, but it was growing dark. The sun was already down, making the shadows all but impenetrable.

Wolves? Bears? This near the swamp, there were bound to be bears. And painters. Merciful saints in heaven, she could be swallowed whole by one of those huge, slinky cats that roamed the dense woods near outlying farms, stealing lambs and calves and chickens.

Lifting her skirts, Sara sailed over the low wrought-iron fence and took off across the fallow field at a run. Next time she visited Louisa, she would bring along a weapon. Or perhaps a nice picnic basket to leave as a bribe at the edge of the woods.

By the time she had finished a supper of sugar cured ham, fried chicken, cornbread, collard greens, and watermelon pickles, Sara had more or less put things into perspective. Beware the wild animals in the woods; beware Ivadelle Moyer in the house.

Sooner or later the woman would have to be dealt with, but at the moment it was all she could do to find her way around her new home. The housekeeper would help show her around, but Sara alone was responsible for hanging onto her own temper.

Miss Moyer took her place at the dinner table as if she had every right. With a pinched expression, she mentioned the likelihood of rain. Sara in turn remarked politely on the lovely row of pecan trees lining the driveway.

When that drew no response, she mentioned a newspaper article she had recently read about a college that had opened its doors to both men and women, which was highly unusual—some said immoral.

"I, myself, never held with colleges for women," said

Ivadelle Moyer with a sniff. She did that a lot, Sara had noticed. Sniff. Sara didn't know if it was an attitude or an allergy.

And then the inquisition set in with a vengeance. Normally as friendly as a Spaniel pup, Sara managed to sidestep the question of how long she had been married, how long she had been engaged, and how she and the captain had first met. Hanging onto her temper by a thread, she introduced the topic of the weather again and the possibility of an early frost.

She was still hanging on by the same thread when her opponent retired from the field of combat. With a look of intense dislike, Ivadelle rose abruptly and stalked from the room.

Alone, Sara dropped all pretense of graciousness. It was a dreadful strain on her system, anyway. She toyed with her dessert and sighed, wondering what kind of briar patch she had landed herself in this time. She might as well have gone back home and taken her chances with Noreen. Without Titus, there was little the woman could do to hurt her. And by now, Titus would have surely had his wings clipped at the very least.

Well. As Maulsie was fond of saying, she had buttered her bread, now she must lie in it. If Miss Renegar could be believed, and Sara was sure the woman was sound as a golden eagle, the Moyer woman had arrived with the overseer and his wife and moved directly into the main house that very day on some pretext about the cottage loft being infested with bats or ants or some such.

"If you ask me, the hussy meant all along to move in here and trick my boy into marriage." Sara still had trouble thinking of Jericho as anyone's "boy." "If that woman wanted herself a husband, why did she have to leave home to find one? Fouled her own nest, if you ask me."

Sara, by force of long habit, took her own dishes out to the kitchen, placating the indignant housekeeper by saying that she might as well start the tour of her new home there as anywhere.

"Well . . . I reckon we can do that. Just let me set this here kettle on to heat. Her Highness'll be screaming for bathwater before long."

Hester Renegar bustled around the large, well-equipped room filling the dishpan, settling the dishes to soak, and refilling the kettle from the rain barrel set conveniently just outside the door. In the process, she muttered about the woman who had moved in without so much as a by-your-leave and made herself right at home.

And while it might not be polite to listen to servants' gossip, Sara prided herself that she was sensible enough to hear both sides of any issue and make up her own mind.

"Some brass, if ye ask me. O' course, it's not my place to say it, but I can tell you the Lord's honest truth, I was that glad when word came this morning that the boy had took hisself a wife."

Then, as if remembering her place, she said, "We don't have a cook no more—money's been hard come by this past year, and now that my boy's done sold his boat, I ain't had time to look for one, but this here's the kitchen, such as it is. New iron stove works real good."

Maulsie, Sara thought. She was selectively hard of

hearing and stubborn as a fence post, but she was a wonderful cook.

Gesturing to a door leading from the kitchen, the housekeeper indicated several points of interest. "This here's the pantry, out yonder's the well and the cool-house, beyond that there broken-down fence is the kitchen garden. Hog leaned on the boards, and now every deer in Pasquotank County comes a-browsing. I told that carpenter the day he come that as soon as he patches the roof where it don't leak all over my good floors, he'll have to mend the garden fence, else there won't be a collard plant left come first frost."

Sara made a mental note to set Big Simon to the task of fence-mending as soon as he arrived. It would make him feel more comfortable, knowing that he was needed.

As the kettle came to a simmer, the housekeeper set a fresh pot of tea to brew, then refilled the kettle and plopped it down on the stove to heat. "No better'n she should be, if you ask me," she muttered, and Sara took they were back to the overseer's sister.

The woman bustled about getting out cups, saucers, and a fat sugar bowl. Then, turning back to Sara, hands twisting in her apron and a stricken look on her long, plain face, she blurted, "Is it over and done yet? Is my boy hurt bad?"

The duel. "I wasn't sure how much you knew. Jericho was just fine when I last saw him, right after breakfast yesterday. Ti—the other party had not yet arrived. Mr. Turbyfill had gone to find him, and I think Jericho was expecting them momentarily."

"Hmph! Weren't for that man, Miss Louisa wouldn't by a-lying out there on the hill with her poor ma and

papa and them other two young'uns that died o' the
flux before they was a year old."

"Mr. *Turbyfill*?"

"Oh, he ain't the one that put a babe in my little
girl's belly and then beat her so bad she laid right down
and died, but if it weren't for that rackety crowd that
comes down to visit him, with their likker drinkin' and
their carryin' on, my little girl never would've met up
with that sweet-talkin' hornswoggler."

Titus. The wretched scoundrel. It was coming back
to Sara now, all the disparaging remarks he had made
about the various women he'd been courting, including
one down here in Pasquotank County. She had
thought at the time that any woman worth her salt
would surely be able to see past his pretty face and
false charm. Certainly, by the time they were of courting age, all her own friends had known him far too
well to be taken in.

As for Rafe Turbyfill, she had only met the man
briefly, but he hadn't seemed all that bad. True, there
was something rather rakish about him, but she had
found him pleasant enough. Years older than Jericho,
of course. And where Jericho was inclined to be sober
to the point of grimness, Rafe Turbyfill was just the
opposite. The devil was in his eyes, unless she was very
much mistaken.

Behind her, Ivadelle Moyer cleared her throat, startling Sara so that she nearly dropped her teacup. In
the harsh glare of the kitchen lamp, she didn't look
quite so young. "Yes? Is there something you wish?
There's fresh tea made . . ."

Ignoring Sara, Ivadelle addressed the housekeeper.

"I can't sleep in that back room. There's drafts, and the stench of smoke makes my eyes burn."

"Ma'am, I can't help that. There's not another room aired out, but I'll set a bowl o' vinegar on the washstand. It'll help chase out the smell."

"There's plenty of empty rooms. Why can't I move?"

Sara's head swung back and forth, attending the battle of wills between the two women. For that was precisely what it was. "Miss Moyer could have—" she began, when Hester interrupted her.

"The other back room's mine. Always was, ever since Miss Louisa was a babe in her cradle. Middle room belongs to her, and I ain't about to move her things out. Your brother's place is—"

"Is just that much closer to that wretched swamp! If I'd known about those everlasting fires, I never would have come here."

Sara was about to retort that she'd been given to understand that it was bats in the loft that bothered her, when something in the woman's face stopped her. For some people—and Sara should know, particularly given her own uncertain position—there was no going back. "I'll swap places with you," she said quietly. "The smoke doesn't really bother me that much. I've had time to get used to it."

She regretted the words almost as soon as they left her mouth, but by the time she heard Hester Renegar's snort of disapproval and saw the flicker of triumph on Miss Moyer's flawless features, it was too late. The overseer's sister would soon be ensconced in one of the two bedrooms that, along with a dressing room and bathing room, made up the master suite. How long would it take her, once the master came home, to cross the threshold into his bedroom?

Sara was no innocent. She knew about such things as mistresses and kept women. She'd heard it whispered more than once that half the men in Norfolk County kept fancy women on the side, and their wives none the wiser.

Oh, she knew all about sex. After all, she herself had done it once and might be with child as a result. The thought of her husband messing around under the covers with another woman was enough to set her blood to boiling, yet there was something about Ivadelle that aroused her reluctant sympathy. Sara knew what it was like to be unwanted in her own home—to be alone, dependent on strangers. Women alone were sometimes forced to make the best of a bad situation, and if Ivadelle's brother had only recently married, why then, his bride might not be too eager to share her home with a third party, even if she were family.

She would do her best to be patient. For a while, at least.

But her last waking thought that night was not of Ivadelle, but of Jericho. *Where are you now? Headed out to sea? Lying wounded, unable to come home? Have you forgotten me already?*

Hours later, Sara lay awake in the narrow room at the back of the house, listening to the night noises. Strange, how they could be so similar and at the same time, so different. All houses had a tendency to creak as night cooled the timbers. At home, she had fallen asleep to the hum of cicadas, the hoot of a barn owl, and the intermittent shrill of tree frogs from down near the branch.

At the hotel there had been the noise of the nightly carousal from the coarser element, as well as the constant din of traffic, both by road and canal.

Here, the night noises were both familiar and unfamiliar. The same creak of cooling wooden timbers. The call of a whippoorwill. But what was that clicking sound in the hallway outside her door? And the snuffling sound? If she were not of such a sensible turn of mind, she might even think there was a large animal loose in the house.

Sometime during the night it set in to rain. Not the driving rain that would quickly flood the creaks and as quickly be gone, but the dismal sort that seemed to hang on for days.

"I swear my head's fit to bust right wide open," Ivadelle muttered, coming in late for her breakfast. "If it's not the everlasting smoke, it's the rain. And I'm sure I heard that dog last night. Renegar! Did you let that dog in the house? I told you dog hair makes my eyes water."

Hester Renegar had just brought in a fresh pot of coffee. She sat down at the table, and Sara passed her the rack of toast. Eyeing the housekeeper, Ivadelle snorted her disapproval. She didn't voice it, but it was clear that she thought a servant had no place at the family table.

"He's too old to stay out in the shed when it rains. Old bones don't take kindly to wet weather." Hester looked pointedly at the overseer's sister, whose age Sara had underestimated the first time she'd seen her in her pale blue sateen with the black gimp trim.

In the harsh light of the kitchen, she'd looked older. In the gray daylight that spilled in through the tall dining room windows, she looked older still. She wore black. And while the gown was fashionable and her silvery pale hair was dressed to a fare-thee-well, with several dainty tendrils curling about her face, black drained the last hint of color from her pale complexion, showing up the faint furrows between her eyebrows and the drooping lines at the corners of her small mouth.

But oh, my, she was elegant. Like a painted white china figurine. Sara had once aspired to such elegance, but over the years she had resigned herself to the fact that she would never be fashionably pale. Along with her father's light brown hair and eyes, she had inherited her mother's golden olive skin. In the summertime, when she worked outside for all hours, she became all one color, which was most definitely *not* fashionable. Her hands were callused and her hair was too straight and too heavy to do more than twist into a coil and anchor the best way she could.

A beauty she was not. Oh, she might pinch her cheeks and splash herself with the scent Maulsie made for her from lemongrass and rose petals, but she had long ago come to terms with the fact that her true value as a woman lay in her frugality, her sensibility, and her willingness to work hard.

No, indeed, Sara told herself, she was not without value. She had always been of a cheerful nature. Somewhat inclined toward a quick temper, but she was working on that failing. A few years ago she had taken great pride in the fact that she could curl her tongue against her two little fingers and let loose a whistle shrill enough to break glass. And while it was not a particularly ladylike talent, it had once earned her a great deal of admiration among the neighborhood boys.

The three women ate silently. Outside, the rain continued to fall relentlessly, hiding all but the nearest of the pecan trees along the driveway. Sara heard the same clicking sound she had heard in the night and glanced around in time to see a big, shaggy red dog appear in the open doorway.

"Botheration!" said the housekeeper. "Set, Brig. I'll let you out in a minute."

The dog sat, and Sara thought, so this is Brig. He was not a friendly creature, according to Jericho. As if to underline that description, the animal curled his lip and growled.

Immediately, Sara recognized the sound. It hadn't been a bear or a painter she'd heard, only poor Louisa's dog guarding his mistress's grave. She determined to make friends with the poor creature, but slowly. Trust couldn't be won in a day. Meanwhile, she had enough sense not to make any sudden moves.

Not so Ivadelle. With another of her loud sniffs, she flung down her napkin and glared at the dog. "If someone doesn't do something about that filthy animal, I'll have Hiram take care of him! Decent people shouldn't have to be exposed to the filthy parasites those creatures carry!"

Parasites? The dog looked clean enough to Sara, but then, what did she know about dogs? The only dog she had ever owned had been the poodle her father had given her the year before he'd died. Within a week, the poor pup had turned up missing. Days later, she had found his ears and his tail nailed to the wall of Titus's tree house.

She had never said a word about it and neither had Titus, but she knew. What's more, Titus had known that she knew.

She shuddered just as someone pounded on the front door. Brig glanced over his shoulder and then turned his small yellow eyes back to the three women seated around the oval mahogany table.

Ivadelle stared right back, but she looked frightened. Sara couldn't much blame her. The dog must weigh well over a hundred pounds.

While Hester Renegar hurried away to answer the door, Sara gazed from Ivadelle to Brig, and was amazed to discover a very real similarity in expression between the furious woman and the massive red Chester duck dog. Either, it occurred to her, might make a formidable enemy.

# Chapter Eleven

Rafael Turbyfill strode into the dining room, looking dark, dangerous, dissipated, and disheveled. With a small yelp, Sara rucked back her chair and raced around the table to grab him by his velvet lapels. "Tell me!" she demanded. "Is he—?"

"Jericho's fine," Rafe assured her. Gently removing her clutching fists, he patted her hands and then smoothed his wine-colored coat back into place. "Leastwise, not precisely fine, but I left him still among the living."

Far from satisfied, Sara had to know every detail. "Where is he? When is he coming home? How badly is he hurt? Is a doctor with him?" And then, grabbing him by the lapels again, she cried, "Rafael, is he outside in your carriage? Oh, mercy, why didn't you say so?"

She was halfway out the door when the words stopped her. "No, Sara, he's still back at the hotel, in no condition to be moved. To answer your other questions, he was knifed in the back, but the blade was partly deflected by a bone. He lost a great deal of blood and he's in considerable pain, but the physician, who was about half sober when he examined him, is of the

opinion that he'll likely heal without too much permanent damage, long's he don't take a fever and die first."

Sara moaned. Taking a deep breath, she willed herself to think of all that needed doing before she could
go to her husband. If she had been in any doubt as to
her feelings—and she had, for the very last thing she'd
ever expected to do was develop tender feelings toward
a perfect stranger—it took only the thought of losing
him to bring home the truth.

*Lord, You look after him real good until I can get
there and take over, will You? I'll hurry as fast as I can.*

The dog came silently to her side and sniffed at her
fingers. Absently, she scratched his ears. From the
other side of the tall, high-ceilinged room, Ivadelle
Moyer was staring at Rafe Turbyfill as if she'd never
before seen a rumpled, dissolutely handsome, middle-
aged man.

Meanwhile, Hester Renegar, elbows on the table,
head in her hands, was sobbing quietly and murmuring. "My boy, my sweet, blessed boy . . ."

"You'll have to drive me there," Sara declared briskly.
"Unless there's a horse here I can borrow? No, I'll need
to take supplies, so a carriage would be better, or at
least a gig. Rafael, do you—"

"Slow up, darling. Princess Anne County's promised
to stay until she has to leave for Liberia. By then, I'll
be back there and I can find another woman. I only
came to tell you the news."

Sara's mouth fell open. "Indeed, you will not find
another woman! Until *who* has to leave for *where*?"

With the suspicion of twinkle in his jaded eyes, he
repeated, "The nurse. Miss County is scheduled to

leave for the colony of Liberia aboard the next ACS ship that sails, which is why—"

"Who—what on earth is an ACS ship?"

"You never heard of the American Colonization Society? They've been around for years, helping any free black who wants to go back to Africa to emigrate. Miss County is of a mind to nurse the good folks of the Liberian colony for a spell. I wouldn't be at all surprised if she don't end up running the whole government in a few years."

"Yes, well . . . that's all very interesting, but if we're going to leave right away, I'd best be gathering up a few things. Miss Renegar?"

The housekeeper rose, dried her tears on her apron and nodded grimly. "Yes'm. We'll need laudanum and willow bark tea, a good healing salve and plenty of bandages. Good thing I made up a fresh batch of my healing oil. Can't beat it for—"

"As it happens, I myself have rather extensive bedside experience," announced the elegant woman in black. Ivadelle flowed across the room to stand between Rafe and Sara.

How does she *do* that, Sara wondered. It's unnatural to be so blasted graceful.

"How do you do, sir, I am Miss Iva—"

"Miss Moyer, Mr. Turbyfill," Sara said bluntly.

Ignoring her, Ivadelle appealed directly to Rafe. "I'm sure Miss—Mrs.—that is, Sara, would be best served by staying home. She only arrived last evening, and the poor child was so exhausted she was barely civil."

Sara bristled. She started to protest when the tall blond cut her off. "I assure you, sir, I'm quite good at tending the ill. My sister-in-law suffers from a poor constitution, and my poor brother has boils that cause him dreadful pain."

Then why, Sara wanted to ask, aren't you looking after your own family instead of meddling with mine? Instead, she quietly left the room and began helping Hester Renegar gather up supplies. After that, she slipped into the small bedroom she had moved into just that morning and crammed a few things into her valise. Whatever else she needed could be sent for later. If she had her way, Jericho would be traveling south just as soon as possible.

And if she had her way, that woman would go home and tend her brother's boils. Which was something she would see to when she returned from helping Jericho.

Presenting herself in the front parlor a short while later, Sara lifted her brows at the sight of Rafael making free with Jericho's brandy. The overseer's sister was ensconced in the best tapestry-covered wing chair, her feet propped on a cushioned stool.

Well. Lifting her chin, she strode into the room. "It was my understanding, Mr. Turbyfill, that we would be leaving right away. Or did I mistake your intentions? If you would prefer, I'm sure I can find something around here to drive."

"Oh, please—Sara has just arrived and hasn't even had time to settle in. I'll be glad to go," Ivadelle said in a voice that was so soft and sweet it made Sara want to throw something. "After all, women who are all alone in the world must earn their keep."

The woman was alone in the world? What about her brother? Sara asked her just that and was ignored for her troubles.

"I would so like to help. You can't know how it feels to be beholden for the very roof over your head."

Sara did know. Noreen had made her feel that way, and in her own home. She came within Ames-ace of weakening, but at the last minute her sense of survival took over. Give some women an inch and they would take a mile. And the mile Miss Moyer would like to take just might include Sara's husband.

"I'm sure Miss Renegar can use your help while I'm away. My own servants will be arriving most any time now, so there'll be rooms to make ready if you'll be so kind."

The two women eyed one another while Rafe finished his brandy and set the glass on the pie-crust table. Sara, arms crossed over her breast, stared at Ivadelle until the woman's eyes fell.

There, she thought. That settled the pecking order in the Wilde household. All that mattered now was Jericho. Getting him home and getting him well.

The dog, Brig, clicked down the hall to stand in the doorway. Ivadelle stiffened and drew back. Dog hair might make her eyes water, but it was terror, not tears, that Sara saw on her face. Acting on impulse, she snapped her fingers and watched warily as the dog made his stiff-legged way to her side. His tail wasn't wagging, but then, neither were his ears laid back.

"Nice dog," she murmured, and to Ivadelle she said, "See? He won't harm you."

Reaching out a hand toward his massive, shaggy head, she stopped just short of touching him and waited. Cautiously, Brig sniffed her knuckles. Then, with what appeared almost to be a sigh, he allowed

one of his ragged ears to be scratched for a count of
perhaps ten seconds before backing away.

Sara let out the breath she hadn't even known she
was holding. Ivadelle sniffed—the woman really must
be allergic—and Rafe grinned like a possum.


"I am not your darling," she told him firmly as soon
as he handed her into the one-horse chaise. He had
called her that more than once.

"Yes'm."

"You're only teasing, I know, but all the same, some
people might get the wrong idea."

"Yes'm."

One of the most irritating things about Rafael Turbyfill, Sara had quickly discovered, was his habit of
grinning for no reason at all.

Which he did nearly all the way to his own farm,
some two miles north of Wilde Oaks.

Oh, he answered her questions soberly enough. Including the one she could not quite bring herself to
ask. Smithers, he told her, had turned and thrown his
knife out of turn, seriously wounding Jericho, who had
nevertheless managed to let fly his own knife, catching
Smithers in the belly. "Not one man in a hundred sur-
vives a gut wound. Doc said he'd not last the night,
even if he made it off the field alive."

Sara swallowed hard. For the next few minutes she
tried to think worthy thoughts about her stepbrother,
who had made her life miserable from the first day he
had crossed her father's threshold. Why should she be
surprised to hear that he had cheated in what was
supposed to be an affair of honor? He was sneaky in
all things. Always had been.

And yet, he was her stepbrother. Or rather, he had been. She supposed she should feel some small touch of remorse for anyone who had died so young, and so unnecessarily. For Noreen's sake, she tried, honestly she did. But Louisa had died young, too. Died tragically. And Titus was solely responsible. Besides which, the wretched coward had nearly killed Jericho!

On the heels of hoping Titus would burn in hell, Sara squinched her eyes shut and offered up a plea for forgiveness, in case the Lord decided to punish her wickedness by taking from her the very thing she valued most in this world.

Jericho.

"Is he in great pain?" she whispered.

From the seat beside her, Rafe twitched the reins, setting the mare into a fast trot. "Sleeps most of the time. I'm not sure if it's laudanum or some conjuring potion out of Miss County's red bag of tricks, but he was resting quiet when I left. Ain't come down with the fever yet, either, which is a good sign."

They traveled fast, and Sara clutched the sides to keep from being tossed tip over tail onto the rutted road. Rafe pulled up before his house, a tall brick affair with a fan-lighted door, and shouted for someone to come trade out his horse. After telling Sara to stay put, he raced inside and was out again before she could even begin to fret over the wasted time.

Waving a basket under her nose, he said, "I've not had supper yet. This way we'll save time by not having to stop. Ham biscuits, raisin cakes, cheese, and wine, darling." And then he grinned that wicked grin that Sara was coming to expect from him. "Not to mention a fresh waistcoat and a stack of clean cravats. Can't afford to ruin my reputation as a dandy."

It was nearing midnight when they reached the hotel. After nearly three miserable hours on the bumpy road, Sara felt as if her bones had disconnected and every tooth in her head was loose.

The night clerk was dozing in an easy chair in the lobby. Ignoring him, Rafe hurried Sara directly to the Carolina wing. She held onto her hat with one hand, the half-empty basket with the other, while Rafe carried her hastily packed valise.

"In here," he said, and then laid a finger over his lips. "Shhh, we don't want to disturb him if he's sleeping."

But no sooner did he turn the knob than the door was yanked open by the most intimidating creature Sara had seen in all her born days. The woman stood every bit of six feet tall, her skin the color of blackstrap molasses. Her generous body was costumed in a colorful panoply of skirts, shawls, half aprons, and overblouses, and decorated with jewelry made of beads, bones, seeds, and a variety of unidentifiable items.

Sara was dismissed with the merest glance. The woman looked Rafe directly in the eye and demanded in a fierce whisper, "Who she? Don' need no picayune white girl messin' around here."

"This is Mrs. Wilde. She's his wife. I went to fetch her when I heard there was an ACS ship leaving out of Hampton Roads within the week."

"She too puny."

Tired of being spoken of as if she weren't even present, Sara pushed herself forward and glared up into the fearsome black face. "I may be small, but I am certainly not puny. Anything you can do, I can do better and faster. Try me!"

If she weren't so furious, she might have seen a twinkle of something akin to respect in those large, ebony eyes. "Kin you talk a fever out'n a body, an' him burnin' fit to die?"

"I know about willow bark tea and cold cloths. I know not to bleed a man who's already lost too much blood. I know . . ."

"You know how to sing de debil spirit out'n a body an' see it don't come back no mo'?"

"Yes! Of course I do! Anyone with a grain of sense knows that!"

Sara was almost, but not quite certain she was being made sport of. She hadn't the least notion what the woman was talking about, but whatever it took to make her husband well again, why then, that was what she would do. The Lord would guide her. If she had to do penance for her own wickedness for the rest of her days, she would do it. She would see that Titus had a headstone any man would be proud of, with an epitaph that . . .

Well. She would think about that later. There was no point in making things worse by promising to have her lies carved in granite.

The next few days were unlike anything Sara could have imagined in her wildest dreams. In the first place, there was her husband's disposition. If she'd thought she had a quick temper, it was nothing compared to Jericho's outbursts.

Of course, he did have the excuse of being forced

to lie on his belly all the time, with no relief. Miss County had cautioned against turning him over onto his back until his wound had stopped seeping.

As for the wound itself, the blade had evidently gone in, struck bone, and then sliced all the way up into his shoulder, tearing through every tissue along the way. The surface wound was relatively small, but the flesh all the way up to his shoulder was outraged and swollen. Sara was cautioned to change the dressings several times a day for as long as it went on seeping, and to watch for the color of the seepage to change from pink to green, which was a bad sign.

So three times a day she soaked the bandages with warm water, peeled them off his tender flesh, and three times a day Jericho cursed her, swore revenge, and tried to reach around behind him with his good arm to swat her away from his bed.

Three times a day, while his wound lay uncovered, she sprinkled the gray musty powder Miss County had left behind into a saucer, lit it, and while it burned, repeated the gibberish she had been made to memorize in case there were any evil spirits waiting to pounce on the unsuspecting victim.

There was no point, she thought sensibly, in taking chances.

That done, she would spread a layer of Hester's healing oil, which smelled mostly of turpentine, over the injured flesh and the surrounding bruises, search for any hint of undue redness, swelling, or any hint of green seepage, and then wrap the area in clean linen.

Three times a day she forced her husband to drink a cupful of fresh-brewed willow bark tea dosed with laudanum. She listened stoically as he called her every wicked name he could think of, most of which she had never even heard, but which must be awful indeed if his expression was anything to go by.

It was impossible not to be aware of his magnificent body. Even wounded and helpless, Jericho positively radiated masculinity. Sara had never even been aware of such a thing as masculinity until the first time she had laid eyes on the man she was later to marry. Even now, lying helpless and half drugged, he was such a powerful presence in the room that she was constantly forced to steel herself against wayward thoughts.

Which meant that she spent a good deal of her waking hours, not to mention those spent turning restlessly in the trundle bed that had been brought into the room, in concentrating on what she was *not* supposed to think about.

*The man is ill, Sara Rebecca! And you're here trying to visualize his* parts?

The man was her husband. If anyone had the right to visualize his parts, surely it was his wife.

Still, she tried not to. Not to think about his private parts, that was. Because theirs wasn't that sort of a marriage. Jericho had offered her a home and a name for her baby, if she found herself carrying Archibald's child, and she had offered him . . .

Precisely what he was getting. Care and whatever duties he required of her.

He watched her. Times when she thought he was asleep, she would feel his gaze on her and turn to find those basilisk eyes focused on her in such a way that heat would come rushing to her face. "Did you want something?" she'd asked him the first time, but he had only closed his eyes and soon his breathing had slowed, and she had been left with her own thoughts.

Which were becoming more and more difficult to deal with.

Late on the third day, Rafe came in and, with Sara's help and two extra pillows, turned Jericho so that he could lie on his back for a change. Which made Sara's lot considerably easier, since helping a grown man to eat and drink while he was lying on his belly was a thankless task.

It was Rafe who spelled her several times a day so that he could tend to Jericho's personal needs while she tended her own. Thus Jericho was always neatly shaved and bathed. Although he muttered that he would almost rather grow a beard than have some cutthroat waving a razor in his face, and him not able to defend himself.

Of an evening, while the patient dozed, muttering frequently in his sleep, Rafe and Sara played games. From somewhere Rafe procured a checker set and a deck of cards, and he taught her to play Monte.

She was good at it. "You'd make right smart of a gambler, darling," he observed, and smiling, she shook her head.

"No thank you. I've already seen one fortune go whistling down the river. I'll not risk another. And don't call me darling."

"Give me leave to call you Sara, and I won't."

"Leave," she cried, and they both laughed.

And they laughed some more, and played some more, with Sara winning three buttons and Rafe swearing to take revenge. Not until she had put away the cards and gathered up her nightclothes to step behind the folding screen did she notice that Jericho was awake.

"Are you in pain? Do you need more medicine?"

"So you mean to hang onto my fortune for me. In that case, I'm obliged to advise you to steer clear of men like Turbyfill."

Sara was puzzled about his reference to *his* fortune. Surely she had told him that she was an heiress in her own right. She knew very well she had told him about the way her own father, and Titus after him, had gambled away all but the roof over their heads and a few acres of worthless land.

"Well?" he prompted, and she noticed then the lines in his brow that had been etched there by pain. His perennial tan, a result of spending years aboard a ship, had quickly faded to be replaced by a grayish pallor that came from loosing too much blood.

"I simply meant that I believe gambling for money is a fool's game. What difference does it make what card turns up next, or what rooster manages to spur another to death, or what horse reaches a certain mark first? Or last? Or even not at all? The world will go right on spinning in any case."

"That's not what I meant, and I suspect you know it. However, I'll take comfort in knowing you don't plan to beggar me just yet."

"Jericho, you're just trying to be difficult. If your shoulder aches, I'll give you a few drops of—"

"No more laudanum. It appears to me, madam, that if I want to guard my interests, I'd do well to keep my wits about me."

"There's no point in hurting when you don't have to," Sara retorted. "It's been a long day. Trying to sleep in a narrow padded box with an ungrateful creature constantly grunting and groaning and muttering in his sleep in the same room is no great pleasure, I assure you."

For a long moment, they stared at each other. Sara regretted her sharp words the moment they left her tongue. That dratted temper of hers. One of these days she really was going to have to do something about it. "Jericho, I'm sorry," she said quietly.

"Come here Sara."

Still clutching her nightclothes, she took a step backward toward the changing screen.

"Sara. Please come here." Jericho held out his left hand, wincing as he did so, for even so small a movement put a strain on the tender tissues of his back.

Warily, she moved to stand beside the bed. No matter how disgruntled he was, she told herself, he could hardly take out his rotten disposition on her. Physically, he lacked the strength.

And then he took her hand in his, studied it for just a moment, and carried it up to his lips. When Sara felt his lips touch her skin, her heart turned completely over in her breast.

She felt the heat rise to her face and knew she must appear a perfect dunce. She had no experience at all with this sort of thing. Archibald didn't count, because Archibald had never ever made her feel all wispy and tingly. Jericho made her feel wispy and tingly with a single touch, which was strange indeed, because she had known Archibald for years. Jericho was still a stranger.

And then she felt his tongue stroke her palm. Her eyes widened. Her breath caught in her throat, and she stared down at him. "Why did you do that?" she whispered.

Was that sheer devilment glittering in his eyes, or was he coming down with a fever?

"Jericho, are you sure you don't need a dose of something?"

He dropped her hand. His eyes closed, and she wondered if she had only imagined those strange lights that had danced there for a moment. His lashes, which were longer than hers, resembled tiny black lace fans against his pale, angular cheekbones.

"Go to sleep, Sara," he said tiredly.

Which made it all the more ironic that hours later, she was still awake, going over in her mind everything that had passed between them since she had first laid eyes on this remarkable, enigmatic man.

# Chapter Twelve

From inside the hotel came the usual night noises. The clink of bottles, the sound of jeers and curses, frequent explosions of laughter. There was the occasional sound of a shrill voice from one wing or another as a female of the more respectable class upbraided her unfortunate spouse.

Rafe preferred to remain outside. The wind blew in from the east, bringing a hint of salt and some relief from the peat fires. In the distance he heard a dog bark. Heard the soft call of an owl on the hunt and the scream of its prey a moment later. From the direction of the livery stable came intermittent stomps and whiffles as a dozen or so horses settled down in the strange environment.

Smithers's horse. Had anyone thought to pay the tab and send the poor beast home?

Rafael Turbyfill, one booted foot propped on the porch railing, drew on his cigar, blew a stream of smoke into the darkness, and pondered the strange position in which he presently found himself.

Rarely in his nearly thirty-nine years had he felt the pinch of conscience. Never to this extent. Seldom had he felt it at all, for since the death of his bride nearly twenty years ago after only three months of marriage, he had lived a purely hedonistic life, free of all constraints.

And now this. Damn all, it wasn't even as if he'd liked the boy! Smithers had been just one more face, albeit prettier than the average, that had made up the scenery for so long. Stoddard, Mayberry—Hilliard, Jamison, and that crowd. Good fellows all, who came and enjoyed his hospitality for a day or a week or a month, bringing friends who in turn returned and brought their own set of friends.

Of which Titus Smithers was one. Ye gods, he knew more about the poor bastard dead than he ever had alive.

Rafe was aware of the fact that over the years his own reputation as a freewheeling, hell-raising host with a damned fine cellar had spread widely throughout the area. But what the devil, he had nothing better to do with his time. The farm ran itself. His overseer was far too efficient to need his help, and as Rafe had no real need to do otherwise, he had gradually fallen into a pattern of gambling, drinking and wenching. He told himself, when he thought about it at all, that it was a harmless enough way of life. A man needed friends. The married friends needed the occasional respite from their families. If he had bothered to think about it at all, he would have said he served the purpose of allowing his friends a safe place to throw off their shackles before putting their noses back to the grindstone.

As for Smithers, he doubted if he had spoken to the boy more than a dozen times at the most.

And then the fool—the shabby bastard—had gone

and committed a heinous crime against an innocent young woman that had resulted in the loss of three lives, including his own.

Damned near four. Rico wasn't out of the woods yet.

Rafe swore at his own stupidity. God, how could he have been so criminally careless as to allow himself to be a party to something like that?

Not that he had known or even suspected. Smithers had mentioned meeting a woman in the neighborhood, which, if Rafe had thought about it, could only have been Louisa. Little pudding-faced Weezie, whom he had teased unmercifully as a child and ignored from then on. Rafe rarely even saw the girl, for all she lived only a couple of miles away. She had always been painfully shy. Then, too, he had never been one to waste his time on respectable females.

Leastwise, not for more than twenty years.

So he had gone on risking a small fortune every night on the turn of a card. Gone on betting on the dogs and the horses. Gone on drinking himself into an early grave, which would be no great loss to anyone, as he himself would be the first to admit.

And then Jericho had come home the first time, wanting to meet the young man his sister was walking out with before he went back to his ship. By the time he returned, the damage was already done.

"I owe him," Rafe said softly around the stump of his cigar.

Only there was no way in hell he could ever replace what had been lost. No way. Weezie was gone. How old had she been? He didn't quite recall, but his own sister would have been about the same age.

God, he'd almost forgotten he'd ever had a sister.

Emma had died at the age of seven, along with his parents, of the smallpox. Since then he had done without family. Who needed family when he had a thriving farm, plenty of friends and a good, reliable staff? It was a hell of a lot more than Rico had.

Although Rico had Sara. He could envy the man Sara if he didn't feel so damned sorry for him. And so guilty.

Crushing the tip of his cigar on his boot sole, Rafe tossed it out into the darkness. He swore and forked his fingers through the thick, iron-gray hair that was one of his few real vanities. There was one thing he *could* do for his friend. It wouldn't make up for the loss of a sister, but it might steer him away from the ruinous path Rafe himself had chosen to follow.

A bachelor's life, while it had much to commend it, was far from perfect. There came a time when a man grew bored with gambling. When his gut couldn't tolerate much more drinking. When his manhood refused to take any interest in a well-turned ankle, a playfully lifted petticoat, or one more plump, rouged breast.

At this rate, he thought ruefully, he might even be forced to spent the rest of his days holed up in his library, reading worthy tomes and writing snide letters to the editor of the *News and Intelligencer*.

If that was to be his role, so be it. He had earned it. But Jericho deserved better, and Rafe was going to see that he damned well got it.

And as it turned out, fate had played right into his hands.

Ivadelle Moyer. Now there was a piece of work, he mused.

Y        ₩        ₩

Oh, for mercy's sake, didn't anyone care that there was a desperately ill man in room number three? How was a body supposed to rest with all this going and coming? Here it was the middle of the night, when decent folks were abed, and boats were still pulling up to the landing, the passengers insisting on being serviced.

Sara sat up in the trundle and shivered. The fire had burned down, and she hadn't bothered to stir it up. She'd always preferred sleeping under a mound of covers with a window cracked open, even in the dead of winter.

Jericho was staring up at the ceiling, which wasn't too surprising. He'd been increasingly restless lately. It was getting to be a problem, just keeping him in bed.

"Sara? Are you awake?"

"Shhh, go to sleep."

"I need to get up for a minute."

"Don't be ridiculous. Whatever needs doing, I can do it for you. That's what I'm here for."

"Sara. I need to get up," he repeated, and it dawned on her what he meant.

"Oh," she said, and scrambled out of bed. The chamber pot was behind the screen. Usually, Rafe helped with the more personal side of nursing.

But before she could fetch the pot and leave the room, Jericho swung his feet off the bed and tried to stand. Scolding under her breath, Sara lunged to catch him and was barely in time to keep him from falling. He staggered, and they might both have fallen in a heap on the floor if she hadn't managed to support him until he could grab a bedpost.

"Stubborn man," she muttered.

"Bossy female," he growled.

"You need Miss County. She would put you in your place and keep you there if she had to sit on you."

Panting with exhaustion, Jericho looked up at her through the unruly shock of dark hair that was forever falling over his brow. "You have my permission to try it, madam, but take my advice—wait until after I've used the necessary."

Sara gasped at his plain speaking. "Well, I never!"

"Then I reckon it's about time you did. I'll go with you."

He tried to get up again, and Sara placed both hands on his shoulders. "If you'll just wait until I get my clothes on, I'll fetch Rafe and he can help you."

If he weren't in so much pain—if his bladder weren't fit to burst, Jericho might even have laughed at the thought of this small, determined woman marching into the taproom and dragging poor Tubby out by his ear.

Not that Rafe wouldn't be willing. Those two seemed to have gotten real chummy these past few days.

*Darling!*

To Jericho's way of thinking, the best thing for all concerned would be to get himself and his wife back home, and send Turbyfill on his way. "I don't need Rafe," he said shortly. "And neither, I might add, do you."

"Well, you might not think so, but if it hadn't been for Rafe, I wouldn't even know where you were, or if you were even still alive. If it hadn't been for Rafe—"

"All right, all right, he's a bleeding saint. Are we all agreed on that point? Now then, damn it, come back here!"

Which made Sara lift her head, jut her chin and back out of reach like a wounded wild animal, wary of being caught.

Which made Jericho feel like dirt. Blast it all, whether he wanted her or not, the woman was his wife! He would never hurt her.

Taking care to keep any hint of impatience from his voice, he said, "Sara, lend me your shoulder. With or without you, I'm going out that back door. And while I'm at it, I might even stay outside long enough to smoke a cigar."

"Over my dead body," she vowed.

"That can be arranged," he shot back, and could have cut out his tongue when he saw the stricken look on her face.

Smithers had been her brother, after all. He kept forgetting that. And he, Jericho had murdered him, never mind that the rat had deserved to die. "Sara, I'm truly sorry. I'm in a foul mood, but there's no call to take it out on you. If you don't mind stepping out to the front desk and asking the clerk to round up Rafe, I'd appreciate it."

"Are you in much pain?" She narrowed her eyes as if suspecting him of a trick.

"Yes, ma'am, I'm in considerable pain."

"Do you want some laudanum?"

Jericho sighed sharply and gazed up at the ceiling, which had not been repaired since the drunk had shot a hole in it. "No, ma'am, I don't want any more pain-killer. What I want is a place to relieve myself, and if you don't quit yammering and help me outside, I might just embarrass the hell out of both of us by committing infancy in my blasted bedclothes!"

What could she do? The man was stubborn as a three-legged mule. "Can you take time to put on your boots?"

"Depends on how big a gambler you are."

Sara moved hastily to his side and lowered her shoulder, edging it under his good arm. "It's cold outside, but I reckon if you were going to take a fever, you'd have done it before now. I only hope your feet are as hard as your head."

"If they're half as hard as your heart, *darling,* I won't feel a thing."

"Wretch," she said with just a hint of a reluctant smile.

"Wife," he shot back, as if to say tit for tat.

She led him to the door of the gentlemen's facility and slipped into the women's room. Bodily functions presented a real problem when one was confined in a small space with a person of the opposite gender. Even when that person was one's spouse. Bathing and dressing behind a folding screen was one thing.

Other things were . . .

Well. Other things.

He was waiting for her when she went back outside, leaning against the rough plank building, arms crossed over his massive chest. Even in the long knit underwear he slept in because a nightshirt would be impossible to deal with when it came to dressing his shoulder, he looked strikingly masculine. She had thought at first it was only because he was so tall, and he always dressed entirely in black—and his skin was dark, and his hair and his eyes. And he had that way of walking that drew one's attention to the width of his shoulders and the

length of his muscular limbs. But that wasn't it at all.
Even in his underwear, he was spectacular.

*Especially* in his underwear.

Oh, my merciful saints alive. "I'm sorry," she said
breathlessly. "I didn't mean to keep you waiting."

He grinned, his teeth flashing white in the light from
the sliver of a moon. Wisps of ground-fog drifted up
from the warmer waters of the canal to swirl about
their nightclothes. "It's damp out here," she said. "I'd
better get you inside before you—"

"Sara."

She paused in the act of positioning herself under
his arm. "Yes?"

"Thank you."

"Oh, for goodness sake, you don't have to thank me.
I had to go—that is, anyone would have—"

And then, Jericho started to chuckle.

And then Sara did, too.

And then, there they stood, the two of them, out
beside the necessary under a silvery quarter moon,
hanging onto one another and laughing fit to wake
the dead.

Oh, my, she did like the clean, musky scent of his
body. Liked the feel of his arms around her and the
strength of his long, lean body hovering over her so
protectively, when if the truth be known, she was the
one who was supposed to protect him.

All the same, she stole a moment to huddle in the
sheltering warmth of his arms before turning to slide
her shoulder under his arm, her own arm around his
taut, narrow waist.

*The man is an invalid, Sara! You ought to be ashamed
of what you were thinking!*

Rafe was waiting outside the door when they got back to their room. "Where the devil have you two been? I came by to see that you were secured for the night, and you were gone."

Scowling, Rafe edged Sara away and took her place at Jericho's side, helping him into the bedroom. She discovered, somewhat to her surprise, that she wanted it back. That she liked being able to hold her husband on any pretext at all.

Which just went to show that not even the most sensible of women were proof against the temptations of the flesh.

"Rico, I checked with the livery a few minutes ago, and the boy says Smithers's horse is running up a tab of three dollars a day."

"Blue?" Sara whispered. "Blue is here?"

Both men stared at her. Rafe had lowered Jericho to sit on the side of the bed. "That's the name of the gelding. Of course, you'd know about Smithers's horse."

"Blue was my father's horse," she explained. "Titus took him over after Papa died."

Rafe looked from one to the other, and then he shook his head. "I'd almost forgot about that. You know, I can't figure out which one of you two is the craziest. Are you sure you want to stay married? I could track down that joiner and see if he wouldn't untie the knot. It ain't like you'd had time to do anything about it." He lifted a nicely arched brow. "Or is it?" he drawled.

If Jericho looked embarrassed, Sara looked ready to sink through the floor. "Titus was not my real brother, he was only my stepbrother," she said stiffly.

Rafe's eyes, which were the exact color of wild chicory, were impossible to read. Sara suspected he was teasing, but she couldn't be sure. "Did you ever stop to think what you're going to tell your young'uns if they start asking why they don't have any aunts and uncles?"

Jericho shrugged, and then winced as his shoulder muscles protested. Sara was busy picturing a miniature Jericho: dark, defiant and too daring for his own good. Or a little girl . . . they could call her Louisa.

"You didn't think about that, did you? Took one look at Sara's big brown eyes and forgot everything else."

"You were there when it happened, damn it! Why didn't you stop me then, if you thought it was so all-fired important?"

"When I rode up, the deed was already done. Smithers was off sharpening his knife, the joiner was cramming his Bible in his hip pocket, and you were stowing your bride aboard the *Albemarle*."

He was teasing. Sara was almost sure he'd been teasing all along. All the same, if Jericho truly felt that way about it—about their marriage—then what chance did they have to make a future together? Or had he even thought about the future?

She searched the eyes of the man she had married in such indecent haste. In the steady light of the oil lamp, the lines etched by pain and exhaustion were clearly visible in his angular face.

"I thought about it, damn it," Jericho snapped. "But it didn't change the way things were. I did what I had to do, and I'll thank you to stay out of my business."

Heart fit to break, Sara started to apologize for her husband's rudeness, even if it had been mostly deserved, when of all unlikely things, Rafael began to grin. And then he started to chuckle. Both Sara and Jericho stared at him as if he had lost his mind.

Sara tightened the sash of her wrapper. "Rafe, are you feeling all right?"

Even Jericho looked concerned. "You've been drinking, haven't you? More than usual, I mean."

Rafe dropped onto the foot of the bed, leaned back against the footboard, and howled. The only coherent word they could get out of him was "fate." He kept repeating it over and over. Finally, he got up and staggered out into the hallway. They could hear his uneven progress as he made his way toward the taproom, still laughing, still muttering about fate.

Jericho turned to Sara. "You reckon I ought to get dressed and go after him?"

Sara sighed. "I reckon you'd better get yourself in that bed before you fall down in a dead faint. I doubt you'd appreciate it if I had to drag you off the floor and finagle your carcass into that bed again."

A gleam of dark amusement crossed Jericho's face and was gone so swiftly she thought she must have imagined it. "Spoken like a wife, madam."

"I am a wife," she said with a baleful look. For now, at least, she added silently.

# Chapter Thirteen

"I've settled the tab for your gelding, Sara. If you'd care to sell him, I think I can find you a buyer with no trouble at all."

"No, don't do that. Let me think, Rafe." When he wasn't in a teasing mood, Sara had found that Jericho's friend could be quite nice.

The three of them sat out on the veranda on one of the long backless benches, enjoying the scant warmth of the hazy October sunshine. Aside from his most recent excursion to the necessary, this was the invalid's first real outing. To judge from his expression, he was not particularly enjoying it.

"I'll take the horse," he muttered. "Sara can use it for her own personal mount until I find her something more suitable."

They were talking across her, which irritated Sara no end. "Blue is perfectly suitable, thank you all the same."

"He's nearly seventeen hands," Jericho argued.

"He's gentle as a lamb," Sara riposted. "I've ridden him for years."

"No need to decide now," Rafe placated. "We'll tie him behind the shay along with your horse, Rico, and you can make up your mind later."

Sara spoke up sharply, ready to put an end to the discussion. "Thank you, but my mind is already made up." She wrapped her shawl more closely around her shoulders, wishing she had thought to bring along a coat when she'd gone haring off into the night to succor a critically wounded husband. At the time, clothes had been the last thing on her mind.

"Rafe's right. The matter don't have to be settled now."

Ignoring her husband, Sara turned to the older man. "Rafe, I've written a letter for my stepmother. Could you possibly find someone to deliver that and Blue? Noreen can sell him if she needs to. There's little enough else left to sell." That last was added somewhat bitterly, but Sara knew she owed it to her father's memory to see that his widow didn't starve. She had written a bank draft, not a letter. Knowing Noreen, the woman would far rather have money than a few false words of sympathy.

The house would probably end up as a boarding establishment. By now, Sara was past caring. Everything she had ever loved about her home was long gone, overlaid with too many bad memories. Including Blue. He was Titus's horse. *Had been* Titus's horse, she amended.

She only hoped Maulsie and Big Simon were at this moment waiting for her at Wilde Oaks.

Rising abruptly, she hurried inside, murmuring something about the chilly weather.

"She's looking weepy," Rafe observed.

"Sara? Didn't look weepy to me."

"You didn't notice how the tip of her nose was starting to turn red?"

"She said it was cold, didn't she? Reason enough for her nose to turn red."

Feeling trapped, Jericho scowled at the toe of his boot. It was the first time he had worn them since the duel. Being fully dressed again after lying around in his blasted underwear should have given him a sense of being back in control of his affairs.

Instead he had never felt less so.

"I don't believe you even looked at her," Rafe said slyly. He had a way of pretending to know more than he actually knew that never failed to set Jericho's teeth on edge.

"I looked at her, damn it! I was about to give her my coat when she upped and left."

"She's fell off some these past few days. You notice the way that frock was hanging off her b—that is, her frame?"

Jericho snorted. "Sara? She's in fine fettle."

With a shrug, Rafe clipped the tip off his cigar. "If you say so."

"Damn it, if the woman needs fattening up, then I'm the one to do it! She's *my* wife, not yours!"

Rafe spread his palms in a placating gesture, turning away to hide the gleam of satisfaction in his bright blue eyes. Fate was all very well, but a little prodding never hurt. "I reckon you've got the papers on her, all right, but that don't mean she can't have friends. You told me yourself it weren't a real marriage."

"You want to know how real it is, try poaching on my territory."

"You know I'd never do that. All the same, while you was sprawled out in bed snoring your head off, the two of us spent more than one night together. Hit it off just fine." He paused. Seeing Jericho's hands curl into fists, he weighed his next remarks carefully. "Damned shame you were in such an all-fired hurry to haul her up before a joiner. I'd have saved you the trouble by marrying her myself if I'd known. Least I could do, under the circumstances."

"You'd take another man's leavings?"

"Hell, Rico, you ain't even had time to set your mark on her yet."

"I'm talking about Ricketts, damn it! He bedded her before his wife came and hauled him away. She might even be breeding."

Rafe shrugged. "Can't blame Sara for that. The old goat hornswoggled her."

"I'm not blaming her, I'm just saying—" Uttering a string of raw profanity, Jericho got to his feet too quickly, swayed and nearly fell back onto the bench. Brushing aside Rafe's offer of help, he stalked into the hotel.

"Rico, my boy, you know as much about women as I do about driving a bloody sailboat," Rafe murmured. Still grinning a few minutes later, he sauntered out to the livery stable to find a boy to deliver the gelding and Sara's letter to Smithers's ma. From the little Sara had let drop during their late-night card games, the woman was a witch of the first order, but if Sara wanted her to have the damned horse, then who was he to argue?

The trouble with Sara Wilde, he was coming to realize, was that she was a real nice woman. And more often than not, nice women got the short end of the straw.

Sara was sitting in the rocking chair that had replaced the straight chair which had been destroyed the

night the three drunks had broken into the room. The
night one of them had shot a hole in the ceiling.

The night her reputation had been shot full of holes.

When Jericho let himself in she was rocking hard,
doing about eighteen knots, as near as he could judge.

"Something worrying you?" he asked cautiously.

"No." She didn't bother to look at him. Neither did
she slow down.

"That's good. Was it something I said?"

"I told you nothing's worrying me," she snapped.

"Cut line, woman. Your nose is red, you're fixing to
cry, and you've been losing weight. That dress of yours
is just hanging off your b—your frame."

"It is not, I am not, and it is not."

Jericho knelt beside her and stopped the motion of
the rocker by gripping the side post. Using his right
hand. He caught his breath sharply. The torn muscles
in his shoulders had not yet healed completely.

Sara heard him gasp. "You go right ahead and tear
your wound open again. I've nothing better to do than
stay here another week and nurse you, for I'm sure
Hester can order the roofers around and see to rebuild-
ing the kitchen garden fence. Ivadelle will likely take
a hand in the redecorating. I don't think she likes the
curtains in the front parlor, and as for the carpet . . ."

During the entire recital, she refused to look directly
at him.

Ivadelle? Jericho's jaw was not hanging, but the effect was just the same. Who the hell was Ivadelle?
What was wrong with the curtains and the carpet?
They'd been good enough for his parents and
grandparents.

Cautiously, still kneeling beside her, he lifted a hand

and held it against her brow. "Are you coming down with a fever?"

And then she did look at him. Her large, golden brown eyes were shimmering, her full lower lip was trembling, and the tip of her nose was indeed a bright pink.

She looked so damned beautiful Jericho felt his lungs seize up in his chest. "Sara," he whispered hoarsely, not at all certain of what he wanted to say, only knowing that he had to say something.

His chest was so full of feelings he could scarcely breathe. Instead of speaking, he did something.

And while the something he chose to do might not have been wise, it was as inevitable as the tides. As the rising sun of a morning. As the falling of leaves in autumn.

He kissed her. And she let him. Not only let him, she kissed him right back. Softly, at first. A mere brushing of moist, warm lips. He felt her breath against his face, and she smelled of soap and dusting powder and the peppermint powders she used on her teeth, and Jericho thought it was surely the most intoxicating scent in the world.

"Ah, God, Sara," he groaned. Sliding her off the armless rocker onto his lap, he bent one knee, bracing his foot on the floor, and leaned her back against the inside of his thigh. His good arm supported her back, his right hand came up to turn her face to his again, and this time when he kissed her there was no softness, no gentleness involved.

He kissed her fiercely, hungrily, as if he couldn't get enough of her. Stroking her neck, his thumbs tangled in her hair. One by one, with trembling fingers, he removed the tortoiseshell pins that held it in place, and it tumbled over the back of his hand like a warm, heavy waterfall.

Her own small capable hands moved over his face and fluttered down to knead the muscles of his shoulders. Both shoulders. He didn't even feel the pain, his whole awareness being centered on another part of his anatomy.

And hers. With an unsteady hand, he traced the delicate line of her jaw. His fingertips trailed down her neck until their progress was impeded by the high collar of her woolen gown. After only a moment's frustration, he slid his hand down over her chastely covered breast and felt her stiffen in his arms. Felt the immediate response of her hardening nipples, and knew a powerful surge of triumph.

*Careful, Wilde, for all she's been bedded, she's still green.*

The weight of her hips pressed against his fiercely aroused flesh while the hard, bare floor pressed against his bony backside, making him exquisitely aware that the floor was hardly the best place for an exercise of this nature. Only how the hell was he going to get her up off the floor and onto the bed without coming to grief? Getting to his feet out on the veranda had nearly done him in.

"Sara," he whispered against her throat. She had to feel him. He was as hard as an oar handle, damned near as big. She had to know what she was doing to him. "Sara, do you think we might edge over near the bed so I can hoist up aboard the mattress?"

She looked at him then, her face flushed with passion.

Or was it embarrassment?

"Oh, merciful saints. What were we thinking about?" she whispered.

"I'm surprised you have to ask."

Before he could figure out his next cautious move, she was scrambling to her feet. In the process she braced her hand right where he was most vulnerable and then jerked it away as if she'd grabbed hold of the business end of a hot poker.

He was still taut as a flying jib in a full gale when, blushing up a storm, she bent over and grabbed him under the arms. "Here we go now—I'll pull, and you grab hold of the back of the rocker and see if you can get to your knees."

"Jesus, woman, I'm not a cripple, you know!"

Ignoring his protest, she said, "Maybe I should make you a pallet on the floor so you could rest first. . . ."

Rest *first*? That might not be such a bad idea, only he wasn't sure he could hold out that long.

She stepped back, her hands on her hips, looking angry and flustered. "I knew it. I *told* you it was too soon to get out of bed!" Then, bending over him again, she started patting and pushing, her soft breast swinging right in his face, and Jericho commenced to sweat. If she said one damned word about fever, he vowed he would bed her right where she stood. Or knelt. Actually, he could envision any number of interesting possibilities, none of which required a mattress.

But before he could act on any of them, someone rapped on the door. "Rico? It's me, Rafe. Are you in there?"

Tarnation. "Get the hell out of here, Turbyfill!"

"Are you all right? You sound like you're in a bind."

"Can't a man get any blasted rest around here?" Jericho muttered. Sara tugged at his elbow and with a mighty effort, he managed to grasp the bedpost and swing himself up and around. Collapsing onto the feather ticking, he yelled, "Go to hell, Turbyfill!"

"Righto. But before I go, send Sara out here a minute, will you? I need to have a word with her."

Jericho would rather have carved out his own liver and sent it out on a silver platter, but that didn't appear to be an option. He flat-out refused to beg. "Go if you're of a mind to, madam," he snapped. "I'm not your blasted keeper."

"No, you're not. What you are, sir, is childish. I thought I had a nasty temper, but you're worse than two tomcats in a tote sack."

Childish was he? Curling his lip, he snarled at her, just to watch those clear eyes of hers shoot sparks. Which they did. Without even bothering to help him lie down, she spun around and marched across the room to the door.

Jericho sighed a sigh that was felt in every torn and half-mended muscle in his body. His gaze followed her as she yanked open the door. In twenty years he had seen more than his share of storms at sea. He'd seen St. Elmo's fire light up the rigging aboard the *Wilde Wind* until she glowed from bowsprit to sternpost.

All that was a summer breeze compared to the way that woman affected him.

Not until the door closed behind her did Jericho let himself relax. And then he groaned. Childish was he? He didn't feel childish. What he felt was horny as a ram and mad as hell because he was still too damned weak to do anything about it!

The truth was, he felt weak as rainwater. The whole right side of his upper back was aching like a rotten tooth. Having never been sick a day in his life, he had expected to mend overnight. In a day or so, at the most. God knows, that blasted conjure woman had smeared enough of her stinking potions on his back and chanted enough gibberish to raise the dead.

She had conjured him good, all right. He'd been forced to lie abed for neigh onto a week, half of it flat on his belly, while the strength seeped right out of his body. He'd told the fool woman that what he needed was a little more brandy and a lot less fermented frog brains.

She'd told him that brandy wouldn't replace all the blood he'd lost. He dimly remembered going a few rounds over that, but then, between the princess's conjuring spells and the doc's laudanum, it was a wonder he could even remember his own name.

And then Sara had come. She had taken up where the other woman left off—bossy little female.

At least she'd gotten his blood to circulating again.

Some thirty minutes later, when Jericho heard Sara's brisk footsteps coming down the hallway, heard the rattle of the doorknob, he was in no sweeter frame of mind. Closing his eyes, he pretended to be asleep.

She came and stood over him. He could feel her heat, smell the special scent that told him she was nearby, even in the dead of a pitch-dark night.

Hell, he even knew the cadence of her breath.

Right now it was quicker than usual. Which made him wonder what she had been up to.

With Rafe.

It would serve her right if he grabbed her by the wrist and flipped her over on top of him. He would do it, too, if he thought he had what it took to make the next move, but bedamned if he was going to ask her to unfasten his breeches and lift him out. Before he would do that, he would wither away like a Mexican pepper that had been strung up to dry.

Instead, he listened to her moving around in the room, tried to envision what she was doing and how she looked doing it as he heard the rustle of cloth and the clink of pitcher against washbowl.

Eventually, he must have drifted off to sleep.

Sara wondered if the man was going to sleep all day. He'd been awake when she had come back to the room last night, but pretended he wasn't, and for reasons she didn't even try to sort out, she had let him believe she believed it.

She told herself it was only because she wanted to avoid another argument. All they seemed to do lately was argue. But it wasn't that. It had something—more than something; more like everything—to do with all the kissing and other things that had been going on.

When he had touched her right smack dab on her bosom, she'd thought she would swoon from all the peculiar feelings that had rushed through her body. She had felt like a glass of cold tea when one stirred a spoonful of honey into it. It was all the same clear color, yet one could actually see the torpid streams and currents swirling around in its amber depths.

Currents of honey. That's what she had felt. And that, for a woman who had always prided herself on her sensibility, was downright frightening.

Oh, she knew what it was all about. She might not be terribly experienced, but she was, after all, a married woman. Twice married, for all intents and purposes. She knew what it was to bed a man.

Actually, it wasn't at all what she'd expected. It hadn't hurt—at least, not down there where it had all happened. Mostly, it had been embarrassing. Sort of like the way one felt when one bathed one's self with a washcloth. All decent girls were taught to think of something else when they bathed their private parts, only sometimes . . .

Well. At any rate, Jericho wasn't Archibald, and he certainly wasn't a washcloth.

"Do you want breakfast served in here, or would you like to try the dining room this morning?" she inquired brightly the moment she detected a sign of life from the bed.

Jericho groaned and flung his good arm up over his eyes. "If there's two things I can't abide of a morning, it's sunlight in my eyes and a chirky woman before breakfast."

"Oh? And how many chirky women have you had before breakfast?"

Easing his arm aside, he cocked an eye at her. "That was a figure of speech, woman. But if you really want to know—"

"I can close the curtains if the sun bothers you," Sara said quickly. She had waked early, bathed and dressed behind the screen, wearing her most flattering gown—well, actually, it was the only other gown she had brought with her—and now she was starving.

"Close the curtains, look to see if there's water in the pitcher, order me up a quart of coffee, and then make yourself scarce. I'll meet you in the dining room in half an hour."

"Are you sure? I could help you—"

"Sara . . ."

"Oh, all right. There's plenty of water. I had the pitcher filled after I—that is, it's full. And I'll ask the dining room to send around a pot of coffee right away."

"One more thing," he said when she was halfway to the door.

Sara glanced over her shoulder. He was sitting up in bed, the covers rumpled down around his hips, his chest bare of all save the fascinating tee-shaped pattern of dark curling hair she had noticed when she had first seen him without a shirt. "What happened to your shirt? You went to bed last night in your clothes."

"My shirt? Now that's about the strangest thing I've ever seen, Sara. Sometime during the night, my clothes just upped and plum disappeared. Every blessed stitch I had on. I reckon I could've got up and looked around some, but I was afraid you might wake up and take fright to see a buck naked man in your bedroom, so I decided to wait until morning. Things don't look near as scary once the sun comes up."

The flash of white teeth in the shadowy morning growth of whiskers made her catch her breath. She had almost forgotten what a wicked sense of humor her husband had. When he bothered to use it.

"Well, at least you seem to be feeling better this morning."

"You might say I've thought of a good reason to get well."

"Of course you have a reason to get well. My mercy, with all that's going on back at Wilde Oaks, I should think you'd want to hurry back there as fast as you could."

"Unhuh," he said, still studying her with that dark, wicked gleam in his eyes.

Well, Sara thought as she hurriedly shut the door behind her.

*Well!*

# Chapter Fourteen

Rafe dragged a chair from another table, straddled it, and propped his elbows on the table. "Morning, Rico. Glad to see you're feeling some better than you were last night. Sara was worried—told me she was afraid you might be having some kind of a relapse." .

Jericho nearly choked on his coffee. "I'll thank you not to talk about me behind my back, madam."

Sara's lips tightened, but she refused to rise to his baiting. The slatternly woman who served their table slapped down three plates of hominy, biscuits and underdone bacon, and Sara hastily averted her eyes. She had woken up feeling unwell and put it down to last night's turtle stew. The gluey gray mess had begun to return on her during the night.

"I've got a plan," said Rafe, attacking his own plate with enthusiasm.

Jericho sipped his coffee and said nothing. His first day dining in public, and he hadn't even touched his breakfast, Sara thought irritably. Didn't the exasperating man even want to regain his strength?

"You want to hear it?"

"I reckon you're going to tell me anyway."

Looking totally unperturbed, the older man slathered

butter on a huge, ragged biscuit and took a big bite. "Mmm, best cooking I've tasted in years. If you don't want your biscuit, Rico, I don't mind taking it off your hands."

"I don't need you to take anything off my hands."

For reasons she didn't dare delve into, Sara felt her face grow warm as both men continued to glare at each other. At least Jericho glared. Rafe looked smug as a cream-fed cat.

Crumpling her napkin, she eased her chair back and stood, bringing them both to their feet. Rafe dusted bread crumbs off his waistcoat, which was of yellow brocade, piped in royal blue to match his coat. He did favor elegant garments.

Jericho was dressed in his usual black.

"If you'll excuse me," she said primly, "I believe I've had enough."

"You didn't even touch your food," Jericho accused.

"She means she's had enough of your grouchy disposition."

Jericho's jaw took on that granitelike quality that Sara had come to recognize, having seen it on more than a few occasions in the short time since she had met him. "I don't need you to tell me what my wife needs or doesn't need."

"You sure as Solomon need somebody to set you straight. That is, if you mean to hang onto her."

Sara didn't linger to hear her husband's response. She was afraid she already knew what it would be. Flinging her napkin onto the table, she spun around and marched from the room. "Oh, for mercy's sake," she muttered. Blinking hard, she barged into a matronly female, bouncing off the well-upholstered bosom.

"Lawks a mercy, look where ye're going, why don't ye?" the woman protested. And then, "Why, ye're crying. Honey, it cain't be all that bad."

Sara brushed past her and hurried across to the door that led to the rooms of the Carolina wing. The woman stared after her. From the dining room beyond, both men followed her progress. Then Rafe turned to Jericho and said, "I reckon she's breeding after all. Damned shame. Last thing you need now is a cuckoo in the nest."

"My nest is none of your bloody business. Now, if you've got something else to say, spit it out." Jericho was behaving badly. He blamed it on a number of things: a sore shoulder, losing Louisa, losing his ship, and then damned near losing his life. It had nothing to do with Sara.

"Speaking of nests, it came to me last night that what with you and Sara and that horse of yours, this place is costing you damned near twenty dollars a week. Now that you're up and about, maybe you ought to start thinking about heading south."

"I can do my own thinking, damn it."

"Just thought I'd mention it. But if you happen to run out of worry-fodder, you might want to chew on this for a spell. You got one horse in the livery. I've got a horse and a shay that'll hold two people. Now, I could drive the shay on back, and you and Sara could double up in the saddle, but it's a long ride. Be rough on that big ugly gelding of yours, even rougher on Sara. Especially if she's breeding. Or I could take Sara up with me in the shay, and you could follow along behind us on—"

"No." Jericho had settled back into his chair and was twisting his thick china cup in his hands.

"No? All right then, what if I was to ride your gelding while you and Sara take the shay? Trouble is, you ain't up to driving all that distance, and I don't know if Sara even drives. You happen to know if she does?"

"How the devil would I know?"

Rafe shrugged as if to say, she's your wife.

"There's always the packet," Jericho said reluctantly.

Leaning forward, Rafe propped his elbows on the table. "Now why didn't I think of that?" he mused, leaving Jericho to suspect that was what the man had been aiming at all along.

In his early days at sea, before he'd become the captain of his own thirty-two ton schooner, Jericho had traveled the canal many a time, hauling lumber, pork and whiskey up through the Albemarle Sound, up the Pasquotank River, rounding the Narrows at Elizabeth City and lock-stepping north to Deep Creek, up to the southern arm of the Elizabeth, through the mouth of the James and into the bay.

With the arrogance of youth, Jericho had stood at the rail with his mates and jeered at the doughty little packet boats plying the canal. Pissants, they'd called them. Mud-kicking pissants.

God, he had owned the world back then. "Tell me something, Tubby—does it strike you that now and again a man can make a royal ass of himself without half trying?"

Appearing to consider the matter, Rafe stroked his jaw, which was, as always, impeccably shaven. A disso-

lute rake he might be, but he prided himself on being
a fastidious dissolute rake. "Come to think of it, I believe you're right."

Sara was all packed by the time Jericho had smoked
a cigar on the veranda, strolled out to the livery to
see how Bones was faring and returned to the room
they shared.

Standing in the open doorway, he frowned at the
valise on the bed. "You had it all planned, didn't you?
You and Rafe. Is that what you had your heads together
over last night?"

"I don't know what you're talking about. Rafe mentioned going home now that you no longer need him,
and I simply thought, since you don't need me any
longer, either, I might as well leave, too."

"I never did need you. It wasn't me that invited
you here."

Up went that small, stubborn chin of hers. Jericho
could see the flash of fire in her eyes all the way across
the room. "You never *wanted* to need me," she cor-
rected. "But you needed me, all right. You couldn't
even turn over in bed without help, and that princess
woman wasn't about to cancel her trip to Libya to—"

"Liberia."

"Wherever!"

"You want to talk about who needs who?" Jericho
drawled. "What were you planning on doing with no
money, no husband and your belly full of baby?"

Sara gasped. "I do so have money! I have more
money than I could ever spend." Which wasn't precisely true; she had enough to live on for the rest of

her life, as long as she wasn't too extravagant. "I certainly didn't marry you for yours."

"That's right, I remember now. You married me to give Rickett's bastard a decent name." Jericho knew she had her own money. The trouble with Sara was that she was just too independent for her own good. Maybe it was time he reminded her of just why she had married him.

Even as he watched her, her face flushed, then drained of all color. It struck him that from the first time he had laid eyes on her, in that ugly brown frock, with her brown hair and her brown eyes and her suntanned face, something about the woman had snagged his keel and held him fast. He still wasn't sure how it could have happened. The way she dressed, she should have looked plain as a slab of salt horse. Instead, she looked as fancy as one of those caged jungle birds he saw for sale at all the South American ports he visited.

He was still considering all that when she lurched for the screen, fell to her knees over the chamber pot and began to wretch. After one moment of feeling totally helpless, he grabbed a clean towel, dipped it into the pitcher, and stood hard by to lend a hand.

"Go away," she groaned, twisting around to glare at his boots.

Jericho knelt beside her and clumsily wiped her face.

"I can't stand for you to see me like this." With one shaky hand, she shoved back a coil of hair that had slipped its mooring. "Rico, please go away."

Rico. It was the first time she had ever called him that. "We always keep a supply of gingerroot and dried peppermint leaves in the lazaret aboard the *Wind*. Every now and then, a green hand comes down with the heaves, mostly after they've been aloft the first few times in a rolling sea. All that pitching and yawing can look mighty fearsome when you're thirty, forty feet above the deck."

Sara closed her eyes and groaned.

"Don't know that it'd serve for your troubles, but it's worth a try."

"Just let me lie down for a few minutes. The packet boat won't be coming for at least an hour, will it?" She put the lid on the chamber pot and rose, thrusting out a hand to steady herself against the wall.

Jericho wanted to sweep her up into his arms, but he restrained himself. For one thing, he suspected she would try to fight him, and right now, she lacked the strength.

For another thing, so did he.

After setting the pot out into the hall to be collected by the potboy, he poured a tumbler full of water. "Here, sip on this while I see if I can find something to settle your belly. What with the slop they serve at mess here, they're bound to have something on hand."

He ventured a smile, and she responded with a weak one of her own. "Lie down, Sara," he said in a voice he scarcely recognized as his own. "Let me unlace your boots for you."

She let him. It was an indication of just how miserable she must be feeling that she settled back on the pillows and allowed him to fold back her skirt and petticoat and unlace her boots. Small, sensible black boots. Nothing frivolous for his Sara, no sirree.

When, rejoicing in their freedom, she wiggled her stocking-clad toes, he stopped himself just short of clasping them in his hands. He figured she had allowed

him about all the freedom of her person she was of a
mind to right now.

"I'll be back directly. Try to sleep."

"Jericho, thank you. I know I'm sharp-spoken. It's a
failing I'm working on."

"We all have our failings, I reckon. I know how it is
with women in your fix."

"How could you possibly know . . . Oh. You must've
had a lot of mistresses."

Halfway to the door, Jericho stopped dead in the
water. He figured it was a shot in the dark, but she'd
been square on target. He'd had him a mistress once
for nearly two and a half years. Which wasn't all that
long considering he'd been at sea most of the time.
The relationship had ended when he'd come in from a
spell of lumber hauling up from South America. Lucy
had greeted him with the news that he was to become
a father in five months' time and he'd best marry her
right away.

The trouble was, he'd been at sea for six months.
When it came to the trade of mistressing, Lucy had
been right up there with the best of them.

When it came to ciphering, she had never been even
middling fair. She had married a redheaded greengrocer, and five months later she presented him with a
redheaded daughter. Jericho had sent the child a
carved wooden box he had picked up on the west coast
of Africa and sworn off mistresses, which he had only
sworn onto in the first place because he'd been scared
of catching a case of the French pox from one of many
prostitutes who prowled every seaport.

"Well? Am I right?" she asked without even opening
her eyes.

"Madam, you sound just like a confounded wife."

"I am a confounded wife." Sara waited for him to deny the charge. It was none of her concern. All men kept mistresses, or so she had been told. And besides, theirs had never been intended as a real marriage.

*So why did it matter so very much?*

Arms crossed over his chest, Jericho regarded her dispassionately. "It's common knowledge, madam. Carrying women are always sickly of a morning."

"So are women who eat stewed turtle that's gone off. And I do wish you would stop calling me madam in that nasty tone of voice."

Sara scrunched her eyes shut and prayed he would leave her in peace. The truth was, she didn't know whether her trouble was what she had eaten the night before or what she had done on her wedding night. Her first wedding night, that was.

There'd been only that single time, and that over and done with almost before she'd known what was happening.

On the other hand, many a time she had planted a whole row of store-bought seeds, only to have nary a one sprout, while a chance-fallen seed tossed out with the kitchen garbage would sprout, flourish and bear fruit.

"Oh, go away," she grumbled.

Somewhat to her disappointment, he did.

Vowing to sleep no more than thirty minutes and then to rise and take her valise out to the landing, Sara concentrated on visualizing a black velvet curtain swaying in the wind.

Swaying . . . and swaying . . .

She had always put herself to sleep this way whenever she was troubled. Usually it worked like a charm.

Swaying . . . swaying . . .

With a groan, she curled over onto her side and swallowed a fresh surge of nausea. "Please, dear God, let it be the turtle," she prayed.

Out by the livery stable, Jericho heard the *Albemarle*'s steam whistle blowing in the distance. From the sound he figured she was somewhere between the Wallaceton locks and the feeder ditch. Traffic was heavy this morning.

Giving his gelding a shriveled carrot he had stolen from the cook, he was headed back to the hotel to rouse Sara when the elderly female she had barged into in the dining room that morning grabbed him by his coat sleeve and shook his arm.

"I'll have a word with you, if you please, sir."

He didn't please, not that he thought it would do him any good to say so. "Ma'am?"

"Any man who makes a helpless woman cry is an abomination before the Lord."

For all she was small, she had the grip of a stevedore. Jericho's backbone ratcheted up another few notches. "Beg pardon, ma'am, but—"

She shook his arm again. "Hush! I'm not finished with you yet. That sweet girl who was taking breakfast with you this morning is only a poor, helpless vessel—"

*A poor helpless vessel?*

"—For your lust, but the Good Book teaches that any man who lifts a hand against his wife will surely burn in—"

Jericho didn't linger to learn the fate of such a man.

Jerking his sleeve from his assailant's determined grip, he hightailed it to the hotel, slammed the door shut and breathed a sigh of relief just as a pigtailed seaman came sailing through the bat-wing doors of the barroom.

God Almighty, what a place, he thought wonderingly. Drunken seamen, evangelizing females, runaway lovers, and men who met at dawn for the sole purpose of ventilating one another with knife or pistol.

The sooner he got her away from here, the better.

Sara was sleeping soundly, her color fully restored, when he let himself quietly into their bedroom. For several minutes he stood watching her, trying to think of the best course to take. Should he send her on ahead on the packet, or escort her home himself? This was no place for any woman, especially not a woman as prone to trouble as his Sara was.

His Sara . . .

He heard the steam whistle again. She was no more than half a mile away by now. With a whispered oath, Jericho let himself out as silently as he had let himself in. How could he chart a sensible course with Sara lying there in the bed, her lips parted, her small hands tucked up under her chin? She was a bloody lodestone, was what she was!

But this was no place for a lady, that much he did know, what with crooks from Carolina laying about in the Virginia wing, and crooks from Virginia holed up in the Carolina wing. And Sara, whatever else she might be, was a lady.

*His* lady. That, too, needed considerable pondering. Now that he had recovered to the point where a few shots of brandy and a little caution in the way he moved were all he required, maybe he'd better rethink this whole marriage business before it was too late. Sara needed a husband, all right, but did he need a wife?

Lost in thought, Jericho sauntered outside. Three cardplayers on the wide veranda lifted a hand to hail him and thought better of it. Two men knelt in a patch of sunshine and rolled dice. One glanced up at him, started to say something, and then looked away.

Jericho saw none of them. Leaning against a giant black gum tree that hung out over the canal, he gazed up at a hovering fish hawk and made an effort to assemble his reasons for marrying Sara Young. Reason number one being that he had spent what he'd thought at the time might well be his last night on earth in her bed, and thus had been responsible for ruining her reputation.

Another reason was that he had failed to protect his own sister, and his conscience had been hurting something fierce.

Then, too, he had told himself that even if he survived his meeting with Smithers, he would eventually go to sea again. Wilde Oaks needed a mistress, if not a master.

He'd had good reasons for marrying, he told himself now, but one thing he was certain of—he hadn't married Sara because he needed her.

The hawk plunged and came up shaking its feathers, a fish gripped fatally in its talons. Some creatures died so that others could live. It happened. As it turned out, he himself had lived.

But then, the damnedest thing had happened. While he'd been lying abed, sore, weak and mad as hell at life in general, he had started thinking of all the things he would miss if he died at the age of thirty-two.

The puzzling thing was that he hadn't thought of all the ports he had yet to visit, all the seas he had yet to sail—he had thought about Wilde Oaks. His home. The place where he'd lived out his boyhood, seeing the greening fields year after year without even noticing them. Seeing the tobacco turn gold in the autumn, the seagulls following the plow each spring as acres of dark, fertile land were turned.

He'd thought about stories he had heard as a boy from an old black man named Moses, who had lived on the farm forever. Tales about old Chief Okisko, and how Moses and Jericho's grandfather had hunted bear in the swamp and run a trotline for giant cooters.

He had thought about all the times he and Tubby had hidden from Louisa by climbing the pecan trees, and how old Vinegar used to fuss at him, telling him he was going to break his bony head, because pecan trees were too brittle for climbing.

Surprisingly, he had not thought once of all the women in the world, waiting to be discovered, to be dallied with, to be pursued and pleasured.

Instead, he had thought of Sara.

They ended up taking the shay, partly because they missed the packet, but mainly because Rafe told Jericho he wasn't up to driving, and naturally, Jericho had to prove that he was. Both Rafe and Sara had argued with him, but in the end, Rafe had agreed to ride Jericho's gelding to Wilde Oaks, where he would wait for them. If they weren't home by dark, he would head north to meet them.

Even Sara knew the ride would likely take longer than that, what with the roads in the condition they were in. If the farmers and the drummers and that rackety old stage racing daily between Norfolk and Elizabeth City weren't enough to wear it out, there was the constant flow of heavily laden log wagons and shingle carts coming out of the swamp, churning up the road so that it was little better than a mud hole in some places.

Rafe didn't care much for Bones, who tried to bite him. Bones cared even less for Rafe. "Should've thought to warn you," Jericho said with a grin. "He's not real partial to the smell of Bay Rum."

Rafe scowled, but got the beast under control and walked him out onto the road. Sara and Jericho watched the ill-suited pair out of sight, then prepared to set off on their more leisurely journey. All signs of Sara's distress had faded. After her unscheduled nap, she was feeling better than she had in days.

Their first argument came when she seated herself and started to take up the reins.

"Madam, I do my own driving."

"That may be true when you're fit to drive, but you're not, and we both know it. Jericho, for once in your life, be sensible."

"Damn it, Sara, for once in your life, *you* be sensible! A woman in your condition has no business driving. It puts a strain on the, uh—on your—"

"My shoulders? They're in better shape than yours, might I remind you? If I can manage old Blossom pulling a rickety farm cart, I can certainly handle a nice little one-horse-chaise."

Jericho drove. Sara fumed. Her belly had settled,

thanks to the gingerroot he had found for her to chew on, but at this rate, he would have her so riled up she would need a peck of the stuff before they got home.

They had hardly gone more than a mile or two when Sara's eyes began to burn. "Is it my imagination, or is the smoke getting worse?"

Jericho concentrated on passing a shanty where children, pigs, chickens, and dogs spilled across the road. "Look over to the southwest. Those aren't rain clouds."

"Fire?" she whispered.

"Looks to be just this side of Lem's horse camp."

"Where is that? Do we go through it?"

"Near enough," he said, and drove in grim silence for a while. Sara decided it was best to let him concentrate. She could patch up any damage he did to his shoulder once they were safely home.

The smoke got worse. It was increasingly hard to see. "Hang on, Sara," Jericho yelled over the clatter of hooves on cypress logs. "I'm going to see if we can't get past before it reaches the road."

And hang on she did. With both hands—one on the side rail, the other on Jericho's hard thigh. If it bothered him, he didn't let on. He drove like a madman, his face taut, his dark clothing gray with ash. Sara felt sorry for Rafe's little mare, who couldn't be accustomed to such a pace, but as the smoke grew ever more dense and fly ash began to settle all around them, she forgot the mare and began to worry about Jericho. His wound had healed over, but it couldn't take too much punishment.

"Maybe we should turn back," she yelled over the rattle of wheels bumping over a rough section of corduroy.

"Too late," he cried grimly.

Holding her hat on with one hand, she twisted around and stared. "Oh, my merciful saints alive," she breathed. Fire had sprung up in several places behind them. Not raging forest fires, for along this section of the swamp, most of the woods consisted of wet-footed trees. Swamp juniper, gum and cypress. The scraggling acres of cleared land had long since been harvested, so there was little fuel there.

Sara knew about the swamp fires, about the layers of peat that had built up for thousands of years—perhaps millions—since a time when the very road they traveled now had been ocean beach. About the dry cycles when lightning could set off fires that burned underground for years, now and then springing up aboveground to burn a few acres of forest . . . or more.

They passed two farm carts, loaded with children and sacks of grain. Jericho called out to the driver of the hindmost cart to ask if the fire had reached the road yet.

"She's sprung up fresh 'bout a mile off to the west. There's a clearing 'twixt the fire and the canal, so the road'll be jest fine, long as some fool don't strangulate on smoke and block the way." He spat a stream of tobacco juice, and without even looking over his shoulder, yelled, "Set down, younguns, or I'll feed ye to the hogs!"

Half a mile farther south, Jericho stopped and jumped down. While Sara rubbed her tender, battered behind, he dipped a handkerchief into the black water at the edge of the road and wrung it out. He handed it to Sara, then removed his coat, swagged it through the ditch, and swung back up into the shay.

"Cover your head with this if it gets any worse," he said, and handed her the sodden garment, which stunk of mud and smoke and worse.

It was deliciously cool to her touch. She hadn't realized how much the temperature had risen. "What about you?"

"I've been through worse."

She didn't doubt it, but they had both started to cough, and she couldn't help but notice the way he grimaced whenever he did. As if it hurt him.

Getting up onto her knees, she wrapped her arms around him to keep from being thrown out and tied the handkerchief over his mouth and nose. He tried to brush her hands away from his face, but controlling the skittish mare was taking all his attention.

He muttered a muffled thanks.

At least, she thought that was what he had said. For all she knew, he could be directing her to fry in hell. From the looks of the spark-laden smoke, they might both be on their way there.

The farmer had been right—the road was untouched. She recognized a certain lightning-struck tree, a massive black gum with roots arching high above the black swamp water from her recent journey north, and knew they were not very far from Wilde Oaks. Another few miles—

And then suddenly everything seemed to happen at once. Sparks were flying all around. A burning brand drifted down onto the mare's hindquarters, and she screamed and rose up on her hind legs. The shay tilted, and Jericho reached out with one hand to grab Sara just as she went sailing over the side.

The fireworks continued, only now her face was wet

and she couldn't breathe and her head was splitting apart.

"Jesus, Jesus, Jesus." The words seemed to echo in some vast, dark brown cavern, repeated over and over in a hoarse, but entirely reverent tone.

Had she fallen asleep in church and woken up suddenly?

But why was she so wet? Why was her head hurting so she could hardly bear it? Why did someone keep praying over her, as if she were laid out in a coffin with a lily in her hands?

# Chapter Fifteen

"Is she dead?"

Sara recognized that voice. She tried to lift her head and glare at the speaker, but it hurt too much. Something was pressing into her belly. Something or someone was jostling her so that her arms were flopping, swinging, brushing against something cold, wet and hard. She slitted one eye open and saw in the flickering lantern light a pair of dangling hands—her own; boot heels—definitely *not* her own—and the familiar wooden steps that led up onto the veranda at Wilde Oaks.

How strange . . .

"What happened?" the voice persisted.

"Hester!" someone shouted. "Get out here, fast!"

She knew that voice, too. It was Jericho's voice, coming from somewhere above where she dangled. Only why was he shouting when her head was about to fall off?

"Is she dead?" the first voice repeated. "What happened?"

"Who the devil are you? Where's Hester?"

"Right here, right here—oh my blessed Lord in heaven, what've you gone and done to her? Is she hurt bad? Is she—?"

"No, damn it, she's not dead, but she might well end up that way if you're going to stand around gawking all night!"

*Well. She wasn't dead, then.*

"Help me get her down."

*Down from where? Heaven? If this was heaven, then the other place must be awful, indeed.*

Hands tugged at her from all sides, grabbing her by the waist, by the hips. She smelled a whiff of spicy, lemony scent—her own, which she was most definitely not wearing as she hadn't even thought to take it with her when she'd gone racing off to care for Jericho.

"What's wrong with her? Captain Wilde? No, wait— let me spread something over the sofa before you set her down, else she'll ruin the cover with all that mud."

Jericho swore. Hester Renegar made that noise with her teeth and tongue that meant she was disgusted. Sara opened her eyes.

She was wet, cold and horizontal. Finally. And ruining the sofa. Dimly aware of the two women hovering over her, she looked wildly around for Jericho. Don't leave me, she wanted to cry. Oh, please, whatever you do don't ever leave me!

He was standing behind the sofa, pale as a sun-bleached bedsheet, his left hand rubbing his right shoulder.

"You're hurting, aren't you? There, I told you you should've let me drive." She hadn't meant to fuss at him, truly she hadn't. For some reason, she didn't seem to have a speck of control over her thoughts, much less her tongue.

"Oh, Miss Sara, hush now, don't try to talk," Hester scolded.

"I'd better get some shears and cut off her hair," said Ivadelle Moyer.

At which Sara blinked the mud from her eyes and said the first thing that popped into her head. "Are you still here?"

"Who the hell *is* this woman? Hester, where's Tubby? Someone's got to go for Doc Withers."

"Shhh, he's already gone. Left out of here not more'n an hour ago, said if you was this late, likely you'd had trouble with that arm of yours, what with the fire and all." The old woman's face puckered up. "Only it weren't your arm at all, it was Miss Sara, poor lamb. Is she burned anywhere?"

Sara really thought someone should show more concern for Jericho. After all, he had got her home, hadn't he? The last thing she remembered was sailing over the side of the shay, feeling her head strike something hard, and then seeing a shower of fireworks. After that, all she could remember was flopping around like a sack of meal.

With her eyes closed, Sara did her best to reconstruct what had happened, but it was hard to think when her head hurt like the very devil. "At least you had the good sense not to strain your shoulder," she whispered, not even knowing if he was still there.

"Sense enough not to risk dropping you on your backside, you mean," Jericho growled, carefully arranging a crocheted spread over her wet body. Turning to the housekeeper, he said, "She's not burned, not so far's I know."

Sara opened her eyes in time to see his hand hovering over her head. She flinched. "Don't touch it! Is it—broken?"

"We'll find out as soon as Doc gets here. Shhh, now . . . don't try to talk. You've got a knot on your noggin big as a dipping gourd, but I don't think you busted anything."

Hester was there with a damp cloth, wiping and blotting, making tsking noises again. Ivadelle kept going on about cutting off her hair and how awful she looked, but Sara was hurting too much to care.

And then a banty rooster of a man wearing a rusty black suit and pinch-nose spectacles burst into the room, shooing everyone away, and she could hear Rafe in the background talking to Jericho. With a sigh, Sara sank into blessed oblivion.

The sun was shining brightly through a crack in the draperies when Jericho opened his eyes. He ached in every inch of his body from having slept in a chair. Or possibly from leaping out of the shay, diving into the swamp after his wife and then carrying her over his shoulder the last few miles. The shay had been hopelessly mired, one wheel hiked up off the road, the other bent and buried. He had cut loose Rafe's mare and the poor creature had gone flying off down the road before he could lay a hand on her, otherwise he might have carried Sara home that way. It would have been a hell of a lot easier on both of them than the way he'd been forced to carry her, slung like a croker sack over his good shoulder with one steadying hand on her backside to keep her aboard.

At the time, all he'd been able to think of was that she might die, and if she did, he didn't think he could bear it.

Or that she might well lose her baby, which didn't

bother him near as much, but all the same, he wouldn't
wish that sadness on any woman. It reminded him too
painfully of what had happened to Louisa.

Instead, he had discovered that the woman he had
lusted for, the woman who had muddled his thinking
ever since he'd looked up and seen her through the
hotel window, had made a fool of him.

An even bigger fool than he had made of himself.

Not that he would ever let her know that he'd been
all ready to give up the sea for her by the time Doc
Withers had let slip her secret. Ready to give up the
one thing he loved most in the world for something he
had come to love even more.

The thought slipped into his mind before he could
guard against it, and he swore. Love Sara?

Like hell he did!

Sara moaned. Without opening her eyes she was
aware of the brilliant sliver of light that fell across her
face. Inch by inch, her fingers explored their immediate
surroundings. These weren't the coarse hotel linens.
Nor the thin hotel mattress. That wasn't the raucous
sound of drinkers and gamesters she was hearing. The
whining noise outside the window was oddly familiar,
although at the moment she couldn't quite place it.

Her head ached furiously, but at least she was dry.
Which was a reminder of just how wet and miserable
she had been only a short while ago. And how she had
got that way.

Now she was dry and miserable.

She must have made some sound, because Jericho
was there when she opened her eyes, almost as if he'd
been waiting for her to wake up. She gazed up into his

face. He looked gray. The lines that bracketed his wide mouth were deeper than ever, and that granite jaw of his was half covered with a dark stubble. "You look dreadful," she rasped. "You haven't been here all night, have you?"

"Hester cleaned you up and fussed over you for a spell. I stood the graveyard watch. Happen I fell asleep in the chair."

Sara hadn't the least notion of what a graveyard watch was, but she didn't much care for the sound of it. Had they expected her to die, for mercy's sake?

"It appears to me that you sat your watch, not stood it."

The look he turned on her would have sent a lesser mortal scurrying for cover. Sara was made of sterner stuff. "Did your wound tear open again?"

"So you remember that, do you? What else do you remember, madam?"

Madam. Well. She didn't much care for the sound of that, either. "I'm sorry to be such a bother. And sorry about the sofa, too—all the mud, I mean. You should've let Ivadelle cover it before you set me down."

And then the door opened and that woman bustled in bearing a tray. She was wearing the same light blue sateen trimmed in black gimp that Sara had once envied.

Now she envied her the fact that she was able to walk and smile instead of lying abed scarcely able to keep her head from falling apart like a broken teapot. "You're still here, I see," Sara said, which was hardly gracious, but then, the woman had no right to be so cheerful when both her host and hostess were in pain.

"It's a good thing, too, what with you and the captain

both ailing. Renegar can't manage all these steps."
Turning to Jericho, her scowl disappeared and was re-
placed by a look of concern. "Are you feeling better,
Captain Jericho? I did offer to sit up with Miss—with
Sara, you'll remember."

Jericho grumbled something and rose stiffly to his
feet. Sara eyed the tray, which held both a teacup and
a glass of some milky liquid. She needed the laudanum,
but would prefer the tea.

Her foot hurt. Why on earth would her foot hurt?

She struggled to sit up. Examining her surroundings
for the first time, she thought, how odd. *I seem to
remember moving into a cubbyhole of a room at the
back of the house before . . .*

Ivadelle reached behind her and punched at the bolster until it was in the most miserable position possible,
and then she stepped back and beamed at Jericho.
"There, now, I do believe she's looking better this
morning, don't you? Of course, she never did have any
color, but at least that hideous lump on her head has
gone down some. Doctor Withers says she'll likely not
even have much of a scar. Have you told her the
news yet?"

Jericho snarled. There was no other way to describe
the sound that began low in his chest and worked its
way up past the thin barrier of his lips. Just like one
of the big black bears that lived in the nearby swamp
that Sara had heard about all her life, and even eaten,
both stewed and roasted, but had never actually seen.

"I'll see she takes her medicine. Tell Hester to make
up something fit to eat. I'll be down for it in a little
while."

Ivadelle brightened. Really, Sara thought, no woman

who looked so pretty should be allowed in the sickroom
of a woman who didn't. A woman who never had and
never would.

"Shall we say bacon, ham, fried potatoes, and scrambled eggs?"

"You can say whatever you damn well please, but
bring me a bowl of burgoo."

"What on earth is—"

"Gruel! Oatmeal or cornmeal—Hester'll know
what's best."

"Oh, but—"

"Scat! On your way, woman!" He clapped his hands,
which made the hammers start up all over again in
Sara's head and made Ivadelle yelp like a scalded cat.

Which was almost worth the pain.

No sooner had Ivadelle scurried through the door
than Rafe poked his head in, bringing with him an
aura of peat smoke, Bay Rum and cigars. "Good morning, Miss Sara. Now why don't you take off that colorful mask you're wearing and give us a proper smile?"

At his cheerful teasing, Sara felt her eyes prickle.
"Oh, Rafe, I'm so glad you're still here."

"Here again, darling, not *still*. Spent the night in my
own bed, but I come right on over first thing. Not
feeling so feisty this morning, are we?" He sauntered
into the room, ignoring Jericho's grim lack of welcome,
and presented Sara with a big bouquet of hothouse
roses that had to have come all the way from Norfolk
by way of stage.

Burying her face in the flowers, which, had she but
known it, clashed wildly with her black-and-blue forehead and her red-scraped cheek, Sara felt her eyes
brim over and cursed her own weakness. "You're not

going to call me madam or threaten to cut off my hair, are you?"

"Cut off that bountiful glory? I should say not. And if I'm not to call you madam, and that husband of yours clouds up every time I call you darling, then we'll have to think of something else. How about—Petunia? I once knew a man who called his woman Petunia. She called him Fart Blossom. Happiest couple in Currituck County."

Sara giggled, even though it hurt something fierce. Her laughter broke off when she noticed Jericho's reaction. Evidently he didn't appreciate Rafe's silly attempt to make her smile, for he'd gone all sour and solemn again. She was beginning to think that was his natural condition.

"You want to leave under your own steam, Turbyfill, or shall I help you out the window?"

"The door, by all means. I never was real partial to being thrown out second-floor windows." He held up a placating hand and said, "I'll see you directly, Sweetpea. Doc says you're going to be just fine. Way I heard it, that belly ache you was suffering from yesterday must have been something you ate."

"Is that all you heard?" Jericho pressed.

"Well, no . . . now that you mention it, I reckon between old Doc Withers and that yeller-haired female that's running tame around here, I heard about all there was to hear. You got something you want to talk about, Rico? Like maybe you need some advice?"

Jericho's eyes narrowed. He reminded Sara of a bull about to charge. She grabbed Rafe's sleeve and whispered, "What? What did he say? Is there something wrong with me? Something you haven't told me?"

"More like something you haven't told Rico," Rafe said gently, smoothing his sleeve. His eyes looked tired, but there was a definite twinkle in them. Which was more than could be said about Jericho.

"Get out."

"If you need some advice—"

"Get out. Just get the hell out of my house!"

Rafe backed toward the door, still grinning, which didn't make a bit of sense to Sara. "I'm going, I'm going, you don't have to get testy. And Rico, about my rig—"

"I'll settle with you later on that count."

"The mare was there in the paddock when I got home last night. Had a burn on her rear end, but—"

"Out."

"But other than being a mite skittish, she was in right fair shape. More'n I can say about my rig. I sent half a dozen hands up the road to—"

"Out! I'll settle with you directly."

Rafe had his hand on the door. He opened it partially, and there was a scurrying sound outside in the hallway, as if someone had been listening outside the door. "Damn right you will. Sweetpea, don't let anybody bully you. If this seagoing baboon turns you out, you come straight to me, y'hear?"

*Turned her out?*

All Sara understood was that she was hurting all over; her head obviously wasn't working right yet, and for some reason Jericho was angry with her. She was madam again.

But surely he wouldn't turn her out.

Moving carefully, she eased over onto her side, closed her eyes, and concentrated on lying perfectly still. If Jericho thought she was asleep, he might leave her alone until she could sort things out. Evidently she had done something dreadful, but for the life of her she couldn't remember what it was.

At the moment she didn't much care. All she wanted to do was sleep until all the pain and confusion went away.

She heard the chair creak, knew he was still there, but they continued to ignore one another until eventually she fell asleep.

From the kitchen came the clatter of pots and pans and the smell of frying bacon. Ivadelle's voice could be heard telling someone or something to scat. A mockingbird ran through a lengthy repertoire, and Brig barked once or twice.

Sara slept on. Slept and dreamed she was dragging her husband out of the swamp by his arms. One arm fell off, and as she was searching for it among the cypress knees and black gum roots, the trees around them caught fire. Cottonmouth moccasins and snapping turtles began to converge on them, and she tried to shout a warning to Jericho, but no sound came forth.

As soon as he was confident that Sara was sleeping soundly, Jericho slipped away. He moved silently past the study, where the Moyer woman was dusting—damn her meddlesome soul—and he ran her out. He didn't allow anyone to mess around in his private quarters.

He finally located Hester in the kitchen. "Who the devil *is* that woman? What's she doing here?" he demanded.

"Her? Hmph! As for who she is, she's your overseer's sister. As for what she's a-doing, I've got me own notions. Claims she can't abide sleeping in a loft. Moved in here bag and baggage, saying she'd go back to the cabin once this smoke died down."

Thinking back, Jericho seemed to remember hearing something about Hiram Moyer's having a sister. He'd had so much on his mind at the time that the farm and the new overseer had been well down on his list of worries. He had assumed, if he'd thought about it at all, that the sister would be an elderly spinster, someone who would hardly make a ripple on the surface of a place as large as Wilde Oaks.

This woman made more than a ripple. She made a damned tidal wave! For the life of him, he couldn't figure out what she was up to, but she was up to something, all right. He could smell it. As if he didn't have enough on his plate, what with learning how to deal with a wife, he now had two troublesome females to contend with.

He should have gone back to sea. He should've taken care of Smithers, bound up his shoulder, hightailed it to the nearest port, and signed on aboard the first outward-bound ship. As an able seaman, if that was the best he could do.

While Hester changed the dressings on his shoulder, fussing about what would've happened if the knife had gone half an inch lower and pierced his lung, Jericho asked a few questions. "What was that female doing in Mama's room?"

"Miz Moyer? Your wife gave her leave just before she ran off with Rafe to fetch you. Turn this way—there now, you're gong to have a fine scar."

"Sara gave her leave to use Mama's room?" As soon as he'd got his second wind, Jericho had carried Sara up to the master suite and laid her on the bed, with both women right on his heels. The confounded Moyer woman kept insisting it was her room and that Sara would be better off in the back where it was quieter.

With a few short words, he had set her straight. He had ordered her to clear out her gear. She hadn't much liked it, but she had gone without making a fuss. Which was a good thing, because if she'd said one more word, she'd have likely found herself escorted to the overseer's cottage with orders to damn well stay put.

With a raisin biscuit in hand and Hester's sharp voice ringing in his ear, Jericho left the kitchen, promising to get some sleep, to come back down for dinner, and not to worry Sara if she was resting.

An hour later he was still pacing the master bedroom, one hand looped in the scarf the housekeeper had fitted on him after rubbing him down with turpentine and camphor. The sling helped, taking the strain off his freshly strained shoulder, but it didn't do one bloody thing to ease what ailed him most.

She had lied to him. His own wife had lied to him. Not only was she not carrying a child, she had never even been bedded. He had taken Doc Withers aside, out of range of any nosy females, and asked him to make certain her baby was all right. The old man had briskly reentered the bedroom where Hester had been left to stand watch. A few minutes later he had brought out the information that not only was there no bun in the oven, but the girl had never even been broached.

"But then, I reckon you know that, seein's she's your

wife." The physician had looked puzzled. Both men had been embarrassed. And then Jericho had felt the anger begin to build inside him.

She had lied to him. He had acted in good faith to protect her reputation and give her a home. He had trusted her because he'd had no reason not to trust her, and she had *lied to him!*

The old man had left him with a final word of wisdom. "If ye're a-wanting to know if she's able, then ye can rest easy, boy. For all she's small, she's got the breadth to 'er. Some women ain't. Miss Louisa weren't built for breeding, but this one'll likely whelp as easy as spittin' out watermelon seeds."

Jericho still hadn't quite believed it. "Are you telling me she's—that my wife is—?"

The doctor had misunderstood him. "Healthy as a horse. As for the lump on her head, it'll likely go down directly. Bruises take a mite longer to fade. Cold cloths. Turpentine poultices. Use the powders on her cheek, and as for the place on her foot where she whacked it, chances are, it'll heal up with no trouble. Feet's got a lot of bones to 'em. Tricky thing, the foot."

Her foot? Jericho hadn't even known about her foot. "What I meant was—"

"Give 'er a few days, boy—she'll be up and about, ready to do her wifely duty."

"But—"

"Now if ye're of a mind to take some advice off an old man that's seen his share of troubles, ye'll send that Moyer female packing before she muddles things up. It ain't none of my business, son, but that one's a troublemaker, sure's the world. I can smell 'em same way I can smell out a fever."

Still stunned by what he had just heard, Jericho had paid no attention. He hadn't even noticed when the old man had let himself out and driven off in his mud-splattered, soot-covered buggy.

Judas priest. A virgin.

She had made a fool of him, all right. He would never even have thought about marrying her if she hadn't told him she might be carrying a child. If he hadn't felt sorry for her. If he hadn't climbed into her bed while she lay sleeping, been discovered there by the world's biggest pair of flap-jaws, and been obliged to do what he could to salvage her reputation.

*If he hadn't undressed her over and over in his mind and enjoyed every sweet, seductive inch of her body in every conceivable way . . . some of which probably hadn't even been invented.*

But she had lied to him. Probably set out to trap him the minute she discovered that Ricketts already had a wife.

Every shred of instinct he possessed told him that Sara wasn't the type to play a man false. Not his Sara. Not the woman who had teased him and confided in him, laughed with him and tenderly cared for him in spite of his surliness.

On the other hand, she was Smithers's sister.

Wrong. She was only his stepsister. No blood kin at all. Hadn't she been running from the bastard herself?

God, what a muddle. Jericho rubbed the back of his neck, then ran his fingers through his hair, leaving windrows falling every whichaway. How had he managed to get himself into such an almighty fix?

More to the point, how was he going to get himself out of it?

At least Smithers was dead. Not that he relished having a man's blood on his hands, but if ever a man deserved to die, that one did. Not only for Louisa, but for Sara.

Sara. What was he going to do about her? He knew what he wanted to do, even now that he knew of her trickery.

He thought about the one and only long-term relationship he'd had with a woman. The same woman who had tried to pass off another man's get as his own because she figured a shipowner had a more promising future than a greengrocer.

There was a rap on the door and before he could respond, Ivadelle opened it and offered him a self-deprecating smile. "I hope you don't mind me interrupting you this way. I thought you could use some coffee."

Hearing again the physician's words, Jericho studied the tall, good-looking woman. Was she a troublemaker? Not the kind he was used to, at any rate—the kind that fomented strife aboard ship. The kind every captain was forced to deal with sooner or later in his career.

"I didn't know if you took sugar," she said in a voice that reminded him of cane syrup.

It was that sweetness that set his teeth on edge. She was *too* bloody sweet. No female was all that sweet unless she wanted something. God knows, Sara never went out of her way to be sweet.

Which meant . . .

Which meant that when it came to women, he was still at sea. "Obliged," he said gruffly, taking the cup and ignoring the bowl full of lumpy brown sugar.

"I happened to overhear what Dr. Withers said about poor Sara," she said diffidently. "I was dusting the window ledge in the next room."

She was a great hand for dusting, he'd hand her that. "She don't look too good now," he allowed grudgingly, "but she'll heal." Regardless of how he, himself, felt about Sara, he wasn't about to criticize her to another woman.

"It's not as if she was any great beauty to start with. Still, I don't suppose the scar on her cheek will even be noticeable in a few years."

Jericho flexed his fingers once or twice. Somehow, he had the feeling his wife had just been insulted. Sara was his problem; he would deal with her in his own time and in his own way.

"I knew a man from Fayetteville once who had his marriage annulled after two years. Did you ever? He said she refused to do her duty, and the judge set him free." She smiled expectantly, as if waiting for him to thank her for opening a door.

"I'm obliged for the coffee, Miss Moyer. Tell your brother for me I'd like to see him in my study first thing tomorrow morning. Now, if that's all?"

Her smile faltered. "Well, actually, I was wanting to be sure I didn't leave anything behind. In Sara's room, that is. I borrowed it on account of how the smoke leaks into the bedroom I was using, but Renegar said—"

Jericho's face took on a look that Sara would have recognized right off, having seen it often enough. "If I run across anything that don't belong there, I'll set it outside," he said grimly.

He had stood by and watched while she'd hauled out

all her gear, including a silver-backed brush and mirror set and a bottle of scent that reminded him of Sara. He had more on his mind than a few women's fripperies.

Such as what he was going to do with a lying, conniving virgin bride.

# *Chapter Sixteen*

Missing Maulsie more than ever before, Sara lay still as long as she dared. She was used to rising early. Being bedridden didn't suit her at all, not with so many matters to be sorted out and settled. Ivadelle was still here. Hester didn't like her, but lacked the authority to turn her out.

As for Jericho . . .

Well. That was another matter. He's good and angry with me, Sara thought, although she hadn't the least notion why. Unless he had taken one look at Ivadelle in her fancy blue sateen and decided that as long as he was marrying, he could do better than to settle for a plain brown wren of a wife who had no more fashion sense than a turnip. Which was sad, but true. She never had. Likely, she never would.

Stung by pride, she sat up too quickly, swung her limbs over the side of the bed and caught her breath as the world suddenly tilted on its side. A lump on her head was bad enough, but the draft she had taken so willingly to dull the pain evidently had a few lingering aftereffects. No wonder Jericho had refused to take it.

Moving cautiously, she eased off the bed until her toes touched the Brussels carpet. She stood, and then nearly collapsed again as pain shot through her left foot.

"Merciful saints, what now?" she grumbled. Lifting the tail of her plain cotton night shift, she examined her foot. It was somewhat bruised on one side, but that was all. If it had been broken, the doctor would have bound it up.

Thus reassured, she limped across to the washstand, supporting herself on first one piece of furniture, then another. It occurred to her that she had swapped bedrooms with Ivadelle shortly before she had ridden north with Rafe, yet here she was again in her original room.

Or perhaps she had only imagined moving her few belongings out so that the overseer's sister could move in. The way her mind was working lately, it was a wonder she could remember her own name. To think she once considered herself so sensible.

There was a large oval cheval glass beside the washstand. Carefully, she averted her gaze. She would wash first and arrange her hair, and then change out of her night shift and into one of her prettiest gowns. Perhaps then she would confront herself in the mirror. Hester had done her best, but short of putting a sack over her head, there wasn't much anyone could do to disguise the lump on her forehead and the scrape on her cheek.

She fingered the shaggy braid that hung over one shoulder. Someone had mentioned cutting it off, and she could see why. With her head pounding like a flock of woodpeckers, brushing it would be agony.

The water was cold. She shivered, telling herself that if cold cloths were good for the headache, then a cold bath might ease the aches she felt all over. So she washed, instinctively following the same pattern she

had followed for years. Down as far as possible, starting
with her ears, and then up as far as possible, starting
with her feet. That was the way Maulsie had taught
her to bathe herself when she'd grown too independent
to let anyone do it for her. She had been all of five
years old at the time. That had been the year she had
insisted on braiding her own hair, too. Crooked parts,
lumpy plaits, tangles and all.

By the time she finished bathing, her cotton lawn
gown was thoroughly damp, but at least she no longer
fancied she smelled like a swamp.

She heard the sound of clicking toenails coming
down the hallway. "Brig," she murmured, half tempted
to let the creature into her room just for a bit of uncrit-
ical company. He might not lick her fingers, but at
least he wouldn't call her madam. She was actually
turning toward the door when she caught sight of her
image in the mirror.

"Dear God in heaven," she gasped. She didn't even
recognize herself!

All thought of canine companionship forgotten, Sara
ruthlessly scrutinized her ruined face. Purple, blue and
red. Not to mention raw and swollen. With dustings
of some grayish white powder. About the only recognizable features left were her eyes, and now even they
were beginning to turn red.

At least she could no longer be called plain, she
thought with bleak amusement.

Tears spilled over her lashes as she stared at the
hideous apparition before her. Adding insult to injury,
the salt tears stung her scraped cheek, making her
weep all the harder.

Standing forlornly before the mirror, she stared at

her ruined face and wept until her throat ached, never even noticing when the door opened.

And then another image joined hers in the cheval glass.

Jericho.

"Why d-didn't you tell me I looked such a fright?" she wailed, never taking her eyes off the ugly, splotched face of the stranger in the mirror.

"You'll heal," Jericho said gruffly. He cupped his hands over her shoulders, as if to lend her some of his own strength, and she thought of how many times she'd been tempted to lean on him for just that same reason. "You'll be as good as ever before you know it."

She laughed, but it came out all broken, more of a sob. "As good as ever. Oh, that'll be a treat."

He began to stroke her arms, and weakly, Sara let him, leaning back against his chest. She was probably getting him all wet, and she didn't even care. At least he hadn't yet called her madam in that nasty tone of voice.

"Shhhh, don't carry on so much, you'll get the headache."

"I already have the headache," she said with a watery smile.

"There's medicine on the bedside table."

"No, thank you. I'd sooner put up with a little pain than muddle what's left of my wits with laudanum."

He broke off rubbing her arms and lifted his hands to her temples, and Sara let her head fall back against his chest. Closing her eyes, she sighed as his fingertips began to massage her scalp.

"I could brush your hair, if it wouldn't hurt too much."

"Mmmm. Just chop it off, it'd be easier . . ."

His face brushed against her hair, and he murmured, "Roses?"

"Roses? Oh. My soap. Roses and lemongrass. Maulsie makes it up for me. At least she used to . . ."

Jericho recognized the scent. He'd smelled it most recently on the Moyer woman. Wondering what else that sticky-fingered wench had removed from the room, he vowed to have Hester go through her things before she left. Which would be just as soon as he could manage it without offending his overseer.

He only hoped the man managed a farm better than he did his own family. There were tenant houses to repair, field hands to secure, as well as house servants. He didn't want Sara trying to do too much too soon, regardless of how things stood between them.

As to that, he hadn't yet settled on a course. He'd consider it after he'd set the ditches to being cleared and arranged to buy more stock. According to Hester, they were down to one old milk cow, a few layers, a team of mules, and two horses, including Bones.

Feeling the heavy weight of responsibility settling on his shoulders, anchoring him to the land whether he willed it or not, Jericho sighed.

"Did you want something?" Sara asked, her voice commendably steady considering the shape she was in. In the mirror he studied the tear tracks on her face. She was a mess, she surely was. She was also right up there at the top of his list of responsibilities. He shuddered to think of just how close he had come to losing her.

Not that he wanted her. How could a man want a woman he couldn't even trust?

A perverse voice whispered that she could have broken her neck. At this very moment he could be digging another grave on the hill. Instead, thank God, she was alive and warm, her soft, yielding body secure in his arms while he struggled to remember all the reasons why it would never serve. This marriage between them.

Meeting her gaze in the mirror, Jericho couldn't help but notice how small and fair she looked against his dark, somber reflection. When he had first come through the doorway after hearing her move around, the sight of her plump, pink buttocks gleaming through the thin stuff of her gown had just about done him in.

Now it was her breasts. He told himself it was only because her gown was wet that her nipples stood out like plump brown raisins. Not because she was aroused. She was in no shape to be bedded, even if he was of a mind to bed her.

Oh, he was of a mind, all right. Even knowing she couldn't be trusted, he was fit to bust right out of his breeches. No matter how many times he reminded himself that she was a lying, conniving little witch, he couldn't seem to forget that she was also his wife.

He wanted her, and that was the plain truth with no bark on it. He'd wanted her ever since he had first laid eyes on her, and he hadn't the least notion why. She wasn't the prettiest woman he had ever seen. Far from it. Right now, she looked a pure fright, yet without even willing it, he watched his own hands slip from her temples down her slender throat and linger there, looking dark and alien against her soft, pale skin.

Her pulse throbbed under his fingertips, echoing his own.

"Sara," he whispered hoarsely as his hands strayed

farther south, easing under the neck of her gown to the rise of her breasts.

He heard the sharp catch of her breath. She stiffened and then seemed to sag in his arms. "Please," she said so low he could hardly make out the word.

His staff leapt eagerly against the warm softness of her buttocks. Damn. How the devil had he ever been able to command a ship when he couldn't even command his own body? Swallowing hard, he searched for one last shred of common sense and came up empty-handed.

"Sara, this is not what I came here for."

"I know," she said with a sad little smile that lent her the look of a painted clown. "You came to call me madam."

"I came to *what*?" He went to turn her in his arms, and her foot gave way under her slight weight. She gasped and fell against him, clinging to his shoulders for support.

"I'm sorry. I'm so sorry, Sara." He would never deliberately hurt her.

Standing on one foot, she gazed up at him with her ruined face and her big golden brown eyes. One of the few unscathed areas of her face was her mouth. Her sweet, tempting mouth. Jericho stared hungrily down at her until her bottom lip began to tremble.

Whatever else she was, he told himself, she was more than enough to tempt a saint, and Jericho had never come even close to being that. Heaving a sigh of resignation, he surrendered to the inevitable.

He had kissed her before. Sara loved his kisses—she admitted it freely, despairingly. But this time, it was different. Oh, the same desire was there, if this heart-pounding, sweating, breathless excitement could be called desire. But this time there was something more.

With his hands at the side of her head, he held her in place as he lowered his own face. One of his fingers accidentally raked over her cheek, and she caught her breath with a gasp just as his mouth covered hers. Then she forgot everything but the immediacy of his kiss. His taste. His tongue.

His tongue. Oh, my . . .

And he was angry with her. She didn't know why, but she could feel it in the way he ravished her mouth, as if he wanted to devour her, only she wanted to devour him right back. They swayed in place, his arms crushing her to him, his mouth punishing hers even as his hands moved over her body, creating glimmering, glittering shards of promise wherever he touched her.

His palms cupped her buttocks, holding her tightly against that part of him that was so essentially male. When his fingertips curled into the crease between her plump cheeks, she wriggled, startled at the sensation. He groaned into her mouth and moved against her in a way that made her trembling limbs want to part.

She felt weak, and it had nothing at all to do with her accident. "My bones have all melted," she whispered breathlessly when his mouth left hers to move down her throat.

The harsh sound of his laughter reverberated on the nerves at the pit of her belly. "I've bone enough for the both of us," he said, and she didn't know quite what he meant, but then again, perhaps she did . . .

"Oh, my," she panted as his teeth closed gently over the tip of her breast. "Oh, my merciful saints in heaven!"

"Don't," he said, lifting his lips for an instant. "Don't say anything." And then he began to suckle her right through her thin lawn shift, and she couldn't have spoken if the earth caught fire beneath her very feet.

As it very nearly did. Jericho swept her up in his arms, and she hid her face against his shoulder. It hurt her cheek, the coarse weave of his shirt, but the hurt was small beside the overwhelming feelings racing through her body like a swarm of butterflies gone mad.

Besides, she didn't want him to see her. Not the way she looked now. "I wish it were night," she whispered as he lowered her onto the bed.

If he heard her, he didn't let on. He was tugging at the buttons on his shirt, his hands shaking as if he had the ague. His eyes glittered feverishly. His cheeks were flushed, and she could have sworn the planes of his face had grown sharper.

When he flung his shirt to the floor and began tugging on his belt, she realized for the first time what was about to happen. Turning her face away, she fumbled to smooth her gown down over her limbs, wishing it were of far finer quality. Wishing she were beautiful. Wishing her head didn't ache quite so much so that she could concentrate on all these other lovely feelings inside her.

"Sara," he said hoarsely just as a familiar voice called through the door.

"Miss Sara? Is you in dere?"

Jericho paced the study, his mood every bit as dark as the walnut paneling that had been grown, sawed, and planed right here on Wilde Oaks more than seventy years ago. It wasn't his nature to drink of a morning, but dinner wasn't on the table yet and already he had lowered the tide in the brandy decanter by more than a few inches.

He still hadn't made up his mind whether the gods had played a monstrous joke on him or spared him from an unwanted entanglement. She was his wife, after all. Whether or not he wanted her, he had her.

Correction. He had *nearly* had her.

He swore at the unassuaged lust that still inflamed his loins, then swore some more, thinking of the comical figure he must have cut, snatching up his clothes and scampering, naked as a plucked chicken, through the door to his own room, just as the big black woman in the shiny black silk gown came in through the other door.

Raking a hand through his hair, he lifted his glass, scowled, and then set it down again.

She would have to go, that was all there was to it. The Moyer woman, not Sara's Maulsie. She had been down there at the bottom of the stairs—dusting—when he had come downstairs.

"Is Sara still feeling puny? It's a good thing she's got that old woman to help look after her, isn't it? I sent her up the minute she got here, thinking you might need her to spell you."

Jericho knew very well what she had been thinking of, and it wasn't his own convenience. "Obliged," he said shortly.

Ivadelle simpered, her dust cloth forgotten. "It was the least I could do, since Sara doesn't seem to like me overmuch. But then, sickly women often resent those of us who are hale and hearty."

"Sara's not sickly. She suffered an accident that

could happen to anyone." Jericho felt obliged to defend his wife.

"Oh, I know she's not really sickly. I expect she just wants to stay out of your way until you've gotten over your disappointment."

"Disappointment?" If she had any notion of what his disappointment was all about, she wouldn't have stood there preening, poking out her small bosom and showing off her small white teeth.

"I mean about the baby and all. I must say, I don't know exactly what went on between you two, but I'm sure Sara never meant to deceive you. Why, marriages have been annulled for less."

Too furious to reply, Jericho had turned and stalked off. Just before he reached the study, she called after him. "Oh, by the way—when Mr. Turbyfill brought the old woman over, he brought along some crippled old man who don't look like he'll be worth his keep. Said they belonged to Sara. Looks to me like you took on more than you bargained for. The woman might be useful, but if I was you, I'd ask Hiram to get rid of the old man the best way he can. Unless you're real strict with your rations, they'll eat you out of house and home."

Natter, natter, natter. No wonder the overseer had thrown her out. The woman was enough to drive a brass monkey to drink.

"I thank you for your advice, but that old man's my new butler," he said, enjoying the way her jaw fell.

"Your new *what*?"

But Jericho had already left. Stalking down the hallway, the sound of his boot heels muffled on the newly cleaned and spread runner, he wondered how his household could have grown so big and unmanageable in such a short time. He had hired one man, and now the place was overrun. It was a good thing Brig was a male dog and not a bitch, else he'd likely find himself wading through a litter of mongrel pups.

An hour later he was still brooding over the situation. Damned if he weren't foundering before he'd even left port. Give him a ship and a crew of good men, set him down in the middle of any sea in the world with neither sextant nor compass, and eventually, he would find his way to the nearest port.

Set him down in a household of females, and he was dead in the water.

# Chapter Seventeen

Maulsie and Big Simon were here. But oh, Jericho—! In a messy muddle of ragged emotions, Sara cried herself senseless while Maulsie bustled around in her noisy silk taffeta gown, inspecting her new domain. She poked in drawers and wardrobes, pulled back draperies, sniffed every medicine bottle and salve jar and loudly pronounced her disapproval while Sara gulped and sniffled, hoping her tears would be taken for tears of joy. "Don't mind the mess, I can't seem to finish unpacking," she said, hoping to distract a woman who knew her far too well.

"Dat man makin' you mis'able, ain't he?"

Sara nodded, dried her eyes, and then changed the subject. Maulsie had demanded to know right off how she could set out for Norfolk and wind up way down in Pasquotank County, married to the wrong man. "I'm just being silly. Now tell me again how you managed to get away. Did Noreen have a tantrum? Is she crushed over Titus's death?"

"Dat boy *dead*? My, my! Reck'n dat's why de missus done lit out in such a hurry. Made me pack up her trunk and den she left out in a big black carriage. Nex' t'ing, dat nice boy fum de livery come fer us, so Simon and me locked de do', turned out de mule, an' come away. We put up in Eliz'buff City wit' a fine family while dat lawyer man looked at our papers, and den I bought me dis here dress, and Simon, he bought hisself a pair o' carpet slippers, and here we is."

And truly, there they were. Simon had taken one look around and got to work mending the garden fence, which drew Hester's approval right off. Maulsie had been less easily satisfied at Sara's sudden change of plans. She had demanded to know every last detail, and Sara, held close in the old woman's arms, had laughed and cried and told her every speck of it. Once satisfied that in no way was Jericho responsible for Sara's present condition, she had settled down to fuss over the woman she had raised from an infant.

And for a little while, Sara had allowed herself to be fussed over. Had even settled briefly into a harmless fantasy in which both her mother and her father were somewhere nearby, and everything was safe and lovely again, just the way it used to be.

Unfortunately, she lacked the temperament to be a successful invalid. As her bruises faded and her strength began to return, her sensible side took over and she began fretting over all the responsibilities she was neglecting. What had seemed so simple when she had boarded the packet boat had somehow become so complicated she no longer knew what was expected of her.

Jericho had a bee in his bonnet, and she hadn't the least notion of what it was all about. She did know he wanted to bed her. He had mentioned once that he was the last of the Wildes.

Well, she wanted to bed him, too, and it had nothing

to do with getting him an heir and everything to do with the fact that she thought about him most all the time, knew the very minute he set foot in the house. Every time he touched her, her heart started fluttering in her chest like a mulberry tree full of mockingbirds.

Oh, she wanted him, all right, but first she had to clear the air between them. Unless she could do that, she would have to leave. Now that she was a woman of independent means, she refused to live in a house where she was barely tolerated. No woman with a grain of sense would choose misery over freedom.

*But, oh, Jericho, why couldn't you learn to love me just a little bit?*

Thanks largely to Maulsie's fierce guardianship, Sara saw almost nothing of her husband over the next few days. Every time she heard him moving about in the room next door, her breathing would go haywire and her heart would kick up a fuss, but the connecting door remained shut. She told herself she was glad he was staying away until her face healed. Being plain was one thing; being downright ugly was something else entirely. She did, after all, have her pride.

But sooner or later, they were going to have to set things straight between them if she intended to stay on at Wilde Oaks.

Meanwhile, Sara tried to convince herself she had all any woman could want. Certainly she had far more than she had ever expected to have when she had run away from home to marry Archibald Ricketts. For the time being, she had a lovely home. Maulsie and Big Simon were safe. And her dresser set had magically reappeared. It had been missing for a little while, but at the time that had been the least of her worries.

By now her face was healing rapidly, her bruises fading, the swelling nearly gone from her forehead. The patch of fine scabs had peeled off her cheek, leaving it shiny and bright pink. She had Rafe and Hester for companionship, and Louisa's dog, Brig. Much to Maulsie's disgust, she had let him into her room once or twice for a little while—not that he was all that much company. All he did was sniff her fingers, then flop and curl up on the floor beside the bed.

Truly, she had everything. So why wasn't it enough?

Part of the trouble was that she was tired of being an invalid. It gave her entirely too much time to brood. She brooded some about the house—about how she could put her own stamp on a place that was already perfect. A few pressed flowers framed and hung on the wall would not be enough. She seemed to have developed a territorial streak, and suspected it had something to do with her lack of security.

Which brought her to another of the things that needed brooding about: *that woman*.

Ivadelle Moyer. She had been here when Sara arrived. She was still here. No one seemed to know why, unless Jericho knew something he wasn't sharing. Hester swore the woman had set her cap to catch herself a husband, but Sara found that hard to believe in light of the fact that Jericho was the only man around, and he was already married. Not that Ivadelle could have known it when she moved in.

Why not set her cap for Rafe? The few times Sara had seen them together, Rafe had looked at her with those laughing, knowing eyes of his, and Ivadelle

turned all huffy, but at least Rafe had the advantage
of being unmarried. Jericho was already taken.

Sara spent hours brooding about it. Was Jericho already regretting their marriage? It had been such a
spur-of-the-moment affair. Now—with Ivadelle and her
blue eyes, her yellow hair and her tall, willowy figure,
making herself available—perhaps he was having second thoughts. What was that old adage? Marry in
haste, repent at leisure?

Jericho had married in haste, all right. He'd been in
such an almighty hurry he had snatched the words
right out of the joiner's mouth, told the man she did,
pronounced them man and wife, and then practically
tossed her aboard the packet boat.

Well, what could not be changed must be endured.
Another old adage. Perhaps she should take up needle-
work and cross-stitch it on a sampler as a reminder.

Never having been sick a day in her life, Sara quickly
discovered that she lacked the patience to lie in bed
and allow other people to wait on her. One day of
coddling was about all she could take, and she'd had
five. Maulsie had told her right off that she wasn't to
set foot on those stairs without permission.

So while Maulsie was busy downstairs in the
kitchen, Sara gave herself permission. Rising from the
chair by the window, where she'd been plotting a dia-
gram of how she wanted the kitchen garden laid out
next year, she tossed aside her wrapper and started
unbraiding her hair.

Ten minutes later she was fastening up her yellow
gown, which clashed horribly with her fading bruises
but even so was more flattering than the brown. Not
for the first time, she wished she hadn't been in such

a rush to get here that she'd passed up the chance to shop for material and a good dressmaker.

But then, at the time she had thought she would soon be needing maternity wear and hadn't been at all excited over the prospect.

She did wish, though, that she had taken time to buy yarn to crochet herself a pair of bed slippers. Her yellow shoes were too tight, and her foot was still tender. The doctor had told her that bones in the feet took forever to mend. She struggled to pull on her black high-tops, took two limping steps, and pulled them off again. "Oh, drat!" If Maulsie caught her limping, she would chase her back to bed with a broom.

Studying her reflection in the mirror, Sara tugged at the waist of her gown, removed her black stockings, and gave a satisfied nod. What Maulsie didn't know wouldn't hurt her. Who ever looked at feet, anyhow?

Before she even reached the head of the stairs, she heard a familiar voice and nearly changed her mind. Ivadelle was on another rampage. She was always on a rampage of some sort, unless Jericho happened to be nearby, in which case she turned all sticky sweet, as if she'd swallowed a mouthful of molasses.

"One of these days," Sara vowed quietly, "I'm going to step on that pesky female and then sweep her right out the door like a big fat spider!"

They were standing in the foyer between the staircase and the front door, the three of them. Jericho, tall and unsmiling, was wearing his usual black. Rafe looked splendid in royal blue with a paisley waistcoat. As for Ivadelle, her face was the most colorful thing about her. It was red.

Well, mercy, things must be in a sad state indeed if

that one was showing her true colors before two of the handsomest gentlemen in creation. Sara found the notion delightful.

Arranging a cheerful smile on her face, she swept gracefully down the stairway, her bare feet silent on the carpeted treads. Pausing halfway, she took the time to enjoy the novelty of looking down on the world rather than up at it for a change. Then, taking a deep breath, she said brightly, "Good morning, all."

Tongues fell still. Three pairs of eyes looked upward. Ivadelle's were all squinched up, as if she'd just seen something distinctly unpleasant. Sara didn't need to guess what that something was.

Rafe was in his usual devilish mood. The man did like to tease. It was part of his rakish charm.

Not until her gaze moved on to Jericho did her smile falter. He looked grim. But then, lately, he always looked grim.

Except for a few unforgettable exceptions.

Sara nearly lost her courage as she met those impenetrable black eyes. There was simply no understanding the man. Lying in bed, with nothing to do but think, she had come to the conclusion that he was far deeper and more complex than he appeared at first glance. Nor was he one to share himself. Underneath that stern, handsome facade she had at various times sensed pain and sadness, and even insecurity and loneliness.

And she knew as well as she knew her own name that he would deny until his dying day that he possessed any such qualities.

Only he would call them weaknesses.

From the way he was looking at her now, she also

knew he was still angry with her. Her smile faltered again, but she held it firmly in place. *Remember the last time we were together,* she wanted to cry—*you came to my room when I was bathing and for a little while you forgot to be angry, and I actually dared to hope . . .*

Well.

Deliberately ignoring Ivadelle's pinched look and Jericho's scowl, Sara assumed her best mistress-of-the-manor expression and swept down the few remaining stairs, her hand extended in a gracious welcome. "Rafe! How nice to see you again. Did you know your roses lasted nearly a week? Hester clipped the stems every morning so they could drink, and now that Maulsie's here, she collects every petal the minute it falls for her potpourri."

It was obvious what had been happening. Rafe was teasing Ivadelle, which was nothing new. He did it to get a rise out of her, and she rose beautifully.

But what about Jericho? He wasn't one to tease, nor to enjoy another's discomfort. Looking back sometime later on the brief encounter, she could almost convince herself he'd been jealous.

Of Ivadelle? Of Rafe?

Surely not of her.

It had happened when Rafe turned to Sara to ask her advice about planning a Thanksgiving party. Jericho looked ready to do battle. At first she thought he was only concerned lest she overdo on her first day downstairs.

"Mercy, I've never planned a party in my life," she said with a breathless laugh. "My mother did, but that was so long ago—and my stepmother was never one to entertain."

Not if it would cost her a penny, she added silently, but refrained from voicing the thought aloud. After all, the poor woman had only recently lost her only son.

"Sara has all she can say grace over right here, Turbyfill. This is her first day out of bed."

Afraid Rafe would be offended by Jericho's abruptness, Sara hurried to smooth things over, which only made it worse.

"Oh, but I don't mind at all. Honestly, I've been so bored."

"Then I suggest, madam, that you concern yourself with putting your own house in order. Those two in the kitchen are squabbling up a storm."

"Maulsie and Hester? Oh, but—"

"Never mind, dear, I'll take care of it." Ivadelle laid a possessive hand on Jericho's black serge sleeve. "Rico, this poor child looks dreadful. If I were you I'd send her back up to bed and see that she stayed there until she's fit to be seen downstairs. Honestly, if it weren't for that awful place on her cheek and those bruises, she wouldn't have a speck of color."

Sara's temper, severely strained from a week's enforced idleness, sprung forth full blown. She opened her mouth to let fly with a few home truths just as Ivadelle reached up to tug at a loosened button on the front of Jericho's shirt.

"Oh, my, you do need someone to look after you, don't you? It's a good thing I'm handy with a needle and thread. I doubt if our little Sara's ever set a single stitch, have you, dear?"

Sara opened her mouth to say that she had set a million stitches, and all of them perfect, which was a big, fat lie, but then she saw Jericho staring down at the dangling button, and it came to her all at once just how that particular button had come to be loose. She clamped her mouth shut again for fear she would tell the other woman just what she could do with her handy needle and thread.

Instead, she turned to Rafe and said with a clenched little smile, "Make me a list of the particulars—how many guests you're inviting, their ages and genders, whether or not you want to have entertainment, and how many servants you have available. I'm sure we can put our heads together and come up with something."

And then, head held high, she turned and fled before she embarrassed herself—or hurt somebody. Evidently, her recovery wasn't quite as far along as she had thought.

Both men stared after her as she marched regally toward the back of the house. Jericho's face was, as usual, expressionless. Rafe's held a look that on another man might have been called wistful. Ivadelle stood her ground until Jericho curtly dismissed her, and then, reluctantly, she left.

"What was that you were saying about building a room onto the overseer's house? If I was you, friend, I'd not put it off much longer."

She was barefooted, Jericho noticed. The pesky little minx was swaddled right up to her chin in that dowdy-looking frock, with her hair heaped on top of her head like a bloody tiara, and she had no shoes on!

Minutes later, still fuming, Jericho saw Rafe off and then battened himself into his study, the one room in the house that was supposed to be off-limits to meddle-some females. Sara could wait. He fully intended to settle with her later, but at the moment he had more pressing things to consider.

The carpenter hired on to see to repairs to the roof and chimneys had come by earlier that morning at his request to talk about adding a room onto the overseer's house. When he'd told Ivadelle about it, thinking she'd be pleased, she'd been mad as a scalded cat. What the devil did the woman want, a bloody mansion all to herself? And then Rafe had stopped by and added his half cent, which had made things worse.

As if all that weren't enough, just this morning he'd had a letter from an acquaintance who owned shares in five merchant ships in the West Indies trade, offering him a captaincy. The seagoing profession being a fairly close-knit community, Jericho happened to know that particular bunch of shareholders was too tight-fisted to lay out blunt to see their fleet in good repair. As for their crews, for the most part they were little but jail sweepings, shanghaied from the lowest waterfront dives.

But God, it was tempting. To have nothing more to deal with than a surly, inexperienced crew, a wallowing old tub, and a flock of greedy shareholders. Throw in a wild Caribbean storm and a few hard nor'easters for good measure . . .

Lord a'mighty, it was tempting.

Moving to one of the two tall windows in the walnut-paneled room, he stared out over the acres that generations of Wildes had reclaimed from the swamp. What did he know about farming? All he knew was the sea.

Yet, could he honestly deny that he was beginning to feel the pull of this rich, fertile land? Land that without careful stewardship would swiftly revert to its

primeval state? Besides, these acres, at least for the
time being, bore his name.

Unfortunately, the land wasn't all that bore his
name.

There was Sara. His wife, taken in haste for reasons
that now seemed flimsy as a muslin mainsail. And the
damnedest part of it was that he was finding it all but
impossible to apply the same cold logic to his marriage
that he applied to every other aspect of his life.

For one thing, he had yet to confront her with the
trick she had played on him. If that Maulsie creature
had anything to do with it, he never would. The woman
hovered over Sara like a broody hen with one chick.

Five days ago he had set out to confront her, only
to stray so far off course he had come damned close to
foundering. He'd been lucky to escape with his clothes,
much less his dignity.

Since then he had come to certain conclusions, the
first of which was that if Sara had lied because she
was frightened of the future—and given her circumstances, if all else she had told him was true, he could
understand that—why, then, he might find it in his
heart to forgive her.

On the other hand, if she had lied simply to trap
herself a husband, he would send her packing so fast
her boot heels would smoke. It had been the Moyer
woman who had set him to thinking about an annulment. The thought hadn't set well at all. Had made
him mad as hell, in fact. He had gone too far to salvage
Sara's good name to now deliberately ruin it, no matter
what she had done.

Besides, the truth was—and it complicated things all
out of reason—he *liked* the woman. No matter what

she was or what she had done, she had more grit than most men he knew. The average woman with a roof over her head would have stayed put and suffered the consequences. Not his Sara. She had far too much pride.

She was kind, too—that much he did know. And loyal.

Not to mention so damned desirable that half the time, she had him clenched up hard as a hickory bowsprit, just thinking about what was under those prim gowns and all those layers of underpinnings.

An annulment . . .

Did that carry the same stigma as a divorce? Not having known anyone whose marriage had been legally set aside by either means, he wasn't sure. At any rate, before he considered either course, he would allow her a hearing, which was only fair. No one had ever said of Jericho Jefferson Wilde that he was not a fair man.

With that worthy thought, Jericho allowed himself a tot of French brandy to celebrate. He even toyed with the notion of logging his decisions, the way he had done when he was captain of his own ship. He would reach a decision, act on it, then log the action taken. It was an orderly process. He was by nature an orderly man.

"Then how the bloody hell did you get yourself in such a disorderly mess?" he muttered. Unfortunately, he was coming to realize more with each passing day that the world he lived in was not an orderly place.

Downing his brandy with no appreciation for its quality, he swore for a while and then poured himself a second drink, half tempted to pack his seabag and set out for the nearest port.

*      *      *

Having declared herself officially recovered, Sara lost no time in assuming her duties. In a council of war with Hester and Maulsie, it was determined that Hester would continue to serve as housekeeper, a position she had held since working her way up from second kitchen maid. She would have two helpers and a man available for heavy work whenever necessary.

Maulsie would run the kitchen with the aid of one or possibly two girls. Sara made a mental note to speak to Jericho right away about securing the needed help.

Big Simon was, strictly speaking, not her problem. Mr. Moyer, whom she had yet to meet, had charge of the outside help, but Simon had special talents and special disabilities, and Sara made up her mind to speak to the overseer at the first opportunity.

But first she would have to speak to Jericho.

Which she would just as soon put off as long as possible.

Not until she came to Ivadelle did she admit defeat. Was the woman a guest, or a servant—or something else altogether? Was she to be a permanent fixture?

Whatever she was—and Sara wasn't at all certain she truly wanted to know—they were going to have to come to terms. Sara had been taught to respect her elders, and for the most part, she did. She had failed when it came to Noreen, and now Ivadelle was making it all but impossible. She had yet to be around the woman for more than two minutes without being made to feel clumsy, stupid and unattractive.

One would almost think it was deliberate.

Silently crossing the foyer, she whispered, "Never put off until tomorrow what scares the bejabbers out of you today." It didn't help. Not until she was about to knock on the study door did she remember her shoes. Or lack of them. However, if she ran upstairs to fetch them now, she might never screw up her courage enough to come down again.

So she rapped on the door and then opened it a crack before Jericho could tell her to shove off, which was what he told Hester whenever she tried to clean his precious sanctum.

"Jericho, I need to speak to you if you can spare me a moment."

Interrupted in the middle of staring blindly out the window at his fallow fields, Jericho scowled, having found it an effective tool when he'd been handed his first command at a time when he'd been barely old enough to grow a beard.

"Man can't even call his home his own," he grumbled. Then, turning away from the window, he said, "Well, don't just stand there, damnit. Come in, take a chair. Might as well get it over with."

Judas priest, she was something to behold. Even in that mud-yellow frock, with half her forehead stained from fading bruises, there was a quality about her that defied description. Exotic, he called it in his mind for want of a better word. Something to do with the shape of her eyes and her coloring, and the way light seemed to glow right through her.

"In here? Mmm, Hester said—"

"Is Hester in command here?"

"Well, no, but—"

"Then come aboard and step lively." Jericho pointed to a straight chair, taking perverse pleasure in seeing her scurrying to obey like the lowliest cabin boy.

Still in her bare feet. The wench had more brass than a British admiral. "Speak up, speak up, I don't have all day," he barked.

"Yes, well . . . it's about Hester," she began, and he waited, "Miss Renegar, that is."

"I do know my housekeeper's name." He was unable to repress a gleam of amusement, and she caught it. What's more, he knew the minute she did. Some of the steam went out of her pipes.

Clever little piece, she didn't miss a thing. "What's she done now? Crossed swords with that battle-ax of yours? I'll tell you here and now, Hester stays. She's been here since before I was born, and as far as I'm concerned, she'll be here until she takes her place on the hill."

The hill, Sara surmised, was the graveyard. It might be all of three feet higher than the surrounding territory. She had gone to pay her respects to the family when she had first arrived. Jericho went there, too. She'd seen him from her window, stalking through the woods with Brig trotting along behind him.

"Well. It's not much of a hill, if you ask me," she retorted, wondering how to regain control of the discussion. She had thought for a moment there that he might be relenting.

"You're right." This time there was no mistaking it. There was a definite thaw in the atmosphere. Taking a deep breath, Sara plunged ahead before he pokered up again. "First, about Hester. She needs help. This house is too much for one woman, even without the laundry and the cooking. I'd like to hire on two women to help her, and at least one girl for Maulsie in the kitchen. Maulsie's a grand cook. Hester hates cooking."

She waited for an argument, and when none was forthcoming, launched her next topic. "Now, about Big Simon—"

"Squared away. He knows his duties and is satisfied with conditions. You might as well know, I hire, I don't buy. Free blacks and slaves don't do well together."

"Oh. Um—well, I agree. Now, as I was saying—"

"You need help in the house. That's not unreasonable. It's a big place, and it hasn't had the care it needs in more than a year. My sister couldn't afford it." It pained him to admit it, which was one of the reasons he did. He didn't believe in sparing himself. "Hire on as many hands as you need. You'll want to send off to Elizabeth City. I'll make arrangements. Now, is that all?"

"Not exactly." Sara screwed up her courage. "About Ivadelle—Jericho, how long—"

He left the window, and for the first time, Sara got a good look at his face. In the weak November sunlight, he looked tired. Older than she knew he was. "Leave Ivadelle to me, if you please."

Well, there was no point in arguing, she did know that much.

"Are you done?" He sounded every bit as yielding as that big iron stove in the kitchen.

Sara nodded. And then she thought better of it. "No, I'm not done. I'd like to thank you. For dragging me out of the swamp, I mean. When I fell out of the buggy." She worried her lower lip, and then plunged ahead. "I might have already thanked you for that, I don't remember, but I do appreciate it. And, um—you sat up with me right at first. Thank you for that, too."

"Hester's an old woman. She can't stand every watch."

"No. I mean, yes, of course." *Get out before you make a great big fool of yourself, Sara!*

"Is that all?"

No, it wasn't all! She wanted to say, what about the last time you came to my room, when you nearly made love to me? What about that? Was it only a mistake?

"I suppose so," she said grudgingly. Rising, she brushed the creases from her skirt. "Thank you for your time." She was tempted to add, *sir*, but didn't quite dare. The very idea of treating her this way. She had married him in good faith, and now he treated her as if she were no more than a stray cat wandered in from the alley.

Not that they even had an alley, but all the same . . .

"Sit down, Sara. You had your say. Now I'll have mine."

Halfway to the door, Sara froze. Her head lifted as if she were balancing a heavy, jeweled crown. "I'd just as soon wait, if it's all the same—you probably have dozens of things . . ."

"Sit!" he commanded, and sit she did.

# Chapter Eighteen

Now she was in for it. A dozen reasons for Jericho's seething anger ran through Sara's mind. One thing above all stood out. He had never truly meant to come back home. If he survived the duel—and he very nearly didn't—he must have planned to go back to sea, leaving her to keep his house in order and him free to take up with all those fancy women that greeted every ship that came into port.

Oh, she knew about them. Every decent woman within a hundred miles of any seaport had heard about what went on when a ship docked after weeks, or even months, at sea.

Only first he'd had to see her settled, and then one thing had led to another, and now they were stuck with the hasty bargain they had struck back at the Halfway Hotel.

"Why did you do it?" he demanded.

Puzzled, she repeated, "Do it?"

"Were you all that eager for a husband, Sara?"

What the dickens was he going on about? Archibald? "I told you why I ran away. And that Archib—"

He cut her off with a sharp gesture. "Why did you lie to me?"

Twisting her hands in her lap, Sara wondered what lie he was talking about. To her knowledge she hadn't told him a single untruth. Not that she couldn't lie with the best if the occasion called for it, but in this case, it simply hadn't. Her gaze focused on his boots as they paced a tight pattern on the bare oak floor. She pleated her skirt, trying to think of an inadvertent lie she might have told that would account for his present attitude.

"Well? Are you going to tell me Doc Withers was mistaken?"

This was getting preposterous. "Mistaken about what? He said I'd heal and I'm healing. I'm as strong as a horse and ready to take up my duties this very minute, but if you're going to complain because I've wasted nearly a week, then you'll just have to trust me to make it up t—"

"*Trust* you!"

More puzzled than ever, she wondered if he could have struck his head when he'd fallen after Titus had stabbed him in the back. It was all she could think of that might explain his weather-vane disposition that could veer from mild to stormy in the blink of an eye.

"For mercy's sake, Jericho, you've been huffing and snorting all week. If I've done something to offend you, why, then just tell me what it is and I'll try to make amends."

The boots stopped pacing. He was standing so close he was practically treading on her toes. Sara jerked her feet back under the chair and gave him back scowl for scowl. She refused to be intimidated, having had enough of that commodity to last her a lifetime.

"All right, all right, so you married in haste and now

you're repenting!" she exclaimed. "Is that my fault?"
She wasn't by nature given to violence, but right now
she wouldn't mind having a go at him with the handiest
weapon she could find.

Unfortunately, there didn't seem to be one.

"I'm *what*?" he drawled.

"Repenting! Regretting! Whatever you want to call
it. I'm sorry if you didn't get quite the bargain you
were hoping for, but, then, if you'll remember, I never
promised you anything but to lo"—she gulped, then
continued—"to honor and obey and look after your
household." His brows lowered until his snapping black
eyes were nearly hidden, but she refused to let him
interrupt until she'd had her say. "You knew when you
married me that I was plain as a mud-dauber's nest,
so you can't claim you were cheated there. I did tell
you I was sensible, and I am, only I hadn't counted on
being laid up for a week. And then there's Ivadelle—"

Her mouth snapped shut. She truly hadn't meant to
mention Ivadelle, but the woman stuck in her craw
like a mouthful of shad bones.

"Ye-ess? What about Ivadelle?" Jericho purred. He
was leaning against the mantel, one arm stretched
along its surface as he toyed with a six-forked candela-
bra. His face was in shadow, which meant that Sara
couldn't see his expression, but he fairly reeked
satisfaction.

What the devil did *he* have to feel so blooming smug
about? "Ivadelle? Well, she—well. Once we hire a
cleaning woman, we won't need her, that's what. She
doesn't do all that much dusting, anyway, if you ask
me."

"Not that I recall asking, but Ivadelle isn't here to do the dusting."

"No? Then why is she here? No, don't answer that. I don't even want to know."

Sara hunched her shoulders, wishing she had never brought up the subject. Wishing she had never come to Wilde Oaks in the first place. Never laid eyes on Jericho Wilde.

No, she didn't wish that. For whatever reason they'd been thrown together by fate, and she could never regret a single moment of what had happened since. Loving him one minute, wanting to lop off his head the next.

"Well. You go right ahead and build your—your love nest if you want to. I don't care what you do with her as long as I don't have to trip over her everywhere I turn." For good measure, she hoisted her chin in the air, which was a tactical error, because it gave her a better look at his face, and—

And he was laughing!

Sara surged to her feet. Unfortunately, she stepped on the hem of her gown, lurched forward and would have fallen on her face had not Jericho moved with the speed of lightning and caught her in his arms.

He was still laughing, which was a rarity in itself, but even before she could push herself away, his laughter faded. "Sara," he said, his arms hardening around her. "Why did you lie to me? I would've married you anyway, since I'm as much to blame for ruining your reputation as Ricketts was."

She had trouble enough breathing, much less speaking coherently. "L-lie? But I explained all that. I never lie—that is, not unless it's absolutely necessary to spare someone's feelings, but in this case I didn't—lie, that is—because I truly didn't know about his wife, else I certainly never would have—"

"You told me there might be a babe. Doc Withers says that's impossible."

"Well, there you are, then. You won't have to give your name to Archibald's baby, and I won't be waddling like a wagon full of watermelons, too fat to do my work."

His hands went to her shoulders where his fingers bit into her tender flesh. It hurt. When he began to shake her, she kicked out and then moaned as her unshod toes connected with his leather-clad shin. "Stop that!" she managed to protest. "We both know you're stronger than I am, you don't have to prove it! Just because you're my lawful husband, that doesn't give you leave to treat me like a—a—"

"Like a lying, conniving female? How else should a man treat a woman who inveigled him into marrying her by claiming she'd been bedded and might be carrying a child?" His eyes were condemning, but his hands had gentled instantly.

"Well, how was I to know I didn't catch? I could have, you know. Right now, you could be facing the possibility of housing and feeding a whole litter of little Ricketts, and you'd have no one to blame but yourself."

Jericho shook his head slowly in disbelief. "Would you care to explain your reasoning?" he asked mildly.

Sara tried desperately to think of a devastating retort, but nothing came to mind. She'd never been quick that way. "No," she whispered.

"I thought not. Madam, if you're going to swell with any man's child, it will be mine."

She swallowed hard and stared at the eye-level button on the front of his collarless shirt. It was still hanging by a thread. She was fairly certain the shirt had been washed since that memorable night, but Hester's eyes weren't what they once were. He could be missing a whole raft of buttons and she probably wouldn't have noticed.

Did he mean that bedding was to be a part of her wifely duty?

One part of her dreaded the notion. Another part, one that had been a complete stranger to her until quite recently, leapt eagerly in anticipation.

Forcing herself to remain calm, she said, "Well, at least the hurting part's over and done with."

"I beg your pardon?" He slipped his hands from her shoulders until they rested on her hips, and then he leaned back against a bookcase, bringing her into dangerously close contact with his . . . parts.

Sara nearly strangled. She could feel her face burning, but somehow she managed to hang onto her composure. She was no longer an ignorant girl, after all. "You probably don't know this," she confided earnestly, "but with women—well, it's different. At least I think it is. But maybe men feel pain the first time, too. Was it that way with you?"

It was Jericho's turn to gape. "Sara, didn't your mother ever, um—explain things to you?"

"You mean about the marriage act?"

Wordlessly, he nodded.

"I was only eleven when she died, and she'd been sickly for years before that, so naturally we didn't talk about—about that sort of thing. Later, after I'd grown up, there was Noreen. My stepmother. We didn't really do all that much talking about anything, but I have this friend who went off to Illinois and got married, and she wrote me all about it." Relieved to be back in control of the situation, she said gently, "I expect you've done the marriage act several times. You're certainly old enough, and I know how it is with sailors."

"You do?"

"And not only sailors. I've heard most men keep mistresses, and now that you're fixing to set up a place for Ivadelle—"

"I am?"

"Well, yes. You said so, didn't you?"

He looked for a moment as if he'd swallowed a plug of tobacco. "Leave Ivadelle to me, if you please."

"That's what I'm trying to tell you," Sara explained patiently. "I'm hardly a child, Jericho. I *do* know how these things work. You probably want an heir, which I can understand, and that's a part of my duty. I just wanted you to know that I understand—"

"Yes? Just what is it you think you understand, Sara?"

"Well, that I—that is, that you and Ivadelle—but first, I reckon you and I need to—ummm . . ."

"I need to get my heir on you first, is that what you're trying to say? And then I can take on as many mistresses as I can satisfy?"

Satisfy. The word brought on a whole raft of emotions, few of which Sara understood. One thing she did understand, however, was that having given her word, she was obligated to stand by it. When a woman had nothing to cling to but pride, her word of honor was everything.

"Then, I suggest we get started on it," Jericho said,

and before she could take in his meaning, he was propelling her toward the door.

Sara grabbed the door frame and held on. "Now?" she protested, peering back over her shoulder.

"Why not?"

"Well—well, for one thing, it's not even dark yet."

"I have it on good authority that heirs can be got around the clock."

"Yes, but—what about tonight's dinner? I was going to talk to Maulsie about what kind of foods you particularly like."

"I'm not all that hard to please."

"You're not?"

She cast him one despairing look over her shoulder, and Jericho came close to relenting. Either she was shockingly ignorant, or she was still trying to deceive him. For the life of him, he couldn't figure out what she had to gain by pretending to be experienced. It wasn't as if he wouldn't discover the truth for himself as soon as he could shuck her out of that hideous gown and spread her thighs.

So it had hurt, had it? He didn't know what Ricketts had done to her, but he knew what the old sot had *not* done.

"Hester?" Sara cried out as he hurried her through the foyer.

"Never mind, Hester," he said when the housekeeper peered around the parlor door. "Sara and I have some unfinished business to attend. We'll be down directly."

"You didn't have to say that," Sara whispered fiercely. "Now they're all going to know what we're doing!"

"You'd rather have an audience?"

"Jericho! For mercy's sake—!"

"Hester'll find some way to keep the other two down-stairs if she has to anchor 'em to the kitchen stove."

Sara's shoulders fell. She sighed. Then, lifting her skirts, plodded barefooted up the stairs with Jericho right behind her, watching the way her hips swayed with every step, inhaling the faint essence of citrus and spice that always seemed to follow her.

He felt his enthusiasm begin to rise. He would bed her, all right. Plain and straightforward, at least the first few times. Once she'd had time to forget whatever perversity Ricketts had practiced on her, he might ex-plore a few of the more pleasurable variations, for he'd been well instructed in how to please a woman by women whose business was pleasure.

Sara had obviously not been instructed on how to please a man, which made it all the more curious that she pleased him so very much. Making no attempt at all to be seductive, she poked up the fire, closed the curtains and then turned down the bed, folding back the covers with mathematical precision and then fluffing up the pillows.

Jericho braced his shoulders against the door, watch-ing in amusement and growing arousal as she marched around the room, checking to see that the pitcher was filled just as if she were an efficient housemaid instead of a woman about to be bedded by her husband for the first time.

She lifted a quilt off the rack and unfolded it. He was about to tell her that she wouldn't be needing that to keep her warm when she flung it over the mirror.

Coming away from the door, he said, "What the devil is that for?"

"The quilt?" And then she blushed. Even in the dim light, he could see her embarrassment. "Oh. Well, my friend from Illinois—remember, I told you about her?" He nodded, wondering what kind of harebrained hoodoo he was going to hear next. "She read this book, all about houses of—*you know*—in London? You probably won't believe it, but there's one that actually has mirrors all around the bed. Can you imagine anything so— well, so embarrassing?"

Jericho could see right off that his bride was going to need a masterly hand to overcome a shocking degree of ignorance, not to mention all the misinformation coming out of the state of Illinois.

"Sara, come here," he commanded in a quiet, commanding tone. Dutifully, she came and stood before him, still buttoned up to the chin, her arms covered all the way to her wrists. "Do you want to undress, or shall I do it for you?"

"Undress?" She screwed up her face, still fiery red, and looked him right in the eye. He gave her half marks for courage. "Are you sure you want to get it done right now? I mean, we could always, um . . . go for a walk or something. With the sun and all, I expect it's real warm outside, and—"

"Sara?"

"What?"

"Kindly hush up. Now turn around and let me unbutton you, and then, if you're of a mind to, you can do the same for me."

Never before had Jericho realized just how little he knew about dealing with a woman. Leastwise, with a decent woman. All his adult life, with a few brief exceptions, he had lived solely among men. It had been his experience that at times like this, a man simply made his choice, paid his money, and followed the whore to her quarters, where nature took its course without all this backing and filling.

The women of his experience had known their business. Invariably, they wore only a few scraps of lace that could be quickly disposed of. When it came to divesting a gentleman of his clothing, their fingers were as nimble as any dockside purse lifter.

With a sigh that gave him some idea of just how much she dreaded what was about to happen, Sara turned her back to him. Jericho was clumsy, but then, the buttons were so blasted small. Frowning, he slowly bared her back, and with each inch of skin revealed, recalled the way she had looked when he had brought her upstairs and lowered her onto the bed in the next room.

Delicate. That was the only word to describe her shoulders. She put him in mind of one of those fine jade carvings he had seen over in China—delicate as lacework, but surprisingly strong for all that.

She smelled good. As he leaned closer for a better whiff, his face brushed over her neck and he felt his shaft thrust painfully against his breeches. *Easy, cap'n. Easy as she goes . . .*

With fingers that might as well have been ten thumbs, he finally managed to unfasten the last of her confounded buttons and ease the gown off her shoulders. Her arms came up to cover the front of the flimsy scrap she was wearing underneath, even though her back was to him.

Jericho's gaze lifted to the quilt-draped mirror across the room. Unbidden, his mind painted a swift picture of what she would look like naked. He had seen her nearly so when Hester had removed her wet, muddy garments that night he had brought her home.

God, he had never been so scared in his life. He had *died* when he'd seen her lying half on her face in that blackwater swamp, her neck bent at an angle on that damned cypress knee. Even after he'd got her home— even when he knew she was still alive, he hadn't been able to leave her side. All night and half the next day he had stayed with her, touching her hand to be certain it was still warm—watching the slow rise and fall of her chest to make sure she was still breathing.

He wanted to tell her how precious she was to him, for against all that was reasonable, she was. With all her odd starts, her stubborn ways and her strange notions, she had somehow managed to get under his skin. Somewhere along the way, he wished he had taken time to learn how to talk to a woman. To really talk to a woman, about something more than how he liked his meals served or how much she charged per hour for her services.

With a soft whisper of sound, the gown slipped down over her hips and billowed out around her feet. He wondered whether to untie her petticoats or take down her hair first. Or if she would rather take down her own hair.

She stood there, still as a statue. What was she thinking? Was she dreading what he was about to do to her? He wanted to tell her not to be afraid, but then, she might be wise to be afraid. He had never before taken a virgin. He'd heard tales, though. With some, it all but took a battering ram. He could never,

ever inflict such pain on any woman. With others, he'd heard it was no more than a mosquito bite.

He hoped Sara was the latter kind, because otherwise, he would never be able to do it. His staff would shrivel right up if she so much as let out a whimper of pain, he was sure of it.

But then, perhaps not, he thought as she lifted her arms and began to take down her hair. Still with her back to him. Still without meeting his eyes.

His hands were shaking. His palms were wet. He wiped them off on his trousers and then fumbled to untie her petticoat. And then, with her hair falling over her shoulders like a heavy silk shawl, she stood before him in nothing more substantial than a pair of long ruffled drawers, a corselette with a doohickey on the stern, and a flimsy little undershirt that barely even covered her shoulder blades.

Jericho found himself shaking like a halyard in a high gale. At this rate he might even lose his priming before he'd fired off his first shot.

"Do—do you want me to help you with your buttons?" she asked in a voice so thready it was barely audible.

He cleared his throat. "No—that is, no thank you. Go to bed, Sara."

Sara peered over her shoulder in time to see him shut his eyes. He looked as if he were in pain, but he was swearing under his breath.

At least his lips were moving, and she caught a word she hadn't heard but once in her life, and that only when the boy who used to help Simon had let the ax slip and chopped off the tip of his own boot.

Obediently, she turned toward the bed, but before

she could go two steps, Jericho caught her and swung her up in his arms. He brought his mouth down on hers in a kiss that was anything but gentle, and within seconds, every rational thought she possessed had scattered.

With his lips covering her, his tongue explored her mouth. He tasted of brandy and something even more intoxicating. Something dark, mysterious, enticing.

Slowly, he lowered her feet to the floor again, and she was acutely aware of the rough, rigid tension of his body as she slithered down over him.

"Ah, Sara, Sara," he whispered against her mouth, "I don't want to hurt you, but—"

She was already hurting in ways she couldn't begin to comprehend, except that the feeling was remarkably similar to the way she felt every single time he touched her. Something between pain and the sweetest kind of pleasure. Like starving and feasting at the same time— which was plainly absurd. She kept wanting to rub against something the way a cat rubbed against a table leg. Only it was Jericho she wanted to rub against, not a piece of furniture. And since she seemed to have lost all control over her actions, she did just that.

Using his mouth, his tongue and his hands, he took her farther and farther from earth, into a strange and exciting new world. Pressing herself against him, she twisted restlessly, feeling his body shift and harden and change even as he moved against her.

Then, spreading his feet widely apart, he held her against that part of him that she had seen swell and change shape before her very eyes on more than one occasion. She grabbed his shoulders and hung on, her senses reeling. "Oh, my—" she gasped.

"Sara, I can't wait," he groaned.

"I want—please—" She didn't know what she wanted, she only knew that Jericho and Jericho alone could give it to her, and if he didn't, then she would die.

"Let me—" He eased her away and began tearing off his clothes. Buttons flew in all directions. Neither of them paid the least attention.

Sara fumbled with the buttons on his trousers. She had a dim recollection of having done this before, and she hurried instinctively, in case something happened again to interfere. "How do they—"

"This way," he rasped, and his hands replaced hers at the front of his breeches. "Don't be frightened."

Grabbing a fistful of black serge and white knitted wool, she tugged it down over his lean flanks. Her knuckles raked over warm firm flesh, roughened with coarse black hair, and she paused to stare down at what she had uncovered.

*Oh, my mercy . . .*

"Don't look at me," he said gruffly.

"But I want to look at you. I want—"

"So do I. Sweet salvation, so do I!"

And then they were both naked, and suddenly stricken with a shyness neither had ever before experienced. It lasted only a moment, but it was long enough for Sara to think, *that's not going to work. There has to be some other way to . . .*

And for Jericho to think, *she's too small. God, she's the most beautiful thing in the world, but she's too small. Her hips—that tiny wisp of curls—there's not room for me inside her.*

He nearly wept.

"Sweetheart, I don't want to hurt you—I'd never do that," he said, sounding strained, sounding hoarse, sounding hungry.

"I don't care, I'm hurting now," she wailed. "Do something. Make it go away . . . please, Rico!"

He could do that for her. At least he could take away the hunger she was feeling. It surprised him that she was even feeling it, for with all the women he had known, it was part of the performance. Part of what a man paid for—the pretense that the woman they had hired for the evening or the hour or the quarter hour felt the same fierce, driving hunger their poor salivating slob of a customer was feeling.

Common logic told him it wasn't so. Over the years, a few such women had taken the time to teach him how to pleasure them, but time was money, and he doubted if very many of them valued their own pleasure above gold.

"You're trembling," he whispered.

"So are you."

We're a fine pair, he thought ruefully. Reaching out, he lifted her carefully into his arms and said, "Don't be frightened, Sara. I'm going to lay you on the bed, and then I'll do—that is, I won't actually—" Judas, how did a man describe such things to an innocent woman without sounding depraved?

He didn't feel depraved. He only wanted to bring her pleasure. Wanted the act to be beautiful for her. Wanted to show her how much she meant to him.

Only how could he explain all that? What were the proper words? God, he was only a rough seaman!

"Sara, what I'm trying to say is that there are ways—"
Swearing silently, he lowered her to the bed. "At any
rate, it won't take long. I'll see to easing your pain,
and then"—and he vowed it was so—"I'll leave you be,
I promise."

# Chapter Nineteen

At first there was only the sound of two people breathing in gasps and small sighs. "Is this the way—?" Sara started to ask when with his hands and his mouth Jericho caused her to gasp again. Only now was she beginning to realize how much she didn't know, and she'd thought she knew everything. She was intelligent. Sensible. How could she *not* have known? Every woman was supposed to know these things, else how did babies get born?

"One of the ways," he said, his voice deep and rough, like torn brown velvet. He placed a chaste kiss on the very tip of her breast, his own flesh leaping to feel her grow turgid under his lips.

One part of Jericho's mind was caught up in wondering exactly what it was Ricketts had done to her—for the man had surely done *something*. He'd been pulling on his clothes when his wife had come for him—his legal wife, that was.

"Sara, tell me what you want," he whispered.

Staring at him helplessly, she said, "But I thought *you* knew."

The scent of her body rose around him. He was kneeling beside the bed she was lying on, when he would far rather be in it. With her. Atop her. Or beneath her, with her astride his hips.

But all that could wait. He had promised to pleasure her without hurting her—without disgusting her. Without repeating whatever perversity Ricketts had practiced on her.

Unless she happened to have liked it.

It wasn't seemly to talk about such things. Even a man of his own limited experience knew that much. Yet there was something inside him—some nasty little worm of curiosity—that kept gnawing away at his brain. Which only went to show that a man could as easily sink below as rise above his own expectations.

"Did he kiss you—here?" he asked, kissing, and then suckling her other breast. Her whole body seemed to lift right off the bed. She shook her head rapidly.

"He didn't do that, but he, um—pinched my bosom."

"That was when he hurt you?"

"N-not really." She was clutching fistfuls of sheet, her body stiff and unyielding, limbs clamped together, arms at her sides. "My night shift was all bunched up over my bosom, so his fingers didn't really hurt very much."

He hadn't even undressed her, then. The bloody old fool. "Where exactly did he hurt you, Sara? If you'll tell me, I'll do my best not to . . ." He had never felt so clumsy in his life. She was so small, so vulnerable. That any man had ever taken indecent liberties with her body infuriated him. That one of the men who intended to do just that was himself, infuriated him even more.

"You're my wife, Sara," he reminded her, reminding himself at the same time.

"I know." She addressed the ceiling instead of him, as if she were embarrassed. "Then if you must know, it was my fingers."

Her fingers.

"Your *fingers?*"

"You see, Archibald's knees—"

Her fingers and his *knees?*

Judas priest, he thought he had heard it all, living cloistered aboard ship for weeks at a time. "I'm sorry, Sara. It's truly none of my business. I only wanted to be sure I didn't hurt you in the same way, or give you a disgust of this whole—er, marital business." He found he couldn't use the crude terms that were common currency aboard ship for what he was about to do to her.

"Yes, well—you probably won't. I mean, you're not even sharing my bed, are you? Archibald didn't mean to hurt me, I'm sure. He was a very kind man. But the bed wasn't very wide, and he was scrambling around and muttering—I believe he must have had too much to drink—and then his nightshirt sort of got tangled up and he fell on top of me, and when I offered to move over to make more room, his knee came down on my hand and bent my fingers backward into the mattress, and it . . . well, it hurt." She was still staring up at the ceiling, her chin thrust out as if to say, laugh if you must bedamned to you!

Instead of laughing, Jericho rested his brow on the mattress, the top of his head brushing her hip as the last piece of the puzzle slipped into place. He had married an idiot. A blooming, blithering innocent who truly thought babies came from mashing fingers. She hadn't lied. Criminally uninformed she might be, but at least she hadn't lied to him.

After a moment he felt something brush against his hair. He froze. His shaft, which was already standing at half-mast after her absurd revelations, drooped farther.

And then he felt her fingertips touch his scalp. Tentatively. As if she weren't sure he would be pleased with the small liberty she was taking.

God, yes, he was pleased! He was thrilled right down to his small toe that she was willing to touch him anywhere. He had a job of educating to do, but it had been his experience that a raw recruit could be shown a task far easier than he could be told.

And so he set out to show her.

Coming up onto the bed, he sat beside her at first, taking her hand in his. One by one, he began to stroke her fingers, dipping in between them, his fingertips straying now and then across her palm. "Sara, I'm going to lie down beside you. I did that before, if you'll remember. I didn't hurt you then, did I?"

"No," she said thoughtfully. "And this time, no one's apt to shoot at us."

It occurred to Jericho that, while he knew his way around any number of whorehouses both here and abroad, when it came to courting a respectable woman, he was in a league with the cat who sat down to tea with the bishop. Somewhat out of his element.

Carefully, he lay down beside her, shifting so that his left leg touched her right one. She was smooth as silk. He was inclined to be hairy. Just one of the many differences between them that excited him almost beyond bearing.

When he was sure he could speak calmly, he said,

"If you were to move closer, you could rest your head on my shoulder."

"Mmm," she murmured, and edged an inch closer.

Jericho forced himself to be patient, to think before he made his next move. But patience didn't come easy. His member had snapped to attention again and was eagerly tenting the bedcovers. Which made him glad he hadn't opened the curtains after all, for he was coming along far too nicely to risk scaring her off.

Kissing. A man could hardly go wrong kissing. So propping himself up on one arm, he leaned over and kissed her lips, and then her eyes, and her temples. Next he allowed his lips to stray down the side of her neck to the small hollow at the base of her throat.

He touched her with the tip of his tongue, savoring the sweet-salt flavor of her skin, which only made him hungry for more. Emboldened by the pulse he felt throbbing there, he eased one hand aboard her belly, spreading his fingers so that his thumb touched her navel at the same time his fingertips tangled in the small nest of golden brown curls between her thighs. He had large hands. She was a small woman.

He was large in other respects, as well, and therein lay the problem. He had vowed not to hurt her, and yet . . . "Sara, can you spread your legs for me?"

She started to speak and then stopped. Started to obey, but then clamped her thighs tightly together, capturing his invading hand. He could hear the breath seething between her teeth, and it thrilled him to know that she might be feeling something of the same sort of excitement that he was.

The scent of sexual arousal drifted up around them,

mingling with the scent of her hair, her skin—his own muskiness. The scent alone nearly did him in.

Patience, he warned himself. You're almost there now. Easy as she goes . . .

He slipped three fingers between her tightly clasped thighs. "There now, shhh," he whispered, soothing her with small murmuring sounds as he continued to explore. Her eyes were shut as if to deny what was happening to her, and he felt a small surge of pity for any maiden setting forth on this particular voyage for the first time without a chart, much less a compass.

God knows what that friend of hers from Illinois had told her, but it had obviously never prepared her for the simple truth. Ricketts, he discounted altogether. The bumbling old fool had probably never even got close to home port.

She was small, hot and slick, her body ready even if she didn't realize it. Finding the nugget of pleasure he sought, he began to stroke the soft folds around it, tugging this way and that, teasing but never quite touching the tiny man in the boat, though it was standing boldly now, eagerly demanding attention.

He entered her with a single finger, feeling her fright as if it were his own. *Easy, mate—warp alongside gently now, and then board her boldly.*

Moving over her, he lowered himself carefully, letting her feel his weight, easing gently into position . . . He had it all laid out in his mind, having gone through more or less the same maneuver scores of times over the years.

But this was Sara. This was his very own wife, not some nameless female whose body he could rut on for a small price and then walk away from without a second thought.

Already fit to burst his own skin, he felt himself grow even larger, felt himself brush against her sweet, steamy jungle. He groaned.

Sara gasped. She pushed against his shoulders and at the same time, clamped his body between her thighs. Jericho recognized the conflicting action as a defensive reflex, meant to keep him from going deeper. Instead, it sent him over the edge. As she began to thrash around beneath him, he eased into her. Gently at first, only far enough to pin her in place. He had barely broached her when the exquisitely sensitive tip of his shaft felt her maiden's veil. Closing his eyes, he whispered a single oath, fighting the compulsive temptation to ram through.

*You promised,* he reminded himself. *You vowed never to hurt her.*

His heart was pounding hard enough to shake the whole bed. His tortured lungs caught and held his breath, and he hovered there for one small eternity, praying he wouldn't disgrace himself by firing off too soon.

And then Sara took things into her own hands, quite literally. He never knew if she meant to help matters along or cover herself against deeper intrusion, but when she wedged a hand down between them, when her fingertips blundered onto the root of his manhood, Jericho lost his last feeble hold on sanity. With one wild cry, he pierced her, then drove into her again and again, deeper and deeper, faster and faster, oblivious to all but the mindless race for release.

The end was inevitable. Almost from the first moment, he could feel it overtaking him. Glowing. Pulsating like the great northern lights. Finally, exploding over him in wave after splendid wave.

With a long, shuddering gasp, he braced himself on his forearms. Buried deeply inside her, he hung on, holding her safe. Holding them both safe against the drugging, drowning power.

Eventually he became aware once more of his surroundings. Of the woman beneath him, nearly crushed under the weight of his sated body. Of the sweat that covered them both. Of her startled eyes staring up at him as if she had never seen him before.

"Is—that it?" she asked finally, her voice no more than a whisper against the harsh rasp of his own breathing.

Jericho swore silently. Holding her tightly, he rolled onto his side, carrying her with him, pressing her soft, hot body against his. He was still inside her and swelling again, but he knew to his vast sorrow that she wasn't ready for another go at it.

Might never be, under the circumstances.

His conscience bade him apologize, but he could no more shape the proper words than he could fly. "I reckon so," he said, which was neither apology nor explanation, but simply the best he could do at the moment.

"Well," she said, and with that one small utterance, stole what was left of his heart right out of his breast.

Sara didn't know whether to feel proud or offended. So this was the true marriage act, she thought. Carrie had been right about the pain, but she had left out all the other feelings. The sense of being a part of another human being—being joined for a little while in ways that had nothing to do with bodies.

Which was fanciful, to say the least. And Sara had never been the least bit fanciful. All her life she had prided herself for her sensibility, but if there was anything sensible about hanging onto a man's body while he did things to her that defied description and passed all understanding—if there was anything sensible about wanting him to do it to her all over again—why, then, she didn't know what it was.

So she settled for curling up in his arms and going to sleep, feeling safe and warm and wanted.

Feeling wanted. It was the next best thing to being loved . . . wasn't it?

Jericho split kindling. He wasn't particularly good at it, as it was a skill not often required of seamen. But it was hard physical work, and he felt a real need for hard physical activity.

The air was warm for November. Brisk, but still warm in the sun. With no wind at all, the smell of burning swamp was barely discernible. He could smell the rich scent of alluvial earth, the sweet, dry smell of corn in the crib. The resinous scent of pines and cedars, and the dusty scent of the pecan trees that lined the drive path and the massive water oaks that gave the place its name. Only now was he beginning to realize how much he had missed the smell of all those things during his years away from home.

Home . . .

Another puzzle that had taken root in his mind. Was home the farm where he had spent the first thirteen years of his life, or the sea, where he had spent the next twenty-odd years?

Or was home the woman whose bed he had so recently left, amazed to discover that it was still broad daylight outside?

Sara. It had seemed so simple when it had all started. She was a decent woman. She had needed him. He'd needed someone to look after Wilde Oaks now that Louisa was gone. So he'd married her, never thinking beyond the duel. And now he had a wife.

Wiping the sweat from his brow, Jericho stared up at the bedroom window, wondering if she was still asleep. Wondering if she'd taken a disgust of him. He wouldn't blame her if she had. He was a great gawking hulk without any of the fancy manners women liked in a man. He didn't know how to choose his waistcoats and cravats and all the colorful trimmings Rafe set such store by, and so he settled for owning two suits, both black, two cravats, both black, and five shirts: three of white linen, two of black wool.

He possessed two pairs of boots, neither with the neat banded tops of contrasting leather that were worn by fancy gentlemen on both sides of the Atlantic. Although one pair did sport a fanciful pattern of salt stains.

Oh, he was a great hand when it came to getting along with menfolk. He could spin a yarn with the best of them. He had earned the respect of those who knew him and those who knew only of his reputation. He knew his ships, he knew his men, his cigars and his whiskey.

But when it came to knowing women, he was dead in the water.

Except in whorehouses. He knew what was expected of him there. The women knew what was expected of them, so without bothering with much in the way of small talk, they got down to the business of fornication.

But none of that was much help to him now. How did a man deal with a woman like Sara? He couldn't deny she heated him up quicker than any high-class whore in the fanciest French bordello, but he could hardly treat her like one. She was a decent woman. She was also stubborn as a harness-galled ox.

On the other hand, he reckoned stubbornness might be called a virtue if it meant giving her word and sticking by it. If it meant loyalty to two old freed blacks who had raised her from a baby. If it meant riding hell-bent for leather to tend to a husband who'd had the misfortune to get himself sliced up in a duel, and who didn't much want to be tended to in the first place.

Stubbornness, Jericho concluded, wasn't entirely a bad thing as long as a person was stubborn about the important things in life.

A flicker of movement caught his attention. Shading his eyes with one hand, he glanced up at the window in time to see the curtains twitch open. There she stood, her hair down over her shoulders. Their eyes met and held, and Jericho thought, not for the first time, that his wife was a beautiful woman.

Beautiful to him at least—even in that brown frock she wore more often than not. Nine men out of ten might pass her by without even seeing her on account of she was so small and she didn't do anything to draw attention to herself the way most women did.

But the tenth man—and by that, Jericho meant himself—would see the depth of her tilted brown eyes and the way the sunlight snagged there and sparkled. The way her small, pointed chin could square up when she was crossed. The way her lips quivered just before she laughed, and the way . . .

He sighed, still gazing up at the woman who was his wedded and bedded wife. She would stay by him, all right, because she was a dutiful woman.

Only suddenly, he found that he wanted more from her than mere duty. He wanted her to feel the way he was beginning to feel. Light-headed. Hollow-chested. Wild as a possum drunk on strong corn mash. He wanted her to feel a pulse throbbing in her groin when she thought about lying naked in a bed with him, and maybe even making a baby together.

She left without even smiling down at him, and Jericho went back to splitting kindling. At this rate they'd soon have enough to fire every stove in Pasquotank County.

The next morning, Ivadelle shoved her hairbrush in the pocket of her best apron, knotted a silk shawl about her shoulders and headed for the second-floor portico. The house faced east. The sun would be slanting across the southeast corner about now, making it a perfect place to dry her hair.

She'd set the old bat to heating water before the breakfast dishes were even washed, as soon as she heard that Rafe was riding over to speak to Jericho about a mare and a team of mules that had come up for sale in the next county.

Ivadelle was nothing if not practical. After yesterday, when Jericho had taken that mousy wife of his to bed in the middle of the day, she had finally faced the fact that he was going to keep her. And while she had no real objection to married men, Hiram would kill her if she got in trouble again.

Besides, why settle for another woman's husband when with a little more effort, she could have one of her own?

Settling herself on the rail, she spread her full skirt and began to brush. She didn't really hold with all this hair-washing nonsense—working talcum powder into her scalp and brushing it out again did just as well, and on hair as pale as hers, it didn't even leave a dulling film. But there was nothing at all romantic about letting a man see clouds of dirty talcum settling on a woman's shoulders.

So she'd washed, using a bar of Sara's scented soap, timing everything so that she would be caught in the act. What could be more innocently seductive than a woman drying her hair in the morning sunshine? It wasn't as if she'd dragged a chair out into the front yard so that anyone riding up the drive path would be sure to see her. A second-floor portico was private, almost an extension of the sleeping rooms, even though it did open out over the front yard.

Rafe wouldn't have been her choice as a husband, or even as a lover. He was too sure of himself, and he had a way of laughing with his eyes that made her feel uncomfortable. As if he knew precisely what she was thinking.

Besides, she wasn't at all certain she could manage him. Jericho now—he was another matter. Strong as a bull, dark and exciting to look at, he was a babe in the woods when it came to women. She could have had him jumping through hoops in no time at all if he hadn't gone and married that little nobody.

It had all sounded so perfect when Hiram had come home and described the place. Within easy driving distance of a nice little town, but set off to itself with only one close neighbor. The two farms, Wilde's and Turbyfill's, took up all the land for five miles in any direction. And both landowners were single. A woman didn't get a chance like that more than once in a lifetime.

"I'll have a free hand," Hiram had told them both, his wife and sister, over supper the night he got back from his interview. "Wilde's been to sea most of his life, don't know much about farming, but that's all to the better. I've got me some ideas I'd like to try out, rotating corn with beans and round about again."

Bess had wanted to know about the house, right off. Hiram had described the main house and the tidy cottage set aside for the overseer. Right way, Ivadelle had known which of the two she preferred.

"Be glad to get away from this town, I can tell you right now. I ain't much for listening to town talk, but when it gets so a man can't walk down the street without hearing tongues a-wagging about his womenfolk, why it's time to pull up stakes and move on."

Ignoring his wife, Bess, who reminded Ivadelle of Sara, come to think of it, he'd glared accusingly at his sister, as if she were to blame for everything.

If anyone was to blame, it was Bess, Ivadelle thought rancorously. She'd been after Ivadelle to find herself a husband ever since Ivadelle had moved in with her newly married brother and his bride three months earlier, after Aunt Martha had died and left everything to

HALFWAY HOME          305

her scapegrace son instead of to the niece who had
nursed the old sow through her last interminable
illness.

"Well, how was I to know Edward was married? Is
it my fault his wife was spending the summer visiting
her folks up in New England and he clean forgot to
mention her existence?"

She had loved Edward, and thought he loved her.
He had told her so. And she had allowed him to teach
her things about her own body that no decent single
woman would even dream about, much less enjoy, until
she screamed with pleasure.

Naturally, the whole town had found out about it,
and Hiram had threatened to send her out to Indian
lands to marry the first man fool enough to take her.

He hadn't really meant it. All the same, it had been
a bad time. Edward's wife had come home and the talk
had started up all over again, and Hiram had quit the
job he had held for seven years to apply for one far
enough away so that no one would have heard about
his immoral sister.

The minute Ivadelle had heard that the owner of
Wilde Oaks was a bachelor, she had set her sights on
marrying him and becoming mistress of the mansion
Hiram had described. Only things hadn't worked out
quite the way she had planned. The place was a mansion, all right, only it was in sad need of refurbishing.
All that dark, heavy old mahogany and walnut would
have to go. She was already planning where to start as
soon as Hiram could supply her with enough house
slaves when that little trollop had turned up, claiming
she was married to Captain Wilde.

At first Ivadelle had thought she was lying. Had

*wanted* her to be lying. It had ruined everything, just when she'd managed to talk Hiram into letting her move into the main house.

Bess, of course, had helped. Her sister-in-law had never liked her, and the feeling was entirely mutual.

For a little while she had thought she might still pull it off. It was a strange marriage, right from the first, with the bride coming home two days after her wedding without her husband.

And then Sara had gone haring off, and a week later, her fool of a husband had come home, bringing his bride over his shoulder as if she were no more than a deer he had field dressed. That was bad enough, because he refused to leave her side.

But the final blow came when he finally bedded the stupid little twit. And in the middle of the afternoon, no less, with people all around to hear what was going on, plain as day.

In Ivadelle's experience, the act had seldom taken more than a few minutes. But then, with Edward, there had always been that certain furtiveness involved. She had lain with him three times before she discovered he was married, and by that time she'd been so deeply in love she would have spread herself for him in the middle of McPherson Road on Market Saturday at high noon.

What a fool she had been. She, who could have taken her pick of the single men, she had the misfortune to fall in love with a married man. Not only a married man, but a married minister.

The sound of a horse trotting up the drive path caught her attention, and she resumed brushing, allowing strands of her pale blond hair to trail across the brush and drift down over her shoulders. *Look at me*, she willed. *Up here, Mr. Turbyfill, you with your knowing look and your fancy clothes. You might not be the man Jericho is, but I'll bet even so, you know what to do with a woman. No wife of yours would have to knock you over the head to get your attention.*

Mr. and Mrs. Rafael Turbyfill. Squire and Mrs. Turbyfill? Well, why not? With her behind him, there was no reason why he couldn't rise to a position of power in this miserable corner of the state.

Jericho, trying to concentrate on all the things he wanted to go over with his overseer later on in the day, heard Brig barking outside the window. Hiram must be early. Brig was fiercely protective of those people he considered his. He tolerated Rafe, just barely, but he still hadn't made up his mind about the Moyers. Except for Ivadelle. She didn't like the dog any better than the dog liked her, which was just as well. Jericho had too much on his mind to worry about how Louisa's dog treated an uninvited guest.

He thought of the way the retriever had taken up with Sara right off, which was strange. And then he thought about Sara herself, forgetting Rafe and Brig and the overseer as he went over what had happened upstairs in his bedroom the day before.

He had bungled it. Like the rawest recruit, he had barged in with guns blazing, fired off a round and then struck his colors before the battle was even engaged.

No wonder she didn't think much of what she called the marriage act. If he were a wife, he wouldn't, either. He had started out so carefully, arousing her slowly until she was almost ready for him. And then he had jumped the gun.

They both had a lot to learn. By all rights, he should be the teacher, she the student. He was the one with experience, after all. On the other hand, he could hardly go wrong if he set to courting her, could he? Not that he was any great hand at courting, either.

Wine . . . he could serve her wine. Ladies liked sweet wine.

And flowers. Rafe wasn't the only man that could being flowers to a woman. He'd get Hester to order him some—she'd likely know how to go about it.

And he'd talk to her, get to know her. Say things like, "I like the way you smell." He could tell her that. Maybe even, I like the way you taste.

No, better start out with something less personal. I like the way you move? I like the way you twitch your behind when you climb the stairs, even though I know damned well you don't mean to do it?

I like your gentleness, your strength? The way you stand by your friends? I like the way you accept the way things are instead of bellyaching about the way they might have been?

He did admire that about her. She was solid as a six-foot oak keelson, but that didn't seem a courtly thing to say to a lady.

Should he tell her he liked the way she sighed when he kissed her and forgot for a little while to close her eyes and then scrunched them up tight so that her lashes stuck out like a hedgerow? That he nearly came apart when her hands went to fluttering over his shoulders like a pair of birds set loose from a cage?

Maybe he would log it all first—write it all out to fix it in his mind.

Watching her while she slept yesterday, lying on her side with one knee drawn up and one fist against her mouth, he had felt himself begin to harden again and wondered what she would say if he told her how he felt when he was inside her. Like he was standing on top of the world and about to jump off.

He'd been tempted to slide into bed beside her and try her again, but she would be too tender.

Outside he heard Rafe's voice, and then Ivadelle's and that reminded him of something else he had to do. Before he set about courting his wife, he was going to get that woman out of his house, if he had to drive her all the way to Elizabeth City and set her up in the Indian Queen Hotel. He'd nearly tripped over her when he'd left the bedroom yesterday. The look on her face had been . . .

He didn't know what it had been. All he knew was that one way or another, she was leaving.

# Chapter Twenty

Some thirty-odd miles away, in the best bedroom of the widow Geppart's house, Titus Smithers sipped his bimbo, a deceptively mild concoction of brandy, sugar and lemon, while he plotted his revenge. On the table beside the bed was a bowl of congealed pork stew and a slab of cold corn bread.

Food did not interest him. Ever since he'd realized that he was not going to die, he had been planning for the future, and those plans were better fueled by drink than by food.

Although he still kept up the pretense of being an invalid, through sheer determination he had managed to regain nearly all his strength. If the widow knew just how far along the road to recovery he'd come, she'd have had him back in her bed long before now. Alice, like her late husband, was known for her hospitality, but sooner or later a man was expected to repay that hospitality, and Titus knew he wouldn't escape scot-free.

He was not looking forward to it. His mind was on more important matters. But he would pay the piper, in case he ever needed to dance to her tune again.

At least his mother had gone back home. If he'd had

to put up with her carping and whining one more day, he might really have turned up his toes. After the duel—after Wilde had knifed him in the belly, John Ladymore had been so certain he was on his way out he had lit out for the Gepparts' place, where they had both spent many a merry time, and dumped him off there instead of carrying him the rest of the way home.

Ladymore was a fool and a coward. Always had been.

But Titus had been in a bad way, all right. More dead than alive. Alice hadn't liked the look of him anymore than Ladymore had, but she had a certain amount of loyalty to the young men who had shared her bed and board—quite literally. So she'd sent for her own physician, and then sent word to his mother to come cart off his remains.

Only he'd fooled them all. He hadn't died. Come damned close to it, with both women snapping over his carcass like two dogs with a single bone. Run a fever that liked to have set the bed on fire, but he'd come through it just fine, in spite of all their broth, brangles and basilicum. It was brandy that finally healed his gut. Plain old applejack brandy, liberally applied inside and out. Good for what ailed a man. Lubricated his thinking machine. It had come to him while he'd still been burning with fever that he'd never before been so clearheaded.

Broth, brangles, basilicum, and brandy. Damned if he weren't clever with words! Clever, clover, cleaver . . .

As clear as day, his whole future spread out before him—what he had to do first. What he had to do next, and so on.

One more day, he calculated. Two, at most. He had

finally got rid of his mother by convincing her to go home and get everything ready for his homecoming. He'd instructed her to sell that worthless pair of darkies and use the money to hire a young maid, giving her the name and direction of a slave taker he'd had dealings with in the past. In the proper hands information was worth money, and Titus was always in need of money.

As for those two lazy old sods, they'd been living off him for years. They owed him something for that. It wouldn't be the first time a free black had been taken up and resold. The old crows wouldn't bring much on the market, but there was nothing else left to sell.

Nothing left to sell. So far, Titus could only dream of a life in which he didn't have to scramble for every penny. No gentleman deserved to live like that.

But all that was about to change. Once he set his brilliant plan in motion he'd be richer than any of them. Richer than Rafe Turbyfill, richer than that railroad fellow up north, richer than President Jackson— and all thanks to some old croaker whose name he didn't even know, who'd been fool enough to hand over his entire fortune to a stupid granddaughter he'd never even laid eyes on.

Titus gulped down the last of his drink, reached for the pitcher to refill his glass and discovered it was empty. He threw it across the room. That ought to bring the old bitch scurrying up here. She ought to know better than to let his pitcher go dry.

Women! Couldn't stand 'em no more. The sight of 'em, the sound of 'em, the smell of 'em made him sick to his stomach. Made his head buzz like a damned hive of bees.

Turbyfill should have told him about Wilde. Louisa—his Wilde woman, he'd called her, the stupid drab. Wild? She was dull as a dead dog.

Or dead as a dull dog.

D-D-D. He cackled at his own wit. That was why Wilde had challenged him, wasn't it? Because Louisa had turned up her toes. Sometimes he had trouble remembering. Other times it was clear as gin. About what had happened when she'd told him she'd got caught and he had to marry her. About how he had tied up her damned dog and then invited her to walk with him in the woods . . .

He'd got more satisfaction from beating her than he ever had from bedding her. She deserved it, the stupid whore, for lying to him—for leading him to believe—

Whatever it was she'd led him to believe. Sometimes it got a bit muddled in his mind. Came from lying abed too long. Muddled a man's mind. There, he'd done it again! Muddled, man, mind. M-M-M. And B-B-B. Brangle, brandy . . . what else? Bitch?

Oh, he was a clever fellow, no doubt about that.

Her house, that was it. All her lovely money and that great big house of hers. It had impressed the devil out of him the first time he'd ridden out from Turbyfill's and seen it through the woods. All those pillars and porticoes, fanlights and dormers with the sunset reflected in every pane of glass. It had looked like a bloody palace.

He hadn't paid much attention to the condition of the place, much less to the condition of the rest of the farm. That was better left to working slubs. Overseers and the like. It was the mansion itself he'd had his heart set on, picturing himself entertaining all the fellows who enjoyed Rafe's hospitality. Yes, and he wouldn't invite Rafe, either. Serve him right for . . .

Something or other. Something unpleasant he couldn't quite put his finger on.

He did remember meeting Louisa, though. Tongue-tied, dough-faced female. He had cleverly got her to talking, though, and like the fool she was, she had told him how many acres she owned, that she was unmarried, and that since her parents had died she'd lived all alone but for one old woman.

All alone . . . He'd nearly shat his breeches. A chance like this, he'd told himself excitedly, comes once in a lifetime. That very day he had set out to court himself into a bloody fortune.

She'd been pathetically easy. He could hardly believe she was still hanging on the vine. She'd been a virgin, of course. Dull as ditch water, but adequate. He'd figured that once he had his hands on her money, he could stuff her in the attic and start living life the way it was meant to be lived. If she behaved herself, he might even allow her to come downstairs and gaze at him from time to time. Women always liked to look at him. His hair, his clothes, his face. They adored him, bless their stupid little hearts.

Oh, God, yes, he'd had it all planned. If Turbyfill had thought *his* house parties were grand, he'd turn green with envy when he saw the kind of house parties Wilde Oaks would support.

He had briefly considered changing the name from Wilde Oaks to something that included Smithers, but he'd been unable to come up with anything that sounded quite right. Smithers, smoke, smart? Smithers, smooth—

Oh, well. There was time, he'd thought. Plenty of time . . .

Time. By the time he'd found out the only dowery Louisa would bring to any marriage was her stupid self—that there was a brother who owned everything, brick, stick, and cornstalk, he had nearly gone too far with his courting. Making a hasty retreat, he had sent word by one of Rafe's grooms that he'd been called to his mother's bedside.

Instead, he'd ridden up to Geppart's for a stay. That had been just about the time—he couldn't recall too clearly at the moment—that his mother had sent word about Sara's fortune. The letter had followed him from place to place and finally caught up with him at Geppart's, just as he was wondering whether or not to settle for Geppart's widow.

Or had he been considering whether or not to try his hand with the James girl again? Old fish face and her papa's bloody fortune.

Damn, damn, damn. He wished his brain wouldn't spin quite so fast. It was one thing to be clever, quite another to be so clever he couldn't even keep up with his own thoughts.

He had gone home then, that was what he had done. And that was when everything had started falling apart. He remembered it all now. Sara had laughed at him. *Laughed* at him!

And then he had gone back to see Rafe, and Louisa had found out he was there and told him about the baby and started pestering him to marry her.

Or was it the other way around? Damn his head, anyway. He couldn't seem to shake it clear.

There was that damned dog of hers, too. Sara had had a little dog once . . .

Ha! But not for very long.

One of the first things he intended to do when he took over Wilde Oaks was tie a sack of bricks to that blasted mutt and dump him into the swamp for snapper bait.

He needed a drink. He needed a goddamned bloody drink! "Alice! Where the devil is everybody? Can't a man get any service around here?"

Slouching against the fat, feather-filled bolster, Titus fumed over the injustice of it all. He had never had a fair shake, not a single one. His own father had ruined his life, and then that mealymouthed creep his mother had married had gone and gambled away all but the roof over his head, and then Louisa had lied to him . . .

Turbyfill. He blamed Turbyfill for misleading him about Louisa. For not setting him straight before he got in too deep.

And Wilde. He could hardly remember all the reasons he hated Jericho Wilde. Owning Wilde Oaks— that was one reason. And gutting him. Leaving him for dead. That was another.

And then, in a moment of sparkling clarity, it came to him why he hated Wilde most of all. Not only did the devil own Wilde Oaks, he had married Sara and her fortune, when by rights, it belonged to Titus. Ladymore had brought him that lovely little scrap of news.

"Alice!" he shouted. Damned bitch, she was no better than the rest of them. Sara and her uppity ways, thinking she was too good for him. The James girl. Louisa and her pasty-faced prissiness. Alice, climbing all over him while he was still half dead, palming him and then mounting him and riding him to hell and back. Taking his seed like she had every right to it.

And his mother. Damn her greedy soul, she had a few things to answer to. If she thought she was going to move into that big house at Wilde Oaks after he married Sara, she was in for a little surprise.

Or maybe a big one . . .

Sara was too restless to remain indoors, even though it was fixing to rain. It had been three days since she had spoken more than a word to Jericho. He'd been avoiding her, which made her self-conscious so that she avoided him. At the rate they were going, they might as well live in different counties.

Did he regret what they had done? Well, my mercy, what were husbands and wives supposed to do with each other? She wasn't very good at it yet, but she was perfectly willing to learn.

Only evidently, he wasn't interested in teaching her.

"Hester, I'm going out for a spell," she called out as she reached for the threadbare old coat that hung behind the back door for quick trips out to the garden or the cool house or the chicken pen.

It was a good day for planting. Maybe she would dig up something in the yard and transplant it to Louisa's grave. Maybe that would please the old sobersides.

"You come right back if it commences to rain, you hear?" the housekeeper called after her, and Sara promised. At least some folks cared about her. Instead of having one woman to fuss over her, she now had two. Hester was as bad as Maulsie. The one thing they both agreed on was that Sara wasn't fit to look after herself.

"Take dat animal," Maulsie advised her, and Sara said she would. She suspected Maulsie only wanted to get him out from underfoot. The big, shaggy creature had taken to hanging around the house lately.

In fact, he had taken to hanging around wherever Sara happened to be. She rather enjoyed it.

"Here, Brig, c'mon, boy, let's go for a walk." At least *someone* appreciated her company.

Jericho had left with Hiram Moyer right after breakfast, according to Hester. Unable to help herself, Sara scanned the vast expanse of forest and fallow fields, the rows of tenant houses that were presently being reroofed, and the cow barn that was being readied for a new milker and maybe a few head of beef cattle.

It was all coming along nicely, she told herself. Evidently, Hiram Moyer was cut from a different bolt of cloth from his useless sister.

Sighing, she stared off in the direction of the overseer's cottage. Not even to herself would she admit she'd been hoping for a glimpse of her husband on that big ugly horse of his. He rode as well as he did everything else these days, now that his wound was almost completely healed.

That is to say, he moved with more grace and strength than a mortal man should be allowed. Especially one who'd spent far more time on a ship than he ever had on a horse.

Lord, he was beautiful. Sara had thought so the first

time she had ever laid eyes on him. By the time he was hers to care for, she had been completely fascinated by everything about the man.

Not that she had taken advantage of his help-lessness. She would never—

And besides, Rafe was always there to perform the most intimate tasks. But she had been the one to sponge off his back, which was broad and tanned and incredibly smooth to touch. And once she had even rubbed down his limbs when he had complained of cramping from lying in one position for too long.

She wasn't surprised. They were knotted with mus-cles under a light covering of crisp, black hair. She had remarked on how powerful they looked, and then turned fiery red at her own boldness, but he hadn't seemed to take it amiss.

"Comes from spending years standing on a moving deck," he had told her. "A body learns to compensate."

Now, swinging the shovel she had taken from the gardening shed, she wondered just how a body learned to compensate for having to do without something it had only just learned to crave.

"Hard work," she muttered, remembering all the time she had worked off her temper by chopping weeds and clumping up and down the rows of her vegetable garden behind old Blossom. "Hard work and worthy thoughts."

She selected a bush that was covered with small red berries now and would be covered with fragrant white blossoms in the spring. It would do for the foot of the grave. Come spring, when everything was in bloom, she would select something showier to go at the head.

Or rather, she would if she was still here come spring.

From a distance Jericho watched the small, industrious figure stomping down the earth around the roots of the shrub she had just set out. She did it as if she were performing a dance, holding her skirts up out of the way, twisting that delectable little rump of hers with every stomp. He had never seen a woman throw herself into her tasks so wholeheartedly. Once she set a course, nothing could sheer her off. Hoisted sail and away she went, and devil take the hindmost.

His eyes warmed in a smile that faded almost as quickly as it was born. What was he going to do about her? More to the point, what was he going to do about himself? It had been nearly twenty years since he had felt this unsure of himself. Twenty years during which he had armored himself against all tender feelings. His rather frivolous mother had been openly dismayed by his loud, boisterous ways as a boy. He had been a great disappointment to his father, and too young to do anything about it even if he'd known what to do. Only Louisa had accepted him as he was, and in the end he had failed her.

Now there was Sara. Would she, too, come to think of him as crude and wild, not fit to be among civilized people? He had long since outgrown the youthful high spirits that had made his mother flinch from him, but he was still stern, hard and unpolished. His father had been a man of letters. Jericho had been fifteen before he could teach himself to write a legible hand. A man in his position had no use for soft music, sweet poetry and drawing room manners—the things that impressed a lady.

And Sara was a lady. She claimed to have plowed behind a mule. Claimed to be able to trap a weasel and then skin the critter out once she'd caught him, but she was a lady, all right. Small, dainty, delicate—softhearted, innocent, and loyal to the bone.

Did he dare take the risk of leaving himself open to a wound that might well prove fatal? What if she came to know him better and decided she didn't want him? He wasn't a polished hand with the ladies, the way Rafe was. Rafe called her darling without even batting an eye.

Jericho's tongue wouldn't even wrap around the word. Darling. Sweetheart. Sweetpea, for God's sake!

Rafe had brought her store-bought roses. For her first wedding, Jericho had gone out and picked a handful of some weeds he found blooming on a ditch bank. For her second one, he hadn't even thought to do that much.

Sara, he thought bleakly. She deserved a gentleman, someone who could appreciate her. Someone who could give her all the things a lady should have. Jericho didn't even know what those things were.

What was he going to do about her? How long could he go on working until he was ready to drop and then drinking until he could sleep, trying to keep from returning to her bed?

"Why, it's Mr. Turbyfill," cried Hester, swinging the door wide. "You can come in and set, but they ain't here. Jericho's gone out with that overseer man, and Sara, she's gone out with Louisa's dog."

"Rain'll likely chase them home before long," Rafe said, flustering the housekeeper by kissing her on her wrinkled cheek. "Matter of fact, I've come to see Miss Ivadelle. Don't tell me she's gone, too."

Hester sniffed. Rafe grinned. Ivadelle appeared in the parlor doorway, looking as calm as if she hadn't seen him ride up on his great gray gelding. Frantically, she smoothed her hair and her skirts and pinched some color into her cheeks.

"You wanted to see me? Goodness, why ever for?"

Ivadelle felt herself begin to simper. She was too old to simper. She knew it, but she couldn't seem to stop. Just let an eligible gentleman come within range, and she began acting like a fifteen-year-old virgin at her first grown-up dance.

He had that laughing look in his eyes again. She wished she had the nerve to swat it right off his face, but she needed him too much. "And how are you this fine morning?" she cooed.

"Damp. Rain started before I even come halfway."

"Oh, dear. Would you like a—that is, shall I have someone make up the fire?" Her hands fluttered use-lessly for a moment, but at his knowing look, all pretense fell away. The man never failed to get under her skin. He did it deliberately. "Oh, for land's sake, you're not all that wet!"

Rafe decided that, with a little training, she would do very well. He liked her better when she wasn't pretending to be something other than what she was. A woman who was still beautiful but no longer young, and who knew it. A woman whose sister-in-law had made it impossible for her to live with her only relative.

A woman whose plans to snare a well-to-do husband had come to a dead end.

"I've come with a business proposition for you, my dear. Before you say anything, I suggest you hear me out."

# Chapter Twenty-one

Sara was muddy. She was also far more tired than she'd expected to be, but then, this was her first real outing since she'd recovered from being thrown from the shay. The day that had started out so fine had turned out rainy.

After a final look at the shrub she had set out, she trudged home through the drizzling rain, thinking of the woman she had never even met who had had such a profound influence on her own life.

Louisa had been tragically young to die. From what little Sara had heard, the poor girl had barely begun to experience life.

It never occurred to Sara that she was far younger than Louisa had been, and that she had never experienced much of life, either. Nor was she apt to do so, married to a man who didn't seem to know what to do with her.

Back at the house, she paused on the sheltered back porch, cracked the kitchen door a bit so that she could reach inside and hung up her coat. Her hair was soaked, for she'd gone out without a hat, and her shoes were finally, once and for all, quite beyond hope.

"Hester, do you need anything from town?" she

called out as she unlaced the poor muddy relics and tugged them off. "I've a mind to go shopping." Shoes were just the excuse she needed. She'd been itching to do something about the dark walls, the dark furniture and the dark floors in this old mausoleum ever since she'd taken her first good look around. It was a lovely home, but it could be lovelier still with a few bright touches.

Through the kitchen door she could hear the sound of Hester's thin cackle and Maulsie's rich, full-bodied laughter. "What's so funny?" Padding into the warm room in her stocking feet, she inhaled the rich smell of ham-bone soup and coffee.

"She done gone," Maulsie chortled.

Sara looked from one to the other, mystified.

"That woman," Hester clarified. "Packed her bags, left out without even saying good-bye, now ain't that a sure enough shame?" Her lined face was as composed as ever, but her faded old eyes sparkled like a pair of wet blue agates.

"But why? Did—did Jericho take her somewhere?" Sinking down onto a bench beside the massive iron range, Sara unpinned her hair and fluffed it around her shoulders to dry while Maulsie poured her a cup of coffee. Normally she would never have taken her hair down outside her own bedroom, and certainly not in the kitchen, but on a rainy day in mid-November, it seemed acceptable.

"Mmmm, I needed this," she said with a sigh, clasping the hot cup in her cold hands as she savored the heat and the aroma.

Brig nudged the door open again and poked his red shaggy head inside. Hester flapped her apron at him.

"Don't you come in here, you wet, stinking dog. Shoo! G'on outside where you belong."

Sara hid a smile when the old woman took a biscuit left over from breakfast from the basket and tossed it after him. "Now who's going to tell me what happened to Ivadelle?"

"Told you. She's gone. Tubby come and fetched her no more'n half hour ago."

"Tubby?"

"Mr. Rafael, that is. He was Tubby when he used to come sneaking into my cool room, stealing ham skins and taking 'em down to the pond to use for bait."

Sara had trouble picturing the dapper Rafe Turbyfill stealing greasy ham skins for any reason at all. At the moment, however, she was more interested in why he had stolen Ivadelle, if steal her he had. "Where were they going? What does he plan to do with her?"

"What do any man do wif a woman like dat?" Maulsie rolled her eyes.

"As to that, I'm sure I couldn't say," Hester said primly, and both women burst out laughing again. Sara wondered if they'd been sampling Jericho's brandy.

"Now, what's all this talk about shopping? Miss Sara, are you barefooted again? Where are your shoes, child? You're going to catch your death, sure's the world."

Maulsie shook her head as if to say, I did my best with her, for all the good it did.

Sara felt a warm glow begin inside her and work its way out to her cold toes and fingers. This was home. This was where she belonged. In the kitchen, drinking hot coffee, being clucked over by Hester and Maulsie. She reached for one of the leftover cold biscuits. Now if only Jericho felt the same way about her . . .

\*    \*    \*

Jericho came in while Sara was on her second cup of coffee. The table wasn't yet laid, but the soup was done. It was well after noon. Both his face and his dark hair gleaming wet, he brought with him the exciting smell of cold rain, wood smoke and horse. Hester dipped him a basin of water, adding to it from the kettle, and handed him the soap and towel. It seemed strange to Sara that anyone would wash up in the kitchen, but then, she supposed it was more sensible than tracking through the house to the washstand in his bedroom upstairs.

He had shucked off his muddy boots on the back porch. There was a bootjack there for just that purpose. He hung his slicker on the peg behind the door to drip on the floor and not a one of the three women present uttered a word of protest.

"Is she gone?" he asked, and Hester nodded.

"Did you help her pack?"

Again she nodded. "Didn't find nothing but a lace-edged handkerchief with a Y and some blue flowers embroidered on it."

Sara bit her lip. She had had a handkerchief like that. It had belonged to her mother. Come to think of it, she hadn't seen it lately.

She started to ask about it and decided against it. If the thing was gone, it was gone. No sense in stirring up unnecessary trouble. A handkerchief was small enough price to pay for peace.

Maulsie dipped two big bowls of soup and set them on the table. Sara sipped her cooling coffee and tried to pretend she wasn't aware of every inch of Jericho's shockingly vital body as he unbuttoned his collar, turned back his cuffs and splashed off his face and arms.

Strictly speaking, she mused, he was not terribly handsome—at least, not in the way Titus had been handsome. His nose was just a tad large, his brows thick and straight, giving him a stern look, and his mouth . . .

Well. Enough about his mouth.

She took a deep breath. "Jericho, I was wondering if I might, um . . . make some new curtains for the front parlor windows? And maybe a few cushions? Hester says there's feathers enough for a whole slew of pillows, and I could pick out some fabric when I go to get my shoes."

He looked at her as if she'd addressed him in a foreign tongue. "Shoes?"

"And curtains and cushions. And maybe some bright paint for the woodwork and a rug or two, something small that would brighten up all the dark old rooms." There were rugs aplenty, but they were mostly brown, with dull, dark designs.

Her heart sank. He was probably one of those people who didn't like change. Some men were like that, or so she'd heard. Never changed so much as an antimacassar after a loved one had died.

Pinning up her hair, which had dried by now, she openly studied the man she had married in such haste. The stranger who could freeze her with a look and then thaw her again with a single touch. Did he still consider her an outsider? Theirs was no longer a marriage of convenience. Whether or not Jericho was willing to admit it, she belonged to him now. This was her home, too.

Only she did wish he would give her some sign that he recognized her right to be here. All he had done lately was avoid her. He watched her when he didn't think she noticed, the same way she watched him. Right now, he looked as if he couldn't make up his mind whether to keep her or throw her back.

"Mistuh Cap'n, dis chile want to go to town. You want I should ask Simon to drive her?" Maulsie had adapted her own version of Jericho's name.

"What for?" Jericho asked, looking at Maulsie and Hester, never once at Sara.

"She tol' you what fo'. She done wore her mama's shoes plum out."

Sara wriggled in her chair and leaned forward. She didn't need a spokesman, she was more than capable of speaking for herself. "It's just that I never had time to finish buying all the things I planned to buy, and I clean forgot about a new pair of good, everyday boots. I did get those yellow slippers to go with my yellow dress, but they're the wrong size, and before I had time to look for something else, Titus—that is, I had to—"

"What she mean is, dat snake done come after her an' run her off," Maulsie finished for her. "Didn't hab no time t'ink 'bout no clothes or no shoes. Now she do."

Jericho leaned over, reached around the corner of the table and lifted Sara's skirt.

She slapped his hand. "Stop that!"

"Barefooted again, hmm?" He grinned, and it occurred to her that he was a different man when he smiled. "Reckon I can spare the time to drive you to town. Moyer's coming along with the hiring, patching and clearing."

"You got me a girl coming?" Hester asked eagerly.

Jericho nodded. "Two for you, two for the kitchen. They'll be living in the cabins out back."

Which meant that their menfolk would be working in the fields. Sara knew that Jericho had no intention of buying workers. What she didn't know was whether it was out of consideration for Maulsie and Simon, because free blacks and slaves never worked well together, or because he truly didn't hold with slavery. There was still so much she didn't know about the man she had married.

"Could we possibly go tomorrow?" she asked, returning to the subject of her shoeless state.

"Why not today? If we leave within the hour, we'll make it soon after dark, and you can have all day tomorrow to do your buying."

All day tomorrow. Which meant they would also be away tonight. Sara refrained from bouncing with joy at the thought of being alone with her husband for an entire day and a night, with no Ivadelle forever dusting right behind them, no Rafe poking his head through the door, and no Hester or Maulsie fussing and fretting over them.

Coolly, she said, "I'm sure Simon could drive me just as well if you're busy."

"And sleep where, in the wagon? I figured on putting up at the Indian Queen."

And of course, there was no place for any black man, free or not, in the town's finest hotel. There were private homes, little more than shanties, where arrangements could be made, but she hated to see the old man have to stay with strangers in a strange town.

"Oh, very well, if you're sure it's no bother," she said

just as if she were reluctantly resigned to her fate. Which was better than jumping up and dancing around the kitchen table the way she felt like doing. "I suppose I'd better go get ready, then, if you're insisting on leaving right away."

"Not wit'out yo' soup. You set right dare and scrape yo' bowl good, child, 'fore I take a willow whip to yo' legs."

Sara sighed. Maulsie had bullied her shamelessly all her life, ever since her mother had grown too ill to look after her. She stared down at the huge chunk of ham swinging in a tomato broth thick with corn and beans, sighed, spread a napkin across her lap, and tried to summon up an appetite. She was too excited to eat.

The minute Maulsie and Hester left the kitchen to go tidy up the downstairs rooms, she excused herself, stepped out onto the back porch and scraped her bowl into Brig's pan.

Evidently Jericho was no hungrier than she was. Idly, he stirred his soup, watching her while she set her dishes to soak. "What'll you give me not to tell on you?" he teased.

Sara stared. Mercy, he was in a strange mood. She had never seen him quite like this, eyes twinkling with devilment, a grin testing the corners of his wide mouth. "What if I promise not to fall out of the shay again?" she ventured.

"I'll hold you to it," he said. His eyes said more, only she felt suddenly too skittish to try and read their message.

Once out of the kitchen, Sara flew up the stairs, ignoring the last faint twinge of discomfort in her bruised foot. They were going to town! She and Jericho, just the two of them! He was taking her to the Indian Queen Hotel, where they had copper bathtubs in every room and an unending supply of hot water for the asking, and where they would quite naturally share a room.

And would they share a bed?

*Well, of course you'll share a bed, you dunce. And you'll turn down the lamp so he can barely see, and sprinkle some of Maulsie's rose-and-lemon grass scent on your hair, and he won't be able to resist you.*

And this time, now that she knew how to do it, she would make sure to get it right. Maybe then, he would want to do it with her again.

Before she had quite finished getting dressed, Sara heard Jericho stirring around in the next room. She was tempted to go in and offer to help him pack, only he would probably refuse. He was a very private person, her husband—a man who preferred to do for himself. She had learned that much when she'd had the care of him for more than a week after he'd been stabbed in the back. If he could have lain on his stomach and changed the dressings on his back, he would have done it.

She slipped into her yellow, which was hardly seasonal, but was prettier than the brown. Her yellow and green bonnet had been chosen to go with the gown, only the yellows were off just enough so that it didn't work. She had never had a scrap of fashion sense. Her friend Carrie had told her that more than once.

That wasn't all Carrie had told her. But by now, Sara thought smugly, she could tell her friend a thing or two.

Carefully, she settled her bonnet over her coiled hair

and anchored it with a jet hat pin. She gathered up her best wool shawl, hoping it would keep her dry, knowing it wouldn't. Her yellow kid slippers were all she had to wear, and she shoved them on her feet. She'd been a fool to buy them in the first place, but they were so lovely, and the store had only had two pairs—one too big and one too small. She'd thought at the time she could scrunch up her toes.

Well. She was older now, and wiser.

*Oh, yes, you're wonderfully wise.* Stifling a giggle, she kicked up her feet and fell back on the bed, bonnet, shawl, and all.

Wouldn't you just know, she thought, embarrassed, that Jericho would choose to come in just then.

He didn't say a word. Sara sat up just as if there were nothing at all unusual about a grown woman wallowing fully dressed on a bed in broad daylight. Standing, she adjusted the waistline of her gown, resettled her bonnet, which had gone crooked, and collected her reticule.

"Ready to cast off?" he asked, a suspicious tremor in his deep voice.

Sara nodded with every appearance of composure. She had already cast off. Cast off every vestige of the common sense she had been so proud of all her life.

As towns went, Elizabeth City was scarcely more than a growing village. All the same, to someone who had lived all her life in the country, seeing lights in the windows of so many houses at once and knowing that there were several shops just waiting for her to explore was thrilling enough. Being shown into the plush hotel by an elegant gentleman made it all the more magical.

And Jericho did look elegant. Compared to all the other men present, which included several dapper gentlemen standing around the lobby of the hotel with their cigars and their colorful silk cravats and waistcoats worn with stand-up collared shirts, he reminded her of an eagle looming over a flock of canaries.

*He's mine,* she wanted to announce to the world. *He might not know it yet—I haven't exactly figured out how to make him realize it—but he's mine!*

After a quiet word to the manager, who obviously recognized a figure of authority when he met one, Jericho led her up the stairs to what surely must be the finest room in the whole establishment. It was three times the size of the room she'd been given when she'd stayed there before, but at that time she'd been newly married and extremely unsure of her place in the world.

"Are you sure you can afford all this?" she murmured, gesturing toward the mahogany tester bed and the matching pair of velvet-covered arm chairs. The chairs were sky blue to match the draperies. The walls were white with deeper blue woodwork. The carpet on the floor was blue and gray and green and pink, and every bit as thick and lovely as the ones she remembered from her childhood, before Noreen had sold them all and replaced them with a few stingy rag rugs.

Jericho scowled. "That's not your concern." *Darling,* he almost added, but couldn't quite bring himself to voice the word. *Darling* was Rafe's style, not his.

He only hoped to God he could figure out what his

style was and get on with this business of courting before he busted a gut.

Sara was opening wardrobe doors and peering behind the curtains, just like a child on Christmas morning. Not that Jericho could remember much about being a child on Christmas morning. He did recall Louisa's expression, however, the year she had received the big china-headed doll. His gift had been a thin volume of inspirational verses. He had hidden it in the attic and claimed he'd misplaced it, which had gotten him a good switching, but it was better than being forced to try and read the blamed thing.

"Oh, my, would you just look at this bathtub," Sara whispered, and he did. Standing beside the folding privacy screen, they both stared down at the biggest copper, slipper-shaped hip bath either of them had ever seen. He had asked for the best accommodations the establishment had to offer, but he hadn't expected something like this.

Slowly, his face gathered heat. He cut his eyes at Sara, wondering if she was thinking the same thing he was. That the bathtub was big enough for two people as long as they arranged their limbs properly. He could think of several ways, and before he could stop himself, he was picturing a wet Sara, her plump pink behind snuggled between his long limbs while he lathered her hair and her . . .

"I'm hungry," he growled, backing away. "I ordered us up a mess of food. Ought to be here most any time."

"You mean we won't have to go downstairs to the dining room?"

"No, ma'am. You can take off your shoes, and I'll

just ease these chairs up a mite closer to the table, and we'll set-to right here."

Carefully, Sara heel-toed her feet out of her cruel kid slippers. Perhaps they would fit Hester, or one of the girls who was coming to work at the house. She removed her coal-skuttle bonnet. Her face, which had been flaming only a moment before as she imagined Jericho seated in the hip bath, with her washing his back, had cooled off until now it felt numb.

She removed her shawl, folded it and placed it in the bottom drawer of the tall, mahogany gentleman's wardrobe. Should she place her night shift there, too, or hang it behind the screen? Suddenly, sharing a man's wardrobe seemed terribly intimate. Which was a ridiculous notion for a woman who had already shared his bed. Shared the beds of two different men, come to that.

She was just being silly. "My, it's warm in here, isn't it?" she asked, striving for a bright, cheerful note. Instead of bright and cheerful, her voice sounded as if it had been strained through two layers of muslin. Thin as whey.

"I'll open a window."

"Oh, no! It might rain in, and besides, it's not all that warm."

He gave her a peculiar look, and she determined to try again.

"Shall I, um—unpack for you?" she offered.

"Thank you kindly, but I'm used to doing for myself."

"Oh," she whispered, looking rebuffed, and Jericho could have kicked himself.

"I'm sorry, I didn't mean—" He broke off and swore, and then apologized again. "Actually, I'm used to having a steward do for me, but that don't mean I can't do for myself. I didn't marry you to wait on me, Sara. Although I reckon it might seem that way, considering how we started out."

*What did you marry me for?* The words went unspoken, but they might as well have been emblazoned on the very air between them.

She stared at him, and then stared at the window. It was pitch-black and raining hard. Hardly an engrossing view.

With two long strides, Jericho crossed to her side and gripped her arms in his big, hard hands. "Sara, I'm not real good at this, but—" He took a deep breath and started all over. "The thing is, we're still strangers in most ways. We know some things about one another, but not the things that are important for the long haul." A wintery smile broke across his face for a moment, making him look years younger. "Such as, I know you have a mole on your left buttock." He paused. "And I knew you were going to blush when I mentioned it."

As, of course, she did.

"There's still a lot of little things I don't know, though—like how many times of a night you roll over. Or if you like to sleep on your left or your right side. Or if you always sneeze three times when you wake up of a morning."

Sara did her best to sound worldly. "I don't have the least idea how many times I roll over. I prefer my left side, and I don't always sneeze three times. Sometimes it's four. Or even five, if the sun's in my face when I wake up."

"There, you see? Now we're getting somewhere."

They were getting nowhere. Those were only super-
ficial things. Things he could tease her about just to
watch her color up, which she invariably did, to his
secret delight.

But there was so much more he had come to know
about her, that it was somehow important that she
knew he knew. Things like her deep sense of loyalty.
Her kindness. Her pride. He had always thought pride
was strictly a masculine attribute, but pride and a
bone-deep sense of honor had guided her as surely as
the North Star guided a mariner.

He wanted her to know that he knew those things
about her so that she would know how much he valued
her, only those weren't things a man discussed. Not
with a woman. Leastwise, not a man who had never
discussed such nebulous things as feelings unless they
had to do with a falling barometer or the uneasy look
of the sky.

He sighed and decided he might as well barge ahead
the best way he could. Things couldn't go on the way
they had for the past three days. He'd go stark-raving
crazy if he had to go on seeing her, hearing her voice,
smelling her scent, and keep his hands off her body.

"So, madam, tell me this, then—if a man was to set
about courting a woman, do you reckon she'd rather
be courted with flowers and pretty trinkets, or with
store-bought sweets and fancy words?"

Sara gaped at him, making him wonder why the devil
he hadn't come right out and asked her about her
own preferences.

"Well, now, I couldn't say what other women would
like. I've never had much cause to think about it," she
said slowly.

He immediately thought of Rafe, with his hothouse roses and his darlings. Clearing his throat, he said, "Yes, well—I didn't mean other women, exactly. I meant you. And I can handle the flowers and trinkets and store-bought sweets, if you'll just let me know your favorings."

"Jericho, you don't have to do any of that, honestly you don't. I'm already your wife. It's not like you had to—to win me."

Damnit, that was *exactly* what he had to do! But before he could make his next move, a rap on the door announced their evening meal. He had ordered the best in the house and hoped their best was better than the Halfway Hotel's stringy turtle and soggy turnips.

While the waiter set out the food and laid the table, Jericho considered Sara's words. No, he didn't have to win her. She was already his, leastwise, so far as the law was concerned. But he knew now that it was no longer enough. Even having her in his bed was no longer enough, although the thought of *not* having her in his bed was unthinkable. He'd been hard-pressed not to come at her again after that first time, but he had made up his mind that before he did that, he'd best sort through all these peculiar feelings he'd been having ever since he'd taken her to bed, and see if he could put it all in proper perspective. A wise captain never set sail without a definite course in mind.

"My, this looks lovely," she murmured. The waiter beamed, and beamed even more when Jericho slipped him two fips.

With a courtly gesture, Jericho held her chair and then slid it under her, trying not to notice too much the faint scent of roses and lemongrass that clung to her hair. One of her hairpins had come loose, and he lifted a hand to shove it back in, then changed his mind. If he touched her now they might never get around to eating supper, and for the task ahead, he needed all the strength he could muster.

"Try that beefsteak, why don't you?" he offered. "And my, don't that roast potato look good? Here, there's plenty of bread. Have some butter, too." She was going to need her strength, as well, if what he had in mind came to pass.

"Oh, doesn't that rain sound good on the roof? I love to sleep with the rain pounding down on the roof. At home I had an attic room, and—"

Her gaze met his, and then they both flushed. The bed loomed behind them, seeming to swell in size. And right behind that screen was the hip bath . . .

Jericho cleared his throat and frowned. "Eat your supper, Sara. It's getting late." Which wasn't particularly subtle, even for a taciturn seaman, he thought ruefully.

He heard her sigh and wondered if it was in eagerness or resignation. She picked up her fork. He thought, *Lord, I think I must love her*. Bemused, he picked up his own.

# *Chapter Twenty-two*

All through the interminable meal, bursts of words alternated with self-conscious silences. Both Sara and Jericho knew precisely what was going to happen, if not precisely when. Jericho toyed with his cutlery as he envisioned undressing her, lowering her onto that big fat feather bed and following her down, burying himself inside her snug harbor and working her until they both collapsed.

He shifted uncomfortably on the overstuffed chair. Doggedly, he cut up his beef into half a dozen bites and began to eat, but it might as well have been the same old shipboard ration of salt horse and burgoo for all the attention he paid.

Sara thought perhaps she might swoon. She never had before, but this might be a good time to try it. How could a body look forward to something so much, and at the same time dread it?

Never had she been so aware of the width of a man's shoulders. Of the way he seemed to fill the room with the force of his presence. Yet, for all his size, he was surprisingly graceful. The first thing she had ever noticed about him was the way he moved, with his shoulders swaying in counterpoint to his hips.

Something to do with balancing on a rolling deck, she suspected, remembering how powerful his limbs had looked when she'd been forced to knead the cramp from his muscular calves.

My, the room had grown warm! You'd think there was a roaring fire on the hearth instead of only the faint glow of one set earlier to take the chill off the air. Surreptitiously, she dried her damp palms on her napkin and proceeded to carve off a tiny portion of potato. Shoving it to the edge of her plate, she carved off another one.

Sara knew as well as she knew her own name that Jericho hadn't driven her all this way on a whim and then hired the best room in the hotel just so that she could shop for a few fripperies. Rafe might have done such a thing. She suspected Rafe was wildly reckless and impulsive, whereas Jericho was sober and practical and steady as a rock.

However, Jericho had killed a man in a duel, had married a total stranger and sent her off alone, had gone to sea at the vulnerable age of thirteen and thereafter lived the life of a sailor—and *everyone* knew what *that* meant.

Well, at least he didn't gamble and smoke stinking cigars and wear flowered satin waistcoats and call every lady he met darling. Sara liked Rafe, she truly did, for he was an entertaining scoundrel, and he'd been a good friend. But when it came to choosing a husband, she would take a man like Jericho over a dozen Rafes.

She managed to force down a few bites of her supper, not because she was hungry but because she suspected Jericho was being far too extravagant. And while she didn't want to encourage it, neither did she want him to think she didn't appreciate it.

Jericho ate because he was hungry, which wasn't particularly romantic, but then, he was not a romantic man. What he was, was a big man who had gone without his breakfast because Sara had already been seated at the table, her face still flushed with sleep. One look and he'd gone stiff as a poker, so he'd headed out to split wood before riding over to Moyer's place.

He had gone without his midday meal because she'd been there when he'd come in through the back door, with her hair down and her damp gown clinging like a second skin. Sitting at the table looking so damned fetching, he'd wanted to devour her instead of his hambone soup.

Damnit, a man had to eat if he wanted to keep up his strength.

Jericho waited for her to rise, and then he stood, stretched, and yawned widely. "If you'd care for a hot bath before you go to bed, madam, I can send for some hot water."

"I'd like that." Her voice came out high and squeaky.

"Stiffens a body up, driving in the rain."

"I do believe you're right. Not that ours isn't a fine carriage." It wasn't a carriage at all, but only a two-seater. Sara happened to know Jericho had ordered a spanking new carriage, but it had yet to be delivered.

He said something that sounded like mumph. Or maybe humph.

"What did you say?"

"I said, madam, that if we're to get any sleep at all tonight, I'd best send for that water."

The word "sleep" seemed to vibrate throughout the

room. Sara busied herself with stacking the plates on
the heavy serving tray. What on earth was happening
to her? You would think she had never shared a room
with a man before. Mercy, she had slept in so many
rooms with so many different men lately she should be
used to it by now.

But this was different. This was Jericho, and for
once, neither of them was an invalid. There was nothing in the world to keep them from . . .

And certainly no reason why they shouldn't . . .

She dropped a fork and knelt to pick it up at the
same time Jericho bent to retrieve it. Their shoulders
bumped. He reached out to steady her with a hand on
her arm, and she half expected to see smoke rising
from the place where he touched her.

*Oh, for heaven's sake, Sara Rebecca, whatever hap-
pened to your good sense? The man is your husband,
not some mysterious dark stranger set on having his way
with you!*

While Jericho left to make arrangements for the hot
water, Sara made a deliberate effort to compose herself. By the time he returned, she had succeeded
quite well.

"Thank you. I do believe I'll sleep better for a nice
hot bath. Shall I leave the water for you, or would you
rather go first?"

There. That sounded sensible enough. They could
probably command enough hot water for two separate
baths, but it would take forever to empty the tub, and
she didn't fancy having a parade of potboys trooping
in and out of the room all night.

While the tub was being filled, Sarah stood at the
window, seeing in the dark glass a reflection of Jericho

sprawled in one of the two sky blue velvet armchairs.
In his black suit, with his dark, angular features, he
looked utterly predatory. She knew he wasn't. Not really. All the same, the notion played havoc with her
heartbeat.

When the tub was filled, he dismissed the boys with
a word of thanks and a few coins, then turned and
regarded her from under the shelf of his level brows.
His eyes glittered. He looked flushed.

"Rico, you never answered my question. Are you
coming down with something?"

Somewhat surprised by her concern—although by
now, he should have been used to it—Jericho nearly
told her just what it was he was coming down with,
but it was still too new to him. This peculiar muddle
of tenderness and protectiveness and desperate sexual
hunger. He couldn't have been any more at sea if he'd
been set down in the middle of a North Atlantic storm
without a compass, a chart, or a spare set of sails. How
did she do it? He could have sworn she was as guileless
as a day old chick.

"Hot water don't stay hot forever, madam. If you're
going to use it, you'd better step to it." His voice was
so gruff you'd have thought she was some raw hand
being hauled up before the mast. "That is, if you're a
mind to," he said, apology in his tone, if not his words.

Without a word Sara went behind the screen, where
she proceeded to undress. Not until she had eased herself into the deep warm water did she remember her
soap. She'd been in such a rush to pack she'd forgotten
to bring it.

As if reading her mind, Jericho asked if she needed
soap. "Yes, but I'm already in the tub."

"Then close your eyes."

Obediently, she squeezed them shut, then popped them wide again. He was standing before her in his shirtsleeves, grinning broadly, a chunk of Hester's best bayberry soap held out in his extended hand.

"Jericho, you're a terrible tease." She was tempted to laugh, but amusement wasn't all she felt. He was still looming over her like a great bird of prey, fists planted on his hips, feet spread apart.

"You look a lot better out of that brown thing than in it."

"You shouldn't be here, and you certainly shouldn't say things like that," she scolded, not meaning a word of it.

"You're my wife, Sara. It's not like I've never seen your body before."

Lowering her head to her bent knees, she groaned. "Yes, well—this is different. I—I want you to leave."

"No, you don't."

No, she didn't. She wanted him to stay. But first she wanted him to say something to break the painful bonds of shyness that afflicted her. She was still pressing her forehead to her wet knees when she felt something slide along her back.

"Shift forward, Sara." With one hand on her shoulders and the other one on her back, he eased her forward on the slick bottom of the tub.

"What are you *doing*?" she hissed.

"Fixing to take a bath."

"But *I'm* in here!"

"Yes, ma'am, I know you are. I did take note of that." His tone was grave, but his voice carried an undercurrent of laughter. She could well imagine the devilment lurking in those wicked black eyes of his. A sober man, he didn't laugh often. When he did, it was usually at her expense.

But then he was settling his body down behind hers, easing one long limb on either side of her hips, and laughter was the very last thing on her mind.

"There now, we fit right fair, wouldn't you say so?"

They fit more than fair, they fit perfectly. But it was all Sara could do to breathe. Speaking was out of the question.

"Don't go sliding under the water, um—darling. I've done with hauling you ashore."

Darling. He had called her darling. Merciful saints, what was he trying to do to her? Finding her voice, she asked him just that.

"As to that, I reckon I'm trying to court you." The soft rumble of his voice sent vibrations coursing through her all the way to the tips of her toes.

He was trying to court her. Sara thought her heart would surely swell up and burst right out of her bosom. "Rico, you don't have to do that," she whispered.

"I'm not doing it because I have to. I'm doing it because I want to. Because you deserve it, only I'm not very good at it." His hands began circling slow and lazy over her skin just above her waist. To Sara's way of thinking, he was very, *very* good at it.

She was clutching the chunk of bayberry soap as if it were a life raft. When it squirted from her fingers, Jericho retrieved it. With slow, soapy strokes, he massaged her sides, her arms and shoulders, and then her stomach. And then his hands slipped to her belly, and she caught her breath at the startling sensations that quivered in her most private parts.

"Rico, I-I'm not sure . . ." she gasped. She wasn't sure of anything except that if he stopped what he was doing, she might die.

She squirmed, aware of the rapidly changing configuration of that portion of his body that was pressed so closely to her own. She knew what it meant. Oh, yes, she did know that much.

"Rico," she murmured at the same time he whispered her name.

And then one of his hands moved up to cover her breast as the other one slipped lower. Her limbs trembled and parted to his gentle urging, and her head fell back onto his shoulder. If the house had been burning down around them, she wouldn't have noticed.

With one last glimmer of sanity, Jericho wondered just where courting left off and rutting began. He suspected he had crossed the line the minute he'd dipped a toe into her bathtub.

Hell, he had probably crossed it the first time he had decided to protect her from the ruffians back at the Halfway Hotel.

His breath was coming hard and heavy, just like the rest of him. He didn't want to rush her, but he wasn't sure just how long he could keep up this pace. He'd never taken a woman in a bathtub before, but there had to be a way.

He eased one leg forward. His foot struck the end. He shifted, wondering if he could slide her up onto his lap, and then his elbow struck the rolled rim a painful blow.

"Sara? Do you reckon we'd better get out before the water gets any colder?"

"Colder?" At the rate they were going, Sara thought, the water would soon be steaming.

He stood and carefully lifted her out. She felt boneless. When he released her just long enough to wrap one of the hotel's huge towels around her, she nearly slithered to the floor.

Jericho swept her up into his arms, murmuring things like, Easy does it, and Steady as she goes. Which weren't particularly romantic, but which sounded wonderfully romantic to Sara's prejudiced ears.

That night Sara became a wife in the fullest sense of the word. With a lover who was both thrilling and tender, she learned things about her own body she would never in this world have dreamed possible.

And then she insisted on knowing all about his body. About whether or not he felt the same things she did, and why. About the stunning effects of touching in a certain way, in a certain place. Together, they explored all the possibilities and invented a few of their own. Sara grew shockingly bold, delighting Jericho, who grew increasingly tender. They laughed together, and once Sara even cried.

No real reason. She simply couldn't contain her happiness, and some of it overflowed in tears.

Jericho was devastated until she reassured him. Which she did, in the most direct way she could think of.

They woke just before morning, starving, and breakfasted on cold biscuits and stale ginger cake from the supper tray that had yet to be collected. They talked about things each considered important, such as those few things from Sara's mother's dresser that repre-

sented home to her. Such as the thin volume of im-
proving verses Jericho had long since retrieved from
the attic at Wilde Oaks, but still hadn't read.

They made love again and again, and early the next
afternoon, just before they set out for home, Jericho
bought Sara three pairs of kid slippers, two with ribbons, and two pairs of high-lows, which he said were
far more practical for country wear. Just as if she had
grown up in the city wearing Roman sandals and silk
stockings.

He promised to drive her all the way to Norfolk to
visit all the drapers and rug merchants and furniture
makers. "Might as well do it up right while you're at it."

"Oh, but you don't have to do that," she had said,
overcome by his generosity.

"I know that, Sara. I'd like to, though."

She nearly wept again. He made her feel as if she
were the most precious thing in the world, and all
without a word of love being spoken.

Sara thought it, though. A hundred times she had
stopped just short of telling him what was in her heart.
The words ached to be spoken, but she just couldn't
bring herself to say it when she wasn't sure he felt the
same way.

Oh, he liked her well enough, she did know that.
And she did know how to please him in bed, but love
was more than that. Love was . . .

Well. Love wasn't learned in a day. She would simply
have to be patient.

The sky had cleared off nicely, and the air was crisp,
not really cold. The smell of peat smoke was hardly
noticeable. Sara was pleasantly sore, pleasantly tired,
and excited by the bustle of shops and traffic. Ships

by the score sailed through the narrows, some anchoring in the local harbor, some bound elsewhere through the canal.

On the way home, Jericho offered to teach her to drive.

"*Teach* me," she crowed. "I've driven a dogcart, a mule cart and once I even drove a team halfway down the lane before Papa caught me and threatened to skin me alive."

She laughed, and he laughed, and Sara thought she had never in her entire life felt so close to another person. It was wonderful.

She drove for the last few miles home. They passed the hedgerow that divided Rafe's place from their own, and Sara asked what had happened to Ivadelle. "I know he didn't really kidnap her. Not even Rafe would go that far."

"As to that, I reckon he might, if he wanted something enough." He sent her an odd look, which Sara missed entirely as she was concentrating on managing the headstrong gelding. "They came to an understanding."

"An understanding! Those two? They spat at one another like two tomcats in a tote sack every time he was over here." Jericho eased the reins from her hands, and Sara flexed her fingers. The gelding was harder to manage than old Blossom.

"All the same," he said calmly, "I reckon they'll suit well enough."

As they neared the place where the lane turned off in the direction of the overseer's house and the tenant houses farther on, Jericho handed Sara back the reins.

"Take her on home, madam." *Beloved Sara. Darling Sara.* "I'll be along directly."

The truth was, he wasn't ready yet to face Hester. She knew him too well. She would know right off what had happened between him and Sara, and it was too new to share.

Proudly, Sara tooled the neat little gig right up to the front door. She wanted Maulsie and Simon to see her. She heard Brig barking from out near the shed, which probably meant that Simon was out there.

"Stand still, sir," she said, climbing down and looping the reins over a low stubbing post. "I'll send Simon out directly."

She dashed up the steps in her brand-new, two-toned high-lows. "*Maul*-sie! *Hes*-ter! I'm *ho*-ome!" she sang out. "Just wait'll you hear what I did—I drove practically . . . all the way . . ."

The kitchen was empty. There was no sign of anyone at all downstairs. The dough bowl was on the floor, and flour was scattered across the table. A chair was overturned.

"Maulsie?" Sara whispered.

At a slight sound behind her, she whirled around. "No." She shook her head in denial. "You can't be here. You're dead."

# Chapter Twenty-three

Sara caught at the back of a chair, nearly overturned it, and slumped weakly down at the table. "Titus, where did you—how did you get here?"

"On that miserable gelding you were so kind as to return to my mother. Overjoyed to see me, sister dear?"

He looked terrible. The bright golden curls of which he had always been so inordinately proud were matted and greasy. There were spots on his waistcoat. His face, always pale, was gray, with liverish shadows beneath his eyes.

"I thought you were dea—that is, you've been ill?"

"Ill. That's it, I came down with a wild fever," he exclaimed, clapping his hands together. The smile that had stood him in such good stead with the young ladies before they saw through it was little more than a nasty sneer.

"But the duel—that is, I understood—"

"Ah, yes, the duel. Did you know our poor dear mother was heartbroke, what with her beloved Sara running off and her precious only son getting gut-stuck by some dirty bastard off a coal barge."

"Off a three-masted schooner," Sara murmured distractedly, "not a coal barge." Her mind worked frantically. Where were Maulsie and Hester? Why had Titus come after her? He could hardly believe she would go away with him, even if she weren't already married.

"Not a coal barge!" he shrieked. "Is that all you have to say for yourself? After all you've done? Mama *told* you you were supposed to marry me! *Me,* not Wilde! It's *my* money! Me, me, my, my, money, money, marry, marry!"

And then he clapped a hand over his mouth and giggled.

Sara's eyes rounded with horror. He was mad. Quite, quite mad. "Titus," she ventured cautiously, "wouldn't you like to lie down? I expect you're tired, what with the long ride and all."

His ruined face, once considered the handsomest in all Norfolk County, was suspiciously guileless. "Where's Wilde, Sara? Where's your husband? Does he know you're promised to me?"

"Oh, but—"

Lunging across the table, Titus caught the high neck of her gown and twisted, cutting off her supply of air. "You belong to *me,* damn your soul! I won't let you cheat me out of what's rightly mine!"

Sara clawed feebly at his hands as dark spots began to swim before her eyes. "No—Titus—can't breathe," she managed to gasp.

"You're going to marry me, Sara, just as soon as I make you a widow, and then it will all be mine." Releasing his grip on her collar, he gestured widely. Then he began to laugh. A feeling of horror crawled over her skin, and she wondered if she could manage to reach the boning knife Hester kept in the dresser drawer.

And then she saw it. The familiar silver-capped stag

handle was lying within inches of Titus's hand, the slim, curved blade half hidden under a stack of newly washed linens waiting to be folded on the end of the table.         .

*Oh, God in heaven, no. Please, no!*

"What have you done with Hester and Maulsie and Simon?" she whispered.

Leaning back in his chair, Titus propped his hands behind his head. The stench that emanated from his body nearly caused her to gag, but she suppressed her revulsion. Titus was not only mad, he was dangerous. Her only chance of escape lay in lulling him into believing she would go with him willingly.

If she got up and sauntered casually past the far end of the table, she might be able to grab the knife before he could stop her. "I'll need to pack a few things if I'm to go with you. Surely, you don't expect me to leave in what I'm wearing."

"Leave? Now why would we be leaving, sister Sara? Sweet sister Sara?"

"I'm not your sister," she retorted, unable to help herself.

Ignoring her disclaimer, Titus rambled on about his plans for the future, which involved marrying Sara and taking over not only her inheritance from her grandfather, but Wilde Oaks, as well. "Louisa was poor. Poor, poor Louisa. Not only poor, but stupid and ugly. You, on the other hand, sweet, sassy sister Sara, are not quite so ugly; and now that Wilde has sold his ship, you're a wealthy widow."

"I'm not a wi—"

"Not wealthy? Ah, but you are," he purred, his bright blue eyes glittering feverishly. "Thought I wouldn't know about that, didn't you? Can't outsmart Titus, Sara. You should know that by now." He waggled a finger in her face. His fingernails were dirty and ragged, which was somehow even more frightening than what he was saying. Titus, while he had never been one to wash where it didn't show, had always taken great pride in being well-groomed in all the parts that did.

"Ladymore, y'know. Old sot told me everything."

*Ladymore? What on earth was a ladymore?* "Titus, wouldn't you like a cup of tea? Or coffee? Or perhaps some of our best brandy?"

If she could distract him for just a moment, she could knock him unconscious with the heavy iron kettle, or at least distract him long enough to run for help.

*Jericho, come quickly!*

And then her gaze fell on that wicked boning knife half hidden beneath the pile of laundry, and she thought, no! Oh, God, no, for he would walk right into a trap, all unsuspecting.

Jericho strode down the leaf-strewn lane, satisfied that he had hired a good man. The clogged ditches were already being dug out. Come planting time, the fields would be properly drained, and Moyer had five more men on board to commence clearing for early spring planting. Hired on just yesterday, they would be here within the week so that most of the work could be accomplished before winter came down hard. Their womenfolk would work up at the house, and according to Moyer, all save two who were breeding were strong, willing and capable.

Which was one hell of a lot more than could be said

of Moyer's own wife. That plump little pigeon was a beauty, all right—he could see how a man might be taken in by her looks. But she was a whining sort of female with more complaints than Brig had fleas. Before she'd even offered him the hospitality of the house, she had set in to carping about a chimney that didn't draw properly and a door that hung crooked. The necessary was too far from the house, and although the cottage had four windows, every one of them was either too high, too small, or in the wrong place.

He understood now why Ivadelle Moyer had moved out and taken up residence in the main house. The cowshed would have been an improvement. At least the milker didn't whine.

Rafe and Ivadelle, he mused, kicking up a flurry of damp leaves. Now, there was a pair to draw to. Either he'd be the making of her, or she'd be the ruination of him. Jericho didn't particularly care which, although he would be forever grateful to the man for taking her off his hands.

Rafe had wanted Sara. Jericho hadn't missed the way he still looked at her when he thought no one was watching. Nor had he been so far under the weather back at the Halfway Hotel that he had failed to notice how friendly the two of them were becoming. Even with the pain and the laudanum, he'd heard them laughing, whispering—heard the slap of cards and Sara's hiccuping giggles whenever she won a trick.

Darling, Rafe had called her. The old jack-a-dandy fancied himself a great hand with the ladies. "Hothouse roses, my darling ass," Jericho snorted. If Sara wanted flowers, why then, she would damned well have flowers. Jericho would bury her in flowers up to her armpits, if that was what she wanted.

And comfits. He would find a place that sold store-bought sweets and buy her a locker full. And jewelry, too. A ring, first off. Something wide, that would show up real well so that every man within range would know she was spoken for.

Under a pink and gray sunset, Jericho paused to watch a ragged formation of honkers fly over, headed for the nearby Currituck Sound. It was then that he heard Brig cutting up, making a noise that was part whine, part howl. "Chafing to go after them, aren't you, old boy," he murmured.

Maybe he would clean up that old fowling piece of his grandfather's and go after a few himself. It had been a long time since he'd spent a day crouched down in a rush-covered dugout, waiting for a good shot.

Brig would enjoy it. Hell, he would enjoy it himself.

His boots were muddy when he came up onto the back porch. The road hadn't had time to dry out since the rains. Jericho was contemplating taking them off outside to spare himself a good raking down by his housekeeper when the dog raced past him, trailing what looked to be a length of harness, to stand quivering at the back door.

"Here, boy, easy as she goes." He laid a steadying hand on the old dog's head. Harness leather? Who the devil would have tied him up with a strip of leather?

Who the devil would've tied him up at all?

Brig focused a pair of small imploring eyes on him and then went back to whining and twisting, trying to nose open the door. Jericho felt the hair on the back of his neck stand up. "Shhh, quiet, boy. Whatever it is, we'll handle it." Silently, he lifted the latch. The dog burst into the kitchen, circled the table twice, and hurled himself at the door that led to the hallway.

Jericho was more thorough. The kitchen was obviously empty. Not even a lamp was lit. He wet a finger and touched the range. It was warm, not hot. By rights there should be pots simmering on top and bread baking in the oven.

A spill of dried beans crunched under his boot sole. A chair lay on its side, another one was raked out away from the table. At the far end of the table and trailing down onto the floor was an untidy heap of laundry.

"Hester? Maulsie?" Jericho mouthed silently.

*Sara. Dear God, he had sent her home alone.*

He started to ease back out the back door and look in the shed to see if the gig was there, but he couldn't leave. Something was wrong. And whatever it was, it was right here in the house. Brig knew it. He should have trusted the dog's intelligence instead of wasting a single moment.

Moving silently in his damp-soled leather boots, Jericho nudged the dog aside and turned the cast-iron doorknob.

"It won't be long now," Titus announced gleefully. As if already seeing himself as lord of the manor, he was seated behind Jericho's desk, drinking Jericho's brandy, smoking one of Jericho's thin, dark cigars. On the desk beside his right hand was Hester's boning knife. He had used it to cut off the end of his cigar, used it again to trim a fingernail, and then amused himself by carving his initials in the gleaming mahogany surface of the desk.

Across the room, Sara tugged painfully at the cord that bound her wrists behind the back of the chair. Her ankles were secured to the chair legs, and Titus's filthy cravat was tied so tightly across her mouth it was all she could do to keep from retching.

Her eyes were dry. She was too frightened, too furious to weep. Besides, Sara knew from past experience that tears only fueled whatever demons drove the mad, wicked creature. Titus wanted her to weep and to beg.

*Jericho, stay away! He means to kill you!*

"Hear that? He's gone up the stairs to hunt for his pretty bride. Don't you want to call him, Sara? Don't you want to tell him where you are? Oh, but never mind. He'll search under every stick of furniture. He'll find you soon enough, won't he, sweet sister Sara? And when he does . . ."

Titus picked up the knife, holding it by the tip of the blade. He frowned. "It ain't balanced. I'll aim for the heart, but I might as well tell you, Sara—sweet, sassy, silly sister Sara—like as not I'll miss and spill his miserable guts all over your nice clean floor. It'll be messy, Sara. You might want to shut your eyes." He giggled, and then clapped a hand over his mouth. "Shhhh," he whispered, and giggled again.

Sara thought she heard something right outside the door, but her heart was pounding so hard, she couldn't be sure. And then Brig barked sharply and began to whimper. The door rattled as he hurled himself against it, but the latch held.

Sara prayed silently, fervently. *Jericho, please, please listen to me. Lord, don't let him come in here. Sooner or later, Titus will fall asleep. The way he's drinking, he can't last much longer.*

Titus swore. "I tied that goddamned animal in the shed!"

Dear God, where were the others? What had he done to them? Were they in the shed, too? Bound hand and foot, the way she was? Sara couldn't allow herself to believe he had murdered them.

"Shh, he's coming downstairs now. Two steps at a time. I hope he don't break his neck. I got plans . . ."

Brig began to growl, an ominous sound that was dredged from the depths of his massive chest. Then he began to howl. Sara had heard that high, keening sound once before, on the day she'd arrived at Wilde Oaks. She'd been standing beside Louisa's grave at the time.

"Shut up! Stop that!" Titus jumped up, staggered, and knocked over the brandy decanter. He began to swear. "I should have killed that hellhound! I should have run him through with a pitchfork! I should've run them all through with a pitchfork! Do you know why I didn't, sweet Sara?"

He lurched forward to where she sat bound and gagged. Swaying on his feet, his eyes wide and quite, quite mad, he told her. "Because I wanted to wait and let you watch me do it. Remember how you used to run screaming whenever I cut my finger and threatened to drip blood on you? You never could stand the sight of blood, could you, sweet sister Sara?"

*It wasn't the blood, you fool, it was you! I must have sensed right from the first that you were a monster!*

Slowly, Titus lifted the blade and held it in front of her face. Crooning, he began to stroke the cold steel surface against her cheek. Sara shifted her weight in a frantic attempt to heave the chair over onto its side.

Suddenly the door burst open. She tried to voice a garbled warning through the strip of cloth that held her mouth wide open.

Reeling to face the door, Titus stared round-eyed down the barrel of Jericho's dueling pistol. As the gun barrel rose, he shifted his grip on the boning knife, lifted his arm to throw, and then everything seemed to happen at once.

A streak of red fury flew through the air. There was the sound of a gun exploding. Someone screamed, and then Sara felt herself toppling just before she was buried under a ton of something heavy, wet and stinking.

They were seated in the front parlor. Jericho, Sara, Maulsie, Hester, and Big Simon. It was obvious that Simon felt acutely uncomfortable. He was not a parlor man. Seated on the edge of a chair, he stared down at the glass of brandy in his big, scarred hands as if it might be poison.

"We're all agreed, then, that this needn't go any farther than right here?" Jericho stood before the fireplace, looking pale and grim, but every inch the captain of this particular ship.

Sara, lying in state on the Beidermeier sofa, blew the hair off her forehead and eased down the coverlet that had her sweating up a storm. With everyone treating her as if she were on the verge of collapse, she'd been cosseted to a fare-the-well. It was a wonder she had even been allowed downstairs.

There was a ragged chorus of agreement from the assembled company. Nothing could be gained from having it told up and down the countryside that Titus had laid a trap for Jericho, using Sara as bait, and that the trap had been sprung prematurely when a red Chester duck dog with particular cause to hate him had torn out his throat before anyone could prevent it.

Jericho had shot the case clock off the mantel. He'd been aiming at Titus when Brig had knocked him off-balance. Sara couldn't help but believe things had turned out for the best. As far as the authorities were concerned, Titus had broken into the house and thinking he was threatening Sara, the dog had attacked him. Brig would not be punished. Everyone knew that red Chester duck dogs were not vicious. Protective, yes. And somewhat territorial, but never vicious.

It was nearly midnight by the time everything had been settled and Titus's body was on its way home. Simon had gone for Hiram Moyer, and Moyer had sent for Rafe Turbyfill, who, along with Jericho, had handled the details. Ivadelle had not come with her new husband.

Although whether or not the two of them were actually married was anyone's guess, not that anyone even bothered to wonder.

"Poor Titus," Sara said now with a sigh. "Poor Noreen. Do you think I should go and see her?"

"And tell her what? That her precious son was as crazy as a bedbug? That he was a murdering scoundrel who didn't deserve to live?"

Sara sighed. She was propped up in bed, having been carried upstairs by Jericho despite her protests. He had stoked up the fire until it was blazing up a storm. "Oh, for mercy's sake, Jericho, you'd think I'd been through a war or something! I'm perfectly all right!"

She might as well have saved her breath. He'd carried her to his own bed, not hers. He had told her that from now on that was where she was to sleep, which suited her just fine, indeed it did. He'd told her he planned to turn her bedroom into a big bathing room, with a double-sized copper bathtub and one of the new patented indoor necessaries.

Sara accepted her fate. He seemed bound and determined to smother her in *something*. He'd promised flowers in every room in the house, and she'd told him she would just as soon grow her own. He had promised sweets, and she'd told him that too many sweets made her break out in spots. He had mentioned jewelry, and she had said she would settle for a wedding band, which seemed to please him no end.

But a nice new oversize bathtub, that was different. That was only sensible.

Her mind drifted back to the previous night as she waited for him to finish hemming and hawing and move on to whatever was bothering him now. It had been a horrendous evening, and she, for one, was exhausted. Then, too, neither of them had had much sleep the night before.

"Mercy, was it only last night?" she murmured, which had the effect of stopping him in his tracks.

"Was what only last night?"

"Well . . . you know. Last night."

"Was last night only last night? Sara, you'd better pull the covers up over your shoulders, I think you might be catching a chill."

"Oh, for heaven's sake, I never caught a chill in my life! Now, will you please scatter those coals?"

Instead of pulling up the covers, she yanked them down around her waist. And then shoved them all the way down to her knees. "Rico, you're going to have to stop trying to turn me into an invalid. There's not a blessed thing wrong with me that a good night's sleep won't cure. As for all the awfulness, well . . ." Sighing, she turned to stare at the reflection of lamplight in the rippled surface of a windowpane. "We'll simply have to put it behind us. I don't know what else we can do, do you?"

Jericho came to sit on the edge of the bed. He was still dressed, but he had removed his coat, unbuttoned his shirt and turned back his sleeves. His muscular forearm lay dark and heavy across the white coverlet.

Boldly, Sara covered his hand with her own. For no real reason she could put her finger on, she felt suddenly secure in her position as Jericho's wife. She loved him too much for him not to love her back. God wouldn't be that unfair.

He turned his hand palm upward to clasp her own. "It's over now, Sara."

"I know. It wasn't before, was it? Not truly."

Shaking his head, he said, "No, it wasn't. Louisa would have liked you." He hiked himself up onto the bed and leaned back against the bolster. "Sara, do you believe in spirits?"

"You mean like brandy and rum? Or like ghosts?"

"Sailors are a superstitious lot. Not me, of course, but I've known seamen who wouldn't sail on a ship after a man had died building her. Some won't sail with a woman on board, and I had a first mate once who swore some woman wearing black veils came to him every time he stood the graveyard watch."

She shuddered. "The graveyard watch?"

"Midnight to four of a morning."

"With a name like that, I can't much blame him for being fanciful."

"I reckon none of us knows all there is to know," he mused.

She waited for him to go on, afraid to lead, not quite daring to hope. "Mercy, no," she murmured.

"Like what makes a body know that without a certain person beside him, the wind in his sails would die out, the stars he steers by would fade. Oh, he might not founder right off, but he'd probably drift for the rest of his days like some abandoned, rudderless hulk."

Sara thought she had never heard anything so beautiful. She thought her heart would swell right up and explode. She thought that there were depths to this man she had married in such haste that would take a lifetime to discover.

"It's a good thing," she ventured, "that we're in no great hurry to learn all the answers, isn't it?"

Turning to her with a look in his dark eyes she had never seen before, he said quietly, "I reckon it is. I reckon we've got all the time in the world, and then some . . ."

# *Author's Note*

In January 1830, the Lake Drummond Hotel, which came to be known as Halfway Hotel for being situated across the state line between North Carolina and Virginia, was advertised in the Norfolk papers. It was 128 feet long, and boasted eight separate chambers, each with its own fireplace. Put up for sale before the end of its first year, it was called "—fully applicable for all the purposes of life, as eating, drinking, sleeping, marrying, dueling &., &., in all its varieties."

Twenty years later, it was still doing business, its dining room serving bacon and hominy to travelers on both the canal and the canal road.

# Another wonderful romance coming in August

**D**evon followed Elizabeth up the stairs to the second floor, then took his leave of her as if retiring to his chamber for the night. Moments later, with his greatcoat over his arm, he slipped quietly back down the stairs to the dining room.

The servants had already cleared away the remains of the dinner and snuffed the candles, leaving the room in darkness except for the moonlight shining through the bank of tall, mullioned windows at the far end of the room. He stepped into the shadows to wait—and to think about the beautiful woman for whom he was waiting.

It had been years since he had looked forward to a liaison with such anticipation. There was a mystery about Moira that drew him like a magnet, and an intelligence so quick and clever, its brilliance outshone the plethora of candles that had earlier decorated the massive table. For, though she had taken but a single taper with her to light the way to Charles's chamber, her leaving had seemed to rob the room of all illumination. And she wanted him as much as he wanted her.

He'd suspected as much since he'd realized the kiss they'd shared had been more than a dream. Tonight his suspicions had been confirmed. In one brief, unguarded moment, her eyes had met his in a look so full of longing and passion, it had been all he could do to keep from leaping across the table, bad leg and all, and taking her in his arms.

From that moment on, he'd been so intensely aware of her presence, everyone else had faded into the background. Oh, he had gone through the motions of conversing with Elizabeth and listening to Blackjack's stories. He had even answered questions put to him and asked a few himself.

But it had all been like a dream. The only reality had been his burning need for the sensuous beauty whose silent invitation had made his palms sweat and his heart pound as if he were a mere stripling about to take his first pleasure with a woman.

He traced his finger along the binding of the slippers he held in his hand—the slippers Elizabeth had said Moira would come seeking. Alone, in the darkened room, he smiled to himself. When she came, she would find him waiting.

Moira tucked both Charles and Alfie into their beds and kissed them goodnight, then made her way to her own suite to collect her warm wool pelisse. The days were pleasantly mild for the first week of March but the night air was still too chilly to walk outside without a wrap.

She'd seen Elizabeth enter her chamber just moments before when she'd returned from the nursery, so she felt certain Devon must have opted for an early night as well. At least she hoped he had. The last thing she wanted was to find herself alone with him.

Just thinking about the magnetic energy the man possessed struck terror in her heart. Try as she might, she had been unable to take her eyes off him during dinner, and he had returned one look that had burned its way into her very soul. Never had she felt more vulnerable nor more filled with a terrible, aching need to know the fulfillment that only this man could give her.

A glance at her bare feet reminded her that, as usual, she had kicked off her shoes during dinner. Knowing her nocturnal habits, her staff would have left them for her to collect before her walk. She smiled. Although just this morning, that cheeky fellow, John Footman, in his new capacity as butler, had hinted he was contemplating hiring a tweeney to do nothing but gather up the shoes she left about the house each day and return them to her chamber.

The dining room was deep in shadow when she entered. Placing her candle on the edge of the table, she knelt down and felt under the chair but found no slippers. She dropped to her knees and was just about to crawl under the table to continue the search when she heard a familiar voice ask, "Could these be what you are looking for?"

She raised her head to find Devon standing over her, her slippers dangling from two fingers of his outstretched hand. A shaft of moonlight caught the glint of gold in his hair, the glint of amusement in his eyes.

Scrambling hastily to her feet, Moira snatched the slippers. "Thank you, my lord St. Gwyre," she said, hopping on one foot while she jammed the other into a slipper that suddenly seemed too small, when it had fit perfectly just a few hours before.

"Let me help," he said, wresting the slipper from her protesting fingers and fitting it neatly onto her foot. He held out his hand. "Now the other." She had no choice but to give it to him and lift her other foot.

"There you are, all properly shod," he declared. "Though I can understand why you find wearing them so annoying. With me it's nightshirts."

"Nightshirts?" she stammered, utterly confused.

"Haven't worn one in years, much to my batman cum valet's disapproval. For an ex-smuggler, Ned can be annoyingly proper at times. To tell the truth, I never could stand the blasted things—nightshirts that is. They have an aggravating tendency to work their way up into—"

"A roll at one's waist," Moira said without thinking. She felt the same way about wearing the silly item English ladies called a nightrail as she did about wearing shoes.

"Are you saying you too choose to sleep au naturel, lovely lady? What a provocative image that inspires."

"I am saying nothing of the sort, my lord." She felt her cheeks flush hotly and was grateful the light was too dim for Devon to see how he'd disconcerted her.

"How disappointing. You deny it then?"

She would have to lie to deny it and she was the world's worst liar. She chose instead to skirt the issue. "This is a most improper conversation, my lord, and apropos of nothing," she declared in her chilliest voice, pushing past him to stride toward the door.

"Ah, but there you are wrong, ma'am. It has definite significance." Devon's laugh had a wicked ring to it. "I am assembling a most fascinating puzzle, you see, and another piece has just fallen into place."

Moira sniffed. "It is plain to see you are either foxed or given to speaking in riddles, and since I feel ill equipped to contend with either circumstance, I shall bid you goodnight."

"What a bouncer! I am convinced you could contend with a herd of stampeding Indian elephants with one hand tied behind your back," Devon said. "But what is this 'my lord' business? I thought we had agreed it was to be Moira and Devon from now on."

Moira stepped from the darkened dining room into the corridor where a footman waited with a branch of candles to light her way to the garden. She stopped long enough to button her pelisse with fingers that had an annoying tendency to tremble, and to her surprise realized that Devon was shoving his arms into the sleeves of a caped greatcoat.

"What are you doing?" she demanded in a hoarse whisper, although she could see very well he was now in the process of fastening the frogs which marched down the front of the garment.

"Preparing to accompany you on your nightly walk," he whispered back, "since I was certain you planned to invite me."

Moira's heartbeat accelerated alarmingly. In her present vulnerable mood, she didn't trust herself to walk in a moonlit garden with the "most notorious rake in London" and she trusted him even less. "I had no such plans," she said coldly. "I always walk alone."

"For shame, madam," Devon declared, cupping her elbow with his strong fingers and propelling her forward past the grinning footman. "When we have that promised talk of ours, we must remember to include the subject of manners. Informal is one thing; rude is another. Now, which way is it to that garden of yours?"

She was never certain how she got there, but moments later Moira found herself walking with Devon along the gravel path that wound through her favorite garden. They passed James Keough, standing silent and watchful beneath the same mulberry tree where she had encountered him each of her previous walks since the brothers had taken on the guarding of the young duke.

Devon passed him without a word, then loosening his grip on Moira's elbow, drew her arm through his. She left it there. What choice did she have? Snatching it away would make her appear nervous and unsure of herself—the last image she wished to project to the arrogant earl.

For some time they strolled in silence, the only light that of the pale spring moon, the only sound, other than the pounding of her heart, the croaking of the bull frogs in the lily pond at the center of the garden. Moira breathed in the rich, earthy scent of the fresh turned flower beds and the delicate fragrance of the early forsythia blossoms sprinkled along the bare tree branches above her head—hoping to find the same sense of peace she usually found in this beautiful spot. It was of no use. There was nothing peaceful about walking with her arm linked in Devon's. She felt like a top whose spring had been wound so tightly, it was about to go flying off in all directions.

With a start, she realized he was talking. "I'm sorry," she said, "I'm afraid I wasn't listening."

He looked taken aback, even shocked, and she found

herself with an almost overwhelming urge to giggle. "The most notorious rake in London" was undoubtedly accustomed to having women hang on his every word.

He watched her out of the corner of his eye, as if to make certain she was listening to him this time. "I said if there was one thing I had learned about you in our brief acquaintance it was that, unlike most females, you meet every issue that confronts you head-on."

"It seems the logical thing to do." Moira held her breath, waiting for his next words and gripped by a strong premonition they would change forever her relationship with the enigmatic earl. He had certainly been acting strangely since she'd encountered him in the darkened dining room, and the look in his eyes could almost be described as predatory.

Devon had done a great deal of soul-searching while waiting for Moira to claim her slippers and had come to the conclusion he wanted to begin his affair with her as he meant to go on. Open. Honest. Without all the ridiculous posturing and subterfuge that he had found so boring in dealing with his previous mistresses. She was that kind of woman. Plain in her tastes and, he suspected, delightfully elemental in her passions. Exactly the kind of woman he needed at this moment in his life.

He stopped beside a fountain into which a gigantic marble fish spat a never ending waterfall of crystal clear water, and smiled down at the lovely woman whose hand was still tucked in the crook of his arm. It was a delicate, slender hand and shockingly bare of glove—which somehow conjured up an image of other, more delectable parts of her body in the same state of undress in his bed. He covered her fingers with his own, absorbing their warmth, and the ache in his aroused body instantly intensified.

"So, lovely Moira," he said, getting right to the point, "what are we to do about this overwhelming attraction we feel for each other?"

"Do?" She looked genuinely surprised, and he felt a moment of uneasiness. She was a woman of the world and as such had to be well aware of how the game of seduction was played. He couldn't believe the fact that he was cutting the chase a bit short would disturb her unduly.

"We cannot simply ignore our passions for the next fourteen years," he said reasonably, wondering at the sudden tenseness he felt in her arm that was linked with his. He cleared his throat. "I, for one, have never found self-torture to be the least bit satisfying."

"I shouldn't imagine you had, my lord, but surely even 'London's most notorious rake' will admit 'our passions' cannot be our only consideration." There was an edge to her voice which surprised Devon. She sounded strangely indignant, almost as if she considered his reference to her passionate nature an insult.

He experienced a touch of annoyance. One expected such prudishness in the insipid little virgins making their come-outs in the London marriage mart; one did not expect it in a practical woman of the world—especially one with Moira's colorful background.

"I am well aware that we must be discreet for Charles's sake," he said. "Though God only knows how our liaison could further blacken two such tarnished reputations as ours."

She continued to regard him with narrowed eyes. "You have a point there, I suppose, such as it is."

She was angry. Definitely angry. Women were strange, unpredictable creatures. Why had he expected Moira to be all *that* different?

Devon swore softly under his breath, his patience growing thinner by the minute. His nose was cold; his fingers colder. What was he doing trading words with this beautiful woman in a chilly garden when they should be tumbling in a warm feather bed?

"Devil take it, madam, what do you want of me?" he asked. "I thought you, of all women, would be above demanding I do the pretty. Must I put it into words? Surely you know I desire you more than I have ever desired any other woman. You haunt my dreams when asleep; you torture my thoughts when awake. If I do not have you soon, I shall be forced to commit myself to Bedlam as a stark, raving lunatic. There, are you satisfied?"

Her face was pale in the moonlight, almost as pale as the marble that surrounded her. "I am satisfied you sound like a spoiled child who wants a new toy simply because it is the one toy he has not yet played with and discarded," she said with such haughtiness, if he hadn't known better, he might believe her a duchess born instead of one created in a bargain with a dying old man. "I will not be your plaything, my lord, nor indeed that of any man. If I have unwittingly led you to believe I would be, I can only apologize."

Devon felt gripped by a terrible coldness, whether anger or shock, he wasn't certain. "I do not want you for my plaything, Moira. Nor even for my mistress." He gritted his teeth. "I want you to be my lover, as I want to be a lover to you. I am not a man who seeks his pleasure without giving full measure to the woman with whom he shares his bed. If I have unwittingly led you to believe otherwise, I can only apologize."

He braced his hands on the cold marble at either side of her face. "Now, Moira Reardon Handley, Dowager Duchess of Sheffield, will you be my lover and my friend for as long as we both shall passionately desire each other?"

For a long moment she searched his face, her exotic eyes dark with emotion. She was his, he thought triumphantly. Her protestations had just been the usual womanish tedium a man had to endure when dealing with the opposite sex. With herculean patience, he waited for her answer.

Finally it came. "No, my lord, I will not be your lover. Nor do I think we could ever be friends. Let us hope for Charles's sake we can avoid becoming enemies."

Devon dropped his hands to his sides and stepped back. "I think you owe me an explanation for that answer, madam, when we both know you want me every bit as much as I want you," he said with barely controlled anger. "Even my poor, naive, young brother was given a reason for his rejection—and in writing too."

Moira pushed away from the marble statue and stepped forward onto the path that led to the manor house. She kept her eyes averted from Devon's gaze, even though her pelisse brushed against his legs as she passed. Only when she was safely beyond his reach did she turn to face him.

"I owed Blaine an explanation," she said in her low, throaty voice. "He loved me—to my everlasting regret.

I owe you nothing, Lord St. Gwyre. You have only joined the long line of men who have lusted after me. I have forgotten most of their names, as I shall soon forget yours."

Then she was gone, fading into the shadows, to leave only a marble fish to register the look of shock and dismay mirrored on his face.

From *The Gypsy Duchess*
by Nadine Miller

Have you read a Signet Regency lately?
Available at your local bookstore or call 1-800-253-6476 to order directly with Visa or Mastercard.

# WE NEED YOUR HELP

To continue to bring you quality romance
that meets your personal expectations,
we at TOPAZ books want to hear from you.
Help us by filling out this questionnaire, and in exchange
we will give you a **free gift** as a token of our gratitude.

- Is this the first TOPAZ book you've purchased? (circle one)

    YES          NO

    The title and author of this book is: _____

- If this was not the first TOPAZ book you've purchased, how many have you bought in the past year?

    a: 0 - 5     b  6 - 10    c:  more than 10     d:  more than 20

- How many romances in total did you buy in the past year?

    a: 0 - 5     b:  6 - 10    c:  more than 10     d:  more than 20 ____

- How would you rate your overall satisfaction with this book?

    a: Excellent    b:  Good    c:  Fair    d:  Poor

- What was the main reason you bought this book?

    a: It is a TOPAZ novel, and I know that TOPAZ stands
       for quality romance fiction
    b: I liked the cover
    c: The story-line intrigued me
    d: I love this author
    e: I really liked the setting
    f: I love the cover models
    g: Other: _____

- Where did you buy this TOPAZ novel?

    a: Bookstore    b:  Airport    c:  Warehouse Club
    d: Department Store    e:  Supermarket    f:  Drugstore
    g: Other: _____

- Did you pay the full cover price for this TOPAZ novel? (circle one)

    YES          NO

    If you did not, what price did you pay? _____

- Who are your favorite TOPAZ authors? (Please list)

- How did you first hear about TOPAZ books?

    a: I saw the books in a bookstore
    b: I saw the TOPAZ Man on TV or at a signing
    c: A friend told me about TOPAZ
    d: I saw an advertisement in_____magazine
    e: Other: _____

- What type of romance do you generally prefer?

    a: Historical    b:  Contemporary
    c: Romantic Suspense    d:  Paranormal (time travel,
       futuristic, vampires, ghosts, warlocks, etc.)
    d: Regency    e:  Other: _____

- What historical settings do you prefer?

    a: England    b:  Regency England          c:  Scotland
    e: Ireland    f:  America    g:  Western Americana
    h: American Indian          i:  Other: _____

- What type of story do you prefer?

  a: Very sexy                b: Sweet, less explicit
  c: Light and humorous       d: More emotionally intense
  e: Dealing with darker issues   f: Other

- What kind of covers do you prefer?

  a: Illustrating both hero and heroine    b: Hero alone
  c: No people (art only)                  d: Other_____

- What other genres do you like to read (circle all that apply)

  Mystery            Medical Thrillers    Science Fiction
  Suspense           Fantasy              Self-help
  Classics           General Fiction      Legal Thrillers
  Historical Fiction

- Who is your favorite author, and why?_____
  _____

- What magazines do you like to read? (circle all that apply)

  a: *People*                b: *Time/Newsweek*
  c: *Entertainment Weekly*  d: *Romantic Times*
  e: *Star*                  f: *National Enquirer*
  g: *Cosmopolitan*          h: *Woman's Day*
  i: *Ladies' Home Journal*  j: *Redbook*
  k: Other:_____

- In which region of the United States do you reside?

  a: Northeast    b: Midatlantic   c: South
  d: Midwest      e: Mountain      f: Southwest
  g: Pacific Coast

- What is your age group/sex?    a: Female    b: Male

  a: under 18     b: 19-25     c: 26-30     d: 31-35    e: 36-40
  f: 41-45        g: 46-50     h: 51-55     i: 56-60    j: Over 60

- What is your marital status?

  a: Married        b: Single      c: No longer married

- What is your current level of education?

  a: High school          b: College Degree
  c: Graduate Degree      d: Other: _____

- Do you receive the TOPAZ *Romantic Liaisons* newsletter, a quarterly
  newsletter with the latest information on Topaz books and authors?

  YES              NO

  If not, would you like to?    YES       NO

Fill in the address where you would like your free gift to be sent:

Name: _____

Address: _____

City:_____Zip Code: _____

You should receive your free gift in 6 to 8 weeks.
Please send the completed survey to:

Penguin USA•Mass Market
Dept. TS
375 Hudson St.
New York, NY 10014

# CELEBRITY TOPAZ MAN
# MARK CONSUELOS

Mark Consuelos is an actor widely known for his portrayal of the seductive Mateo Santos on ABC-TV's daytime drama "All My Children." He was voted Outstanding Newcomer by *Soap Opera Digest*. Fluent in both Spanish and Italian, Mark is also well-versed in the language of love.

Visit the Topaz area on our website
http://www.penguin.com